"Since you're going to bed, you won't be needing any clothes."

"I have no intention of getting into your bed!" she stated firmly. "I have a stage to catch."

"I'm afraid you'll have to change your plans. The stage left over an hour ago."

"An hour . . ." She swayed lightly and he reached out to grab her. With a determined effort she fought off the darkness that began to close around her. "Don't touch me!"

He was startled by her outburst. Her fragile appearance was deceiving. "I'm not going to hurt you."

The woman remained stubbornly in place while he debated how best to convince her to lie down. He wasn't used to bargaining, especially with a woman. Normally, he wouldn't be all that tempted to do so now. But given the woman's circumstances, he was willing to allow her some leeway in obeying his commands.

"I'll give you exactly thirty seconds to get back in that bed or . . ."

"Or what?" she whispered, her bold blue-green eyes making up for any failure of her voice.

Finding her open defiance surprising, if not altogether disconcerting, he clenched his fists at his side. What was she doing challenging him? Only a few brave souls had ever dared to challenge him before, and they had lived to regret it. "I'll put you there myself." When his warning drew no more than a reproachful glare, he began counting. "One . . ."

RAWHIDE AND LACE

~

Margaret Brownley

A TOPAZ BOOK

TOPAZ

Published by the Penguin Group
Penguin Books USA Inc, 375 Hudson Street,
New York, New York 10014, U.S.A.
Penguin Books Ltd, 27 Wrights Lane,
London W8 5TZ, England
Penguin Books Australia Ltd, Ringwood,
Victoria, Australia
Penguin Books Canada Ltd, 10 Alcorn Avenue,
Toronto, Ontario, Canada M4V 3B2
Penguin Books (N.Z.) Ltd, 182-190 Wairau Road,
Auckland 10, New Zealand

Penguin Books Ltd, Registered Offices:
Harmondsworth, Middlesex, England
First published by Topaz, an imprint of Dutton Signet,
a division of Penguin Books USA Inc.

First Printing, March, 1994
10 9 8 7 6 5 4 3 2 1

Topaz Man photo © Charles William Bush

 Topaz is a trademark of Dutton Signet,
a division of Penguin Books USA Inc.

Printed in the United States of America

To Natsuko,
who knows how to tame bold men
and wild frontiers

Chapter 1

THE last glimmer of daylight had long disappeared by the time the horse-drawn wagon swung onto the narrow dirt road that led to Deadman's Gulch, one of the many towns that had sprung up overnight since last year's discovery of gold in California.

The recent rains had washed away anything favorable about the road, leaving behind endless ruts and rocks and an occasional tree root held in place with more luck than soil.

It was for this reason that Libby Summerfield cried out with relief when the springless wagon finally came to a grinding halt after five hours of the most torturous journey she had ever endured.

"Are we there?" The question lingered on her lips and when no reply was forthcoming from the cheerless driver, she struggled to sit upright in the back of the wagon. Peering between the rough slatted sides, she narrowed her eyes in an effort to pick out signs of the town. Darkness surrounded her like a black shroud.

A cramp shot through her calf. "Oh, rot!" she murmured beneath her breath. What a nuisance one's body could be at times. Impatiently she rubbed the affected area, then reached behind to relieve the ache in her lower back. The threadbare blanket tossed to her by the driver at the beginning of the journey was barely adequate to cover her and did nothing to cushion her body from the battering jolts.

"This can't be Deadman's Gulch!" She expected more of the town, at least a hotel or boardinghouse, but as far as she could discern there was nothing but the whispering rustle from the trees and the rush of a nearby creek.

The grizzled driver took a long swig from the cask he kept beneath the buckboard seat and wiped his hand across his mouth. "This is as close as I'm gittin'," he drawled. "You're on your own from here on in."

She gasped in alarm. "I paid you good money to take me to Deadman's Gulch."

The driver hopped to the ground and reached for her luggage, a weather-beaten leather valise that held a change of clothing, a few sparse toiletries, a baby's layette, and a lock of hair that had belonged to her late husband. The valise fell to the ground with an unceremonious thud.

Everything she owned was in that valise.

"Wait! You can't do that." It took a great deal of effort, but she managed to heave her somewhat awkward bulk over the splintered sideboards of the wagon. Skirts and petticoats aflutter, her high-buttoned boots scrambled recklessly until she found a foothold above the back wheel.

Despite her somewhat precarious position atop the sides of the wagon, she kept her wits about her and managed to bombard the driver with a thorough tongue-wagging. "Of all the despicable things I've ever heard. You cowardly, spineless, no-good, two-timing . . . Just wait until I report you to the proper authorities!"

The driver seemed unperturbed by her threats, as well he might. If there was a proper authority anywhere in California, Libby had not seen him, nor, as far as she knew, had anyone else.

But it made her feel better to say it. Without thought of decorum or grace, she managed to reach the ground, ripping the one dress she owned that still accommodated her ungainly figure.

She didn't bother checking out the tear; she had more important things to worry about. Her hand flew to her swollen belly. Lord, what a belly it was, as big or bigger than the watermelons her grandpapa grew the summer she turned fifteen, and almost as hard to the touch.

Assured that everything was as it should be inside, she turned to the dark form of the driver. "You promised to take me into town!" Oh, the nerve of the man, throwing her precious belongings around like a sack of rubbish! Then threatening to leave her stranded only God knows where. "I paid you good money to take me into town!"

"You paid me 'nuff to pay for my likker and 'bacco, but not 'nuff to get me head blowed off."

So that was it, she fumed. He wanted more money. "You're nothing but a two-timing thief, that's what you are." The thought of being left stranded filled her with horror. Fighting both fear and panic, her tirade escalated. "You should be ashamed of yourself for taking advantage of a woman about to give birth. A deal is a deal, you . . ."

She threw out every insulting word she could think of in rapid-fire succession.

She ran out of breath before she ran out of suitable barbs, but it probably didn't matter. He was obviously immune to insults, if indeed he even understood half of what she'd said, which she doubted. She clamped her mouth shut and decided that contrary to her nature, she'd better think before she acted. The life of the baby she carried depended on it. Unfortunately, the more she thought, the worst her plight became. She cast an uneasy glance toward the menacing shadows and shivered against the icy chill that touched her heart.

Lord Almighty, she was going to have to bargain with the man. She cleared her voice. Your name is?"

"Roseborough. Harvey Roseborough."

It was her opinion that *Thorn*borough would be a more appropriate name, but she fought against the urge to tell him so. Her best chance was to throw herself at his mercy and hope that the man was capable of some small measure of human kindness. "Mr. Roseborough, I'm sure you are a reasonable man," she began beseechingly. "I don't have much gold left, but I'm sure we can work out an agreement. Please. I beg of you."

The man snorted and spit, a stream of tobacco juice hitting the ground with a little whooshing sound. "I ain't goin' nowhere near that town. Makes no diff'rence how much you pay me. The last time I drove there, I darn near got meself kilt. No one goes there unless they is crazy." The man reclaimed the driver's seat and reached for the reins.

"Wait!" she pleaded. *Oh, Lord, don't let him leave me here!* She considered planting herself in the middle of the street, but wisely decided against it. A man so determined to leave as to refuse money couldn't be trusted to let a human life stand in the way of his departure.

The driver swung the wagon around in a frenzied arc sending pebbles and dust flying up in her face. She jumped back and waved the dust away with her hand. The wagon tore back in the direction they'd come. Its wheels rumbled loudly.

Hands on her waist, Libby stared after the retreating wagon. "You can't leave me here!" she called at the top of her lungs. "Think of the baby!"

"Quit your belly-achin'," the driver yelled back. "You only have a mile to walk."

"A mile . . .?" She turned and stared in the opposite direction. That's when she saw it, a tiny light glimmering in the far distance, no larger than a pinhole.

Behind her the sound of the wagon faded away. From the distant hills came the yipping sounds of a lone coyote howling at the winter moon that was darting in and out of the clouds gathered overhead.

Shivering, she drew her fringed woolen shawl around her shoulders and glanced anxiously at the shadows that loomed on either side of her. Swallowing hard, she chided herself for giving in to her fears.

Since arriving in California seven months earlier

she'd been through hell. Surely nothing that awaited her in Deadman's Gulch could be worse than losing a husband and being left stranded in an untamed land some thousands of miles from home or friends, penniless and heartbroken, with a child on the way, and no immediate prospect of improving her lot.

Thoughts of the baby filled her with anxiety. There were scant few women in this part of the state, and no midwives. The only doctor in the area was in Nevada City. With a little bit of luck, she should be able to catch the morning stage out of Deadman's Gulch and be in Nevada City by the following night.

A sharp pain shot though her distended abdomen. She held her breath until the pain subsided, then felt her way in the dark until she located her valise. Her only hope was to make it to Nevada City before it was time for the baby's birth.

It was December and the wind blowing off the snow-covered peaks of the upper Sierra Mountains sliced through the thin fabric of her calico dress like the hard cold blade of a knife. Shivering, she forced herself to concentrate on the tiny speck of light ahead, telling herself that it was only a mile away and trying not to think of how much her back ached.

It was slow going, mainly because of her bulk. The road was dangerously rutted and several times she stumbled and almost fell. The tiny circle of light gradually grew larger. The outlines of wooden structures loomed ahead and she could hear the unmistakable sounds of civilization: dogs barking, a fiddle playing, the shouting of male voices. An argument?

Unable to catch her breath, she stopped to rest. That's when she heard it: the sharp quick sound of a gun.

A gripping fear surged through her body, making it almost impossible for her to breathe. Frozen to the spot, she shivered in the darkness, her senses alert. Despite her earlier resolve, every bone-chilling tale she'd ever heard about the wild and lawless inhabitants of Deadman's Gulch came back to haunt her.

The bullet had soared over the head of the tall, bearded man dressed in buckskins and ripped a hole through the canvased ceiling of the Golden Hind Saloon. The sharp report of the gun had commanded the full attention of the three dozen or more miners who were packed into the place. Not even the clink of a gold piece had stirred the silence as all eyes lifted from the green baize gambling tables and riveted upon the short, stocky man with the black eye patch.

With a demonic grin, the man lowered the barrel of the gun until it pointed straight at the chest of his intended victim.

"I should have warned you, St. John," the gunman slurred. "I'm a bad loser." Yellow teeth parted a mangy beard as his forefinger played with the trigger. His fiendish grin failed to reach his one bloodshot eye.

Logan St. John regarded the man with contempt. There was nothing he hated more than being on the down side of a gun. Unless it was to have his poker game interrupted. Flint was guilty of both. But that wasn't all he was guilty of. The man had been pushing his weight around town since his arrival a week ago. More than one man had been found with a bullet in his back and St. John was willing to bet that Flint was the culprit. It was time to teach the man a lesson.

"You know what they say, Flint," St. John drawled lazily, so lazily in fact, one would think he was the one with the gun, the one who held the advantage. "There's nothing worse than a poor loser." He paused before delivering the final line. "Unless it's two poor losers."

With that, he kicked the under part of a game table with his foot, catching the man off-guard. Poker chips and playing cards flew from one end of the small crowded saloon to the other. A snapping tension filled the air, followed by shuffling feet as the other patrons grabbed their drinks and moved to the sides of the canvased walls, leaving the center free.

Before Flint recovered from his surprise, St. John had knocked the gun from his pudgy, small hand. Flint reacted with a violent thrust of a fist, but St. John ducked and threw his weight against Flint's legs. Flint hit the floor with a grunt, then managed to push St. John away with a thrust of his worn Jack boots.

Grunting, St. John flew backward against the bar.

Flint jumped to his feet and charged after St. John, snorting like an angry bull. But he was no match for the bold mountain man and in an embarrassingly short time, he was sprawled on the floor, winded and humiliated.

Logan St. John stood over him, looking none the worse for wear. Grimacing his dislike of the man, he picked up Flint's tattered felt hat and tossed it to him. "If you know what's good for you, Flint, you'll not let me see your ugly face around here again."

Flint rose unsteadily to his feet, holding his stomach with both hands. Amid laughter and jeers, he made his way to the open door of the saloon and staggered outside to his piebald horse.

Libby scowled at the seemingly deserted buildings on the outskirts of town. Her feet were beginning to ache. A mile, indeed! If she ever got her hands on that no-good driver ...

Relishing the thought of what she would do to him, she was completely taken by surprise by the appearance of a horse that loomed without warning from seemingly nowhere and was heading straight at her.

With a startled cry, she jumped out of the way, but even so, she felt a strong current of moving air as the horse flew by. Her foot slipped, followed by a moment of confusion as the ground gave way beneath her.

Her senses spun as she tumbled down the embankment and was swallowed by icy waters. Arms and legs flailing, she thrashed about, gasping for air. Several seconds passed before she realized the water ran less than a foot deep.

Sputtering, she pushed herself upward. She had fallen into the creek that meandered along the side of the road. Her arms and legs numbed from the bitingly cold water, she crawled up the slight incline and collapsed in a clump of tall grass, grasping for breath. The ba . . . by. Oh, Lordy . . . the . . . baby.

As soon as she caught her breath, she rolled over on her back and pressed her frozen fingers ever so gently against her swollen belly. Please be all right. Oh, please, God . . .

Her simple calico dress clung to her, the wet fabric sheathing her like a thin coat of ice. Her teeth chattered. Never had she felt so cold in her life.

A terrorizing thought filled her head; if the fall hadn't hurt the baby, certainly the cold would. Oh, if she ever got her hands on that driver!

Thinking she'd freeze to death if she lay there much longer, she forced herself to her feet. She wandered around in a daze until she located her valise. She tugged on the leather handle, but she couldn't seem to lift the luggage off the ground. Indeed, she barely had enough strength left to stand on her own two feet. Her heart ached at the thought of leaving her precious belongings by the wayside. But she had no choice.

Tears blurred her vision as she stumbled forward. Shivering with fear and cold, she fought against the panic that was building inside her.

The unwieldly shapes of hastily built shacks rose on both sides of the narrow dirt road that ran through the center of town. Canvased saloons teeming with shadowy men quivered and glowed like golden balloons about to take flight.

The incessant cries of monte dealers rose from the various tents. "Make your bets, gentlemen. Make your bets!" This was met with shouts of "Come down with your dust" and "Bar the porte."

The high-pitched scream of a fiddle soared above

the rowdy sounds of argumentative voices and loud, mirthless guffaws.

The noisy street was empty except for the horses that were tied to the wooden hitching posts in front of the various canvas saloons. A black stallion nodded its head and neighed softly as she passed. A mule hee-hawed.

She nearly stumbled over a prone body that lay in the middle of the dirt road. Not knowing if the man was dead or merely drunk, Libby held her breath as she stepped around him.

Where was it? The hotel. There had to be a hotel someplace. Or a boardinghouse or something besides a saloon.

She reached the end of the town, passing no less than seven rowdy saloons on the way, but not one hotel.

A nearby shout startled her.

"Why you son of a . . ."

This was followed by a thud and a groan. Panicking, she ran. Gunshots sounded behind her. Something grazed her shoulder. A hand? Not a hand . . .

Terrified for her baby, she grabbed on to the wooden post of the nearest building and clambered up the uneven steps to the porch. Something pulled her downward. She fought against the invisible force until she could fight no more.

Chapter 2

MOST men would not have heard the soft sound coming from outside the door, but Logan St. John was not like most men. He had senses as sharp as any wild animal; this was not surprising considering he'd spent all but five of his thirty-six years living in some of the wildest, rawest land in the northwest.

His hard, lean body ready to spring into action with the slightest provocation, Logan pulled his Colt Walker from his waistband and turned to face the door. All this was done in one smooth, efficient move.

It was Flint. It had to be Flint. Damned, bothersome man. Back looking for trouble, no doubt. Well, Logan was just the man to give it to him.

Despite his resolve, he viewed the prospect as more of a nuisance than something he relished. Logan had had a hard day in the diggings, and an even harder night at the gambling tables. To make matters worse, the cold wintry air had settled in his injured leg, causing it to ache worse than a mouthful of rotten teeth.

What he wanted to do was to climb into the warmth of his fur-lined pallet and get some shut-eye. He did not want to mess with the likes of Flint.

His every sense alert, he stood perfectly still. Nothing. Obviously, Flint was timing his ambush carefully, waiting no doubt for Logan to douse his lantern and fall asleep. Fool man. Showed how much he knew. Even when a trapper slept, his senses remained ever alert.

Chiding himself for not being done with the man

when he had the chance earlier, Logan decided to get the matter over with quickly. He moved toward the door, his moccasined feet soundless against the dirt-packed floor.

An ear pressed next to the door, he shut his eyes and waited. It was dark outside, and Flint wasn't likely to wait for Logan's eyes to adjust before he waged his attack. He ignored the sounds of gunfire and the wild whoops of miners in the distance. It was the sound of human breathing that he listened for, the sound of a bending knee or a hushed footstep. Sounds too soft for most men to hear.

When he was certain he'd acquired his night vision, he held his gun cocked and posed, then ripped the door open with such force that the entire flimsy shanty shook on its foundation and threatened to collapse around him in a heap of splintered wood.

Nothing. Eyes sharp, he rapidly scanned the dark shadows for the least movement or suspicious form.

That's when he saw the body lying at the edge of his porch. Shaking his head in disgust, he shoved his gun into the belt at his waist. Just another drunk.

Having learned at an early age not to turn his back, he stepped aft into the cabin and stopped just short of the open doorway upon hearing a soft sigh, no louder than a kitten's mew. Frowning, he glanced again at the dark form, not sure he'd heard right.

Another sound, barely above a whisper, convinced him to to have a closer look.

Thinking it was a trick, he moved cautiously to the side of the prone body and dropped on his one good knee. His touch elicited another soft moan and this time there was no mistake; it was a woman!

"What the hell . . .?"

Stunned by the thought of a woman in Deadman's Gulch, he touched her forehead and let the sensitive tips of his fingers trail down her cool yet silky skin to the slight pulse at her neck. His finely tuned fingertips told him that she was barely holding on to life. Her flesh was colder than any human flesh should be. It was no trick.

Without further hesitation, he scooped the woman up in his arms and carried her inside, kicking the door shut behind him.

He laid her gently on the thick bear robe spread out in front of the stone fireplace. He had already banked the fire for the night and though the grate glowed with red-hot embers, the room had grown noticeably colder. Hunching down, Logan tossed in some dry kindling and added another log. In seconds, bright flames tongued upward and sparks began to crackle and fly, landing upon the brick hearth like red glowing stars.

He then devoted his full attention to the woman. Not even the spattering of mud on her fine pale face detracted from her delicate features. Long lashes fanned across the soft curves of her cheeks. Her wet hair was a soft brown color, tumbling about her shoulders in tangled curls. She looked so pale in the soft glow of the room, he feared he'd already lost her.

With two fingers, he once again checked her pulse and was alarmed to find it had dropped another beat or two. It would take quick action to save her. He glanced at her sopping wet clothes and frowned at the red bloodstain on her shoulder.

Reaching for the leather sheath that hung from the back of a chair, he pulled out his skinning knife. He inserted the tip of the blade beneath the high neckline of her sopping wet gown and with a flick of his wrist sliced the thin fabric away from her shoulder as easily as he skinned a rabbit.

He examined the wound with a practiced eye. Unless he missed his guess, she'd been grazed by a bullet. Fortunately, the wound was only superficial. He was more concerned about the temperature of her skin than he was with the wound. Indeed, in the soft glow of the fire, her lips appeared to be turning purple.

He peeled the remainder of the wet dress off her and tossed it aside. He then slit the fabric of her lace-trimmed camisole until the lovely soft curves of her breasts were fully exposed.

On some level, he recorded her breathtaking beauty, but his hands never once faltered, never once lost their urgency. Not until he slit away her ruffled pantaloons and revealed the thickness of her waist.

He was so startled by the sight of her swollen belly, he sat back on his heel and stared in utter disbelief. Between the dimly lit room and his haste to save her, he'd failed to notice what was now astoundingly obvious: she was with child.

He didn't know much about such matters, but enough to guess she was pretty far along.

His face set in lines of consternation, he finished ripping the last of her soaked clothing away, then immediately covered her with a woolen Indian blanket.

Her pulse was dropping rapidly. Rushing over to the fireplace, he reached for the kettle hanging on the spit and poured hot water into a small porcelain basin.

He dipped a soft piece of deerskin into the basin, squeezed out the excess water, and rubbed the hot chamois vigorously up and down her body, working around the blanket. When the water had cooled and it was clear that she still suffered from exposure, he tossed the blanket aside and rubbed her briskly with his hands, letting the warmth from his own flesh warm hers.

A profound relief washed over him when at last her skin began to grow warmer as a result of the vigorous massage.

She sighed softly as he rubbed his hands across her lovely full breasts and over her belly. Her eyes fluttered, but never fully opened.

"You'll be fine," he murmured softly. "Just as soon as we get you warm." There was no indication that she heard him, but he kept talking to her, just the same. It was important to try to reach her, to pull her back to consciousness.

He tried, he really tried to keep his eyes averted

from her nakedness, to not take advantage of her vulnerability. But it was hard. Not hard; impossible. Logan St. John was many things, but he was no saint where women were concerned.

And it had been so long since he'd touched a woman.

But he was touching a woman now. Indeed, he rubbed his hands over pretty near every square inch of her body until the worrisome blue left her lips, and her skin lost its icy cold feel.

He could not have poured more of himself into the woman had he been her lover.

Satisfied that she was past the danger point, he drew back on his heels and turned the edges of the bearskin over her, covering her nakedness and wrapping her into its warmth.

Grabbing his emergency supplies from the buckskin bag he called a possibles bag, he set to work dressing her wound. He cleansed her shoulder with alcohol before applying a small patch of beaver fur. A touch of sticky resin that he'd collected fresh that very day from the weepy trunk of a cypress held the fur in place and provided a seal against infection.

She needed something warm to wear. He glanced around the room, his gaze falling upon one of his buckskin shirts that hung from a wooden peg. He quickly grabbed it and worked it over her head and arms. It was far too big for her, but it would help to keep in her body heat. He then wrapped her again in the tightly woven Indian blanket, the only man-made blanket he deemed warm enough.

A quick check of her pulse confirmed that her breathing was normal, but she still trembled slightly beneath his touch.

Sucking in his breath, he picked her up in his arms and carried her to his pallet. He laid her on the pelts of beaver and fox that made up the mattress, taking the utmost care not to jostle her more than necessary. Covering her with a buffalo robe, he then brushed her still-damp hair away from her forehead.

Her eyes remained closed but a shadow touched her lovely smooth brow, telling him that subconsciously she could feel his hand. It was an encouraging sign. He ran the knuckle of his finger across her velvety soft cheek. On impulse he leaned over and touched his lips to hers. To check the temperature of her skin, he told himself, for the lips were more sensitive to the touch than were the fingers, enabling him to better monitor her condition. That's all he meant to do—check her body heat. Therefore, he was totally unprepared for the jolt that followed the touch of his lips to hers.

He pulled back as if he were burned and caught his breath. After a moment he shook his head. It had been a long day and he was bone-weary tired. Was it any wonder he was imagining things?

Straightening, he extinguished the oil lantern on the table by the bed. His way lit only by the soft burning fire, he reached for a bedroll and since the bearskin robe was still damp from her body, he spread his roll out on the hard dirt floor.

He pulled off his moccasins and stripped to his long johns, then settled himself down for the night. He never had trouble sleeping until he moved indoors. Had, on occasion, slept on hard rock, in mountain caves, and in the saddle. Once when he was being tracked by a band of unfriendly Indians, he'd been forced to sleep inside a stick and mud beaver lodge. But tonight he couldn't seem to find a comfortable position. The chilling dampness in the air cut through to the bone of his bad leg like an iron stake.

His leg had been mangled by a grizzly bear when he was but fifteen. At first the injury was barely noticeable, but it had grown progressively worse in recent years. Knowing that he could never survive another winter in the wild, he was forced to seek shelter in this makeshift shack, one of many in the area that had been hastily built by a company of gold miners who later abandoned the town and moved on to try their luck elsewhere.

He didn't dare admit, even to himself, that his chances of returning to the wilderness looked grim. If he couldn't continue his life as a free trapper, he had nothing. That was the only life he knew. The only life, for that matter, that he ever wanted.

It had been difficult to learn to sleep inside a man-made shelter. He was not accustomed to sleeping in close quarters, with a roof over his head, unable to monitor the safety of his surroundings. No owl could be heard to signal a change in the weather. Nor was he able to detect the sound of creaking boughs or the rustle of branches. The still air inside the wooden dwelling offered no changing scents to tell him what animals crept near, or to warn him if, by chance, a man hid in the darkness.

Any foreshadowing of danger was denied him, and he decided it took a great deal of faith, not to mention courage, to sleep soundly inside a man-made dwelling.

Still, as he lay there it occurred to him that the woman's presence was comforting and soothing in a way that both surprised and puzzled him. He soon abandoned his efforts to monitor outside for possible dangers. It was far more pleasant to concentrate on her. He listened to her soft breathing and it stunned him to think he'd never actually listened to a woman sleep before. He could smell the soft fragrance of her damp hair, as if she had rubbed the petals of a flower through each silken strand.

As the heat of her body became trapped beneath the covers, he grew more aware of the lovely sweet fragrance of her warming skin. The skills he'd perfected through the years as a matter of survival served him well in tracking her recovery.

There was really no reason to climb out of his warm bedroll and check on her. No reason at all to subject his already painful leg to the cold night air. Yet, he couldn't seem to help himself. And so, throughout the seemingly endless night that followed, he made numerous trips to her side.

His leg grew progressively stiffer with each passing hour, until, at last, he was forced to hobble. But neither the piercing leg pains nor biting cold air diminished his satisfaction upon feeling her forehead or touching his knuckles to her now warm cheeks.

Who was she? he wondered. Where did she come from? And why, with all the man-made structures in town, had she found her way to his?

CHAPTER 3

S HE was dead. It was the only explanation Libby could think of that would explain the feeling of weightlessness she felt upon opening her eyes to the strange, unfamiliar surroundings.

Afraid to move, she let her gaze roam freely about the small, cluttered room. The word coffin came to mind as she stared up at the low wood ceiling. The room had no windows and only a single door.

Pieces of canvas were stuffed between the rough-hewn planks that made up all four walls. Even so, cold air blew through the cracks, and glimpses of the dull cloudy sky could be seen through the tiny openings in the roof. The one bright spot in the room was the orange glow from the slow-burning fire.

Little by little, her senses awakened. She smelled burning cedar and coffee. It was the latter that convinced her that perhaps she was only half-dead.

A flutter at her side just below the waist, a tiny movement of hand or foot, and the events of the past began to come back.

She turned her thoughts inward, to the precious life she carried that was now letting its presence be known in the most comforting way possible. Relief flooded through her, followed quickly by a sense of urgency. She couldn't stay here; it was imperative that she reach Nevada City as soon as possible.

Her head felt as heavy as a lead ball as she lifted it from the pillow and pushed the covers aside. Moving with uncharacteristic caution, she inched her legs across the fur that lay in valleys and peaks beneath her. She felt stiff, disjointed, so unlike herself.

Her feet firmly in place on the fur rug by the bed, she pushed herself forward, aware of a stiffness in her left shoulder. Standing upright, she stared down in astonishment at her clothing.

Lord Almighty! She was dressed like an Indian!

She ran her hand along the soft deerskin tunic that fell loosely from her shoulders. It was far too big for her, even with her swollen belly. The shoulder seams fell halfway down her arm, the fringe at the cuffs reached beyond her fingertips.

She straightened and although the bulk of her abdomen prevented her from seeing her toes or even her feet it was clear to her that the fringe at the hem did not quite cover her knees. She added indecent exposure to the growing list of things to worry about.

Not that there was anyone in the room to see her bare legs. But the room was rather masculine. *Extremely* masculine. It was the sort of room that made a woman think twice before exposing her limbs or anything else for that matter to view.

She tried to remember where she was. She recalled running down a dark street. Could taste fear, feel a sense of panic—desperation. Then something strange happened; a vision of warmth and softness washed over her.

In a moment of confusion, she imagined hands, gentle yet firm loving hands, running up and down her body, stroking her back, her shoulders, her breasts . . .

Horrified by the unseemly thoughts that assailed her, she lowered herself onto the edge of the bed. It was a dream. She was recalling a dream. A vivid one, to be sure, but a dream, nonetheless. She wondered if such dreams were yet another symptom of her condition, like the strange cravings she'd had in recent months for sardines and pickles.

Just thinking of such yearnings made her mouth feel dry, parched. She needed a drink.

Planting her hands firmly on the whiskey keg that served as a table next to the bed, she stood. The room seemed to whirl around her. She waited for the dizziness to pass before she ventured to the part of the room that served as a kitchen.

She found a bucket of water and ladled some into a tin cup. The water was fresh and tasted cool and sweet in her mouth. Drinking her fill, she took in her surroundings with interest.

The single room of the cabin was no more than ten feet by twenty feet long. A large stone fireplace dominated one wall. A crude wooden table flanked by two birchwood chairs served as the only barrier between the kitchen and the rest of the living quarters. A bearskin was centered in the middle of the dirt floor.

Her gaze lingered on the dark fur rug for a moment before she perused the rest of the room.

Without warning, the door flew open, startling her. Jerking her head around, Libby found herself drowning for the second time in less than a day. Only this time it was not water that absorbed her; it was dark, piercing eyes that glinted with a familiarity that made her gasp. She knew at that moment that the hands she imagined had taken such liberties with her had been no dream.

Logan St. John gave the woman a quick once-over, surprised to see her on her feet. "What are you doing out of bed?"

His voice was sharp, curt, designed to discourage conversation. He was a loner, not given to having company. Not since . . .

The name that came to his mind startled him. Damn the woman. Intruding into his life. Making him remember things he didn't want to remember, think thoughts no man should have to think. The sooner the woman had recovered and was on her way, the sooner he could forget the past and concentrate on getting his leg back to normal so he could head up north to set his traps before it was too late.

He slammed the door shut behind him. It was already too late, dammit! Winter was the time to trap beavers, when furs were thick and the colors rich. That's when they brought the best prices.

Apparently thinking the anger on his face was directed at her, the woman shrank back, pressing herself against the cookstove.

He limped toward her and stopped in front of the table. His eyes quickly adjusted to the dim light inside the cabin. Seeing her clearly now, he was ill-prepared for the fetching way his fringed buckskin shirt looked on her. He let his startled gaze drop to the unlaced neckline that had fallen in such a way as to reveal one lovely white shoulder. The shirt was large enough to hide the fullness of her waist and short enough to reveal her long, shapely legs.

She tugged at the sleeve and pulled it back over her shoulder, but her attempts at modesty only succeeded in exposing more of her lovely full breasts. And hard as she tried, there was nothing much she could do about her lower limbs.

He was sorely tempted to throw a blanket around her, cover her up so he didn't have to be subjected to so much feminine flesh, but she was so wide-eyed with fear, he thought it best to avoid any sudden movement on his part that might further alarm her.

"You'd better lie down," he said. He gave a curt nod toward the pallet and concentrated on keeping his gaze riveted to the relative safety of her lovely pale face. But she wasn't making it easy on him. Indeed, the more she clutched at the opening at her neckline, the more vividly he recalled the soft feel of her skin.

She stared longingly at the pile of furs he indicated. "I . . . I have no intention of lying down." Her pale lips trembled as she spoke, her eyes dark with suspicion.

"You need your rest," he said gently. What he didn't say was that if she didn't lie down, she would probably

fall down. He took a step backward thinking she'd relax with more distance between them. "If you get into
bed, I'll bring you some hot tea."

Libby watched him warily, not certain what to make
of the unexpected gentleness in his voice. It occurred
to her that he wasn't as dangerous as he looked. Or
was it the soft pile of furs beckoning to her from
across the room that made her so willing to let down
her guard?

Fortunately, before she succumbed to the temptation
of climbing into bed, the kick of a tiny foot next to her
rib cage snapped her back to reality. With reality came
the memory of bold firm hands on her body the previous night. How could she forget, even for a moment,
how he'd taken advantage of her? Just thinking about
it infuriated her. How dare he think he could rub his
hands up and down her body anytime he chose. No
more! Not as long as she had a breath of air left in her
would she ever again allow him to touch her.

Fists on her hips, she lifted her chin and stood
ramrod-straight, intent upon making the most of her
five-foot-four height. "I'm quite capable of taking care
of myself."

His gaze dropped to her waist, or at least to the area
that one would normally expect to find a waist. "I
knew from the moment I first laid eyes on you that you
were a woman who could take care of herself," he said
lightly.

Disdain made her act bolder. "For your information,
my name is Libby Summerfield. *Mrs.* Libby Summerfield."

He didn't seem the least surprised that she was married. If anything his face remained remarkably passive
as he spoke. "If you're a married woman as you say,
you won't have any trouble taking orders."

This statement incensed her almost as much as the
knowledge that he'd taken advantage of her the previous night. She felt her cheeks grow hot with fury. "I
have never taken orders in my life!"

"I guess that explains your present predicament."

"It explains nothing of the sort!" she retorted. "Now if you would be kind enough to give me back my own clothes."

"Since you're going to bed, you won't be needing any clothes."

"I have no intention of getting into your bed!" she stated firmly. "I have a stage to catch."

"I'm afraid you'll have to change your plans. The stage left over an hour ago."

"An hour ..." She swayed lightly and he reached out to grab her. With a determined effort, she fought off the darkness that began to close around her. "Don't touch me!"

He was startled by her outburst. Her fragile appearance was deceiving. "I'm not going to hurt you."

The woman remained stubbornly in place while he debated how best to convince her to lie down. He wasn't used to bargaining, especially with a woman. Normally, he wouldn't be all that tempted to do so now. But given the woman's circumstances, he was willing to allow her some leeway in obeying his commands.

"I'll give you exactly thirty seconds to get back in that bed or ... "

"Or what?" she squeaked out, her bold blue-green eyes making up for any failure of her voice.

Finding her open defiance surprising, if not altogether disconcerting, he clenched his fists at his side. What the sam hill was she doing challenging him? Only a few brave souls had ever dared to challenge him before, and they had lived to regret it. "I'll put you there myself." When his warning drew no more than a reproachful glare, he began counting. "One ..."

It amused him to watch her act so nonchalantly. His height alone made him an imposing figure.

"Five ..."

She never as much as flinched.

"Twelve ..." fool of a woman. All he wanted her to

do was to get into the damned bed. He kept counting, hoping she would accept the inevitable. "Twenty-seven . . ."

He never had a chance to get to the final count for she practically swooned before his very eyes. Intent on grabbing her before she reached the ground, he pushed a chair out of his way and rushed toward her.

She moved with a speed of a wild animal. Before he could comprehend what she was doing, she grabbed the Green River knife he'd left on the table earlier and raised it over her head, its lethal blade pointed straight at him.

He stopped midstep, flabbergasted. Never would he have thought it possible for someone to recover so quickly. Gathering his wits, he tried another tactic. "Is this the way you show your appreciation to me for giving you shelter?"

"Don't come near me," she warned.

He scowled. What a damned nuisance she was turning out to be. It riled him that she had him over a barrel. If she were a man, she'd be flat on the floor by now and thinking twice about ever trying to get the best of him again. But a woman, especially one who is with child . . . How the sam hill was a man supposed to defend himself against such a combination?

"I think you'd better put the knife down." He held his hands out, palms toward her. "I don't want to hurt you."

"And I don't want to hurt you," the woman countered.

He almost laughed aloud. Did she really think that was a possibility? "I'm mighty relieved to find we're in accord."

"Just tell me where my clothes are."

"I'm afraid what's left of your clothes will be of no use to you. I had to cut them off."

"You what?" The knife lowered an inch.

"It was the only way I could undress you quickly to take care of your wound."

Suspicion crossed her face. "What wound?"

"The one on your left shoulder. I believe you were shot."

Her eyes rounded in disbelief. "Shot?"

He nodded toward her arm. "It was just a graze. You were lucky. It was your left shoulder or you'd have more of a disadvantage than you do now."

"It seems to me that you're the one with the disadvantage," she said.

"Not really. You see I could shoot the knife out of your hand like this." In a flash he drew his Colt Walker from his belt and shot the lid off the metal coffeepot on the woodstove next to her.

Startled, the woman jumped. Her lips quivered and her eyes flashed with cold fear, but the knife remained stubbornly in place.

Feeling a begrudging admiration for her, he dropped his arm to his side. "I hesitate to show you my full talents with a gun, being that you're ..." His eyes dropped down to her waist. "I've never yet missed my mark, but of course"—he blew on the barrel of his gun—"there's always a first time."

He paused, but when it appeared he'd failed to force her into submission, he decided to try yet another tactic. "I'll make a deal with you. You put the knife on the table and I'll put my gun back in my belt."

They glared at each other in silence for several long minutes. The knife remained in place, as did the gun.

"Take your time," he ventured. Considering his irritation at her stubbornness, his voice was surprisingly mild. "I'll give you the count of thirty. One ..."

She waited until he got clear up to twenty-seven before making her move. With a mighty swing of her arm, she released the knife and it sped toward him.

He ducked, but not in time. The pointed blade nicked his cheek before falling to the dirt floor.

Cursing, he grabbed his face and glanced at his bloodied fingers. "Damned woman!"

Face dark with fury, he shoved the table aside and advanced toward her.

"Don't you touch me!" she warned.

"Keep still, dammit! I'm not going to hurt you."

He grabbed her right shoulder, then slipped an arm behind her legs and lifted her next to his massive chest.

"Let me go, you brute, you . . ." Before she had time to spew out more than a half-dozen choice words, he had whisked her across the room and set her down on the pallet.

"You can't hold me against my will," she said indignantly, and he held back the urge to point out he was doing exactly that. In fact, he was on the bed with her, both his knees pinning her hips down as he held her hands over her head.

Biting back the pain in his leg, he grimaced and adjusted his weight. "If you promise to stay put, I'll let you go." He couldn't believe it. He was bargaining with her. His only salvation was that there were no other trappers around to witness his disconcerting predicament. He'd never live this one down, that's for sure.

Wanting to give her every opportunity to comply to his wishes, he waited with a patience foreign to him. It wasn't altogether an unpleasant wait, despite the added discomfort to his leg. His head was so close to hers, he could feel her warm soft breath against his skin.

He'd all but decided he was going to have to tie her to the bed for her own good when she nodded ever so slightly. Relieved that he would not have to resort to such drastic tactics, he immediately released her wrists and stood.

She scrambled beneath the covers and pulled the Indian blanket to her chin. He wondered what she'd say if he told her that the look and feel of her nakedness had been forever etched into his memory and no amount of hiding would ever erase it.

He grabbed a chair and set it down next to the bed,

straddling it backward. It felt good to get the weight off his leg. He laid his arms across the back.

"I think we need to get a few things straight. Mrs. Summerfield, is it? My name is St. John. Logan St. John. As long as you remain with me, you'll do as you're told. Now, suppose you tell me where Mr. Summerfield might be?" If her husband had a sensible bone in his body, he'd be on a foreign continent somewhere, living under an assumed name. No matter. He intended to track the man down and make him live up to his responsibilities. And the sooner, the better.

His face stung from the cut, his arms burned from where her fingers had dug into him. His leg ached from holding her down on the bed. Her strength had surprised him. She was an absolute wildcat. Kicking and carrying on like he was out to harm her. He'd known grizzlies that had put up less fight.

She eyed him cautiously. "My husband is waiting for me in Nevada City." She folded her arms across her chest. "And when he finds out how you manhandled me, he'll come after you."

Logan considered this for a moment. "And your baby . . ." He hesitated. He'd never discussed such a delicate matter with a woman before.

At mention of the baby, the hostility left her face and was replaced with a look of desperation that made him ache. He didn't want her to be afraid of him. But who could blame her? Perhaps he'd been too hard on her. It wasn't as if they were in the northern wilds, where the ability to follow a command could make the difference between life and death.

This was not the wilderness, nor was she his responsibility. He felt ashamed that he'd been so hard-nosed and rough with her. He was also aware of how he must look.

His thick black hair fell clear down to his shoulders in an unruly mane. Despite the Indian blood that ran through his veins and had chiseled his strong-boned features, he'd inherited the ability to grow a beard from his trapper father. He couldn't remember the last time he'd shaved. "When is your baby due?"

"At the end of the month."

He considered this a moment. "Now suppose you tell me what brought you to my doorstep."

Surprised by the sudden gentleness of his voice, she lowered her thick, golden-tipped lashes and tried once again to recall the hazy events of the previous night. She recalled the fear, the panic. But now, as before, she also remembered warm hands stroking her body, pressing into her flesh.

Clutching the blanket to her chin in an effort to ward off the sudden shiver that ran along her spine, she stole a glance at the considerable size of his hands. Could such large, powerful hands really be that gentle?

She lifted her eyes to find him watching her, staring at her from a rugged face that was framed by dark straight hair that was brushed back from the forehead, and anchored by a dark, bushy beard. Oddly enough, she suddenly was no longer afraid of him, and whether it was the softness in his eyes as he looked at her generous waistline or the worried frown that touched his brow as he considered her predicament, she didn't know. All she knew was that contrary to her earlier belief, this man was not going to hurt her.

Encouraged by the thought, she told him how her driver had abandoned her outside of town. "If I ever get my hands on that man, I won't be responsible for my actions!" she declared, sniffing in contempt.

He rubbed his cheek and chuckled. "If indeed you and this driver do have occasion to meet again, my only hope is that I am there to see it."

Regretting her previous behavior, she studied the still bleeding wound on his cheek. "I didn't intend to throw the knife at you."

"There's no need to apologize."

She studied him for a long moment before asking, "Do you have any medical supplies?"

"None that you would be familiar with." He stood.

"I think it would be a good idea for you to get some rest while I rustle up something to eat."

Nodding, she settled her head on the straw-filled pillow. She realized suddenly how hungry she was, but exhaustion took precedence and she soon felt herself grow drowsy. Through the haziness of her vision, she imagined a softening of the hard lines that fanned from his eyes as he leaned over and drew the covers up to her shoulders.

She stilled his hand with her own. "My valise," she whispered, knowing she had no right to ask him for anything. "Please ..."

Chapter 4

THE light between the narrow cracks of the cabin had turned from silver to gray by the time she awakened. She lay on her side, waiting for her eyes to adjust. It surprised her that she'd slept so long.

Her valise stood on the floor next to her bed. Tears of relief sprang to her eyes. Wiping them away impatiently, she pushed herself up on her elbows. The man—Logan St. John—was nowhere in sight.

She glanced toward the door. The problem was she needed to relieve herself. She climbed out of bed and opened her valise.

She lifted the only dress she now owned and held it next to her. She fingered the soft blue fabric and recalled the long hours she'd sat by candlelight in her room at the miners' boardinghouse, sewing the garment together. It was a simple dress, its only concession to fashion being a dust ruffle and a row of tiny mother-of-pearl buttons, a gift from one of the miners. She'd allowed extra room for her waist and she only hoped that the generous gathers would conceal at least part of her bulky form.

Casting an anxious glance toward the door, she quickly pulled off the fringed shirt and slipped the gown over her head. It was a tight squeeze but she finally managed to work the dress down the length of her. She breathed a sigh of relief that quickly turned into a cry of frustration upon discovering that the front of her bodice was separated by a two-inch gap. It was impossible to fasten the buttons.

Lord Almighty, it wasn't only her middle that had expanded. Now what was she going to do?

Before a plan occurred to her, the door flew open. Gasping aloud, she crossed her arms in front of her bared bosom to cover herself and gaped at the mountain man, whose impressive form filled the doorway.

It wasn't only his sudden appearance that startled her. He'd shaved off his beard and the results were astounding. She realized that the bronzed color of his skin was natural and not caused by the sun as she had earlier supposed. His smooth skin stretched over his high cheekbones. He was younger than she'd first thought, somewhere in his mid to late thirties. Without his beard, he certainly appeared less formidable, and this made her earlier fears that much more preposterous.

"I apologize . . . I . . ." His eyes traveled to her gaping chest that was still apparent despite her efforts to cover herself. A small bandage was centered on his cheek. He drew his eyes away and nodded to where a buckskin shirt hung from a wooden peg near the bed. "Feel free to help yourself to any of my shirts."

His gaze dropped to the floor as he backed outside again and shut the door after him.

Mortified to be found in such an embarrassing state, she fought her way out of the gown and slipped back into the same buckskin shirt she'd worn earlier. It was tempting to stay put, safe from his probing eyes, but nature's call left her no choice but to swallow her humiliation and step outside.

Mr. St. John was on the porch skinning a rabbit. At sight of her, he stood. Outlined against the distant mountains, he looked even less menacing than he had earlier in the confines of the cabin, but no less intimidating. He was the tallest man she had ever seen and his broad shoulders seemed to challenge the fur-lined jacket he wore. His upper thighs bulged above the deerskin leggings that were held in place by leather garters.

She took a deep breath. "I . . . I need to use the facilities."

"The outhouse is in the back."

"My boots . . ."

"Are soaking wet." With a toss of his head, he indicated a corner of the porch where her boots were located. "I stuffed them with straw and left them to dry."

Shivering, she rubbed her hands up and down her arms.

"Here," he said, pulling off his fur-lined coat. He held it out and waited for her to slip her arms through the oversize sleeves. The coat was far too large and its weight almost pulled her down. But she was grateful for the warmth it offered.

"It's getting mighty cold. May even snow." He glanced down at her bare feet. "Here." He doubled over and picked up a pair of moccasins. "Wear these."

"Thank you." She worked the sleeve up her arm so she could take them from him. He nodded and turned back to the rabbit. Glancing at the hapless animal, she shuddered and grabbed hold of the railing, fighting back a sudden wave of nausea.

As soon as her stomach settled down, she searched for a place to sit. There was only the wooden steps, but she decided if she sat down, she'd never manage to get back on her feet.

She tried to raise one foot to no avail. She couldn't even see her feet, let alone raise them high enough to put the moccasins on. This really was the last straw. Frustrated, she burst into tears.

Glancing over his shoulder, St. John looked positively startled. "Now what's the matter?"

His forehead was creased in what looked suspiciously like sympathy. This only made matters worse. When near strangers began to sympathize, a person really was in a sorrowful state.

"Everything!" she sputtered. She hated to admit it but she felt sorry for herself, and she didn't care one iota what he thought. "I can't fit into my own clothes.

I don't bend in the middle. I can't see my feet. My back aches and . . . I'm ugly."

"Ugly?" He straightened and looked at her aghast. "Why that's the most ridiculous thing I've ever heard of in my life."

His astonishment was obviously genuine and this only added confusion to her dejected state of mind. "How would you feel if you were as helpless as I am?"

He surprised her by bursting into laughter. "Helpless?" He touched the bandage at his cheek. "Lady, if you're helpless now, I'm eternally grateful for not having met you before."

Feeling utterly foolish, Libby struggled to compose herself. Lord Almighty, she never cried. Well, almost never. There was that one awful day when she had dug her husband's grave with her very own hands. She'd cried that day. Oh, yes, indeed. Long and hard, she'd cried, and her prayers had been muffled by uncontrolled sobs.

But never before had she attacked anyone with a knife. Not even during the entire six months she lived at that barbaric miners' boardinghouse and was subjected to all manner of unwanted advances. Not once in all that time had she resorted to violence or tears. So why suddenly, in the course of a single day, had she resorted to both?

"Let me," he said. Holding her gaze in his, he took the moccasins from her trembling hands and knelt at her feet. His fingers around her slim ankle felt warm and firm as he lifted her foot.

The familiarity of his touch settled it once and for all. The hands on her body had not been a dream. And if it wasn't a dream, then she was wrong to trust him. What she should be doing is concentrating on making her escape before he had a chance to finish what he'd begun.

He quickly slipped a moccasin on her cold foot, then lifted her other ankle. After completing the task, he stood.

Libby wiggled her toes in the depth of the warming softness. The moccasins were several sizes too large, but they did offer a measure of protection and at the moment she needed this. "I'm much obliged to you," she murmured, brushing aside her tears with a sleeve.

"Ready?" he asked.

"I . . ." She glanced around.

He held her face in his steadying gaze. "There's no one in town, if that's what you're worried about. Everyone's at the diggings. No one will see you."

"Oh." She sensed he was trying to allay her fears, but he only succeeded in making her more nervous. It was just the two of them. Alone in the town.

He didn't look like he meant to harm her, but it could be a ploy, this concern of his, a way of making her lower her guard. Well, she had no intention of lowering her guard. Or anything else, for that matter.

She lifted her head defiantly. "I'm ready."

He tilted his head as if puzzling over something, then held out his arm for her benefit.

Feeling as if she were about to burst, she slipped her hand into the crook of his elbow. For now, at least, physical need took precedence over fear.

"Careful," he cautioned.

The heels of the moccasins flip-flopped up and down as she walked by his side, down the wooden steps, around to the back of the house. Gopher holes dotted the area, gullies crisscrossed it. More than once, her foot slipped on a patch of ice, and had Mr. St. John not been holding on to her, she would have fallen.

He held her so steadily, she was surprised to see him limp. "Is there something wrong with your leg?"

"Just an old injury," he said brusquely.

A quick glance at the hard lines of his profile was enough to convince her not to pursue the matter any further.

The outhouse was nothing more than a tiny shed that had been hastily built from weathered boards.

"I'll wait here," he said. The last ten feet were fairly flat and free of obstacles.

She stepped inside the drafty structure and slid the wooden bar down to lock the door. Partly because of the cold but mostly because there was no way of escaping, she quickly answered nature's call and rejoined him. He once again offered his arm and they walked side by side back to the welcome warmth of the cabin.

After washing her hands in a basin of hot water, she held them in front of the fire to dry, feeling the warmth penetrate her palms while Logan made fresh coffee.

"Is there a hotel in town?" she asked.

"No."

She cleared her voice. "I can't stay here."

"Don't seem like you have a whole lot of choice."

She glanced nervously at the door. The door was bolted, and she couldn't help but wonder if it was to keep others out or to keep her in. "I'll wait at the stage stop for the next stage."

"That'll be a long wait. The next stage isn't due until the day after tomorrow."

"Nevertheless . . ." She walked over to the bed where her valise gaped open. She picked up her gown and held it in front of her. Maybe if she wore the buckskin shirt on top of the frock. It would look strange, but at least it would offer some measure of modesty.

"That's a mighty pretty dress," he said from behind her.

Her heart thudded nervously. He was blocking her way to the door. "If you'd be kind enough to leave, I wish to get dressed."

"No sense putting yourself through that again. If it didn't fit you the first time, it sure isn't going to fit you the second time."

He reached over her shoulder and took the gown from her. "It's a mighty pretty dress, though, ma'am. Mighty pretty." He folded it as if he'd folded a woman's dress before, and laid it in the open valise on top

of her other belongings. "Since you're not going anywhere, I suggest you get back in bed."

"You can't keep me against my will," she said.

He straightened. "It seems to me that you're stuck
here whether you want to be or not. Will has nothing
to do with it."

She hated the feeling that she had no say in the matter. Ever since coming to California, her life had followed an erratic path over which she had no control.
The fact that she was stranded in this stranger's cabin
was the last straw. Something snapped inside. Fueled
by an irrational need to take control once again over
her life, she bolted toward the door with more determination than speed, not sure what she would do once
she got there.

He caught her by the wrist as she fumbled with the
bolt. "You don't want to go out there. It's cold."

"Let me go!"

"Now there." He turned her toward him and wrapped
his arms around her. Fortunately, her belly kept him
somewhat at a distance, but the tender protection he offered touched the aching need inside, and like a frightened child, she clung to him.

"I think you'd better get back in bed where it's
warm," he murmured into her hair.

Feeling dazed by his heady masculinity, she pulled
away from his arms. "I don't need you telling me what
I should or should not do!"

"Are you always this emotional?"

"I'm not emotional!" she cried out emotionally, and
to prove that she was perfectly rational and in control,
she stood by the door, refusing to budge.

"Have it your way," he said impatiently. Without another word, he walked across the room and tossed another log onto the fire.

Feeling cold and more than a little foolish, she
walked to the bed and crawled beneath the covers.
"I'm sorry," she said.

He poked at the fire with a stick. "To what do I owe this apology?"

"I had no right talking to you like that."

He straightened. "I'll agree with that."

She swallowed hard. "And I shouldn't have thrown a knife at you."

He turned to face her. "Why did you? I told you I had no intention of hurting you."

"There's hurting and there's taking advantage."

He considered this a moment. 'Do you think I took advantage of you?"

She blushed and turned away.

"Well?" he persisted.

It was clear by the tone of his voice he wasn't going to let the matter drop. Very well, she thought, neither would she. She lifted her chin with more rancor than courage, and unflinchingly met his gaze. "Do you deny stripping me naked and . . ." She couldn't say the rest.

She didn't have to. He finished the sentence for her. "Rubbing my hands up and down your body?"

No amount of willpower could keep the flush from coloring her cheeks. "So you admit it?"

His face hardened. "The thing I admit to, Mrs. Summerfield, is saving your life. When I found you, your body temperature was dangerously low. I doubt that either you or the child would have survived much longer, certainly not through the night. I make no apology for stripping off your wet clothes or rubbing the circulation back into your body."

Mortified by her own naiveté, she was momentarily speechless. Face burning with embarrassment, she struggled to find her voice. But all she could manage was an inadequate "Oh."

Chapter 5

DURING the next hour, she lay on the lumpy bed, amid the confusion of pelts and blankets, and fought the urge to cover her head.

For the most part, he ignored her, and for this, she was grateful. For it allowed her to suffer her humiliation in private misery. It also freed her to study him at will.

Keeping her lashes lowered, she first stole one or two furtive glances in his direction before she abandoned any pretense of indifference and openly watched him work.

The artistry of his hands mesmerized her. She marveled at his skill as he expertly cut the freshly skinned rabbit into pieces with a sharply honed knife.

The grill of the woodstove sizzled as he placed the meat upon the red-hot surface.

Soon, the cabin was filled with a tantalizing smell, and Libby was reminded of how long it had been since she'd last eaten.

She couldn't recall ever having watched a man prepare a meal. Her mother and grandmother had done all the cooking while she was growing up, and if her father ever stepped foot in the kitchen, he had done so without her knowledge.

The delicious smell that filled the cabin made her heady with hunger and her mouth water. It occurred to her that this strange unpredictable man was already beginning to chip away at her carefully nurtured beliefs.

After all the edible meat was on the grill, he cleaned

up the leftovers. He then turned to face her, dangling one rabbit foot in the air. "There's a lot of fur on the bottom. Means a cold winter is on the way."

She stared at the foot curiously. "It's true then? You can tell the weather by an animal's fur?"

The question seemed to surprise him. "Why wouldn't it be true?"

"I don't know. It just seems a bit hard to believe that animals would know in advance how much fur to grow."

"If you lived in the wilds, you'd make it your business to know how to keep yourself warm."

"I suppose." His simplistic logic surprised her. Partly because he struck her as a complex man, not given to whimsical notions.

"Do you feel well enough to sit at the table?"

"I'm perfectly fit to sit anywhere I want," she said. It annoyed her to be treated like an invalid. She was expecting a baby, not nursing a dread disease.

After he set the table with two tin plates and coffee cups, she slipped her feet into the oversize moccasins and padded noiselessly to the table. She chose the chair closest to the fire, and watched as he served out portions of meat and beans onto their plates.

He sat down opposite her. She'd been taught not to begin a meal before a host began his. But being that she was famished, she was sorely tempted to break even that cardinal rule of etiquette. Fortunately, Mr. St. John prevented her fall from grace. For he wasted no time before digging into his own meal. Indeed, he'd no sooner sat down than he skewered a piece of meat with a small knife and lifted the pointed blade to his mouth.

Appalled, she watched him. Never had she seen such lack of good manners.

He continued in this vein for a moment or two before he even acknowledged her presence. "Why aren't you eating?"

"I would if I had eating utensils."

He held his knife toward her. "Use mine."

She shook her head. "Don't you have a fork?"

"Never saw a need for one."

She looked at him curiously. "What about a spoon?"

He picked up a piece of bark. "It does the job perfectly," he explained. He then demonstrated, scooping up a portion of beans onto the bark and raising it to his mouth.

She took a piece of bark and followed suit. He grinned at her. "What did I tell you? Works perfectly."

The bark served its purpose, but the only way she could eat the rabbit was by using her fingers. She heaved a sigh and began tugging the meat from a bone. She was too hungry to let propriety stand between her and much needed nutrition.

They finished eating in silence. The food was delicious, and once she'd overcome her aversion to eating with her fingers, she had no trouble finishing off every last morsel. "That was most delicious, Mr. St. John."

He looked pleased. "There's more if you like."

"I couldn't eat another bite." She mulled over the problem of how to apologize for accusing him of taking advantage of her. "I'm obliged to you for offering me shelter," she began tentatively.

He shrugged. "I could hardly leave you lying out on the porch, now, could I?"

"I really do apologize for your cheek."

He chuckled softly. "Well, now ... makes a man wonder why they call your condition delicate. As far as I can tell, there isn't anything delicate about it." He pointed to her plate. "Including your appetite."

Lowering her eyes, she blushed. "My valise ... How did you know?"

He dropped the last of the rabbit bones onto his plate and pushed it aside. "You talk in your sleep."

"I'm obliged to you." She looked up. "I truly am obliged. About my accusing you of taking advantage ..."

"I've been accused of worse, believe me."

She met his eyes, but after seeing something flare in their depths, she quickly looked away. "It's most urgent that I reach Nevada City before my baby comes. There's a doctor there."

"And of course your husband is there too." Something in his voice challenged her.

She lowered her lashes, feeling guilty for the lie. But at the time she told it, she really did believe the man meant to harm her. "Yes, of course."

He watched her quietly for a moment. "I'll see to it myself that you make the next stage."

She gave him a grateful smile. "I'm most obliged."

After they cleared the table and washed the dishes, she sat in the soft-cushioned chair next to the fire and read from the Good Book that she had carried with her all the way from Boston.

Mostly she made trips to the outhouse. Numerous trips.

"Is this normal?" Mr. St. John inquired after he'd escorted her outside at least a dozen times.

She nodded. "I expect so. The way the baby keeps kicking."

His eyes dropped down to her waist. "It must feel strange. I mean, little feet kicking you from the inside."

Something in his eyes caught her off-guard. A softness, perhaps a wistfulness. She wondered how she could have so thoroughly misjudged the man, and the need to make it up to him nearly overwhelmed her. "Would . . ." She bit her lip before continuing. "Would you like to feel the baby?"

"Now!" He looked shocked.

"I just thought maybe . . . It's really quite amazing."

"It doesn't seem quite proper for a man's hands to be touching a woman who's expecting a little one. I mean . . ." He looked away. "Unless, of course, it's to save her life."

"It doesn't seem proper that a man shouldn't share in a miracle if he has a chance. Seems to me that miracles don't happen very often."

He turned back to regard her. "Never thought about it like that before."

"Well, then?"

He cleared his throat. "Well, then what?"

"Do you want to feel a miracle or don't you?"

"I think, Mrs. Summerfield, that a miracle would be a mighty nice thing to feel."

He stepped forward, gazed into her face, and quickly looked away. After a moment he took another step forward and reached out his hand. She guided his hand to the place where only seconds earlier she'd felt a rippling movement. The warmth of his palm filtered through the buckskin shirt and seemed to radiate inward until it touched some needy part of her.

It was the first time since her husband died that she had been able to share with anyone such an intimate part of her life.

The baby kicked and Logan yanked his hand away. He stared at her stomach in amazement.

"I felt that," he said, clearly awed. "No wonder you have to . . . you know . . ." He nodded his head in the general direction of the outhouse. "How do you sleep with all that goings-on inside?"

She laughed and was surprised at the pleasure she felt. How long had it been since she'd laughed or even smiled? "It's not easy at times." His gaze dropped to her middle as if he expected to see some movement or change as they talked. "Do you want to feel it again?"

He lifted his eyes until they met hers. "I don't want to intrude."

Her cheeks grew warm. "You're not intruding."

"Are you positive?"

"Absolutely."

The corner of his mouth twitched upward. It wasn't a smile, exactly, but it brought a softness to his granitelike features that quickened her pulse.

Once again, he lifted his hand and laid it gingerly on her stomach. This time a full smile spread across his face. "I felt it!" he exclaimed. "He must be wearing boots."

His enthusiasm warmed her. "It could be a girl."

He looked at her dubiously. "I don't think a girl would carry on like that, do you?"

"She might."

He pulled his hand away and touched the bandage on his cheek. "You mean she might be a wildcat like her mother?"

Not wanting to think about her sorry behavior, she dropped her gaze.

"Do you mind?" he asked, and when she nodded her consent, his fingers worked across her belly once again, gentle, this time, as a breeze on a warm sunny day. Gentle as the hands that had caressed her body the previous night. He'd saved her life and for that she was grateful. Still, feminine vanity made her wish that he hadn't been privy to the full extent of her bulky shape.

He looked up suddenly and she was surprised by the look he gave her, a look of reverence that made her feel special and, strangely enough, even beautiful. The latter shocked her. She'd never felt beautiful in her life. Her mother was the beauty in the family, as was Libby's sister, Josie. So why on earth should she feel beautiful now? In the presence of this man? This stranger? This wild trapper?

He glanced at her parted lips and yanked his hand away from her as if the intimate nature of what they shared suddenly occurred to him. Without a word of explanation, he turned on his heels and walked outside, slamming the door shut behind him.

Libby stared after him with pursed lips. What a strange man, she thought. One moment so friendly, the next so brusque. The thought made her laugh. Lord Almighty, he could very well be thinking the same about her!

She couldn't remember having met a man like Mr. St. John. He was so different from her husband. The son of a preacher, Jeffrey had been every bit a gentleman. His strict religious upbringing influenced everything he'd done from conducting business to making love.

Her cheeks reddened as she considered Mr. St. John's personality and the possible influences his background might have on ... his activities.

Shocked by the direction her thoughts were taking, she decided to take advantage of his absence and rest. Since it was obvious she could no longer control her thoughts, she could only assume that the trip had taken more out of her than she had supposed.

It was late afternoon when she was awakened abruptly by the sounds of guns and wild whoops. Clutching the blankets to her chin, she sat up on the pallet and glanced nervously at the door.

Mr. St. John was sitting at the table, his head bent over what appeared to be a sheet of soft fabric. "Just the miners returning to town, is all. Letting off a bit of steam."

He seemed totally unconcerned by the mayhem waging outside his walls. Obviously, such wild behavior was common practice among the residents of Deadman's Gulch. As bad as the rumors and tales had been about this town, nothing had prepared her for the reality of it.

Rapid gunfire lambasted the air, followed by a silence that was no less frightening, and only made the blasts to follow seem that much louder. She needed to use the facilities again, but she'd die before setting foot outside the cabin.

The wild whoops and hollers continued for the remainder of the afternoon; horses stampeded past the cabin, shaking the very walls around Libby. Gruff male voices bellowed, guns fired.

Lord, if it didn't sound like war. Not that she knew what war sounded like, of course. But she did remember her father vividly describing his own experiences and the death of his brother during the War of 1812.

Fearing that a stray bullet would enter the cabin, she

sat huddled on a chair against the wall farthest away from the road. As was her usual habit during moments of anger or fear, she talked incessantly.

"I've never heard such rowdiness in all my born days. It's a wonder they haven't killed each other by now. Why ..."

She continued expressing her indignation and disgust, not to mention fear, for a full half hour without as much as a breather.

Logan couldn't help but laugh at the stern angry face tilted in his direction. She looked like an angry magpie. Sakes alive, he never knew anyone could talk so much. He'd heard that women in a "delicate condition" ate for two, but never had he heard tell that they talked for two.

At last he interrupted her tirade to ask, "Do you need to ..." He nodded his head in a way that had come to be understood by both.

Tearing her eyes away from the direction of rapid gunfire, she gave him a scowling look. "There isn't any way I'm going outside."

He shrugged and hesitated before adding, "I have something for you." He lifted the fabric he had been working on and shook it out in front of her.

It was a buckskin dress that was long enough to reach to her ankles. "It'll keep your legs warmer than my shirt," he said. "It'll also fit better."

She stared at the dress, her eyes incredulous. "You made that for me?"

He nodded. "As soon as I finish lacing up the seams, you can try it on."

She looked close to tears again. "I'm most ... obliged to you. I only wish I knew how to repay you for your kindness."

"There's no need," he said. It surprised him that she considered the garment a kindness. In his estimation, it was a necessity. He gave his full attention to the dress despite the escalating fracas outside. The entire time he worked, she fretted and fumed over the shocking wild behavior of the town's residents.

He responded to any direct question in a polite voice that showed no more concern than if they were discussing the weather. But mostly he let her talk unimpeded, although he did cast a speculative glance at her on occasion. He wasn't at all certain that a woman in her condition should be getting herself so worked up. Why didn't she settle down and rest? Why did she persist in asking him the same questions after every gun blast, and then think it necessary to restate her unfettered opinion of the town and its inhabitants as if he didn't already know it by rote.

"Did you hear that, Mr. St. John?"

"Yes, ma'am, just like the last time."

"I've never heard such unbecoming behavior in all my born days!"

"So you said."

"And I'll tell you another thing I've never heard of . . ."

He found it utterly amazing that she could ramble on so long without once stopping for air or taking the time to gather her thoughts. This probably explained why she kept repeating herself.

The daylight had begun to fade by the time he stood and shook out the finished garment and held it up for her inspection. "You can try it on now, if you like." He tossed the gown onto her lap. "I'll go outside while you change."

"Don't do that!" she exclaimed. He looked at her in bewilderment and she blushed. "I mean . . . Do you think you should? With all that gunfire? You might be hurt."

"One of the requirements for living in this town is to learn to dodge the bullets." He donned his fur-lined coat and lifted the hood over his head. With an empty wooden bucket in each hand, he headed for the door. "I'll be back in short order."

"You really don't need to leave. I trust you not to invade my privacy."

His back to her, he hesitated, then jerked open the door and was gone.

She listened anxiously for any gunfire, but to her relief all was quiet. She quickly pulled off his shirt, stopping momentarily to examine the bandaged wound on her shoulder, before she wiggled into the dress.

The shoulders and the top of the dress molded her body perfectly. Below the chest, the dress flared out with just enough fullness to accommodate her bulky shape without binding. Not only did the dress fit her width-wise, but the length was perfect. The hem reached clear down to her ankles.

Feeling less awkward, she glanced around the room searching for some smooth surface that would permit her to see her reflection. She'd not had the luxury of a looking glass since leaving Boston, and after Jeffrey died, the lack of such things hadn't seemed to matter.

She could well imagine what her prudish parents would say if they saw her now. The thought made her laugh. Her mother was always so particular about fashion and considered appearances of prime importance. Not one thought had been given to the practical nature of a garment.

As a result of this upbringing, Libby was ill prepared for her trip west. Her velvet traveling suits and satin gowns had been quickly replaced with sturdy calicos. She could only imagine what her mother would think upon seeing her arrive back in Boston dressed in buckskins!

As amused as she was by this last thought, memories of her family caused her spirits to sink.

Take our baby home, Jeffrey had said on his deathbed. It had been such an easy promise to make and such a difficult one to keep. She'd hoped to be back in Boston before the baby's birth. Now, she'd be lucky if she made it to Nevada City in time. Sighing, she reached into her valise for her silver-handled hairbrush and worked the soft bristles through her tangled curls until her hair fell in smooth waves around her shoulders.

She tossed the hairbrush back into her valise and picked up the gold locket that held a lock of her deceased husband's gold-colored hair. Memories. For the last several months she'd been sustained by memories. Memories of Jeffrey, of their life together, their dreams. It was the last dream, the dream Jeffrey had for his child, that kept her going.

"Oh, Jeffrey," she whispered half in prayer and half in determination. "I'll take our baby home. Just like I promised."

Chapter 6

LOGAN finished chopping wood, then carried the two buckets to the swift-running creek that zigzagged behind the cabin. Dipping first one bucket and then the other into the icy waters, he filled each one to capacity. Water sloshed over each brim as he carried the buckets back and set them on the porch to be used as needed.

He paused momentarily to stare at the cabin door. So she trusted him not to invade her privacy, did she? The woman gave him more credit than he deserved. He hadn't wanted to leave; he wanted to watch her undress. He wanted to touch her abdomen once again and to feel the soft rippling movements of the baby, this time with only her bare flesh beneath his hands.

It never occurred to him that a woman could be so beautiful while carrying out nature's purpose. How could such an astounding truth escape him all these years?

He was jolted out of his reverie by a bone-searing ache. For once it wasn't his leg that ached, it was his groin. It was his heart. It was his soul. He ached with loneliness and need. He ached with guilt for feeling such things. She needed his protection, not his lust. She trusted him and, by God, he meant to see that he never betrayed that trust.

Disgusted by the surge of desire that he seemed to have so little control over, he backed away from the house and glanced up and down the street. The town was relatively quiet, with no sound of guns or angry voices to break the solitude. Logan knew it was only a temporary quiet and that the miners would soon be racing through town again, their guns blasting.

Overhead, the sky was dark with heavy clouds. The wind had picked up considerably in the last hour or so, bringing with it the smell and taste of rain.

Logan absorbed all the subtle and not so subtle storm warnings as easily as a flower absorbs the sun. He listened to the birds, watched a squirrel frantically forge for acorns, sensed the heaviness in the air. Reading the weather was not a gift, it was a skill that had been taught to him by his father, who had learned it from his own father, Logan's grandfather. Predicting the weather was the first step to learning how to survive in the wilderness.

He estimated that the approaching storm would last anywhere from three to five days. It was his habit to stock supplies to last longer than the storm. He had enough fresh meat stored in the tiny smokehouse behind the shack, but he was running low on staples.

He didn't want to admit to himself that it wasn't supplies he needed as much as time for the inner fire of desire to run its course.

He shoved his hands down into the soft fur-lined pockets of his jacket and traipsed to the tiny general store that was squeezed between two tented saloons.

The wind blew against the canvas walls of the store with such force, the nails began to pull away from the rough wooden frames. A red-hot brazier provided some heat, but only if a person stood up close.

Seemingly oblivious to the impending collapse of his store, the store's proprietor, Hap Montana, looked up from his three-month-old newspaper and grunted. A short man with a bushy beard and head as bald as a hen's egg, he wasn't particularly friendly or talkative and that's exactly how Logan liked it.

Hap never concerned himself with neatness. The shelves were never stocked the same way twice; the goods were in no particular order. It irritated Logan to find a bottle of molasses lying on the shelf next to a block of beeswax and four rotting apples.

Knowing from past experience that Hap would be no help in locating the items he needed, Logan scanned the untidy shelves until he found what he was looking for. His arms filled with tinned goods, tallow candles, and lye soap, he dumped the items onto the rough-hewn counter.

Hap folded his paper. "Anything else?"

"You'd better give me some illuminating oil."

Hap stood on a wooden crate to reach the shelf over his head where a single can of oil stood next to an iron skillet.

Logan glanced around. "You don't happen to have any eating utensils, do you?"

Hap stepped off the crate and pointed to a wooden keg. "You might find a few pieces in there."

Logan walked over to the deep barrel and started digging through a wide assortment of goods. Amid a hodgepodge of tin cups, spools of flaxen thread, playing cards, and a book on the life of Franklin, he found a knife and fork forged out of steel. Neither matched, but they would serve the purpose. On impulse, he reached for the book. Perhaps if Mrs. Summerfield was occupied with a book, she would be less inclined to talk so much.

Hap sorted through the supplies Logan selected with great interest, holding up the eating utensils. "What's the matter, St. John? Ain't your fingers good enough anymore?" He laughed aloud and wet the tip of his lead pencil with his tongue, then proceeded to add up the purchases. He glanced up. "Holy smokes, how long do you think this storm is gonna last? You got 'nough supplies here to last a month."

Logan had no intention of revealing the fact that he was entertaining a guest. He shuddered to think how the miners would react upon finding a woman in their midst. They'd all be pounding on his door demanding to see her, and he'd be obliged to stand guard over her twenty-four hours a day. "If the storm lasts that long, I'll be ready."

"That'll come to thirty-two dollars even."

Logan frowned. It was highway robbery, that's what it was, the prices Hap charged. He paid for his purchases and headed for the door.

"Enjoy your eating utensils," Hap called after him. The man's laughter followed Logan outside.

A few raindrops fell as he hastened down the dirt road toward his cabin. Upon reaching the porch, he hesitated and wondered if he should knock. Suddenly he felt like an intruder in his own house.

He hated this, hated having to share his space. It was bad enough that his leg forced him to hole up in a cabin, but it was only for the winter. Once the danger of snow had passed, he would be on his way again, in search of open spaces. He could hardly wait to head north again, away from the madness that had suddenly descended upon California. It was getting so a man couldn't think anymore without noise clogging up his thought processes.

He decided against knocking, but he did pound his feet against the porch to rid the soles of his moccasins from any loose dirt. When at last his moccasins were clean and he was convinced she'd had adequate warning, he stomped inside.

She stood facing the door, looking prettier than a field of summer wildflowers. Even he was surprised at the perfect fit of the dress. He'd relied on memory alone to determine size. Using the only tools of measurement a free trapper ever needed, his hands and his fingers, he had depended on the memory of running his hands over her body to judge her shoulders, arm, and breast size.

"Do you like it?" she asked, turning around so he could see the dress to full advantage. "It couldn't be more perfect."

He watched her cheeks grow flushed, and was surprised by her reserved manner. It was difficult to equate the woman in front of him with the wildcat who had only a short time earlier thrown a knife at him.

"How did you know my size? You'll never know how I used to dread the endless fittings my mama insisted upon with each new outfit. But even with all the careful measurements and pinning, I don't think I ever had a dress fit so perfectly."

"I'm a trapper," he said brusquely, as if this were explanation enough. He let the door slam shut behind him. He hadn't counted on her looking every bit as fetching in her new dress as she had in his old shirt. Damned woman would probably look good in a flour bag. He carried his packages across the room and dropped them on the table. "Are you hungry?"

"Come to think of it, I am. Can you imagine? After the meal I ate earlier ... why I never knew myself to have such a healthy appetite. Not since ..."

"Can't you just answer a question with a simple yes or no?"

She looked hurt. "Don't you like to talk?"

"I have nothing against talking." He hated her habit of making him feel guilty. He had no idea how she managed it, but she did it on purpose, he was certain of it. "I don't think a person should talk more than is necessary."

"How can you let the other person know what you're thinking if you don't come out and say it?"

"If you have to beat someone over the head with words, I reckon they don't want to know what you're thinking."

A shadow of a frown touched her otherwise smooth forehead. "Why don't you just say that you're not interested in knowing anything about me?"

"I know everything there is to know about you," he said, tearing into his packages. Recalling with startling clarity how her naked flesh had looked by firelight, he decided he knew too damned much.

She folded her arms across her chest and lifted her

chin in bold challenge. "Just exactly what do you know about me?"

He narrowed his eyes. "I know that you're from Boston, are dangerous with a knife, and probably never worked a day in your life before coming to California."

"Ha! And you think you know everything!"

He couldn't resist the challenge. "I also know that you don't have a husband waiting for you in Nevada City—or any other city for that matter."

This got a reaction, as he knew it would. She stared at him dumbfounded, not saying a word, her velvet-soft mouth parted and her beautiful eyes as round as saucers.

He couldn't help but laugh. "Why, Mrs. Summerfield, in the short time I've known you, you've never been more articulate." He touched the patch on his cheek. "Save the time you attacked me with a knife." He chuckled to himself as he stooped to toss kindling into the firebox of the woodstove. He glanced at her briefly as he reached for the tinderbox and flint.

"How did you know?" Her voice was strained, coming out in a half whisper.

"About your husband?" He lit the fire and closed the door of the firebox, adjusting the vent. "A man would have to be a fool to leave his wife alone in a place like this."

She was silent for a long time, so long, in fact, he glanced over his shoulder to see whether she was still in the room. The look on her face made him regret his careless words. So much in fact, he was pretty near tempted to apologize. Fortunately, she spoke and saved him the trouble of having to figure out what the sam hill he should say.

"He died shortly after we arrived here," she said. "Malaria."

He frowned, thinking about his own wife and her untimely death. "Did he know about the baby?"

She nodded. "He made me promise to take the baby home."

"Why'd you come to California?"

The question seemed to surprise her. "The same reason as everyone else. Gold."

He didn't miss the tight edge of her voice, or the look on her face. It was obviously a decision she'd not only come to regret, but had come to hate. It wasn't surprising. It amazed him how many city-bred men came to this untamed wilderness to try their hand at mining for gold. He'd actually found some of these men on the trail starving to death because they had no knowledge of how to hunt or fish or even how to use a weapon. Fools, all of them.

"Most wives stay home and let their men come alone."

"I guess I'm not like most wives. I believe a woman's place is with her husband. What about you?"

He was ill-prepared for this sudden turn of conversation. "What *about* me?"

"Why don't you have a wife?"

He slammed the skillet onto the stove. He had a wife. Once. But she didn't want any part of him. Not that he blamed her. He was a trapper, a mountain man. What did he have to offer a woman? Still, he was surprised by the anger and bitterness the question provoked. He'd thought that after all this time, there was nothing in the past left to haunt him. And until Libby Summerfield showed up on his doorstep, there hadn't been.

"Did I say something wrong?" Her voice caressed his ears with velvetlike softness. "I didn't mean to pry into your private affairs . . ."

But she had, dammit! Just her presence seemed to pry holes in the protective shield that separated him from the unwanted memories of the past. She asked too many questions, that's what she did. How could a man concentrate on what he was doing with all the tongue flapping going on? He grabbed a package containing the eating utensils he'd purchased and shoved it into her hands.

As predicted, the small gift surprised her into silence once more. At least it was comforting to know that peace and quiet could be bought.

Later, they sat at the table and ate the rest of the rabbit that Logan had cooked up and something he called sweet potatoes.

"All the way from the Sandwich Islands," he explained. "Cost me seventy-five cents apiece." He watched her lift the fork to her mouth as she tasted the yellow meat inside the potato. The dainty way she ate made him frown. Once again, he was reminded of Catherine.

"It was worth every cent," she said softly.

He drew his eyes away and concentrated on his own meal. He stabbed the food on his plate with his knife and pretended not to notice the look of disapproval she gave him each time he drew the blade to his mouth. He was used to eating in silence. It was too damned difficult to work conversation around the business of chewing. He tried to foil any attempt on her part to force polite conversation. But the woman didn't give up that easily and much to his dismay, her questions persisted, forcing him into reluctant participation.

"Why aren't there any windows in your cabin?"

"Don't see no need for windows."

"Windows let in air and light," she persisted.

"All the air and light a man could ever need comes in through the cracks."

"But you can't see much through the cracks."

He shrugged. "That's the point. If no one can see you, they can't go using you for target practice."

Libby shuddered at the thought. "What a strange place this is, where a man's not even safe in his own home." How she hated this land, this barbaric hellhole that had deprived her of her husband. How she hated the town that had put her unborn child in jeopardy and now held her prisoner.

His face was inscrutable as he watched her. "A man

who lives inside a building is at a disadvantage. The very walls that offer shelter also hide the enemy."

She regarded him curiously. She'd heard about men like this. Mountain men. Men who roamed the wild. "What do you do when it rains?"

"Catch up on my sleep." After a moment's pause he explained. "Indians never attack in the rain. Nor for that matter do animals. Rain is the safest time to sleep. Of course, one can always find a warm cave. Ever stay in one?"

"No, I never did."

The corner of his mouth quirked upward as if he suddenly saw humor in the question. "What a pity. Caves stay warm in the winter, cool in the summer, and need no maintenance. You don't have to worry about leaky roofs." He reached for the empty plate in front of her, but she stayed his hand with her own.

"Let me," she said. "I'm not exactly helpless."

He looked down at the small pale hand against his own dark skin and felt a strange stirring inside. "No, ma'am, I don't suppose you are. What do you say we work together?"

He rose to his feet and walked to the fireplace to fetch the steaming hot kettle. Grabbing the handle with a piece of soft leather he kept for the purpose, he poured hot water into two metal basins, one for washing and one for rinsing.

She washed the dishes while he dried and set the plates on the shelf over the sink. At one point, he inadvertently brushed against her hair with his hand. She glanced up at him and their eyes locked for a moment before they both turned away and pretended to be absorbed by something else. He added yet another log to an already blazing fire and she scrubbed a knothole at the center of the wooden table as if it were a stain to be removed.

Presently, he reached for his fur jacket that hung from a wooden peg and shrugged it onto his massive shoulders. "I'll be gone for a while. I'll be just across the way. The boys and I like to play cards. The fire should last until I get back." He walked to the door and hesitated. "There's a chamber pot beneath the bed." He kept his back to her as he spoke. "You'll be safe inside." He closed the door after him.

She abandoned the table and stood the scrub brush on end to dry. She wiped her hands on an empty flour sack, and not wanting to chance stepping outside to dump the dishwater, she left it.

The cabin suddenly seemed very cold and lonely. Strange as it seemed, she actually missed the mountain man with his abrupt mannerisms and peculiar ways. Shivering, she stoked the fire and drew a chair closer to its warmth.

The town grew noisier as the night progressed. Raucous voices rose over the sound of foot stomping and fiddle playing. But it was the intermittent gunfire that gripped her with fear. Each shot sent her heart racing. To think that before coming to California, she'd never heard a gun except on holidays or special occasions. As a child, she associated the firing of guns and cannons with joyful occasions, and it wasn't until she was old enough to understand the war stories her father told that she knew guns could be used to harm people.

Her nerves taut, she picked up the Good Book and searched the dog-eared pages for words of comfort. But if there was any consolation to be found among the revered Scriptures, she wouldn't know. She couldn't concentrate enough to read, not with all the wild hollering and shooting outside. Finally, she closed the leather cover and tucked the little Bible back into a corner of her valise. She ran her hand across the tiny nightgown she'd made for the baby. Smiling to herself, she lifted the gown and held the soft fabric to her cheek. When she married Jeffrey, she had dreamed about the day she would present him with a son. They had so many dreams, the two of them, dreams of finding gold, of going back to Boston and opening up a business of their own.

Jeffrey had been determined to strike it rich. He had some crazy notion that he'd failed her. No matter how many times she'd told him that she didn't blame him for the failure of the bank where he'd worked, he still blamed himself. All she wanted was for him to get the gold fever out of his system so they could go home and raise the family they both wanted.

At the time they made their plans, they had been so in love, it had never occurred to either of them that fate would step in and deal them a cruel hand.

She shivered at the thought of what fate might still have in store for her. Even if she made it to Nevada City in time for the birth of her baby, there was still the journey to Sacramento City and the dreaded six-month ocean voyage before she reached Boston.

Startled by a sudden loud blast just outside the cabin, she jumped involuntarily. She covered her face with her hands. What a dreadful place this was. Home had never seemed farther away than it did at that moment.

Chapter 7

SHE woke with a start. The room was lit softly by the red embers from the dying fire. A quick glance at the dark form on the floor confirmed that Mr. St. John was asleep in his bedroll. It surprised her that his presence had such a calming effect on her. Now that she'd gotten over her initial fear of him, she felt completely safe in his company.

Something—a soft plopping sound—startled her. Tensing, she strained her ears. It dawned on her finally that it was raining outside and the sound came from a leak in the roof.

"Mr. St. John," she whispered.

When he didn't move, she settled back. She supposed the leak could wait until morning. Besides, the rhythmical drips had a lulling effect on her. Her life was so filled with uncertainties, the constant dripping provided a small, but no less comforting measure of reassurance. Mr. St. John's presence provided yet another.

She woke the following morning to the sound of her host moving around the room. The floor was dotted with every possible receptacle to catch the many leaks that had sprung up in the night.

Mr. St. John greeted her with a nod of the head. "Like I said, never had to worry much about leaks in a cave."

"You're beginning to make a believer out of me."

He glanced up at the ceiling that was barely four inches above his head. "I do believe it's raining harder inside than it is outside."

She shared a spontaneous laugh with him, which faded into a self-conscious smile when she realized he was no longer laughing. Instead, he was perfectly still, like a man about to net a rare butterfly.

As if to catch himself staring at her, he turned suddenly and poured a cup of fresh-brewed coffee, which he handed to her. It was strong and bitter, but she welcomed the warmth. The air was cold and damp, turning her every breath into tiny clouds of white mist. The wind whistled through the cracks behind her, and shivering, she moved away from the wall. She drank her coffee in silence and after he announced that breakfast was ready, she inched her feet over the side of the bed and into his oversize moccasins.

"Walk on the planks." He pointed to the strips of wood that he'd arranged on the muddied floor while she slept.

She sat at the table in a chair closest to the fire. "What time is the stage due to arrive?" she asked.

"Won't be any stage. Not till the rain stops."

Dismayed by the news, a moment passed before she protested it. "But there has to be a stage. I have to get to Nevada City."

"In this part of the country it's best if you don't try to get anywhere fast." He studied her a moment. "Don't look so worried. The rain won't last more than three days."

He spoke with enough authority to pique her curiosity. "How do you know that?"

"Night before last I saw a ring around the moon. Counted three stars in the ring. That's a pretty good indication of how long it will rain." After breakfast, which consisted of flapjacks and strips of dried beef, Mr. St. John changed the dressing on her wound. His touch was as gentle as a butterfly's wing against her skin as he washed her shoulder with a soft chamois dipped in warm water.

"There's no infection," he said. "In no time at all your shoulder should be as good as new."

Her eyes met his. "I could have been killed."

"You were lucky."

"This is a barbaric, hateful town." She shuddered. "Why do you live here?"

He cut off a piece of gauze with his knife and placed it gently on her shoulder. "There's a wild group here, all right. But for the most part you know where you stand. A man might kill you, but at least he'll do it to your face."

"I didn't see the man who shot me the other night."

"That was an accident." He finished bandaging her wound and rolled down her buckskin sleeve to cover it.

She thanked him and, unable to find a comfortable position in which to sit, spent the remainder of the morning waddling across the wooden planks that criss-crossed the room. Her disposition grew worse with each passing hour. She walked like a duck and felt as unattractive as a full-grown bear. She was imprisoned in a dangerous town with only a mountain man for company. And any day now, she could give birth to Jeffrey's child.

She stopped next to the table where Mr. St. John sat sharpening his knives. "What if the rain lasts more than three days? It's possible I won't make it to Nevada City in time and . . . Do you realize that my baby could be born right here? In this town? In this . . ." She glanced in dismay at the drafty cabin walls and the muddied dirt floor that was dotted with little pools of water. "Here?"

He studied the blade of his dagger-type hunting knife. "It's possible."

"And what happens if something goes wrong? If the baby is turned around and . . ." On and on she went, recalling every possible complication of birth she'd ever heard of, and they were considerable. It was not proper, of course, to discuss such things in polite company and if the subject ever did come up in a proper Boston home, it was quickly shunned.

When the thought occurred to her that it might be

improper to talk of such things to Mr. St. John, she immediately decided that by Boston standards, he would not by any stretch of the imagination be considered polite company. Relieved, she gave full rein to repeating every god-awful tale she'd ever heard.

During the time of this unsettling discourse, Mr. St. John remained seated and kept busy sharpening his knives on an obsidian rock he used as a whetstone. He paused only on occasion to glance at her or shake his head in disbelief at something she said. "I never heard of a baby with two heads," he said at one point. Another time he put down his knife and stared at her aghast. "Are you sure?"

Finally, he'd had quite his fill of horror stories. "I told you the rain will stop in three days. You'll make it to Nevada City in time and by the way that baby kicks I would say it's probably going to be as healthy as a wild bull."

She thought about this for a moment. "Are wild bulls always healthy?"

"Never saw one that wasn't."

"We have no guarantee that the rain will last only three days."

"If you can't trust the stars, what can you trust?"

"Are you always so trusting?"

He shook his head. "Only as far as nature is concerned."

"Does that mean you don't trust people?"

"I discovered a long time ago that it's a whole lot better for the health of a free trapper not to."

Not wanting to argue the issue, she reached behind to rub her aching back. "I wish Jeffrey were here," she said. "He'd know what to do."

Just thinking about her dear beloved husband filled her with pain. The pain was so intense that it seemed to cut her in two. She let out a low cry and grabbed her stomach.

Mr. St. John shot to his feet, sending his chair flying across the room. "Are you all right?"

Surprised by the concern on his face, she shook her head. "It was a sharp pain. They come and go. There isn't by chance a doctor in town, is there?" She'd been told that the only practicing doctor in the area could be found in Nevada City, but it was possible that there was a nonpracticing doctor locally. No profession was immune to the lust of gold fever.

"A doctor? In Deadman's Gulch?" The surprise in his voice suppressed any hope she harbored to the contrary. "No, ma'am, 'fraid not."

The pain subsided and Libby continued to pace back and forth along the wooden planks, stopping on occasion to move a pot or pan to better catch a drip.

"Maybe if you don't move around so much, you'll keep from stirring things up inside until you get to Nevada City."

"I don't think moving around has anything to do with it."

"You can't be sure about that. I've seen animals in the wild get riled just before their time. Move around in circles, back and forth. Maybe that's nature's way of triggering things." He grabbed a chair and set it down beside her. "Sit!"

Unwilling to argue with him, she did as she was told.

He grabbed a footstool and propped it under her feet. "From now on, you're not to move. Do you hear?" He handed her the book on Franklin. "Read this."

She hated the idea of sitting for any length of time in one place. But since there didn't seem to be anything else to do, she settled down to read. It didn't take long for her to decide that her strange host was far more interesting than Benjamin Franklin. "You said you were a free trapper. What does that mean?"

He glanced up from the knife he was working on. "My father and I trapped beavers. Isn't much call for beaver, anymore."

"So you came to California to look for gold?"

"Not me. I plan to spend the winter here and then head up north at the first sign of spring."

"What made you move to Deadman's Gulch?"

"Didn't have much choice. I came to California because of the relatively milder winters. The mountains were taken over by strangers. Every time I left my cave, someone would sneak inside and start digging up the floor. One night, I returned home and fell into a fifteen-foot hole." What he didn't say was how that fall had caused further injuries to his already bad leg. "Trust me, ma'am, it's a whole lot safer in Deadman's Gulch."

"Did you ever think about moving to a more civilized town?"

He looked startled by the idea. "Now why would I be doing that?"

"You could take a stroll without having to dodge bullets, for one thing. You could also go to the theater and even attend church."

"Church, uh? Well, now, that sounds like a whole lot more civilization than I care to handle."

"You might be surprised."

The golden lights in his eyes disappeared as if an inner candle had been blown out. "It's been my experience, Mrs. Summerfield, that some people were born to live in the city and some of us were born to live outside it. That's nature and you best try not to fool around with nature."

Without another word, he stood, grabbed his coat, and left the cabin.

He was gone for the rest of the day, leaving Libby with a lot of time to puzzle over what she had said to offend him.

It wasn't all she puzzled over. She was intrigued by him, drawn to him. Not that this was all that surprising, she supposed. Oddly enough, they had a lot in common. They were both in Deadman's Gulch against their wills. He wanted to go back up north, she to Boston. Although she knew very little about his past, she was willing to bet that he'd lost someone as she had lost Jeffrey. That would explain the loneliness she sensed in him. Explain why her own deep-rooted and private feelings of longing struck a responsive chord whenever she was with him.

It was a comforting thought, and one she readily accepted. Her dear sweet Jeffrey had only been dead seven months. It was too soon, far too soon, to think about anyone else in her life, except as a friend. And never had she needed a friend more.

Now that she understood why she reacted so favorably toward the trapper, she felt considerably relieved. She made herself some tea and nibbled on a piece of tasteless nail-hard pilot bread.

She sat huddled in front of the fireplace, trying to stay dry and not to think about the gunshots that sounded outside. No amount of rain, it seemed, kept the residents of Deadman's Gulch from riding through town with their guns blasting and raising bedlam.

It was well after midnight by the time Mr. St. John returned.

Feigning sleep, Libby watched him strip off his buckskins until he was dressed only in his long underwear. In the dying light of the fire, he looked taller than usual. The fabric of his long johns clung to his lean, yet well-muscled body, straining against the rich outlines of his masculine form. A shiver ran through her; her heart pounded erratically. Horrified at this unexpected response to his undressed state, she shut her eyes tight and tried in desperation to conjure up Jeffrey's face.

The following morning she woke with a gnawing ache in the center of her back. "Oh, rot!"

"What are you rotting about?" Logan asked. He sat up in his bedroll and rubbed his eyes. The faint gray light of dawn filtered through the cracks. "Do you always wake up this early?"

"Only when I have a backache."

"I'll trade you your backache for my headache."

"Your headache will probably be gone by the end of the day."

He groaned. "Maybe your backache will be too."

"You'd better hope not," she said. "Otherwise we'll *both* have a headache."

"Can you lay on your stomach?"

"Can you turn a mountain upside-down?"

He climbed out of his bedroll. His leg had stiffened during the night and he rubbed it briskly before limping over to the side of her bed. "How about lying on your side?"

Keenly aware that he was dressed only in his long johns, she kept her eyes averted as she turned toward the wall. The feel of his hands on her back was heaven. His fingers were firm yet gentle, seeming to know instinctively where to press. She found herself relaxing. In no time at all, the pain felt less acute.

"How's that feel?" he asked, pulling his hands away.

"It feels . . . better." She moved her back to test it. "Much better."

"I'll make us some fresh coffee."

"You'd better put something on," she called. "Before you catch a chill."

He made no reply, but she breathed a sigh of relief when a soft rustling sound told her he was getting dressed. She waited until she heard the clamoring sound of pots and pans before she dared to turn over. Once she did, she couldn't take her eyes off him. She reminded herself on occasion that her interest in him was friendly in nature. Who in their right mind wouldn't be curious about the strange, tall mountain man? she reasoned. So rough, so gentle, so unlike any man she'd ever met.

The rain continued for the next two days, sometimes pelting the cabin so hard, Libby feared the roof would cave in. At other times the rain scurried across the roof like the racing feet of a thousand little mice.

To while away the seemingly endless hours, she read all of the Franklin book and then devoted her time to the Good Book. She reread the book of Matthew and had just begun to read Mark when Mr. St. John questioned her about what she was reading.

"I'm reading the story of Christmas," she replied.

"I heard of Christmas." He was working on his wooden gold-mining cradle. He had been working on it for the better part of the morning.

"Don't you celebrate Christmas?" she asked.

"Celebrate?"

"You know, cut down a tree. Have a special dinner."

"In the winter months, I cut down plenty of trees. It's the only way to keep warm. As for dinner, anytime you eat in the winter, it's special." He fell silent for a moment, before adding, "Come to think about it, I guess I do celebrate Christmas." He grinned across the table at her. "And I didn't even know it." After a while, he asked her to read aloud to him.

She looked surprised by the request, but complied, her lovely clear voice gliding over the words as easily as water over rocks. He was struck by the beauty of the Christmas story. It was a surprisingly simple story, nowhere near as complicated as he'd imagined.

Sometime later she closed the Bible and stared wistfully into the fire. "Christmas is next week."

"Next week, uh?"

Feeling overwhelmed by a wave of homesickness, she fell silent. Had it only been a year ago that she and Jeff had celebrated their last Christmas together at her parents' Boston home? Jeff had cut down the perfect spruce and the family had decorated it with dozens of tiny little candles.

Everyone—including her brothers and sisters, grandparents, aunts, uncles, nieces, and nephews—had gathered around the table for roast duckling with all the trimmings. After dinner, they had crowded around the spinet piano in the parlor to sing Christmas carols.

She recalled that after the festivities were over, she and Jeffrey had sat alone by the Christmas tree. It was the night he'd first mentioned his idea of traveling out west to try his hand at gold mining. At first she refused to take him seriously; she was convinced it was some sort of joke.

For months the newspapers had been filled with news of the gold found in California and many of their friends and neighbors had already left jobs and family to head west. But it had never occurred to her that Jeffrey would want to follow. He was so serious-minded, always talking about investments and savings, and planning his life with the same precision a mapmaker charted land.

"Don't you see?" he'd asked that last Christmas they would ever spend together. "We'll be rich."

"What do you know about gold mining?" she asked. Unable to find suitable employment when his bank failed, he'd helped her father in his printing business. Jeffrey hated the work. It was too tedious, he said, and offered no challenge or opportunity to exercise his mathematical skills.

"What does anyone know about mining for gold?" he'd asked. "That little detail is not stopping anyone else from traveling to California. Look at old man Mullins. All he knows is blacksmithing. And what about O'Henry? The man's an actor."

"But neither one of those men has a wife," she pointed out.

"Not every man can be as lucky as I am." She recalled with aching heart how lovingly he had spoken those words. She also remembered what else he'd said. "I wouldn't expect you to give up everything and go with me. In fact, I insist that you stay here."

"I will not stay here while you go gallivanting clear around the world." How determined she'd been. How naive.

"I'm not going clear around the world. I'm only going to California. Please, Libby. I don't want to have to worry about you. I'll only be gone a year or two."

It hurt that he made such a long separation from her seem trivial. "If you go, I intend to go with you!"

Her family was scandalized at the idea. Indians and

diseases were cited as reasons to abandon the idea and stay home. Who knew what other perils awaited the unseasoned traveler? But Libby had made up her mind and in the end, even Jeffrey relented.

"I'll make arrangements as soon as the holidays are over," he'd said as they stood on the balcony listening to the church bells peal in the new year. And with those few words, their fates were sealed.

He booked passage on a ship heading for Panama. From there, they made the nightmarish three-day journey to the Pacific Ocean by way of a mule train and a lot of luck. Even so, it was a difficult route and Libby was convinced the mosquito-infested Chagres River was responsible for the illness leading to Jeffrey's eventual death. They arrived in San Francisco one dismal day in late April, nearly four months after leaving Boston.

Libby didn't want to think about the rest. But try as she might to stop herself, snatches of past memories weaved a dark path through her thoughts. Jeffrey passing out in the stage that carried them to the Sierras. The night she sat bathing his feverishly hot forehead, knowing the end was near. The dreary gray morning she'd buried him with her own two hands, with nothing more than a crude wooden cross to mark his grave.

During the long lonely months that followed, she worked at a miners' boardinghouse, washing clothes and scrubbing floors. She took in mending in her spare time and managed to save practically every penny she earned until she had enough to pay her way back home to Boston.

Shaking herself from the memories of the last year, Libby watched Mr. St. John dress the wood of the gold rocker he had built. He shaved away tiny chips with the blade of his knife, then ran his long sensitive fingers over the smooth surface to check for any rough edges.

Reminded how he'd once run those same sinewy

fingers up and down her body, she felt a shiver travel down her spine.

Although she held herself perfectly still and, as far as she knew, gave nothing away, he paused as if to sense something. "Another pain?"

She nodded mutely, not trusting herself to speak. It worried her that they were so closely tuned to each other. Jeffrey was never one to pick up on subtleties.

"It looks like a baby cradle," she said, trying to draw his attention away from her and back to his handiwork.

He grinned, and rocked it back and forth. "Who'd ever think that an old unmarried man like me would spend so much time rocking a cradle?"

The cradle reminded her of all the things she wanted and lacked for her baby. Depressed by the thought, she fell silent again.

Presently, Logan stood and stretched. "I think the rain has stopped. Maybe I'll mosey on over to the saloon. My hands are itching for a good card game." When she said nothing, he studied her thoughtfully. "You don't think there'll be a problem."

"Why should there be?"

"You've hardly spoken a word all afternoon. That alone suggests something's afoot."

"The baby isn't due till the end of the month." Anxious for some time alone, she sounded more confident than she felt. "I'll be fine."

"Well, now." He put another log on the fire and donned his fur jacket. He hesitated at the door. Maybe he shouldn't leave her. She looked pale and listless, her usually bright eyes lacked sparkle. On the other hand, she didn't seem to be particularly interested in his company. With an uneasy glance at her pale, rigid face, he promised himself to make it an early night, and walked outside.

After he was gone, she decided that some fresh air might perk up her spirits. It was still light outside, and

judging by the quiet, the street deserted. She decided if
she hurried, she could sneak some fresh air before the
men began their usual nighttime fracas. She opened the
door cautiously and, seeing no one in sight, stepped
outside.

The sky was gray with clouds, but for now, at least,
the rain had stopped. The air had turned colder but it
felt invigorating against her skin, and smelled as fresh
as a field of daisies. She walked over to the wood railing and inhaled until her lungs were filled.

Suddenly a man ran out of the cabin across the way,
followed by another. Before she had a chance to rush
back into the house, a fistfight was in full swing directly in front of Mr. St. John's cabin.

Men spilled onto the street like an army of ants. In
a blink of an eye, a fair-sized crowd had gathered
around the battling duo. Amid the shouts and hand
clapping, the spectators were forced to jump back on
occasion to avoid being splashed by mud.

Libby was so startled by the suddenness of the fight,
she stood motionless in the shadows of the porch out
of fear of drawing attention to herself.

One of the miners, a man with a red beard and red
curly hair, suddenly pointed in her direction. "Look
over there!"

It took Libby a moment before she realized she was
the object of his interest. The boisterous shouts and
curses faded as the startled men turned to gape at her.

"A woman!" someone exclaimed, and this was
enough to gain the attention of even the two mud-
covered opponents. The battling foes stopped in
midswing and joined the others to stare at Libby in
wide-eyed astonishment.

"Well, I'll be!" said one, rubbing his battered cheek.

"Come on, men!" yelled the red-bearded man. "After her!"

Chapter 8

LIBBY'S heart pounded in terror as she fled inside and slammed the door shut. Fingers trembling, she reached for the rusty metal bolt. After a frantic but futile attempt to slide it into the wooden hinge, she spun around in search of something to prop in front of the door.

Her stomach clenched in a tight knot, she stumbled across the room just as the door flew open. She cried out in protest as the roughest, meanest, and scruffiest men she had ever seen pushed their way inside.

Impaled by their drunken eyes, she felt like a piece of meat up for grabs. Anger replaced some if not all of her fear as she stared back at them.

"Well, well, what have we got here?" This was from a barrel-shaped man with a ragged beard. "Logan's been holding out on us."

"I'll say," said a rail-thin man who hiccuped and took a swig from a half-filled whiskey bottle.

With more defiance than confidence, she held her ground. "You'd better go."

One man laughed. "Will you listen to that? The little lady is telling us what to do."

His mocking tone made her blood boil and she forgot her fear completely. Fists planted firmly at her waist, her eyes flashed with turquoise fire. "This is private property. You have no right to force your way in here."

The man who seemed to be the leader looked momentarily taken aback. It was clear he hadn't expected

her to stand up to them. "Well, now, would you listen
to that? The woman is a stranger to these parts and
she's telling us what our rights are."

A short man with a skinny mustache was the first to
notice Libby's ungainly shape. "Will you look at this?
Logan's going to have himself a family and he didn't
even think to tell his friends."

Another man spoke. "It seems to me that St. John's
been mighty unneighborly, wouldn't you say, boys?
Keeping such a pretty little thing to hisself."

A chorus of agreement rose and the men moved
closer. The smell of alcohol, tobacco, and unwashed
bodies filled the room, seeming to take the very oxy-
gen out of the air. Libby was having a difficult time
breathing, and the faces were beginning to blur together.

"I say we teach Logan a lesson," someone slurred,
taking a swallow from a flask.

"I say it would serve him right!"

The barrel grinned an evil smile. "Maybe it would at
that."

Libby's brave facade suddenly deserted her. Backed
up to the wall, she had no hope of escape. She grabbed
a piece of rawhide that hung from a nail. "Don't come
any closer," she warned, and when the men laughed at
her, she flung out every unflattering name she could
think of. "You bullying, no-good, two-timing . . ." She
whipped the rawhide through the air, catching one man
on the cheek.

"Ouch!" The injured man jumped back and grabbed
his face.

Libby lashed the leathery strap back and forth and
for a time the men stared at her incredulously.

"Watch it!" yelled one grizzly man, ducking low to
avoid a leathery blow.

"Come on, men. We can't let her get away with
this!"

Shouting out a warning, she sliced the air in one direction and back in the next.

But there were too many of them to keep at bay for long. Soon, one of the men ducked beneath her swinging arm and wrapped his hand around her waist.

"Let go of me, you . . ." She turned on him, but it was a mistake, for it allowed the others to grab her from behind. The men overwhelmed her and held her captive. One man put his dirty hand over her mouth to keep her from screaming. "Now, miss, just you calm down."

A loud blast filled the room, followed by a startled silence. An angry voice ripped through the room. It took a moment for Libby to recognize the voice as belonging to Mr. St. John.

"I said release her at once!" he repeated. Not only was his voice impressive, but he towered over the tallest man by at least three inches. Clearly intimidated by him, the miners dropped their hands, freeing her.

St. John's face was as dark as a thundercloud, his voice twice as menacing. "What's the matter with you men? Have you forgotten how to behave in front of a woman? Now suppose you apologize to Mrs. Summerfield. All of you." He glanced at each of their faces before he settled his full attention on the barrel-shaped man closest to Libby. "Let's start with you, Choo-Choo."

His real name was Pete Jenkins, but like most miners, many of whom couldn't afford to have their rightful names known, he'd earned himself a nickname based on the strange choo-choo sound he made when he panned for gold.

Choo-Choo stared at his feet. "I apologize, ma'am."

"Big Sam?"

The hands of the ex-slave played nervously with the felt hat. "Never meant you no harm, ma'am."

"Next."

Logan saw to it that every last man apologized. "Now, get out of here, all of you, and don't let me catch you here again."

One by one, the men left, their feet shuffling against the wooden planks as they filed silently out the door.

Shaking violently, Libby glared after them. "I'm not staying in this town another minute!" she shouted. "Not with those . . . those barbarians!"

Mr. St. John looked grim. "They wouldn't have hurt you. They were just having fun."

"Fun!" Libby fumed. "They have a very strange idea what constitutes fun. And furthermore . . ."

St. John listened patiently to her outburst, then patted her soothingly. "Don't go getting yourself all riled up. They won't bother you anymore. If you're worried, lock the door after me. All you have to do is slip the bolt into the catch."

She gave him a thunderous look and pushed his hand away. "I tried, dammit! But I couldn't get it to budge."

He examined the bolt, poured bear grease on it, and worked it back and forth until it moved freely. "Try this."

He stepped back from the door so she could try the bolt herself. When it slipped into place at her touch, he nodded in satisfaction.

Feeling suddenly weary, she laid her forehead against the cool hard wood of the door. "How did you know to come back?"

"Someone told me he saw a bunch of men stampeding my house. As soon as I finished playing the hand, I came home."

She spun around to face him. "You finished playing your hand first?"

He seemed confused by her reaction. "What did you expect me to do, Mrs. Summerfield? I was winning."

Libby could barely contain her anger. "Why you inconsiderate, selfish . . . I could have been killed."

It was his turn to look aghast. "Must you always think the worst? I told you, they meant you no harm."

"May I remind you that one of them shot me the other night?"

"And I told you it was an accident."

"Dead is dead whether by accident or otherwise!"

"I don't know what you're all worked up about. You had everything under control with your whip." He chuckled and shook his head. "I swear I don't know why they call it a delicate condition." Just thinking of Libby in those terms made him laugh louder until the cabin rang with the unexpected sound of his merriment. "We should all be as delicate."

Seeing nothing amusing about the situation, Libby could only stare at him perplexed.

"You'd better get some rest," he said, pointing to her middle. "We don't want to stir things up."

"You aren't going to leave me alone, again. I mean, now that they know I'm here . . ."

Logan thought about the card game that was already in progress. He was on a winning streak, and it wasn't his intention to stop before Lady Luck had a chance to grant him the full extent of her favors. But Mrs. Summerfield looked so downright agitated, he was afraid if he left her alone, she might stir things up and then where would they be?

"I'm not going anywhere," he said, cursing silently. No one had ever before interfered with his life. He was used to doing what he wanted, when he wanted. He planted himself on a chair and glowered at the thought of playing bodyguard. What in the name of sam hill would be next?

He didn't have to wonder for long. No longer in fact than the following morning.

Thinking that she'd had time to put the unfortunate incident out of her mind, he announced that he was going up to the diggings to try out his gold rocker.

Much to his horror, she countered with plans of her own to accompany him.

"The diggings is no place for a woman," he said reasonably, convinced she would soon change her mind.

"This town is no place for a woman."

"You'll be perfectly safe here. Now that the rain has stopped everyone will hightail it to the diggings."

"I'm not staying here by myself."

"All that exercise might stir things up."

"Some fresh air will do me good," she insisted. "I mean it, Mr. St. John, I'm not staying in this cabin alone!"

He weighed his options. The rain had stopped for the time being. But this was only the start of the rainy season. Besides, it was almost cold enough to snow. Already the upper peaks of the Sierras were covered in snow.

He needed gold and he needed it now. It would cost him a couple of thousand dollars to miss the winter trapping season. If his leg improved, he could make back some but not all of that money this coming spring. Beavers still had their prime coats in early spring, but as soon as the weather warmed and the animals lost their thick fur, the colors began to fade, and the pelts lost their market value.

"All right," he said. He tossed her a fur jacket that was far too big for her. "You can come with me on the condition that you speak only when you have something of importance to say. And ..." he added with emphasis. "You will do exactly as you're told."

He allowed her no opportunity to argue as he grabbed his saddle and lugged it outside.

By the time she had made one last trip to the outhouse and joined him, he had already tied his rocker to the saddle.

He frowned at the sight of her as if he'd expected her to change her mind and stay behind. But he said nothing as he lifted her onto his saddle.

"It's a lovely horse," she said, patting the animal's neck. "Does it have a name?"

"I call him Jim Bridger. Named him after the best mountain man that ever walked the earth."

"Well, Jim Bridger, I'm very pleased to make your acquaintance."

He studied her thoughtfully. "Are you sure this isn't going to stir things up too much?"

Sighing, Libby shook her head in exasperation. "Not unless you intend to race the horse."

"Let me know if you feel anything." He slipped his foot into the stirrup and heaved himself onto the saddle behind her.

Libby felt plenty, but nothing that she wished to share with him. She felt the strength of his thighs press against the curve of her hips. She felt his hard muscular chest against her quivering back, his warm moist breath sending tremors along her nape.

But when he wrapped his arms around her to gather the reins, she felt more than anything safe and secure.

Afraid that he would hear the loud thumping sounds of her heart, she forced herself to concentrate on the scenery.

She had never been to the gold-mining fields. Jeffrey had died soon after they'd arrived in California. After that, she had worked sixteen hours a day at the boardinghouse, which barely left enough time to eat and sleep, let alone explore.

She was totally amazed at the crowds that dotted the mining area. Men were lined up along both banks of the swift-running river. Most had metal pans, but some used Indian baskets, old hats, skillets, and even blankets to pan for gold.

The air reverberated with the rattling sounds of rock against metal and the grating rhythm of gold-mining cradles.

Farther up, men were waist deep in water. "They're constructing a dam," Mr. St. John explained, his voice soft in her ear.

"What are those men over there doing?" Libby asked, pointing to the men who were entrenched in a hole. Their heads were barely above ground level. If it weren't for the picks moving up and down, she might not have noticed them.

"They're working their way down to the bedrock," he explained.

The miners stopped to stare as they passed by. The men rubbed their eyes and craned their necks as if they didn't believe what they saw.

"Lordy be! Are my eyes deceiving me or was that a woman?" one male voice called out.

Another cupped his hands around his mouth and shouted, "I think I died and went to heaven."

Libby had learned from her experience at the miners' boardinghouse that the best defense against unwanted male attention was to ignore it. She kept her head lowered and her eyes firmly planted on the back of the horse's head, and was relieved when Mr. St. John veered away from the river and urged his gelding across a narrow channel to a more secluded area.

"Damn, wouldn't you know?"

"What is it?" she asked.

"The trail is under water. We'll have to go around." He surveyed the rocky incline and dismounted. "We'll have to go the rest of the way by foot. You'd better stay here."

She watched him rub his leg. "If you can make it I can." And to prove her point, she dismounted without his assistance.

He frowned but didn't debate the point. "If we go slow, we should be all right." His eyes met hers as he held out his hand.

Taking a deep breath, she laid her hand in his and felt a slight tug deep inside as his fingers wrapped around hers. He led her up a narrow trail that cut through the chaparral. It was an easy climb, with rocks and half-buried roots providing convenient footholds.

Halfway up, he released her hand and glanced around. His hand was posed, ready to grab his gun or knife should the need arise. Eyes sharp as a wolf's, he searched out each bush and rock before grabbing her hand again. "Let's go."

They followed an abandoned deer path. The dry flat

deer droppings told him that no animal had used this trail since summer. Already nature was reacting to the influx of miners to the area. Judging by the lack of animal droppings, he guessed that some animals had migrated away from the area altogether. He wondered what other impact man's intrusion would have on nature.

They reached the top of the incline. "Stay here," he said. "I'll be back." Without another word, he followed the same trail back to his horse. He slipped the strap of his Hawken rifle over his shoulder and grabbed his gold rocker. He followed the trail back up and set the rocker down by her side.

"Do you want to rest some more before we continue?" he asked.

She shook her head, but she did need to relieve herself. "How much farther do we have to go?"

"Not far. My claim is just beyond that bend."

She turned to look in the direction he indicated. "I have to . . ." She nodded in the way that they had both come to understand. It struck her as strange that already they had devised an unspoken code by which to communicate.

"Don't go beyond that oak." He pointed to a tree a short distance away. "I'll head toward my claim."

She walked dutifully toward the tree, but not wanting to be seen from the river, she decided to move farther away from the main path. Spotting a grove of trees in the distance, she followed a muddied channel down a gentle slope.

A squirrel eyed her momentarily before scampering up a tree. A single ouzel was busily turning over tiny pebbles and decaying leaves along the bottom of a narrow gully, looking for insects. A screeching scrub jay drowned out the distant sounds of gold mining.

Libby inhaled deeply. The air was fresh and scented with pine. She reached a knoll where the trees parted, allowing a breathtaking view of the snow-covered mountains beyond. She was so engrossed with the lovely scenery, she wandered farther away from the trail than she realized. It wasn't until she caught a glimpse of the now distant river through the trees did she realize how far away she'd roamed. The baby gave a firm kick, and she was all at once reminded of the reason she'd wandered from the trail. After a quick glance around, she ducked behind a clump of wild berry bushes.

Startled by a low menacing growl, she froze. Much to her horror, a snarling brown bear stood no more than ten feet away.

Falling backward on her posterior, she let out a bloodcurdling scream.

She was still screaming when Mr. St. John came bounding through the trees a moment later, his face deathly white. "Mrs. Summerfield!"

She pointed to the bear, which, strangely enough, hadn't moved. He took one quick glance at the animal before rushing to her side.

"The bear can't hurt you. It's caught in a trap." He knelt by her side and placed a steady hand on her trembling shoulder. "Calm down before you go stirring things up inside."

"Would you stop worrying about what I'm stirring up?" Although she fought for control, her voice sounded high and strained. "I could have been mauled."

"I told you the bear is trapped. You're lucky. Maybe next time I tell you to stay close at hand, you'll listen to me."

"If you knew the bear was here, why didn't you tell me?"

"I didn't know. By right grizzlies should be in hibernation by now." His expression grew tight. "It's the miners. It's got to be. They're making the poor bear too nervous to hibernate."

"Poor bear, indeed! It pretty near scared the life out of me."

He arched an eyebrow as he looked pointedly at her

waist. "Let's be glad that it didn't. From now on, you will do exactly as I say. Is that clear?"

She folded her arms across her chest and glared at him. She looked like she intended to sit there forever and might well have done so had the bear not let out a deafening roar.

With a cry of alarm, she accepted Mr. St. John's outstretched hand and rose to her feet. Clutching his arm, she eyed the bear with a wary look. "Are you sure it's secure?"

"That trap is strong enough for a full-grown grizzly."

Clearly relieved, she withdrew her hand.

"This is still a cub," he added. "Probably was born in early summer."

At this declaration, Libby's fear immediately melted into compassion. "Oh, no. Poor thing."

"Save your sympathy," he said. "It probably weighs close to five hundred pounds. Come on, we'd better leave before company arrives."

"You're not going to leave it to die, are you?" Libby was scandalized by the thought.

"One thing you learn pretty fast in this neck of the woods is not to go messing around with another man's trap."

"But you said it's a young one."

He made a quick check of the surrounding area. "Which means there could be a big one somewhere nearby." He grabbed her by the arm. "Let's go before we both live to regret it."

No sooner had he spoken than a sound unlike anything she'd ever heard rose from the nearby woods.

With a curse, Mr. St. John pulled his rifle from his shoulder holster, spun around, and took aim.

Eyes wide with fear, Libby glanced back. Her mouth dropped open in horror. A full-grown bear was less than a hundred yards away and closing in fast.

Chapter 9

WITHOUT warning, the bear stopped in its tracks, rose on its hind legs, and clawed the air with its powerful paws. It was a massive beast that stood nearly twelve feet tall.

Logan prepared to fire, but he knew he had little chance of doing much damage.

The convex-shaped head of the grizzly made it a difficult animal to kill. The beast was burdened with only three vulnerable parts: the ears, the spine, and the heart. A bear could live a long time with a bullet in the heart. Logan knew the names of more than a half-dozen dead men to prove it. One of them his father.

Keeping his finger firmly on the trigger, Logan weighed his options. Since his chances of bringing the animal down were slim, there were few alternatives left.

They could try running, but between Mrs. Summerfield's awkward bulk and his own stiff leg, the odds were undeniably in the bear's favor. Also in the bear's favor was the fact that Mrs. Summerfield was clinging to his arm in such a way, it was all but impossible for him to take proper aim. He tried pulling his arm from her clutches to no avail.

"We could climb a tree," she cried.

"There's only one size tree that's grizzly-proof, and it doesn't grow around here." He measured the distance behind him. "Listen carefully. What I want you to do is to head toward the river and yell for help.

Don't make any fast movements. Once you're out of sight, you should be safe."

"What about you?"

He gave her a rough shove. "Go, dammit."

The bear dropped on all fours and advanced. Logan aimed for the ear, fired, and missed.

"Mr. St. John!" Libby yelled behind him.

"Dammit, Mrs. Summerfield, get the hell out of here!"

"I can't! My foot's caught."

Logan cursed and fired. Again he missed, but he came close enough that the bear stopped in its tracks. With a mighty roar, the massive animal rose up once more and tottered on its thick hind legs.

In an effort to divert the bear away from Mrs. Summerfield, Logan circled around slowly. As predicted, the bear followed his progress until its back was turned to her. Logan then lifted his gun and aimed, waiting for the precise moment to fire. He waited too long.

Libby watched in horror as the bear swiped at Mr. St. John's arm with one mighty paw, sending him flying in one direction, the rifle in another.

Fearing he was dead, she screamed. Her loud piercing voice seemed to confuse the bear, but the reprieve was only temporary. Seconds later the bear pawed the air and moved closer to Logan's prone body.

Her voice grew shrill. "Mr. St. John!"

Certain that the bear would finish what it had started, she searched desperately for a weapon. She grabbed a rock and heaved it at the bear, hitting the animal on its hefty rump. The bear stopped just short of Mr. St. John and turned on all fours to face her. She pelted the animal with rocks in an attempt to drive it away. *"Mr. St. John!"*

Her high-pitched shrieks brought Logan staggering to his feet.

"Do something," she cried. "Quick!"

He pulled out his Colt Walker and aimed for the

spine. The bear took an unexpected step to the right, and the bullet missed its mark, barely grazing the thick tough hide. But it was enough to make the bear lose interest in Libby and change directions. With a thunderous roar, it turned toward Mr. St. John.

Libby held her breath as she watched Mr. St. John aim his gun and fire. Much to her horror, the bear advanced.

Seeing that Mr. St. John was in trouble again, Libby threw another rock. This one sailed past the bear and hit the startled man on the forehead.

Undaunted, she found her target with the second missile, and the rock hit the bear squarely on its rump.

The grizzly swayed back and forth on its hind legs, then dropped down. Again it turned in her direction. Behind the bear, Mr. St. John shook his head as if to ward off dizziness and took aim.

"Hurry!" she cried.

The animal ran straight toward her. In a desperate attempt to save her baby, she bombarded it with rocks while Mr. St. John fired. Confused, the bear suddenly veered off in another direction. Much to Libby's profound relief, the bear lumbered away through the trees, whimpering like an injured child.

Sinking down to her knees, Libby's body shook so violently, her teeth chattered.

Mr. St. John dropped his weapon and wiped his hand across his bloodied forehead. With great difficulty, he stood, picked up his hat, and staggered toward Libby.

"Are you all right?" he asked.

She nodded and wiped away her tears so that she could better assess his injuries. "I think so. What about you?"

"How do you think I feel, dammit! I've been battered by a bear and, thanks to your terrible aim, knocked senseless by a damned rock."

Libby was so relieved that the ordeal was over, she welcomed even his anger. "I'm sorry," she squeaked out.

He pulled out his revolver and pointed it at her foot. "Hold still!"

Libby's eyes widened with horror. "My God, Mr. St. John! Don't shoot!"

Ignoring her plea, he pulled the trigger. The bullet hit the locking mechanism and the trap fell away. He slid his gun in his belt and dropped to one knee to carefully lift her leg from the steel clamp. "Are you sure you're all right?"

"If you're through shooting at me, I am!" she gasped. Her heart was beating so fast, she feared it would jump out of her chest. Lord Almighty, what would be next?

She looked about to throttle him and he couldn't help but laugh. "Sorry, Mrs. Summerfield. But we don't have much time. As long as its offspring is trapped, you can bet that bear will be back. Next time we might not be so lucky."

She laid her hand on his arm and beseeched him with blue-green eyes that were still brimming with tears. "It's only a cub," she whispered.

He knew it would do no good to explain the unwritten code that free trappers abided by, the law that forbid them to tamper with another's man's traps. Besides, freeing the cub might be the best chance they had to escape unharmed. With no further discussion, he limped toward the imprisoned bear. He raised his gun, aimed at the trap, and fired.

The cub jumped back, and inadvertently pulled free. With a high whining sound, it lumbered away on all fours, looking like a dark furry ball as it disappeared among the tall pines.

"That was a very kind thing you did," she said softly.

"I'm always kind," he said. "Providing it's prudent." He knelt on his good leg to check her ankle. He gently worked the boot off her foot and pressed his fingers around her slim ankle as he examined the red skin. "It'll be tender for a day or two. Better not walk on it."

He slipped one arm around her shoulder and another beneath her legs and lifted her to his chest. "Hold on."

She worked her arms around his neck, even as she protested. "I can walk."

"The question is, can you run?"

She glanced worriedly over his shoulder. "Do you really think the bear will come back so soon?"

"No, but the trapper might." He carried her away from the area and it wasn't until they had reached the trail leading down the rocky incline to his horse that he stopped to rest. He set her on a fallen log and sank down on the ground to rub his leg. "How did you know that a bear will turn in the direction of its attacker."

She gasped when the full implication of what she'd done hit her. "I didn't know that. I was trying to chase it away."

He arched a brow. "With a rock?"

"The Good Book tells the story of a boy who brought down a giant with a tiny stone. Besides, it worked, didn't it?"

"It worked," he agreed. The combative look on her face brought a lopsided grin to his face, followed by a grimace. "My head's killing me." He gingerly touched the red bump on his forehead. "Too bad your aim isn't as good as your throw."

She sniffed. "We can't all be perfect."

"I suppose not." He rubbed his sore shoulder, then worked his hand back down the length of his leg.

He looked exhausted and in pain, and her heart went out to him. "You stay here and I'll go and get the horse. I think I can bring it around the long way." She put her boot back on, leaving it unbuttoned to accommodate her swollen ankle. She then limped back and forth to test her ability to walk.

Watching her, he shook his head in disbelief. "I wish I had your so-called delicate condition."

Looking back over her shoulder, she smiled. "Now wouldn't that be something to see?"

Despite his growing discomfort, he laughed again and this time his merry, though restrained, guffaws filled the air. "Indeed it would."

That afternoon, Logan sat sprawled in front of a blazing fire, his sore arm and elbow deep in a bucket of hot water. His aching leg was propped up on a stack of cushions. A damp cloth was wrapped around his throbbing head. He looked and felt like a casualty of war.

Libby's ankle was bruised and slightly swollen, but otherwise she seemed none the worse for wear. Had in fact insisted upon preparing their meal, despite Logan's constant reminders to not "stir things up inside."

"If coming face-to-face with a grizzly didn't stir things up, I don't suppose cooking a simple meal will," she declared.

He had to admit she had a point. And even if she didn't, he was in no condition to argue with her. His left shoulder hurt where the bear had swiped him, and his backside was sore from being tossed to the ground. At the back of his head was a large lump where his head had hit the ground, matching the bump over his left eye where she'd thrown a rock at him. His head felt like someone had crawled inside and was demanding with pounding fists to be let out.

His discomfort increased as the day wore on, as did his ill temper. It irked him to find himself dependent on someone. And the fact that it was a woman in a "delicate" condition only made his disposition that much worse. By the end of the day, he was quite willing to believe she'd orchestrated the entire episode for the sole purpose of rendering him helpless.

But in his more rational moments, he was more angry at himself than at Mrs. Summerfield. He was a mountain man. There was no excuse for him not being on guard against any possible danger.

True, under most normal circumstances, bears hibernate at this time of year. But he knew enough about nature to know how unpredictable it can be at times. No, he had only himself to blame, and he was more convinced than ever that living these past few weeks in that damned man-made dwelling had dulled his survival skills.

Knowing how indolent he'd become in so short a time only increased his restlessness and made him more anxious to return to his former life. The fustration of knowing that he wasn't going anywhere in a hurry made him more ornery, as his friend Jim Bridger used to say, than a cornered rattler.

"You can plead all you want," he growled during one heated dispute with Libby. "That was the last time I'm ever taking you to the diggings."

"You make it sound like it was my fault we got attacked by that bear."

"I have been to that part of the mountain more times than I can enumerate, and I've never as much as seen a bear in those parts."

Incensed that he would place the blame entirely on her shoulders, she folded her arms across her chest and glowered at him. "Considering the difficulties you were having defending yourself, I would say you were most fortunate to have me along during your one lone encounter."

For the remainder of that day and night, she ignored him, except to give him an occasional look of reproach. Invariably, she found him glowering back and after a visual but no less combative duel, she looked away.

On some level, she was grateful for his bad temper. At least while they were growling at each other, he wasn't looking at her in that certain way of his that caused her heart to flutter so, and that made her forget her bulky shape and clumsy movements. She was a widow in mourning and she best not forget it.

By the next morning, most of the swelling had gone down, but Logan's disposition had not improved. Dur-

ing the long painful night, he'd used up the remains of
the healing plants he'd gathered during his travels.
He'd also chewed the last of his willow bark for the
medicine it contained that was known to ease muscle
soreness.

He was left with no choice but to hobble to the general store to purchase man-made salves and soothing
balms for his injuries. He was willing to bet they were
less effective than the natural remedies he preferred.

No sooner had he entered Hap's store than, to his
profound irritation, he found himself the subject of rid-
icule.

"Looks like you had yourself one wild night." Hap
winked at the other customers, who joined in the fun.

Big Sam's white teeth flashed next to his dark shiny
skin. "You sure do know how to pick 'em. No wonder
you didn't show up at the Golden Hind last night."

A man named Sharkey took a swig of whiskey from
a brown necked bottle and wiped his mouth with the
back of his hand. He had a long, pointed face and ears
that stood straight out like the handles of a sugar bowl.
"Heard tell from some of the other men that your
woman is a regular wildcat. This more or less proves
it."

Hap glanced over to a tall, rail-thin man with a
drooping mustache. "Didn't that fellow Shakespeare
have something to say about taming a wild woman?"

The man immediately acquired the stance of an ora-
tor. The palm of his hand flat on his chest, his eyes
gazed past the others as if he were addressing an audience. His name was Conrad Peters, but the miners
called him Shakespeare due to his habit of quoting the
English bard. If Conrad ever had a thought that was
not inspired by the playwright, no one had ever heard
it. "Every man can tame a shrew but he that hath her."

Big Sam looked dubious. "I don't suppose this man
of yours ever met the likes of Logan's woman. No man
can tame her. I'd bet my life on it."

Ignoring the lively exchange that followed, along

Chapter 10

FOR two days Libby put up with his ill humor, and held her tongue against his endless complaints. It seemed she could do nothing right. The water that she used to bathe his arm and leg was either too hot or too cold. His meals were too spicy or too bland. The fire was too big, too smoky, or needed more wood.

By the third day, she'd taken about all she was going to take from him. When the opportunity presented itself to lock him outside the cabin, she didn't hesitate.

Mr. St. John accepted being locked out of his own abode with as much grace as a weasel locked out of a chicken coop. "Open up, Mrs. Summerfield! Do you hear me? This is my house. My house! So help me, if you don't open the door, I swear . . ."

A small crowd was beginning to gather in front. Big Sam and Choo-Choo were among the miners who stood jawing away like a bunch of frenzied bluejays. The man they called Shakespeare joined them.

"So what did the Bard have to say about a man being thrown out of house and home?" Choo-Choo asked.

Shakespeare grinned and began reciting. It turned out that old William had plenty to say about shrewish women and their henpecked men.

Gritting his teeth, Logan dropped his fists, but made no attempts to hide his ill humor. Since it was obvious to the crowd of curious spectators that he'd been thrown out of his own house, it seemed like a waste of time to try to pretend otherwise. He hobbled down the steps and started for the Golden Hind. "Don't just stand there!" he growled. "Let's play cards!"

It was much later that night before he crept back into the cabin. Much to his relief, Mrs. Summerfield had left the door unbolted. He tiptoed inside and stood by her bed.

In the orange glow of the slow-burning fire, she looked young and vulnerable. Since she was asleep, it was safe for him to forsake the facade of ill humor that had served to keep his integrity intact. As long as he acted like a spoiled child, she wanted nothing to do with him. This relieved him of having to control the worrisome urges that her presence incited in him.

Tonight, however, as he stood looking at the wispy tendrils that framed her fine smooth forehead and the long silky strands that fanned across her pillow, he realized just how strong his uncontrolled impulses were.

She looked beautiful to him, desirable. His loins ached with need and want that was almost unbearable in its intensity. It was all he could do to keep from climbing into bed with her, taking her in his arms, and pressing his lips to hers.

Startled by the explicit nature of the thoughts that followed, he stepped away from her, disgusted with himself.

It had been a mistake to let down his guard, if only while she slept. She was going to have a baby! She deserved a man's respect and protection, not his lustful greed!

Once his amorous thoughts had taken root, however, they were hard to shake. Impossible. Long after he'd settled in his bedroll, he thought about the night he had rubbed her naked flesh with his own bare hands.

Trying to shake the memory, he turned over and visions of her delicate pink lips flashing that lovely wide smile of hers came to the fore. Another turn of his heated body and he recalled the softness of her touch when she administered to his wounds.

Despite the bitter cold night, his body was burning up. He wanted her more than he'd ever wanted another woman. Abandoning his efforts to control his thoughts, he finally stared at the shadows that played upon the dark ceiling and contemplated the things he would like to do to her if given the chance. His imagination had never been so keen, his thoughts so graphic.

Despite the physical discomforts that plagued him, a wide smile spread across his face as the most delectable thoughts came to mind.

Wouldn't that stir up a few things inside of her? In the name of sam hill, would it ever!

By the next morning, Logan's disposition was worse than ever. He spent the entire night thinking about her in a way that was not right, and his body still hadn't recovered. He found it necessary to pick an argument with her before either had gotten out of bed. The tension was so taut between them as they ate breakfast, he felt certain he could dull a knife by simply slicing it through the air. That was fine by him. Her hostile glares were a far cry from the soft luminous looks he'd envisioned during the night, and he could almost believe that her presence was nothing more than an annoying imposition.

Without bothering to have his usual second cup of coffee, he grabbed his gold rocker and slammed out of the house.

It was much later, as he stood on his claim, absorbed by the peace and quiet around him, that it hit him.

Perhaps he could keep his distance without being so hard on her.

He didn't often feel guilty and couldn't imagine why he should feel guilty now. True, it was his own carelessness that had nearly gotten them killed by that bear. But had she obeyed his wishes, the bear would not have bothered them. Still, he did have to give her credit; at least she didn't stand idly by, like most

women would have done, while the bear tore him limb
from limb.

In retrospect, it struck him as comical the way she
attacked that old grizzly like a fastidious housewife
trying to rid the house of flies. Come to think of it, a
housewife would be better armed.

He set his cradle along the side of the water. The
open-ended wooden box was mounted on rockers. One
side was fitted with a sieve. Wooden cleats were nailed
along the bottom to catch the gold.

Down on his knees, he rocked the cradle with one
hand and ladled water in with the other. His shoulder
was still sore, which meant he had to stop every few
minutes or so to work out the knots. But it was his leg
that was killing him.

The damned woman had only been with him for less
than a week and his body felt like he'd been in combat.
One would think he was the one in a "delicate" condition.

The more he thought of his wounds, the less guilty
he felt for giving her a hard time. He should have left
her on the porch, that's what he should have done. He
should never have rescued her, never assumed responsibility. Now he felt obligated to see that she reached
her destination, and it was a burden that weighed heavily on him. He wasn't used to being responsible for another person.

He wished to God she'd never found her way to his
doorstep that night. He wished he'd never undressed
her or worked his hands up and down her soft womanly curves.

His mouth went dry as a vision of her lovely firm
breasts came to mind. His hand stilled and the gold
rocker came to a stop. The thoughts that had tortured
him through the long endless night came back to inflict
him anew. His heart beat faster as he remembered
pressing his lips against hers and feeling her warm
breath mingle with his own. With a slight rebuke, he

reminded himself that he hadn't kissed her. Not really. He'd only checked her temperature.

Oh, but it felt like a kiss. Tasted like a kiss. Excited like a kiss.

He shook the thought away and rocked his cradle as if his life depended on it.

By noon, his head was damp with perspiration. Even so, he had less than half an ounce of gold to show for his efforts. A cold wind swept down from the upper reaches of the Sierras and shot clear through to the bone of his leg.

He decided to call it a day. The only problem was that without his work to distract him, his thoughts turned to Libby quicker, as Jim Bridger would say, than hell scorched a feather. Just as quickly the cold wind seemed to fade away and a warm feeling spread over him as visions of flashing blue-green eyes and honey gold hair took its place.

The fact that he hankered for such a woman reminded him how long it had been since he'd visited a whorehouse. Not since early summer. He stopped what he was doing. Had it really been that long? Six months? Well, now, he thought with relief, that explained it.

Gathering up his rocker, he attached it to his saddle and rode back into town, intent upon making peace. He only hoped he didn't have to do anything so drastic as apologize.

The door was firmly bolted, requiring him to knock and identify himself before he was allowed in. She claimed that being alone made her nervous, but he was convinced she locked the door just to make him beg for entry.

She looked all flushed and pink and his heart started jumping about like kernels of corn in a hot skillet.

He was momentarily distracted from his objective by a smell strong enough and putrid enough to make the hairs of a buffalo robe stand on end. After unbolting

the door for him, she immediately rushed back to the
stove to stir a large black kettle with a wooden paddle.

His fervent hope was that whatever was in that pot,
it wasn't supper.

She glanced over her shoulder. "You're early," she
said.

He closed the door and set his cradle on the floor.
"The water's high," he said curtly. He had no intention
of going into detail about his leg.

"Oh."

He glanced at the stove and eyed a black ropelike
thing hanging over the rim of the pot. It looked like a
mangled caterpillar. A strange feeling came over him.
He groaned as the source of the stench suddenly occurred to him.

"My clothes," he said hoarsely. He swallowed hard.
The thought was like a sharp knife ripping through his
skull.

He cleared his throat, not willing to believe what his
nose and eyes told him was true. "My buckskins . . .
aren't . . ."

She looked at him curiously. "I'm only washing the
ones I used . . ."

"Washing!" he exploded.

Paling, she nodded. "I didn't want to return them
unwashed and I didn't know how else to get out the
grease."

He stared at her in astonishment. "That grease is
what made my clothes waterproof. Do you know how
many hours it took me to rub that grease into the
leather?"

Mutely, she shook her head.

"Of course you don't know," he thundered. "I don't
imagine people in Boston have to worry about water-
proofing their clothes. But us folks out here worry
about it a lot."

"So I gather," she said, resenting his tone.

"How could you do such a thing?"

"I was only trying to help," she explained. "They were soiled."

He blinked in disbelief. "Mrs. Summerfield, there's no way those clothes could have been soiled. Not with the layers of grease I put on them. Dirt rolled off quicker than an old maid can crawl under a bed."

"The dirt might have rolled off," Libby said with a haughty toss of the head, "but I can assure you that the smell stayed behind. It's a wonder there weren't any vermins hiding in the things."

"If it's vermins you're worried about, then all you had to do is lay the clothes over an anthill."

Libby frowned. "Did you say anthill?"

"And I'll say it again. Anthill, anthill, anthill! There's no better way to rid yourself of vermin."

Libby looked quite taken back. "I never in all my born days heard of such a thing."

"And I never in all my born days heard of anyone boiling the daylights out of perfectly good buckskins."

He plopped down on his chair and found, much to his horror, that the only thing between the floor and his sore posterior was thin air. Sprawled on the floor with his legs straight up, he gritted his teeth against the pain that shot up his spine.

Libby hurried over to him, gasping with concern. "Mr. St. John! Are you all right?"

"Stay away!" he growled. "Or I won't be responsible for my actions."

She looked hurt. "You don't have to be so ornery."

"You'll have to forgive me. I find it difficult to be civil when I'm lying on the floor, fork side up."

"I was just organizing the cabin for you ... I thought ..." She looked close to tears. "Are you all right?"

He was hurting too much to feel sorry for her. Instead, he rose to his feet and rubbed his lower back. "No, I am not all right, Mrs. Summerfield." He reached for her hand and pulled her to the nearest chair. "Do me a favor. Sit there and don't move until I get back."

"Where are you going?" she asked.

"I'm going to inquire as to when the stage will resume its run."

Her face lit up. "I do hope it's soon. I would feel so much better knowing that a doctor was nearby."

Logan rubbed his aching back and limped toward the door. "So would I, Mrs. Summerfield. So would I."

He staggered back into the cabin late that night. It was obvious he'd been drinking.

She closed her Bible and tugged at the shawl around her shoulders to ward off the cold air he brought in with him. "Did you find out about the stage?"

"It's not expected to resume running until the first of next month." He lumbered around the room, bumping into the furniture. Damn, not one thing was where it should be. "Just think, Mrs. Summerfield. You are stuck in Deadman's Gulch for another couple of weeks."

She stared at him with horror-filled eyes. "But there has to be another way to Nevada City."

"The stage road was washed away. Completely." He demonstrated with his hand. "Just like that. The entire mountainside decided to relocate to the valley below." He grimaced as a pain shot through his knee. "Damn, where's the soothing salve."

She reached for the bottle of salve and handed it to him. "Do you want me to help you with that?"

"No. The stuff is as useless as a bucket under a bull. What I need is mullein leaves."

She waited for him to sit down. "I was thinking that I could rent a horse and ride to Nevada City."

Logan rolled up the cuffs of his trousers and rubbed the balm onto his knee. "By yourself?"

"I could hire someone to accompany me."

He set the bottle on the table. "I don't think so. Not in your 'delicate' condition."

"But my baby is due next week. On the twenty-eighth. There's got to be a way to get to Nevada City."

"On the twenty-eighth?" He looked at her in astonishment. "You mean you can figure out a baby's birth to the exact date?"

"More or less."

"What do you mean more or less?"

"The baby could come before or after that date."

"Well, now. Isn't that a fine kettle of fish? Why didn't you tell me this before?"

"I told you that it was due at the end of the month. Besides, I thought I would be in Nevada City by now."

He rubbed his aching head. "Do me a favor. Don't do any more thinking."

She gave him an icy glare.

He stared into the fire and considered his options. One thing was sure: he had no intention of letting his cabin become anyone's birthplace. "Start packing. Tomorrow morning, I'm taking you to Nevada City myself."

Chapter 11

NOT a cloud marred the azure-blue sky that Friday morning when they began their journey. The air was fresh with the scent of pine, its icy edge nipping at the skin like a playful puppy.

Logan had rented two mules, one for Mrs. Summerfield and the other for her valise. After helping her onto the most passive of the two mules, he mounted his own horse.

Libby clung to the pommel of the saddle with both hands. She'd never been on a mule in her life. Nor had she imagined that a mule could be so erratic in its behavior. The animal started forward, stopped, and then turned in the opposite direction. "Whoa," she cried.

Mr. St. John turned in his saddle and reached back for the reins of her mule. "Don't look so worried," he said. "Crazy Sam here won't do you any harm."

"Why . . . why do you suppose he's called Crazy Sam?" she stammered.

"Probably for the same reason all mules are named. It suits his personality."

"Well, if that's the case, I insist upon riding the other mule."

"You mean Man Killer?"

"Never mind!" she snapped.

He shrugged. "Whatever you say. Hold on tight." With a slight kick, he urged his horse forward and braced himself for the journey ahead. It was a journey he had made numerous times, but never under these circumstances.

Still, he was ready—more than ready—to be rid of her; like it or not, he felt responsible for her.

He hated having to go to Nevada City. He hated the crowds and all those highfalutin city folks who gawked at him like he was some sort of unearthly creature.

On the other hand, it offered him a chance to stop at one of the many whorehouses in town. He never much cared for the sort of impersonal attention offered at such places. Having to pay for female companionship was one of the few drawbacks of being a trapper.

Logan forced his horse up a narrow dirt trail that would take them over sixteen miles of rough terrain to Nevada City. Mrs. Summerfield and the mules followed close behind.

Depending on how much damage the storm had done, he estimated that they should reach the city by nightfall at the latest. The trail switched back, allowing a clear view of the valley they'd left behind.

Logan stopped for a moment to watch a half dozen or so cattle walking in a line.

"Is there something wrong?" Mrs. Summerfield called from behind.

He pointed to the cattle. "Cattle always walk toward the wind. They just changed direction and are heading north." He glanced ahead, his eyes narrowed in concentration. There wasn't a cloud in the sky, but his instincts told him that another storm was on the way. However, if the wind continued on its present course, the storm shouldn't reach the area until late that night or possibly the following day.

"Let's go," he said, tugging on Crazy Sam's reins.

Their progress was slow; landslides and uprooted trees from the recent rains impeded their progress. To make matters worse, Crazy Sam needed constant prodding.

Even so, they would have made better time had Libby not had so many nature calls. No sooner would they start up again than she was tugging at the reins for him to stop. In between times she kept him duly informed of her uncensored opinion on the difficult and sometimes dangerous trail.

"Lord Almighty!" she gasped during one particular hazardous section where they were forced to follow a narrow shelf that hugged the side of a sheer rocky cliff.

"Don't look down!" Logan called back to her, during yet another dangerous area. His warning was unnecessary as he discovered when he glanced back to find her eyes squeezed firmly shut. Smiling to himself, he steadied his gaze on to the difficult trail ahead.

As they rose higher, the air grew thinner and colder, and patches of snow dotted the landscape.

Ahead, glints of golden sunlight danced upon the snow-cloaked slopes, glittering like newly polished silver upon sparkling white linen.

Measuring the depth of the snow, Logan sensed the wind velocity increase. No sooner had the wind picked up speed than ominous dark clouds began to drift over the northern peaks. Worried now, he cursed himself for not turning back when he first noticed the wind change.

Behind him, Libby sat on the mule, bundled in a blanket. Never in her life had she felt so cold and utterly miserable. She gasped in terror as the path narrowed and large clumps of ice and snow slid down the mountain. All she needed was for Crazy Sam to pull one of his stunts.

But to her relief, the mule, for once, plodded after Mr. St. John's horse without a single hesitation. But it was a long while before she could catch her breath.

Lord Almighty, all the times she had read the story of Christmas, she never once thought to give the mother of the Christ child her due.

Libby harbored no desire of ever gaining sainthood. It wasn't her nature to suffer in silence. Dutifully, she continued to keep Mr. St. John fully informed of every discomfort. Not only was she as cold as a corpse, she ached all over.

For the most part, he took her complaints with good grace, stopping every half hour or so to allow her a moment to rest and make her call to nature.

But his patience was wearing thin. It had taken them three hours just to reach the summit. He'd counted on it taking them no more than an hour. But then he had no idea the trail would be so bad. On more than one occasion, the ground had begun to slip beneath them. He dreaded the return trip.

Logan reined in his horse and held his palm up, certain he'd felt a drop of rain. He caught another drop and grimaced. The worry lines at his brow deepened as he dismounted and walked back to help Libby off the mule.

"What? No aches and pains?"

She cast him a withering look. Her face was pale. Her lips trembled. Feeling a rush of sympathy, he led her over to a fallen tree trunk.

"I think we best spend the night in Grass Valley," he said.

"You said there were no doctors in Grass Valley."

"There wasn't the last time I was there. But there is a hotel. We'll spend the night and depending on the weather, we'll continue on to Nevada City in the morning."

She was silent for a long while before she spoke. "I don't think that's a good idea."

He studied the clouds that were now directly overhead. "You won't want to hear the alternative."

"Nor will you."

Something in her voice made his hackles rise. "Would you care to explain that?"

She started to say something, then stopped. A shadow crossed her face. Her hands flew to her swollen waist.

Logan's mouth went dry. He wasn't a religious man, but suddenly he had the urge to pray. "Mrs.

Summerfield?" He slipped his arm around her bent-over body. "You . . . you aren't thinking about having your baby today. You wouldn't be thinking about that now, would you?"

She lifted her lashes and looked up at him like a child about to admit to some inexcusable offense. Her lips parted in a whispered apology. "I'm afraid, Mr. St. John, the thought had occurred to me."

Chapter 12

Logan paced around in a circle, telling himself to calm down. He'd been in difficult situations before and he'd managed to handle them. Most of them, at least. So why should this time be any different?

He glanced upward at the ever-darkening clouds, and searched around for possible shelter. There were no visible caves, but providing the wind didn't change directions, they could stand in the shelter of a rocky headland that jutted out of the upper cliffs.

As he considered the possibilities, it suddenly occurred to him that Mrs. Summerfield was unusually quiet.

Alarmed, he spun around. She looked pale, anguished, her attention focused inward. He rushed to her side and dropped to one knee. "Mrs. Summerfield?" Then, "Libby?" He squeezed her hand and held her until her tense body began to relax.

She took a deep breath and gave him a grateful smile. "Lord Almighty, that was a strong one."

"We're going to have to go back."

She shook her head. "I don't think there's time."

He inhaled. This wasn't what he wanted to hear. He considered ways to shorten the return trip. But even if he took her back on his horse, leaving the mules behind, the rain could wash away more of the dangerously unstable ground.

When it appeared she had recovered from the last pain, he walked over to the edge of the cliff. A funnel of smoke rising from the valley floor pinpointed the town of Deadman's Gulch below. As the crow flies, the town was probably no more than thirty minutes away.

His gaze followed the wooden flume that carried water from Nevada City to Deadman's Gulch. The flume had been built during the last summer to solve the water shortage. Without water, gold mining had practically come to a standstill. Everyone agreed that the flume was a mighty fine engineering feat. It saved the town, and it might very well save a young woman's life.

He walked back to her and helped her through yet another painful episode. Should the pains be this close together? he wondered. Wasn't there a way to help her through them? He cursed his own ignorance. "I have an idea." He helped her to her feet.

She looked so profoundly relieved, he was almost afraid to tell her what her what it was for fear of shattering her hopes.

"I want to show you something." He led her to the edge of the cliff. "See that flume? Brings water all the way from Nevada City. Did you ever see a more welcome sight?"

Libby raked him over with the same look of distrust she had earlier accorded Crazy Sam. "I could think of a few sights that would be more welcome. Now tell me, what is your idea?"

"We're crossing over."

Libby stared in horror at the steep drop. "You want me to climb down this mountain?"

"Of course not. I want you to walk across the flume."

Libby swung her gaze to the flume and her mouth dropped open. Wooden stilts rose several hundred feet or more into the air, supporting a foot-wide canvas-lined channel filled with rushing water. Halfway across the canyon the flume sloped downward until it reached Deadman's Gulch.

She glanced back at Logan in disbelief. "You want me to walk across that?"

He lifted his voice to be heard over the sound of rushing water. "Have you a better idea?"

"Are you out of your mind?"

Their voices continued to rise as they stood face-to-face, glaring at each other.

He pointed upward. "Have you noticed that damned sky up there?"

"Have you noticed the drop down there?" she shouted back.

"We can't go back the way we came. It's too dangerous."

"It can't be more dangerous than . . ." She grimaced and he quickly took her in his arms.

"Hold on tight," he urged, feeling her body tense next to his. "Try breathing through your mouth." This was the advice trappers gave to injured men. Whether the same advice applied under the present circumstances, he had no idea. But it couldn't hurt.

She breathed as he'd instructed and soon the deep lines left her forehead. Taking a deep breath, she pulled away from him, amazing him with her resilience. The argument resumed as if nothing had happened.

"I'm not walking on that flume!"

"You'll do what I tell you to do."

"Over my dead body!"

"Dammit, don't tempt me."

The argument waged for several minutes longer before she slumped against him for a second time, both hands on her belly.

He held her steady. "Does it help if I rub your back?"

"It helps if I can hold on to something."

"Hold on to my arm."

She wrapped her fingers around his forearm and squeezed. Her grip felt like steel as her fingers pressed through the sleeve of his coat clear down to the bone. Seldom before had he witnessed pain strong enough to sustain such a powerful grip.

Sweat broke out on his forehead as he absorbed her agonizing hold. He shared in her relief when at last the contraction subsided and she released his arm.

"Let's go," he said, hoping to make some headway before the next pain.

"I am not going!" she said stubbornly. A bullheaded look settled on her face as she pulled away from him.

The last time he'd witnessed such out and out obstinacy was on the face of a dead man. It astonished him that even while in the throes of labor, she was a force to be reckoned with. Under normal circumstances, this wouldn't have fazed him. He was growing accustomed to her obstinance. But the cold was affecting his leg and the clouds overhead were downright ominous-looking. The bitter bile of fear coated his mouth. He felt a moment of helplessness before rallying in anger.

The damned fool woman had been nothing but trouble since arriving on his doorstep. He had stood about all he was going to stand from her. Besides, this was for her own good. With no further ado, he lifted her in his arms. Gritting his teeth against the additional pain the physical burden brought to bear on his leg, he carried her to the flume.

"Dammit, Libby. Keep still!"

Screaming louder than a bull in a briar patch, she kicked her feet and pounded his chest. Underestimating her as usual, he was ill-prepared for the display of strength, and they both almost fell down the side of the mountain. If it weren't for the fortuitous timing of a contraction, he might not have managed to ease her onto the flume.

Terrified of heights, she clung to him for dear life.

"Libby, put your foot next to mine. Come on, that's a girl. Now the other one." He breathed a sigh of relief. At least the frame was supporting her, which took some of the burden off his sore leg. "Don't whatever you do look down."

There was no way she was going to look down or

anywhere else for that matter. Lord, she was so terrified, she couldn't even breathe, let alone move.

"Now when I say go, slide your right foot forward."

"I can't . . . Logan . . ." She glanced at the water that rushed through the narrow channel between her legs and cried out in terror.

"Don't look, dammit!" When she didn't move, he nudged her foot for her. "Trust me, Libby. I'm not going to let go of you. All right, now the other foot."

Inch by torturous inch, he forced her across the narrow flume. Flume walkers crossed these lofty channels on a regular basis. Until now, he'd not given a moment's thought to the brave men whose jobs required them to check for debris or signs of wear.

At one point, he pulled off his fur jacket and tossed it to the canyon below. Without the jacket, he had more freedom of movement.

Each time he felt her body stiffen next to his, he stopped, knowing another pain was on the way. His arms around her waist, he grimaced as her fingers dug into his hands.

He pressed his body against hers. He could feel the ebb and flow of each contraction, the tempo and dissonance. He could taste something akin to metal that each pain brought to his mouth. Unwittingly, he began to anticipate each stage and relaxed or tensed his body accordingly, until it seemed that the pains were as much his as they were hers.

Although the air was freezing cold, heat poured out of his body. He was vaguely conscious of the strange rhythm that had seemed to develop. So many steps forward, pain, steps, pain.

Halfway across, it began to rain.

He looked down at the rugged tree-lined canyon below them and wondered what in the name of sam hill he was doing suspended hundreds of feet in midair with a woman about to give birth.

In front of him, Libby kept her eyes firmly shut. She

was convinced that she was going to have her baby right there on the spot, on a foot-wide platform suspended over a deep and deadly drop.

Never had she hated anyone more than Logan, the man responsible for her present predicament.

Feeling the pain begin to rise again, she pressed her fingers into the firm strong arms that were clamped securely around her waist. Never had she needed a man more.

The rain began to fall so hard it beat down on them like icy needles.

"One good thing to be said about the rain," he shouted in her ear. "We don't have to worry about being attacked by Indians or wild animals."

"What a blessing," she yelled back. As if an Indian or wild animal would be crazy enough to cross a flume.

The flume began to slope downward, slowing their progress considerably. Logan kept a firm arm around Libby as she reached for one of the flimsy wooden posts that were spaced at three-foot intervals. She clung to the splintered stake until he joined her.

"That was perfect," he said, taking her trembling body in his arms. "Now grab the next one."

"I can't!" she sobbed.

"Libby, you must. For the baby's sake!"

It took some prodding, but he finally managed to get her to reach for the next stake, and the next. "Come on, Libby. You can do it. That's a girl."

When at last they reached the end of the flume, they were both soaked to the skin from the rain and perspiration.

He helped her climb down the wooden frame of the flutter wheel, and they stood clinging to each other beneath the heavy downpour. "Let's get you back to the cabin," he said, alarmed by how she trembled in his arms.

It was only a short walk to his cabin, but it was obvious to him that Libby was in no condition to walk.

He picked her up in his arms and held her close to his chest. His foot slipped in the mud, but he managed to regain his balance.

With a pronounced limp, he carried her the short distance to his cabin and set her down in front of the fire.

He stripped the buckskin dress off her and handed her a dry one. He dried her hair with a towel and helped her onto the pallet, arranging the pelts and blankets on top of her.

He then added kindling to the hot ashes in the fireplace, and when the pieces of dry wood caught fire, he threw in a large log. As soon as the flames took hold, he returned to her side.

"Stay here." He squeezed her icy cold hand and tucked it beneath the blankets. "I'll be back in a minute."

"Don't leave me," she pleaded.

"I'm going to find someone who knows about delivering babies," he explained. He ran a knuckle across her pale cheek. "I won't be long. Trust me."

Her large liquid eyes searched his face. "I do trust you, Logan."

He took in a deep breath. Her trust in him humbled him like nothing else ever could. He vowed to do everything in his power to validate her belief in him.

It was still raining hard, and already the dirt street running through town was under a foot of muddy water. He waded through the stream and into the Golden Hind Saloon.

It was crowded inside, and noisy. At the first sign of rain, the men had abandoned their claims and headed for town, intent upon spending the rest of the day gambling and drinking.

Logan threaded his way through the crowd toward the bar where a man named Luke Appleby was playing a tune on his mouth organ.

"Need to talk to you," Logan said.

Appleby looked at him curiously, wiped the mouth of his mouth organ along his red flannel shirt, and slipped it into the pocket of his canvas pants. He was in his late twenties, but his Irish good looks and shaggy blond hair made him appear younger.

"You married, right?"

"That's right."

"And you have a child, right?"

"Two. A boy and a girl."

"Two, uh? Then you're the right man to be talking to. What do you know about birthing?"

Appleby scratched his temple. "Birthing?"

"You know, what happened when your wife—you know—was ready to have the babies?"

"I don't know."

Logan frowned with impatience. He was in no mood to play games. "What do you mean you don't know?"

"That birthing as you call it, that's something only women know about."

Logan considered this for a moment. "Why do you suppose that is?"

"That's the way the women like it."

"Is that so?"

"I have it on good authority. Women don't want anything to do with men when their time comes. Why do you want to know? You worried about your woman?"

"She's not my woman. But yeah, I'm worried about her. It's her time. Anyone else here who's married?"

"Keefer is. Has eleven children." Appleby raised his hand and motioned to a short, red-faced man with muttonchop side whiskers. "Keefer. Come over here a minute." He waited for Keefer to join them. "Logan here, says it's his woman's time. Do you know anything about birthing?"

Keefer slapped Logan on the shoulder. "Congratulations, boy. How far 'long is she?"

"A couple of hours is all."

"Well, don't expect much to happen before morning."

"Anything I can do to help her along."

"Boil water. Lots and lots of water."

That made sense to Logan. Come to think of it, he'd heard something about babies and boiling water. "And ..."

Keefer frowned. "And what?"

"What do I do with the water?"

"How the hell would I know?"

Logan grabbed Keefer by the collar. "Dammit, Keefer, think! What do they do with the water?"

Keefer's eyes grew wide. "They ain't a whole lot you can do with boiling water, 'cept drink it."

Logan released him. "Drink it? You mean like tea?"

Keefer shrugged. "Why not? I've heard tell that tea has magical healing powers."

"You could be right," Logan said.

Keefer brightened. "Maybe the hot water softens up the bones. You know, so the baby has room to move around more."

Logan had never heard of anything so ridiculous, but Appleby, who had been listening to this exchange, concurred with this theory. "Makes perfect sense to me." Appleby pulled out his harmonica and mouthed a scale. "Makes perfect sense."

Logan put aside his misgivings. If these two experienced men believed it was possible to soften bones, then who was he to argue?

Chapter 13

Logan raced out of the Golden Hind as fast as his leg
would allow.

Back at his cabin, he pulled off his dripping wet
clothes. Rivulets of water streamed from the fringes of
his shirt.

Libby watched him from the pallet, her eyes filled
with hope. "You found someone?"

He forced a smile for the purpose of offering encouragement. It made no sense to alarm her. "Found
myself two experts," he said cheerfully. "Now I know
exactly what to do."

She looked unconvinced, but before she could question him further, he explained. "Hot water, that's the
secret."

He hauled a bucket of water to the fireplace and
filled the large black iron kettle with water. He then
hung the kettle on the hinged bar that ran the length of
the fireplace, and added another log. While the water
heated, he did what he could to make Libby comfortable. Mainly, he talked her through the pains. "Come
on, now. You can do it," he'd say, or "Breathe through
your mouth."

It seemed to take forever for the water to heat, but
finally steam shot out of the spout and the fire sizzled
from the drops of water that bubbled over the sides of
the kettle. He filled a cup and carried it to Libby.

"I have it on good authority that this will help," he
explained. "Drink up."

For once in her life, she did as he commanded without argument or undue discussion. She stopped drinking only when a pain gripped her, but resumed once it had subsided. No sooner would she finish one cup than he promptly refilled it.

"No more," she whispered after the fifth or sixth cup.

"Come on, now," he coaxed, "this will help soften the bones."

Rather than comfort her, this only made the lines of worry on her face more pronounced. "I don't want soft bones."

"Trust me on this, Libby. You want soft bones. Come on, now, drink up."

Around midnight, a knock came at the door. It was Appleby. "Just wanted to know how your woman is doing?"

Logan hushed him and stepped onto the porch, closing the door softly behind him. During the last hour or so, the rain had turned to snow and patches of white had drifted onto his porch. "She seems to be having a hard time," Logan explained. It was cold outside and he hugged himself to keep warm as they talked. "A real hard time."

Appleby nodded, his breath a white mist in the darkness. "All women have a hard time."

This was encouraging news. Damned encouraging. "Is that right?"

"Yep. Like I said, I've gone through this twice already. You giving her 'nuf boiling water?"

"Every twenty minutes or so."

"That should do the trick."

Upon hearing her call his name, Logan said a hasty good night and hurried inside. "What is it, Libby?" he asked anxiously. He rushed to her bedside and dropped to his knees, ignoring the pain that shot through the one. He couldn't think about his bad leg. Not tonight.

"I didn't know where you were," she whispered so softly he had to lean over her to make out the words.

"I'm right here," he whispered back. He brushed a lock of damp hair from her forehead.

In the soft glow of the oil light, she looked exhausted and pale. Her eyes were bright, almost feverish in appearance.

"I'm afraid for the baby," she whispered through parched lips. "It's taking so long."

"It's supposed to take this long," he said. "I have it on good authority. What you need is more bone softener."

Her pains came at five-minute intervals for the rest of the night. At first Logan thought he'd imagined the regularity by which the pains struck. But when he started timing them, counting off the minutes in his head, he discovered he'd been right; the pains were exactly five minutes apart. It was absolutely amazing.

Toward dawn the pains grew worse and were coming at three-minute intervals. Her disposition had changed considerably in the last hour or so. She was downright ornery. Not only did she refuse to drink the hot water, she kept kicking off the covers.

He did his best to try to keep her calm, but her strength amazed him. Both of his arms were black and blue from where she'd pressed her fingers into his flesh during the night.

No wonder men stayed away during a birthing, he thought. It was too damned dangerous. After one particular painful onslaught, he handed her a rawhide strap and told her to bite down on it.

He used the increasingly short time between each contraction to best advantage. He sponged her damp forehead with cool water and straightened the pelts around her. He added more wood to the fire and checked the wall for drafts, plugging up even the tiniest crack with pieces of fur or rawhide. Now that the rain had turned to snow, the ceiling was no longer dripping. But puddles of water still dotted the floor, making it difficult to walk.

She dozed between contractions, but as soon as her

body began to writhe, he rushed to her side and took her in his arms. Holding her next to his massive chest, he rocked her until the pain subsided.

"Make it go away," she cried at one point.

"I wish I could," he said, feeling inadequate and as useless, as Jim Bridger would say, as a four-card flush. It had been a long time since he wanted anything as much as he wanted to make her pains go away.

By midmorning, snow covered the streets of Deadman's Gulch. He made his way to the rising creek behind his cabin, stepping over the patches of ice that had formed along the banks. Filling his bucket with the freezing cold water, he carried it back to the cabin, his moccasins sinking into the new-fallen snow.

For the last two hours, Libby's pains had been only a minute or two apart, giving her little chance to rest in-between times. It didn't seem possible that a human body could survive such torture. He stood by her bed and feared for her life.

It suddenly occurred to him how very little he knew about her. She could die in his cabin and he wouldn't even know who to write to, who to send her pitiful few belongings to. It had never occurred to him to ask her about her family, or what to do should something unforeseen happen. She seemed so vital, so alive. So unlike Catherine who had seemed fragile from the start. It didn't seem fair that something as natural as birthing could put a young woman at such risk. Why didn't nature prepare women better?

Libby moaned and called his name. "Logan . . ."

"I'm here," he said softly, kneeling by her side and taking her hand. "Do you want some more water?"

"God, no!"

He couldn't help but smile at the stubborn and determined look she gave him. She still had some fight left and that was encouraging. His spirits lifted and he squeezed her hand.

"Libby, I've been meaning to ask you. Where did you get such a name."

She smiled. "My name is Elizabeth, but my sister couldn't pronounce it so she called me Libby. I'm afraid it stuck."

"It's a lovely name," he hastened to assure her. "I never knew a Libby before."

"I never knew a Logan."

"I was named Kwatoko my by Indian mother. It means eagle."

"How did you get Logan out of Kwatoko?"

"My father was a terrible speller." He grinned. "He also had a hearing problem. He swore to his dying day that my mother called me Logan."

"Don't make me laugh," she pleaded.

"I'm sorry."

"Logan." She tugged at his shirt, drawing him closer. "If anything happens to me . . ." She stiffened and shut her eyes.

Watching the shadow of pain darken her face, he wrapped his arms around her. She gripped his hand until he thought the bones in his fingers would break. Her earlier moans had long since been replaced with loud cries. But this last pain brought a gut-wrenching scream.

Finally, her body stilled and she loosened her grip on him. "Should anything happen to me . . ."

"Don't talk like that."

"Please . . . the baby?"

He searched her face, hoping he'd misunderstood. He hadn't considered the possibility that the baby might survive all this, even if Libby did not. That he might be left with an orphan to care for.

What did he know about a baby? What did he know about anything? He'd lived thirty-six years and suddenly he realized how little he knew about life.

"Would you take care of . . . of the baby."

He stared at her. It was as if she were holding back the pain until she had his answer. What could he say to her? Yes, he would take care of her baby? Him? A mountain man? A mountain man with a bad leg and no future?

Another pain gripped her and he sensed that this one was different from the others. Why he thought this, he couldn't say. But he did and as her body lashed back and forth and the cries seemed to claw at the walls like frantic talons, he leaned toward her and whispered in her ear.

"I'll take care of your baby."

No sooner had he spoken than something quieted inside her. A smile touched her pale lips, then faded slowly as she escaped into sleep.

Knowing that he had only a minute or two until the next pain, he quickly wrung out a cloth in tepid water and wiped the beads of perspiration off her forehead. Her hair was soaked, her dress clung to her body. He wondered if she would be more comfortable if he removed it.

He rubbed his hand against the two-day growth on his chin. It seemed like he should be doing something more for her.

He felt the same frustration now as he had years earlier when he was fifteen and his father lay dying from the wounds suffered from a grizzly attack. With the invincibility of youth, he'd been convinced he could save his father. What a jarring experience it had been to face the truth.

He'd felt utterly alone that long-ago night watching his father die in his arms. Alone and helpless. He felt just as alone and just as helpless several years later watching his young English bride fade away before his very eyes.

The daughter of a British businessman who purchased pelts from Logan, she'd been captured by the Paiute Indians. Catherine's father was an honest, hardworking man who preferred Logan's prime pelts to the less expensive lower grade ones peddled by some free trappers. When he asked for Logan's help in rescuing his daughter, Logan didn't hesitate a moment. He knew the chief and his Indian blood from his mother's side made him close enough to the tribe to give him bargaining power. It cost him an entire season's worth of prime beaver pelts, but he made the trade. Unfortunately, Catherine had already been ravished by several braves. Knowing that she would be marked a fallen woman, she refused to return home.

At the time Logan felt he had no choice but to marry her. Indeed, wanted to. He never thought of her as anything but a perfect lady. She was not responsible for what had happened and he never understood how anyone could think otherwise. But even she blamed herself. She'd been accosted by a band of seven braves in their prime and she berated herself for not putting up more of a fight!

He knew from the start that she married him out of gratitude and desperation. He also suspected that she thought she deserved no better than a wild, uncivilized mountain man. He never had a chance to prove himself more. Truth to tell, there never was more, and in her eyes considerably less.

She hated the wilderness, hated the home he built for her, hated the isolation. Out of desperation, he agreed to move to St. Louis, but strangely enough, they were just as isolated in the city as they were in the wilderness. No respectable citizen would think of socializing with a woman who had *allowed* herself to be ravished by savages.

Much to his horror, she grew thinner and more listless each day, until even her eyes lost their luster.

Alarmed, he booked passage on a liner, thinking to take her back to London. She'd rallied during the preparations for their trip, and he thought the worst was over. He thought wrong. She died en route, and some said it was from a broken heart. He was convinced she willed herself to die.

A knock at the door brought him out of his reverie. He brushed his hand across Libby's forehead before leaving her side. It was Appleby.

Appleby looked embarrassed. He waved his arm to indicate the small gathering of men in front of the cabin. Sharkey staggered as he gulped from a flask. Even Hap had closed the doors to the general store to join the others. Next to him, the man named Shakespeare blew on his hands to keep warm.

"Me and the boys were wondering," Appleby began awkwardly, "how your woman is."

"She's not my . . ." Logan stopped. "I don't think she can hold on much longer."

"That's a crying shame." Appleby tucked his cold, chapped hands beneath his armpits. "Seems especially sad, this being Christmas Day and all."

"I guess there's no good day for dying," Logan replied grimly.

"Guess not. I just want you to know that out of respect for your woman, the boys and me will make sure there's no shooting off of guns or whooping it up."

"I'm mighty obliged."

"It's the least we can do." Appleby turned and rejoined the group of huddled men.

Logan closed the door and returned to Libby's side. Christmas. He thought about the story Libby had read to him from the Good Book. He recalled the soft faraway look in her eyes as she spoke about Christmas in Boston.

He'd never celebrated Christmas in his life. Catherine had made mention of it, but during that one dismal December they'd spent together, they'd been snowed in in their cabin and she had taken to her bed with fever. He never really understood what all the fuss was about until Libby read that story to him.

He reached over and picked up the worn little Bible that lay on the whiskey-keg table by her bedside. As he sat fingering the thin leather cover, an idea began to form.

He replaced the book just as she began thrashing around. "Hold on, Libby," he said. He held her until she grew still again. He leaned over and whispered in her ear. "Today is Christmas." And when she didn't respond, he tried again. "Did you hear what I said, Libby? It's Christmas Day."

"Christmas?" She repeated the word softly, a half smile touched her lips before she drifted off to sleep. He sat back on his chair and rested his chin in his hands.

What did he have to lose? he thought. Making a quick decision, he jumped to his feet and tore open the door. The men were still standing out front, huddled together to ward off the cold, their faces looking grim and forlorn.

"Appleby!"

Appleby broke from the huddle and hurried to the door. "Is she . . .?"

Logan shook his head. "You said today was Christmas."

"Yeah."

"I think that Christmas is important to Libby."

Appleby didn't seem a bit surprised by this. "It's important to a lot of people."

"Is there something I can do? To let her know what day this is. I told her but . . . I think I need to do something that would comfort her in some small way."

Appleby thought for a moment. "I have an idea." He pulled out his mouth organ and beckoned the men closer. To Logan, he said, "You go inside and leave everything to me and the boys."

Logan nodded his thanks. Shuddering against the cold, he shut the door and added another log to the fire. Outside, the strident harsh voices of the miners lifted in song. " 'O come, all ye faithful . . .' "

Logan grimaced in distaste. It was the worst damned singing he'd ever heard.

Chapter 14

WOULD it ever end? Libby wondered feverishly. She tensed as the pain began to build again. Like a volcano erupting inside, the pain shot from some inner source and held her in its relentless grip until it seemed that her last breath had been wrung from her. She had nothing left to give, yet the pain remained relentless in its taking.

It was hard to know when one pain began and another ended. Time had no meaning. Night. Day. It mattered none. She was consumed with the monstrous pain.

Something soft and cool touched her forehead. Her eyes fluttered open to find Logan as usual by her side. He smiled at her as he held a cool wet cloth to her brow.

His fingers felt like heaven. It worried her, though, to see his face lined with fatigue and anguish. She wanted so much to say something, do something that would erase the deep ridges in his forehead, soften the wild, almost desperate look in his eyes.

"Logan." Her voice barely a whisper, she clutched at his hand and held it to her chest.

"Don't talk," he said. "Save your strength." He leaned closer. "Can you hear them?"

She wasn't sure what he meant at first, but then she heard the voices. Convinced that it was the singing of angels, she was no longer afraid.

Without the fear, she relaxed, and her mind drifted away, severing itself from her body. She was in Boston, and it was Christmas Day. Everyone was there. Her mother, father. Her brothers and sisters . . .

" 'Come and behold Him . . .' " came the angels' voices.

Her eyes closed as a soothing peacefulness washed over her. She was back home where she belonged, and the air was filled with the succulent smells of roasted duck and the tangy pine scent of the Christmas tree.

The angels' voices lifted, " 'Born the King of Angels . . .' "

The vision cleared and she was once again faced with reality. A soul-gripping pain began to build. Tensing, she clawed frantically at the tireless arms that held her down.

The pain exploded, seeming to rip her body into a million little fragments.

Then, mercifully, it was over.

Logan stared down at the slippery red baby in his hands. He was afraid to move for fear the tiny body would go shooting across the room. The little fellow had a pair of lungs on him that would make a brass band seem quiet. He was positively squawking to high heaven, and sounded remarkably like a baby beaver. Even so, Logan couldn't remember hearing anything that sounded more musical or wondrous in his entire life.

The baby's cry was greeted by a burst of applause from outside, followed by joyous shouts and loud laughter. The congenial celebration in the street was a striking contrast to the noisy brawls and gunfire that usually rang through the town.

"You can put him here," Libby said, patting her middle.

He laid the baby on her bare abdomen and watched her face soften and glow as she ran a finger across the infant's tiny head. "He's beautiful," she whispered. Her eyes glistened with tears. At her loving touch, the baby stopped crying and turned his head toward her finger.

Relieved that the little fellow was now his mother's responsibility, Logan collapsed, exhausted, in the nearest chair. What he needed was a drink. Maybe a game of cards to clear his head. Some shut-eye wouldn't be a bad idea.

"Isn't he the most beautiful thing you ever did see?" Libby's voice was hushed in awe.

Logan stared at the scrawny, wrinkled, arrow-headed, bloodied, red-skinned baby, and as crazy as it sounded, he had to agree. He was the damnedest, most beautiful thing Logan had ever feasted his eyes upon.

Libby gazed at Logan, her eyes overly bright from fatigue. "You have to cut the cord."

This was dismaying news, indeed. Logan sat forward, hoping he'd heard wrong. "Cut? You mean with a knife."

Libby nodded. "You need to put the knife in boiling water."

"Boiling . . ." Confound it! Wouldn't you know? He was clear out of boiling water. He shot out of his chair, quickly grabbed a bucket of water, and poured it into the empty kettle.

He tossed another log onto the grate, then squatted in front of the hearth. It would take forever for the water to boil. He couldn't let the little fellow dangle forever from his mother, that's for sure. He leaned over and ran his knife blade through the flames.

"That should do it," he said, returning to the bedside. He held his knife up for her to see. The baby was making funny little sucking sounds with its tiny rosebud mouth.

"You have to cut it about here," Libby said, pointing.

His eyes followed her finger. "Are you sure?" he asked. It didn't seem right, somehow, to go cutting around babies.

She nodded. "I'm sure."

He cleared his throat. Suddenly the knife felt all wrong. Or was it his hands that were all wrong? His thumbs felt strange, disjointed. His usual capable fingers felt as stiff and rusty as old nails.

He stared at the ropelike cord. It couldn't have been more than an inch round. It was nothing. Not to a man who, at various times in his past, had pumped bullets into his share of grizzlies, rattlers, and a rabid mountain lion to save his own skin. Nothing.

"You need to tie something around it first," she said.

He pulled a piece of rawhide lacing from a nail and held it up. "Will this work?"

She nodded and watched in silence as he tied a piece around the cord.

He looked up at her. "Are you sure this isn't going to hurt?"

Libby smiled faintly. "Positive."

Holding the blade of the knife inches away from the cord, he sucked in his breath. "What about the baby?"

"What?"

"It won't hurt the baby? Cut some important nerve?"

"No, Logan." She studied his face. "Do you want me to do it?"

"Certainly not! You've . . . you've done enough already."

Legs apart, he held the knife steady. "Ready?"

"Ready."

The chore was done in no time at all.

Grinning like a schoolboy, Logan wiped the blade of his knife and slipped it back into its sheath. "There, that wasn't so bad, was it?" He looked ridiculously pleased with himself.

Libby stroked the dark hair of her baby's head. "I never thought it would be."

"Well now!" He slumped in a chair, feet apart. He felt like he could sleep for a week.

"Logan, the baby . . ."

He straightened. "What about the baby?"

"He needs to be . . . oh, no!"

Looking startled, he shot to her side. "What is it, Libby? Are you in pain?"

She shook her head. "I just remembered that we left the baby's clothes in the mountains. We have nothing for the baby to wear."

"Why of course we do," he said. He pulled an Indian blanket from the foot of her bed. He took a few swipes at it with his knife and held it up for her approval. "The head goes in here and these pointed ends wrap around the baby cocoonlike."

"Why, Logan! That's absolutely ingenious of you!"

He grinned. He didn't bother to tell her that he had learned this trick from the Indians. "Well, now . . ."

"When you finish bathing the baby, I need you to . . ."

"You want *me* to bathe the baby?"

"If you wouldn't mind."

"No," he rasped. "I don't mind."

"And then I'll need you to . . . help me." She blushed. "We're not quite finished yet."

"Good, God, Libby! There's more?"

It took him the rest of the morning to take care of mother and child. He bathed them, dressed them, changed the bed, and while Libby nursed her son, he carried the bucket with the afterbirth outside and buried it behind the smokehouse.

Appleby intercepted him upon his return to the cabin. "Everything all right?"

Logan grinned. "Couldn't be better."

"What is it?"

Logan looked puzzled. "What is what?"

"The baby. Is it a boy or a girl?"

"A boy. A big healthy boy. Weighs as much as a good rifle and is about as long as one."

Appleby was impressed. "That big, uh." He slapped Logan on the back. "Congratulations."

"I'm mighty obliged to you and the others for helping out. As soon as you started singing, things started moving along nicely. You ought to hire yourselves out as midwives."

Appleby laughed. "Wouldn't that be something? The Singing Midwives. Wait till my wife hears that one."

"Would you tell the others how much the baby's mother and I are obliged to them?"

Appleby looked almost as proud of himself as did Logan. "Glad to be of service. Listen, why don't you come over to the Golden Hind and tell the boys yourself?"

"Maybe I'll do that. Let me check to see if the little mother needs anything."

Inside the cabin, Libby was asleep, the baby nursing quietly at her breast. He checked the fire and tiptoed out of the cabin. He felt so proud, he thought his chest would burst clear open. He didn't want to leave her for long. Only long enough to break the good news to the others.

As soon as Logan walked into the saloon, he was greeted with whoops and applause.

"Drinks all around," he called to Moe the bartender. This brought more cheers, more hand clapping, and more foot stomping.

Sharkey grabbed hold of Logan's arm. "So tell us about the baby," he slurred, his breath a hundred percent proof.

Freeing himself from Sharkey's drunken grip, Logan described the baby's weight and height, holding his hands the appropriate distance to illustrate. He then described how he'd caught the baby and detached its mother without causing injury.

Appleby looked over at Shakespeare. "I'm sure you must have something you can quote that would be appropriate for the occasion."

Pleased to be the center of attention, Shakespeare thought for a moment, then grinned mischievously. "To err is human."

Not everyone caught the pun, but he got a hearty applause just the same.

"So when do we get to see this wondrous sight?" Keefer asked, chomping down on his cigar.

Fanning the smoke away from his face, Logan frowned. "Well, now, I don't know . . ." He felt fiercely protective suddenly. Crazy as it sounded, he felt like a mother bear with a newborn cub.

"What do you mean you don't know?" Big Sam's voice boomed from the back of the saloon. "Deadman's Gulch has its very own baby and you plan to keep it to yerself?"

The voices died down and all eyes turned to Logan.

Logan gave an apologetic cough. "You have to understand that babies are susceptible to disease."

"Ain't none of us harboring diseases," Keefer drawled. He glanced over at the big black man. "Hey, Big Sam, you harboring disease?"

"Not me," Big Sam replied with a scowl.

"What about you, Shakespeare? You harboring disease?"

Shakespeare looked positively offended. "Certainly not!" he sniffed.

Keefer turned back to Logan. "What I hear you saying is, we ain't good enough to see your young'un."

"That's not what I'm saying, Keefer." Logan looked about the room, beseeching each man in turn. "Put yourself in my place. If this was your baby would you want to let the lot of you anywhere near it? Most of you haven't had a bath since who knows when . . . look at your hair, your beards. Who knows what vermins you're carrying."

"He's right," Appleby said, stepping away from the bar. "I wouldn't even visit my own two children looking like this."

Satisfied that he'd made his point, Logan took a swallow of beer and assumed the discussion was over.

Next to him, Keefer rubbed his hands together. "All right, men, what do you say we clean up? Baths, haircuts, the works."

Logan choked, spraying beer across the bar. "Now hold on there . . ."

His voice disappeared in the pandemonium that followed. The men were already checking out one another's credentials. "Anyone here know how to give a haircut and shave?"

Beaker McGrath, so-called for his long pointed nose, grabbed hold of Sharkey by the scruff of his neck and lifted the man's drunken head off the table. "I bet you men don't know that Sharkey here was a barber before coming to Californ'a."

"Is that so?" Big Sam ran his hand over the black kinks of his unkempt hair. "Is he any good?"

"Of course he's good." Beaker gave Sharkey a good shaking. "Show them."

Sharkey's head flopped back and forth like a rag doll, but he did finally manage to move his fingers to emulate a pair of scissors.

A look of satisfaction settled on Beaker's face. "What did I tell you?" He let Sharkey's head drop back on the table.

"Then it's settled," Appleby said. "Now what about baths?"

"Wait a minute," Logan protested. "I don't think this is a good idea."

"You got a problem with us getting all gussied up?" Big Sam demanded. "You think your woman and baby's too good for us?"

All eyes turned from Big Sam to Logan. Logan forced a friendly though halfhearted grin. "No, I don't think that. It's just not a good idea for a baby to have too much company. Besides, the last time you men paid your respects, you scared Libby half out of her wits. I doubt she'll want to see you again."

Hap stuck his bald head in Logan's face. "Need I remind you that we stood outside freezing our balls off singing Christmas carols?"

Appleby concurred. "You said it yourself. It was us who made your woman's time easier at the end."

"Yes, it was. Christmas is important to her. I'm mighty obliged to all of you, but . . ."

"Then she'll want company," Appleby insisted. "It's not Christmas without company. Why where I come from, we have company all the way to the Twelfth Night."

"Is that so? Company, uh?"

Logan recalled the story Libby had read aloud from the Good Book. All the company that came to visit the baby Jesus. He wondered if the shepherds had taken the time to gussy themselves up for the occasion. He'd have to remember to ask Libby. "All right. You can visit the baby. But only on one condition. You check your weapons at the door."

"Our knives as well?"

"Last I heard, knives are weapons. And you mind your manners, all of you. No cussing. No spitting and no pushing."

"You drive a hard bargain," Big Sam complained.

"If you want to see the baby, you do it my way. Agreed?"

The men looked at each other. Finally, as if by mutual consent, they raised their drinks in unison. "Agreed!"

The town had, as Sharkey described it, "never seen such a preening and a primping in all its born days." This was quite a statement coming from a man who normally allowed himself only two sober hours in a week's time.

But that was before the miners took it upon themselves to monitor his drinking. Twenty-four hours a day they watched his every move. His flask was confiscated and his tent searched. A coffeepot was kept brewing for the sole purpose of keeping the town's only barber sober.

"It ain't fair!" Sharkey protested bitterly to Logan, whom he blamed for this sorry state of affairs.

"It's fair," Logan assured him, although secretly

he'd hoped that the miners would have forgotten the idea of visiting Libby and the baby by now. "No one wants to trust themselves to a drunk barber."

Sharkey resigned himself, at least temporarily. It appeared his only recourse was to give the men their damned haircuts and shaves. Maybe then they would leave him alone and let him resume his drinking in peace.

He set up business beneath the sagging canvas overhang in front of the general store. This was after he and Hap had hammered out an agreement as to the cost of renting space. Hap was the clear loser in the bargain, until Sharkey generously offered to trim Hap's beard for free. It was the best he could do since the man had no hair to speak of. Had, in fact, no more than one or two strays, which he insisted on keeping.

"A man's not 'fficially bald as long he has a single hair left," Hap said, ready to fight anyone who disagreed.

"And that," Shakespeare said, borrowing from the *Merry Wives of Windsor,* "is the long and the short of it."

Afraid to argue with Hap for fear he'd raise the rent, Sharkey trimmed him first while all the miners watched.

Satisfied that Sharkey knew what he was doing, the miners took their turns sitting upon an empty whiskey keg.

Hair and whiskers flew in every direction as Sharkey shaved, cut, snipped, and trimmed. In no time at all he cut what he said was enough hair to sink a ship.

Although he'd complained about the miners' vigilance in monitoring his drinking, he enjoyed being the center of attention while he worked. He put on quite a show for the benefit of the men who stood patiently, waiting their turns.

He lathered and shaved and lathered again, explaining that only the finest of barbers bothered with a second shaving. He then gleaned each newly bared chin for stray hairs.

When it began to snow again, Hap Montana allowed Sharkey to move his business inside the general store with only a slight increase in rent, providing he cleaned up after every customer and not get stray hairs in the pickle barrel.

Watching all the fuss, Logan didn't know quite what to think. He never would have thought that one small baby could turn a town upside-down in such a way. He didn't recognize half the men without their facial hair. Why the whole town was sporting faces as smooth s a baby's bottom!

Appleby slapped Logan on the back. "How's it feel to be a family man?"

Logan frowned. "I wouldn't know, since I'm not one and never intend to be one."

Appleby nodded. "Yeah, it takes a little getting used to. Especially in the middle of the night."

Logan watched Appleby from the corner of his eye and assured that the man wasn't mocking him, he lowered his voice. It wouldn't do to let the other miners hear him talk about subjects that should be of primary concern only to womenfolk. "Is that normal? I mean for babies to confuse their nights with their days?"

"Normal as can be. I didn't get a decent night's sleep for three months after our last one."

"Three months? That long?"

"I figured it this way. Babies don't get their day eyes until around that time."

"What do you mean day eyes?"

"I mean they don't see day until their eyes develop fully."

"Is that so?"

"If they can't see day, there's no way they know when to squawk and when not to squawk."

"That makes sense to me." Logan offered Appleby his hand. "I'm mighty obliged to you for sharing your vast knowledge and experience with me."

Appleby gave Logan's hand a solemn shake. "I'm glad to be of service."

Logan turned as a large strapping man with a face as wrinkled as a boiled shirt walked into the store.

"Don't tell me you're getting a haircut," Appleby said.

Cast-Iron Peters lived in a cabin outside of town. He cast a disapproving eye at the goings-on and growled, "I ain't gettin' all gussied up for no woman and her young'un."

Libby sat on the coarse thick bear robe next to Noel and swung the gold locket gently from its chain. The embossed surface caught the firelight and miniature flames danced upon the burnished metal of the locket.

Noel gazed at the locket in fascination, his blue eyes bright and alert. Libby felt such tenderness toward her young son that at times she thought her heart would burst with motherly pride. Everything about him from his tiny little toes to the dot of his button nose was perfect in her eyes.

"Your father gave me this locket," she said softly. She carefully cupped the locket in her hand and sprang the clasp open. Almost at once she felt a pang. Noel's hair was almost identical in color to his father's hair. It's what she'd hoped for, of course, but she couldn't help but feel a deep sadness. Noel needed a father and all she could give him was a snippet of hair. *Oh, Jeffrey. If only you could see your son . . .*

Some inner sense made her lift her eyes toward the door of the cabin. Logan stood watching her. His eyes were leveled beneath his dark furrowed brow. A look of withdrawal shuttered his face.

He'd gone to fetch fresh water, but she'd been so intent in her thoughts, she'd not heard him return.

She searched his face for some remnants of the laughter that had been there moments earlier, before he left on his errand. All she could find were harsh and relentless lines. Why had he returned from his errand looking so grim? What could have happened in such a short time?

Feeling awkward and self-conscious beneath his hard scrutiny, she pocketed the locket. This simple movement on her part broke the brittle tension in the air. He ducked beneath the clothesline that was stretched across the room and filled the kettle with fresh water.

"Logan? Is everything all right?"

"Everything is fine!" His answer was short and curt and left no room for discussion.

Puzzled and feeling more than a bit rebuffed, she stayed out of his way for the remainder of the day.

That night, after Libby and the baby were asleep, and the seemingly endless chores had been done for the day, Logan left the cabin and walked through the falling snow to his favorite saloon. How could he have been so foolish as to become emotionally involved with Libby and her baby? The way he'd been carrying on these last few days, one would have thought that Noel was his child; that Libby was his . . .

Well, she wasn't.

So there was no excuse for the way he felt upon finding her staring at that locket and looking like the grieving widow she had every right to be. He had no right to feel hurt and rejected. No right at all.

But he had, dammit! He not only felt hurt and rejected, he felt cheated and even a bit angry. For the first time ever, he'd felt like he belonged. Like he had a family. A home.

He never felt that way before. Certainly not while growing up. He'd been raised by his mother, and after her death, he'd lived with his father. It had been a good life, and until these last few days spent with Libby and Noel, he never once thought his upbringing had been in any way lacking.

Maybe he was just tired. Maybe that would explain the strange thoughts that plagued him. He'd not slept much in recent nights. No one sleeps much with a new baby in the house. That had to be it. *That better be it.*

He stepped inside the saloon and stared in astonishment at the empty tables and chairs.

Only the bartender and Cast-Iron were there, and a monte dealer playing a game of solitaire. Logan had never seen the place so empty, except during the day when the miners were up in the hills mining gold.

"Where is everybody?"

Cast-Iron made a disgusted gesture. "Damned fool men. They're all home washin' clothes and takin' baths."

Logan couldn't believe his ears. The men had agreed to clean up at his insistence, but he never meant for it to interfere with his card game. The truth was, he'd hoped that after their initial attempt to achieve proper hygiene, the men would abandon the idea of visiting Libby and the baby.

Previously, the miners seldom washed their clothes and never during the middle of the week. Any bathing that was done was purely by chance if someone happened to fall into a stream or some other body of water.

"How long do you think it's going to take them?" Logan asked. His hands itched for the feel of cards.

"Forever!" Cast-Iron spit out. "Some men were complaining 'cuz it was taking so long for their clothes to dry. 'Fraid that everyone would see the baby before they do."

Swearing under his breath, Logan ordered a beer. What was happening here? Libby and the baby had already taken over his cabin.

He could barely move for the rope that stretched from one end of the cabin to the other, filled with Noel's flannel nightgowns and the endless diapers cut from red and blue flannel that he called breeches.

He'd paid one of the miners good money to go up to the mountain and fetch his horse and the two rented mules. Libby's valise was ruined, but the clothes inside, though soaked, were otherwise salvageable.

Bolts of flannel had been purchased from Hap, and Logan had spent hours cutting the fabric into little squares. It got so he couldn't look at a flannel shirt without plotting out how many breeches he could cut from it.

It amazed him how much time and attention a baby required. His days were filled with fetching water, boiling water, washing clothes, folding clothes. This combined with his lack of sleep was a volatile combination.

And now he couldn't even enjoy a game of cards with the boys. Libby had somehow managed to take over the saloon, and was taking over his life. He had to talk to someone.

He glanced around on the outside chance someone else might have entered the saloon. No such luck. "I don't understand any of this," he said for Cast-Iron's benefit. "One minute I'm living a perfectly normal life. Before I know it, my house is taken over by two perfect strangers. I can't sleep. There's no time to eat, and now I can't even enjoy a game of cards." His depression increased as he glanced at the grizzled man. What in the world was he doing unloading his burdens on the likes of Cast-Iron Peters? "How could a man's life get so mixed up?"

Cast-Iron grunted and spit out one word, "Women!" as if that explained everything. Logan was beginning to think the man knew what he was talking about.

Chapter 15

IT stopped snowing four days after Christmas, but the temperature was below freezing. The sky was as gray as an old tin wash barrel, pressing against the land with a heavy haze that hid the upper peaks of the Sierras.

A long line of men stood in front of Logan's cabin. The line stretched the length of Main Street, clear to the other side of town. The men jumped up and down and blew on their hands in an effort to keep warm as they waited their turn to see the baby.

Only those passing Logan's stringent inspection were allowed inside his cabin to pay their respects. Having just let Appleby enter, Logan turned his attention to the next man in line. Beaker McGrath stood, patiently holding a wooden cradle.

"Your hat's dusty. Leave it outside."

"Aw shucks, Logan, I don't go anywhere without me hat. You know what they say, you can always tell where a man's been by his hat."

"That's another good reason to leave your hat outside. There're some things it would be better for the little fellow not to know yet."

Beaker's gruff voice exploded with laughter. "Maybe you're right." He set the cradle down and good-naturedly tossed his hat on the porch.

After Appleby had paid his respects, Beaker walked inside and set the cradle at Libby's feet.

She was sitting on a chair next to the fireplace,

wearing her pretty blue dress. Despite her best efforts to keep Noel awake, he was sound asleep in her arms.

She ran her hand along the silky smooth wood of the cradle. "It's beautiful!"

Beaker beamed, revealing two missing teeth. "Beaker McGrath at your service, ma'am."

"How do you do, Mr. McGrath. Did you make this cradle?"

"That I did, ma'am." He leaned over her chair to get a closer look at the sleeping baby. "So that's the little fellow, eh? Mighty handsome."

Libby smiled with motherly pride.

"Looks just like his father."

Surprised, Libby looked up at him. "Now how would you be knowing that? His father's been dead for several months."

Beaker rubbed his nose and looked embarrassed. "Well, I just assumed . . . Logan don't say much about himself. But when a man suddenly acquires himself a family, you just put two and two together."

"Mr. St. John is just a friend."

"If I said anything untoward, I heartily apologize."

"No need," Libby said, smiling to put him at ease. "It was only logical that you should draw such a conclusion."

"Your time's up, McGrath," Logan called from the door.

"Thanks you for coming," Libby said. "And I know Noel will enjoy having his very own bed."

"Noel. Is that the little fellow's name?" When Libby nodded, Beaker shook his head. "Never heard that name before."

"It's French for Christmas," she explained.

Beaker looked impressed. "Is that right?"

"I thought it was a good name for a baby born on Christmas Day."

"You take care of that little fellow, you hear?"

Next to enter the cabin was a well-spoken man named Thornton Wellerton. Unlike the other miners,

who were dressed in canvaslike pants and flannel
shirts, this man was dressed in a fine brown cutaway
coat with square-cut tails, deerskin breeches, and a
gold-colored brocade vest. Upon entering the cabin, he
took off his top hat and laid it on the table with his kid-
skin gloves. He looked and spoke like a gentleman as
he introduced himself to Libby.

"I have a little something for your son's future." He
pulled a soft leather bag from inside his vest. "Gold
dust. Worth at least fifty dollars."

Libby gasped. "I couldn't possibly accept such a
generous gift."

"Of course you can. I insist."

"I don't know what to say. I'll put it in the bank for
him as soon as we arrive in Boston."

"Boston, ma'am. That wouldn't be Boston, Massa-
chusetts, would it?"

"Why, yes."

"I should have know. A lady like yourself. I would
say that makes us practically neighbors."

"Why, Mr. Wellerton, don't tell me that you are
from Boston?" Libby was so delighted, she could
barely believe her good fortune. She held out her hand
and he immediately took it in his own. "I should have
known."

He lifted her hand to his mouth and planted a kiss
below her wrist. She blushed and lowered her lashes.
"Why, Mr. Wellerton."

He continued to hold her hand. "Do tell me how a
fellow Bostonian found herself in such a dreadful place
as Deadman's Gulch."

Libby quickly explained her husband's death and
how she was on the way to Nevada City when she became stranded in Deadman's Gulch. "What about
yourself?" she asked.

"There isn't a lot to tell," he said, but he settled himself on a chair and proceeded to tell her, starting with
how he was the head of a mining company.

From the doorway of the cabin, Logan watched

Libby's animated face and frowned. She had definitely been more circumspect with the previous miners. But there were no sign of reserve on her face now. If anything, she was quick to smile at the least little thing that fool dandy, Thornton, said. Too quick, Logan decided after her hearty laugh rang out. The man couldn't be *that* amusing!

"Your time's up, Wellerton," Logan announced, although in reality the irksome man had another minute or two left.

Logan turned his attention to the next man in line. "Guns on the table."

"Anything you say," Shakespeare said.

"And the knife," Logan said, casting a quick glance inside at Libby and Thornton. It couldn't be healthy for a woman just giving birth to be smiling so much. For that matter, it seemed downright indecent for a new mother to look so pretty. Her eyes sparkled as bright as stars on a cold wintry night. Her cheeks were flushed pink, her laughter was like music. Why in the name of sam hill hadn't she acquired a more maternal look that would be more befitting of her new station in life?

"Your time's up, Wellerton!" Logan's voice echoed through the room, waking the baby.

Libby looked at Logan in dismay. "Logan, really. Must you raise your voice?" She placed Noel over her shoulder and rubbed his back.

"Some people don't seem to be able to hear," Logan said, glaring at Wellerton.

Wellerton seemed oblivious to Logan's disparaging remark, or even to Noel, who was making quite a racket. He seemed only to have eyes and ears for Libby. "Would you mind if I come calling again?" he asked. "It's such a relief to talk to a fine cultured lady like yourself."

"It would be my pleasure, Mr. Wellerton."

"Thornton, please."

Libby smiled up at him. "Thornton."

Hearing this exchange, Logan tightened his jaw. He

remembered how long it had been before Libby had called him by his given name. "I believe you were leaving, *Mr.* Wellerton."

As if to shake himself out of a daze, Thornton grabbed his hat and gloves, took one last lingering look at Libby, and left.

By this time, Noel was positively wailing, forcing Libby to raise her voice to make herself heard. "It's time for his feeding."

Delighted to put an end to all the gawking and ogling that was going on beneath his very own roof, Logan stepped outside. It seemed to him that the men showed entirely too much interest in the mother and nowhere near as much consideration for the baby. "All right, men. That's all for now. It's time for the baby's feeding."

A collective groan started at the front of the line and swept clear to the back.

A Chinese man who had been standing to the side hobbled toward the porch in his wooden shoes. He was dressed in baggy pants and a square tunic top that reached to his knees. His hair fell from beneath his conical hat in a single braided queue down his back. "Pleeze, would you give this to your little one." He spoke in a singsong voice and kept his eyes lowered.

A man with a protruding stomach and a squat red face stepped out of line and shoved the Chinese man aside. "The little one doesn't need anything from the likes of you." The man's name was Benjamin Jacobs. His hatred for the Celestials living in the area was well known.

"Yeah, get out of here," someone called from the back of the line. "We don't need any chinks around here."

The crowd grew noisy as verbal barbs began to fly, all directed at the slightly built coolie.

"Stop it, all of you!" At the sound of Libby's voice, the men fell silent. All eyes turned in her direction as she stood on the porch with Noel in her arms. This was the first glimpse of Libby for the majority of the miners still in line. The men stared at her in a daze as they absorbed every inch of her delicate features, her lovely golden hair, and her fine womanly curves.

Libby, totally unaware of the power she held, motioned the frightened Chinese man inside.

The man glanced anxiously at the others, and when no one made an objection, he crossed his arms in front, slipped his hands into the opposite sleeves, and followed her inside the cabin.

"What is your name?" Libby asked.

"Macao."

"It's good of you to come, Macao."

"I brought a gift for your son." He reached into the pocket of his tunic and drew out a tiny carved wooden box.

"It's beautiful," Libby said, fingering the intricate design.

"It's a dream holder," Macao explained. "You put your dreams for your baby inside and they will come true."

Libby was enchanted. "The first dream I will put inside is my dream to take him home."

Macao nodded in understanding. "That is my dream, also. To go back to my country."

A look of wistfulness and longing crossed his face and her heart went out to him. "Perhaps, if we're lucky, we'll both get our wish."

Later that night, Libby laid Noel in his lovely new cradle and sang the same soft lullaby her mother had sung to her when she was a child.

Meanwhile, Logan prepared their supper and after Noel had fallen asleep, she joined him at the table.

"What a day," Libby said. "Everyone was so kind. Just look at all the presents."

Logan was looking. He couldn't believe how much stuff had accumulated in a single day. He could barely move in his own cabin. Some of it was useful, he supposed. But most of the gifts were a bit ridiculous. What in the name of sam hill would Noel do with a pickax, for example? Or a year's worth of haircuts and shaves? Not to mention a mouth organ.

"And wasn't that Mr. Thornton nice?" Libby continued. "All the way from Boston."

"Humph."

"Why, it's hard to believe that we were practically neighbors at one time."

"So you said earlier."

"And he's very educated. Why, he's the head of a mining company."

"Amazing."

"I still can't believe it. Finding someone here in Deadman's Gulch who was practically a neighbor?"

"Hard to believe."

After supper, Logan left the cabin and trudged across the hard-packed snow to the Golden Hind Saloon. The place was filled, and the miners in high spirits. Relieved that everything was back to normal, Logan ordered a beer and settled himself down for a full night of cards. He hadn't had a decent game of poker since Libby arrived in town and tonight he meant to make the most of it.

He soon discovered, however, that the miners weren't thinking about their bids. Talk centered around Libby and the baby.

"Look at this," Beaker said, pulling a wood block from his pocket. "When I finish with it, it'll be one of those . . . what do you call them . . .?"

"Pull toys?" Thornton offered in his fine cultured voice.

Just hearing Thornton's voice irritated Logan. And seeing him look all spit and polished made Logan's blood positively boil. It wasn't normal to be living in a town like Deadman's Gulch and still maintain a spiffy appearance. You would think someone as intelligent as Libby would see through the man.

"Would you put that damned toy away and deal the cards?" Logan growled.

"Do you know what the baby needs . . .?" One of the other men began.

"The baby doesn't need a thing!" Logan snapped. He fanned out the cards and sorted his hand.

Luke Appleby pushed his chair back on two legs. "Don't be such a spoilsport, St. John."

"I'm being practical," Logan argued. "How do you think Libby is going to carry all that stuff back to Boston?"

"Boston?" Appleby's chair fell forward.

A stunned silence circled the table, then leapt like a wildfire to the other tables until the entire saloon had fallen into a hushed stillness. For once, even the monte dealers were silent.

Thornton was the first to speak. "She's going back to Boston?"

It gave Logan great pleasure to dash the dandy's hopes. "As soon as the baby can travel."

"Why that's mighty disappointing," Appleby said. "I think having a woman and a baby around brings a little culture to this town."

Thornton agreed. "Indeed it does. Of course, we can hardly blame her for wanting to leave." He stared straight at Logan. "It's a shame that a fine lady like that would find herself holed up in a ramshackled excuse for a house."

"I don't hear Libby complaining," Logan said, feeling defensive.

"That's because she's a lady."

Logan glared at him. "Are we going to play cards or are we going to while away the night jawing like a bunch of old shoes?"

The bidding resumed, but there was a definite gloom in the air, and after it was apparent that the men were more interested in discussing Libby's impending departure than in playing cards, Logan finally threw his hand down and left.

Chapter 16

"I don't know if you remember me, ma'am, I'm Luke Appleby."

Libby greeted the miner with a smile. "Of course I remember you, Mr. Appleby. You led the choir that sang to me on Christmas Day."

Luke's face lit up. "That I did, ma'am. That I did."

"You also brought the baby a mouth organ."

His grin almost reached his ears. "I'm most honored that you remember."

"Won't you please come in?"

Libby had just finished giving Noel his bath and had put him down for his morning nap. Logan was out hunting and she was looking forward to a few quiet hours to herself.

Luke pulled off his hat and stepped inside. "I'm sorry to bother you."

"It's no bother," Libby said. "Would you like some coffee? I just made a fresh pot."

"If you don't mind."

"I don't mind at all."

Luke glanced around. "It's mighty cozy in here." His eyes fell on a glass filled with freshly cut snowdrops. "There's nothing like a woman's touch. Reminds me of home."

Libby poured him a cup and set it on the table, then poured herself one. "Where's your home, Mr. Appleby?"

"Illinois. The reason I'm here, ma'am. Logan said you was going home to Boston."

"That's right. As soon as the baby is old enough to travel and the weather clears up."

"Me and the boys are going to hate to see you go. We think a woman and baby adds a homey touch to the town."

"That's very kind of you to say."

"Oh, I wasn't saying it to be kind. I'm saying it because it's true. Only last night I walked past your cabin and I heard your young'un cry. It reminded me of my own family." His face grew wistful. "I can't tell you how much I miss my wife and children."

Sympathizing, she tried to think of something to say to cheer him. "Tell me about your children."

"I have two of them. A boy and a girl. One and three years old. Course we had two more, but they got this fever and . . ."

"How awful for you."

"Yes, well. Like I said, I sure do miss my family. I was hoping to find enough gold and return by now. It's not working out quite like I hoped."

"You haven't found any gold?"

"Oh, I've found gold all right. But it costs a man a lot to live. Look at this." He held up a foot. "I paid twelve dollars for these boots. Why back home my family could live an entire month on twelve dollars."

"I know. I was shocked at the prices myself. I hope it works out for you soon."

"I hope so too. But meanwhile, ma'am. I hope you'll reconsider and stay. It would mean a lot to me and the boys."

Libby hated having to disappoint him. "It's very nice of you to want me to stay . . . But I'm sure you must understand that Deadman's Gulch is not the kind of place that one wishes to raise a child."

"I can't argue with that, ma'am, but since you've been here, the town has improved one hundred percent. Why the boys said they actually enjoyed having a reason to get themselves all prettied up."

"That's very considerate of them, Mr. Appleby, but

I'm sure that having children of your own, you understand that I must put Noel's needs first. There're no schools here, no churches. Why a person could get shot just walking down the street."

She then described the events of that cold December night when she'd arrived in town.

Mr. Appleby looked positively aghast. "Why that's terrible."

"Indeed it is," Libby said. "I could have been killed."

"Or worse!" he exclaimed. He didn't explain what could be worse than being killed, and Libby had no intention of asking him.

Instead, she explained her promise to her dear departed husband. "Noel's father made me swear to him on his deathbed to take Noel home."

"Of course you're obligated to keep a promise like that," Mr. Appleby agreed. "But I wasn't suggesting you stay indefinitely. Only for a while. You're a good influence on the men, and I'm not just saying that to hear myself talk. I hardly recognize some of them with their beards all trimmed and their clothes washed. The best thing of all is that they seem to be less, I don't know, rowdy."

"This is all very nice, but you have to understand that Noel and I are imposing upon Mr. St. John's kind hospitality."

"Do you think so? I mean, I've never heard him complain, 'cept to say he didn't get much sleep."

"He has been extremely patient. But it's obvious to me he would prefer to have his privacy back. He's not used to being around people much."

"It takes some getting used to, that's for sure, having a baby around."

"Yes, and another thing." She blushed. "It's rather a delicate matter."

"I've discussed a few delicate matters in my life," he assured her. "One can hardly father as many children as I have without touching upon a delicate matter or two."

"I suppose you're right," Libby said. "It doesn't seem proper for me to be sharing quarters with a man who's not my husband."

"I see what you mean. That could definitely be considered improper."

"Not that anything improper has happened," she assured him. "Why, Mr. St. John has been a perfect gentlemen."

"I should hope so!" Mr. Appleby declared, but he looked rather skeptical, as if he couldn't imagine Logan behaving himself in the presence of a woman. "Of course, it helps that you're a lady."

"I suppose so. But now that I have Noel to think about, it's essential that I consider my reputation."

"Absolutely." He stood. "I'd better be going. I'm glad we had this talk."

"I am too," Libby said. "Thank you for coming, Mr. Appleby."

"I'd feel a whole lot better if you'd call me Luke."

"Very well. Luke it shall be."

Logan was convinced that once everyone had paid proper respects to the baby, things would return to normal. He was so confident of this, he was astonished to discover the saloon empty that Friday night when he walked in, primed for a night of poker.

Thinking the men had gathered somewhere else, he walked in and out of each of the other six saloons. They were all empty, except for one, where he found Cast-Iron Peters huddled over a drink.

"Where the hell is everyone?" Logan demanded.

Cast-Iron stared into his glass. "At Luke's place. Some sort of meeting."

Logan frowned. "Now's not the time to be having meetings. It's time to play cards. What's the meeting about?"

"Search me," Cast-Iron said. "Something about your woman."

"Libby?" Puzzled, Logan walked stiff-legged out of the saloon and across the street toward Luke's cabin. If a meeting was being held about his wo . . . uh, Libby, then he meant to make it his business to find out what the hell was going on.

Luke's place was packed. Several men were huddled by the open door, craning their necks up and down to see inside. A few men were gathered around the single window that had been cut in the side wall and covered in canvas. One man was on the roof, trying to listen through the chimney.

Logan shouldered his way through the crowd until he made his way through the door. "What's going on?" he demanded.

Luke Appleby, who was giving a speech from atop a wooden box, stopped midsentence and glared at Logan. From all outward appearances, he was addressing the crowd with the same earnestness of a politician during a tight race. It was obvious he did not take kindly to Logan for interrupting the most persuasive part of his speech.

"Mrs. Summerfield is getting ready to leave Deadman's Gulch and we're trying to figure out a way to make her stay longer."

Logan was taken aback. He knew she was planning to leave of course, but he hadn't realized her departure was imminent. "Libby is leaving?"

Big Sam glanced back over his shoulder. "Hell, you're the one who told us that."

"Eh, yes, but I didn't mean she was leaving . . . so soon. Noel's too young to travel."

"But she's leaving soon enough and that's what me and the boys are trying to prevent," Luke said. "When Libby hears our plans, she may well change her mind."

Logan dismissed this with a wave of his hand. "There's nothing that you can come up with to make her change her mind. She hates it here."

Luke remained undaunted. "We're going to change all that. Right, men?"

The crowd shouted, "Right!"

Luke turned to Choo-Choo, who was sitting next to him keeping notes. "Choo-Choo, would you read Logan our town proclamation?"

Looking important, Choo-Choo stood, cleared his voice, and read from his notebook. "It is hereby decided that the city of Deadman's Gulch will have itself respectable laws."

Luke nodded in approval. "Did you hear that, Logan? Respectable." Turning back to Choo-Choo, he wagged a finger. "Continue."

"From here on in, any altercation must be confined to outside the town boundaries."

"Altercations meaning fights," Luke explained to Logan. "Neither the flying of bullets nor fists will be allowed to ruffle one hair of that little baby's head." Pleased with himself, he pointed to Choo-Choo's notes. "Write that down. Neither bullets . . . that's right . . . Nor fists . . . the baby's head."

Choo-Choo finished writing and then continued to read. "It was further decided that from here on in the citizens of Deadman's Gulch will adhere to a curfew."

Logan cringed. "What sort of curfew?"

"Now don't go getting yourself all riled up. This is for the sake of the baby. The boys and I were thinking that ten o'clock seems pretty respectable."

"Ten o'clock!" Logan glanced around the room. "Are you all gone plumb loco? Do you have any idea what kind of hours that baby keeps? I haven't had a decent night's sleep since he was born."

Appleby addressed his comments to the crowd at large. "What did I tell you? We've been making so much gosh-darn ruckus. That's why the little fellow can't sleep." He turned back to Logan. "You watch, with a proper curfew, we'll all sleep like babies."

"Good grief, I hope not!" Logan grumbled. "I hate

to think of grown men waking up every two hours and demanding to have their breeches changed."

Everyone began talking at once. Luke banged two pots together. "Order. Order. That means quiet everyone. That's better. Now we'll discuss living arrangements for Libby and the baby."

Logan had heard just about enough of this foolishness. He walked to the front of the room and planted himself next to Luke. "You can make all the curfews and rules you want. But it isn't going to make one bit of difference to Libby."

The debate continued for the better part of the next hour. But no matter what Logan said, the men had made up their minds.

"From here on in," Appleby announced, "that little fella is going to have himself a proper town to grow up in."

"Deadman's Gulch can be as proper as it wants," Logan argued back. "I'm telling you, Libby's mind is made up. As soon as the stage resumes running, she and the baby will be on it and there's nothing you can say to change her mind."

"We'll see about that," Beaker shouted. "Won't we, boys?"

"You said it, Beaker!"

"Hear, hear!"

Chapter 17

NO question about it; the town was, as Jim Bridger would say, crazy as a bedbug.

Logan was convinced of this the following morning when he was rudely awakened out of a sound sleep by the sound of hammering. He lay on the floor in front of a dying fire and peered through slotted eyes.

Noel had been awake pretty much all night long, and Logan and Libby had taken turns walking the floor with him. It had been close to dawn by the time the little fellow had finally nodded off. Logan had just drifted off to sleep himself when the loud hammering nearly blasted him out of his bedroll.

What the sam hill was going on? Eyes open wide now, he fought his way out of his covers and tiptoed past the baby's cradle to the front door. Astonishingly enough, the ruckus had awakened neither Noel nor his mother.

Dressed in only his red woolen long johns, he slipped out the door and closed it softly behind him. He stood on the porch rubbing his eyes in disbelief as he stared at the crowd gathered in front.

The canvas lean-to that had littered the lot across from his had disappeared sometime during the night. In it's place was a wood-framed skeleton of a house.

Despite the early hour, it appeared that every miner in town was gathered on the spot. Some were heaving logs across the snow with the help of thick-flanked mules. Others were hammering or sawing. Most were standing around a large bonfire issuing orders or drinking coffee out of steaming tin cups.

Logan limped across the street, oblivious to the fact that in his red long johns he stood out like a polecat at a picnic. "What the hell is going on here?" he demanded, addressing no one in particular.

Appleby, who was bent over some rough drawings, straightened and lifted a hand in greeting. "Good morning, St. John. How nice of you to drop by." He nodded toward the framework. "Wouldn't you say that it is going to be a mighty fine house?"

"The very best," Sharkey said. "Look a' here. This here is gonna be the first glass window in town."

Not to be outdone, Big Sam pointed to the opposite wall. "And over there will be a fine stone fireplace."

"This is all very interesting," Logan said. "But why are you going to all this trouble?"

"It's no trouble," Appleby assured him. "Why when Libby and Noel see their new house . . ."

"What did you say?" Logan stared at the men aghast. "You're building this for Libby?"

"With our very own hands."

Logan threw back his head and laughed. "Have you men gone loco? It was only a short time ago that the bunch of you couldn't be in the same room together without coming to blows. Do you actually believe you're going to build a house together?"

"That we do," Appleby said, looking offended. "That we do."

Logan shook his head. "This I've got to see." He never heard of such a foolish notion, but convinced that the men would soon get into a fight and call the whole thing off—or better yet kill each other—he limped back to the cabin. He meant to get some shut-eye and he pitied anyone who dared to interfere!

No sooner had he slipped back between the folds of his bedroll when Noel let out an ear-piercing cry.

* * *

For the remainder of the week, the sound of hammering and sawing reverberated through the little town of Deadman's Gulch.

Logan longed for some good old-fashioned peace and quiet, but what he got was constant noise. Noel's loud lusty cries filled the hours between bedtime and dawn, at which time the hammering and sawing began and continued throughout the day until it was time for Noel's lungs to take over the night shift again. Logan couldn't believe it. Twenty-four hours a day of nonstop uproar.

Logan had every intention of heading for the hills to find himself a nice quiet cave where he could catch up on some shut-eye. But his plans were thwarted by Libby, who insisted he watch Noel while she kept the construction workers plied with hot coffee, flapjacks, and rabbit stew.

Her biscuits were the talk of the town. Even Logan couldn't get enough of them.

"Made them with baking soda," Libby explained. "I was lucky to find some cans of it at the general store." Baking soda, or saleratus as some called it, had many uses, the most prevalent being to clean butter churns. But Libby much preferred to use it as a leavening agent. "Mr. Montana said I was the only one in town who knew what to do with it. Said he never sold a can until I came along."

"Is that so?" Logan said. He had no idea that biscuits could be so light. "I'm going to have to get me some of that baking soda."

His cabin became a regular chow station, with people stomping through from morn till night. As word of Libby's amazing baking soda biscuits spread, there seemed to be a never-ending line winding its way to Logan's front door.

As good as the biscuits were, Logan nevertheless suspected that the men were using the biscuits as an excuse to get closer to Libby, and he felt obligated to watch over her. He kept the line moving and allowed no conversation to last more than fifteen seconds.

Some of the miners took exception to Logan's over-bearing tactics. Even Libby complained.

"I swear, Logan St. John, I don't know what gets into you at times. You were rude to Luke."

"I was not rude to Luke. He's a married man and I mean to see that he stays married."

Libby shook her head in confusion. "You think his asking for seconds will hurt his marriage in some way?"

Put in those terms, it did sound ridiculous, but he could hardly confess his real concern that Luke was taking a liking to her. "It's that baking soda," he said. "Too much of it and a man can get forgetful."

"I never heard of such a thing."

"Well, I daresay there's a lot of things you haven't heard. I think we owe it to Appleby's family to cut down on the biscuits."

She narrowed her eyes and studied him through the thick fringe of her eyelashes. "You're not jealous, are you?"

He stared at her in astonishment. "Jealous? Whatever gave you that idea?"

"I don't know, it's just the way you've been acting lately."

"I haven't been acting any special way," he protested. "Besides, if I were jealous it would mean that . . ."

She held her breath and for a moment they stared at each other. He glanced down at the floor and she stared down at her flour-covered table. "And of course that's not true," he said thickly.

"Of course not," she said, a voice barely above a whisper.

He stole a quick glance at her. Her cheeks had grown flushed and he wondered if this meant her heart was pounding as fast as his. "You going to Boston and all . . ."

"And you up north to resume trapping."

Their eyes met and held, and became locked in a

conversation that ran contrary to their spoken words. "It was a foolish thing for me to say," she stammered. *But I hoped it was true,* said her eyes. "Please accept my apology."

"No need to apologize," he said, but the message he sent with his eyes was far less magnanimous. *If I am jealous, it's because you made me have feelings I've no right to have.* "The idea wasn't *that* foolish. Under any other conditions, we might have . . . you know."

"If you weren't a mountain man, you mean?"

He'd been thinking about his leg, but he would never admit such a thing aloud. His leg made him feel less of a man, and he hated feeling that way around her. "That too. But I was thinking more along the lines of you being a city-bred woman and all."

She wiped her hands along the folds of her apron and reached for her rolling pin. "You're quite right," she said. Her voice was suddenly prim, clipped, coming between them like a slamming door. "Would you mind changing Noel's breeches while I finish up here?"

He backed away from the table. Somehow he felt there was something more to be said. But he couldn't for the life of him think what that something else could be.

He gave Noel his morning bath, then stood guard in front of the cabin so that Libby could nurse the baby in private. All the while he wondered how in the name of sam hill he ever got himself in such a family way.

One day he was living a quiet and contented existence, and the next day his entire life had been turned upside-down, sideways, and every other which way possible. It was the damnedest thing that had ever happened to him. All this stuff about him being jealous. Is this what a man gets for moving to civilization? If so, he wanted no part of it. As soon as the snow melted, he was going back to the peace and quiet of nature, and that is where he intended to stay!

Despite Logan's skepticism, the miners managed to build Libby's cabin without killing each other. They did, however, on occasion fall back on old habits and an argument ensued. But before fists began to fly, Libby hurried outside and stood on the front porch.

Her presence was all that was required to calm things down. The miners became so busy smiling and whipping off their hats to capture her attention, they forgot what it was they'd been arguing about.

In no time at all, the men built the loveliest little cabin imaginable, complete with hardwood floors and a separate bedroom. A porch complete with an overhang ran the width of the house. Since there was no glass yet available in town, the windows were covered with heavy canvas that had been tacked neatly to the frames.

Each window could be opened for air if necessary, and was anchored by a wooden box for flowers.

Upon completion of the cabin, the miners invited Libby inside for a grand tour. Logan volunteered to stay home and keep an eye on Noel. "Go on," he said. "Noel and me will be just fine."

At these words, Libby rewarded him with a dazzling smile that made his heart beat like a beaver signaling trouble with its broad flat tail. He didn't miss the significance of the analogy. His heart was sending a warning that he knew damned well he should heed. He knew from past experience that the quickest and safest way to avoid danger was to head in the opposite direction.

As as soon as his leg permitted, that's exactly what he intended to do.

Libby followed the crowd of miners across the way and into the lovely cabin. Inside, the fresh smell of newly sawed wood filled the air.

"It's lovely! Absolutely beautiful." She squealed with delight and clapped her hands together with every new discovery.

Each man took special pride in pointing out his own contribution. Sharkey opened and closed the windows to demonstrate. "You won't find windows this free and easy in Boston," he said without modesty.

Recalling the heavy framed windows of her childhood home, Libby agreed. "You are absolutely right." She hugged the slender man. "Oh, Sharkey, how can I ever thank you?"

"Now step over here, Miz Libby," Big Sam said, pulling her away from Sharkey. He ran his oversize hand across the face of the stone fireplace. "I handpicked every stone myself," he explained. "Notice how they all fit together like family."

Libby trailed her hand after his, feeling the smooth stone against her palm. "It's beautiful. Oh, Big Sam . . ." She threw her arms around his thick dark neck, bringing a wide beam to his face.

"You ain't seen nothing yet," Beaker insisted. "Wait till you see the bedroom."

The room was small, but well built with one high window. "So the little fellow won't go crawling through," Appleby explained. "My own son Daniel once crawled through the window and disappeared. It wasn't till two days later we found him in the cornfield, fast asleep."

At the thought of Noel escaping the safety of his home, Libby shuddered. "You were lucky you found him."

"That I was."

Thornton, dressed in his usual elegant attire, pointed to the lovely oak bookshelves that lined one wall of the bedroom. "I had my men build these," he explained. "It's never too early to start Noel appreciating literature."

"I quite agree," Libby said, rubbing her hand across the lovely smooth oak. "I can't thank all of you enough."

They returned to the main room. "Well, what do you think?" Sharkey asked.

"I think this is the loveliest house I've ever seen." Libby's eyes shone with tears of gratitude. It was the sort of house she had once dreamed of sharing with Jeffrey.

Beaker held up his hand. "You haven't seen everything yet." He opened the front door to reveal Hap on the porch, his arms circled around a large wooden tub that had been sealed with pitch to prevent leakage.

Libby gasped in delight. "I can't believe it. A bathtub."

Hap stepped through the doorway and set the bathtub in front of the fireplace. "I've been using it for storage, but the men, here, convinced me that you would put it to better use."

Luke gave the tub a quick swipe with a red bandanna. "Of course it took an experienced married man to suggest it," he said, taking full credit.

"I am most grateful to all of you," Libby said. Words seemed so inadequate that for the longest while she stood and stared around her, too overwhelmed with emotion to speak.

After a while, Luke stepped forward. "I guess we can ask you the question that's uppermost in our minds. Will you stay?"

She was touched that the miners had gone to so much trouble on her behalf, and it was all she could do to swallow the lump that rose in her throat. "You do know I plan to leave as soon as the weather permits," she said gently. She didn't want to appear unappreciative for all their hard work, but her first consideration had to be for Noel.

"That won't be for two more months," Luke pointed out. "It's mighty chancy traveling at this time of the year. You know we're going to have a few more bad storms before spring."

"I know," Libby agreed. "But I have to be honest with you. I *will* be leaving in the spring."

"Spring lasts all the way up to June," Big Sam said.

Thornton frowned. "June is too late to start the jour-

ney back home. The trip to Boston is six months by
overland. Longer if you go around the cape."

Libby dreaded the thought of making that long awful
trip with a baby. It had been difficult enough when she
made it with Jeffrey. "Thornton is right. The timing is
critical."

Appleby signaled the other men not to push her any
further. "We have a few weeks before you have to
make any decisions. Meanwhile, you can enjoy your
new home."

More discussion followed and soon it was settled.
Libby and Noel would move into the house first thing
the following morning. She would stay until spring.
The exact date would be determined by the weather.
Meanwhile, the little town of Deadman's Gulch had it-
self a mighty fine little family.

As soon as the tour was over, Libby returned to the
cabin to find Logan fast asleep on the chair in front of
the fire. Noel was nestled peacefully in the crook of
Logan's arm.

The sight of man and child warmed her heart, and
she stood absorbing the peaceful scene and trying for
all the world to keep her feelings under control. She'd
felt so much for this man in the short time she'd
known him. Fear, distrust, gratitude. But that wasn't
all.

Her cheeks burned as she recalled how the mere
glimpse of him getting ready for bed never failed to set
her body on fire. Her heart quickened at the memory of
his touch. Even the slightest brush of his fingertips
made her literally ache for more.

But this . . . this sudden tug of her heartstrings was
something else again. Not brave enough to put a name
to it, she decided it was a very good thing that she
would be moving into her own home. Not that she had
anything to worry about, she told herself. She could
never have serious feelings for a man like Logan.

It was true that the untamed part of him appealed to
her adventurous nature. But she sensed in him a rest-

lessness that would forever be pulling him away. She'd already loved and lost one man. Lost him because, like Logan, he, too, had to answer the call of the wild. She could never again go through what she'd been through the last year as a result. What she wanted, needed, was a man who could settle into a quiet family life. A man who loved Boston as much as she did. Who could share her same dreams and hopes for the future. Logan could never be that man.

It occurred to her, however, that she would miss this sometimes brusque, often gentle man. Without realizing it, she had grown to depend on him; had learned to tolerate, even understand his strange ways.

She was painfully aware that after tonight, she would no longer be able to lie in bed and listen to his soft even breathing.

Or covertly watch him undress by the fire.

Or share her endless joy over Noel.

Logan stirred and she quickly averted her gaze and quickly began to check the rope that stretched across the room to see if Noel's clothes were dry. It wouldn't do to let him catch her watching him.

She waited until late that afternoon before informing Logan that she and Noel would be moving into the finished house across the way. She assumed he would be delighted to hear what she had to tell him. Instead, he gaped at her like she'd taken leave of her senses.

"You what!"

"I said I've decided to stay in Deadman's Gulch until March or April. No longer though."

"April? That's over two months away. I thought you hated it here."

"Now that I've gotten to know the men, I've discovered they have hearts of gold. Why Thornton even promised to sing the entire aria from *Carmen*. I don't know many men who could do that, do you?"

He had no idea what an aria was, but if Thornton could do it, that was reason enough to loathe it.

"And the house is so lovely," Libby continued, her

eyes shining with anticipation. "Just think, Noel will have his very own room. The men went to so much trouble, I simply can't disappoint them."

"Heaven forbid," Logan grunted.

"I'll be moving in first thing tomorrow morning."

"Tomorrow!"

She looked at him with uncertainty. "If you like, I'll move tonight. That way you won't have your sleep disturbed again."

"Tomorrow will be fine," Logan said, his voice clipped. He ran his fingers through his hair. "I changed Noel's breeches. He should sleep for a while."

She nodded. "Logan, I . . ." She bit her lower lip before continuing. "There aren't many men who would have taken me in and taken care of me and Noel as you have."

He shrugged and looked embarrassed. "Well, now."

"I'll never forget everything you've done . . ." Her eyes burned with tears she was not, absolutely not, going to shed. "If there is any way I can repay you for your kindness."

Much to her dismay, he began backing toward the door as if he couldn't wait to make his escape. "I reckon I'll mosey on over to the Golden Hind."

It hurt her that he wouldn't want to stay, this being their last night together. But she would die rather than let him know how she felt. If he thought it more important to play cards, then let him. See if she cared! "You do that!" she said icily. "I have a lot to do myself tonight."

He glanced at Noel, who was lying on the bear robe. It hurt him that she didn't ask him to stay, this being their last night together. He searched her face. "If you want me to stay I will."

So now he's feeling sorry for her. "Absolutely not!" she insisted, shooing him out the door with her hands. It seemed urgent that she get rid of him as quickly as possible. Before he saw her tears. Before he guessed how much she dreaded the thought of leaving his house. Before he suspected how much he'd come to mean to her.

She barely managed to close the door behind him before her eyes blurred and a stream of tears ran down her cheeks.

Lord Almighty, what was the matter with her? she lamented as she paced back and forth, wringing her hands together. How could she have such feelings? Her husband had been dead for only a few months. Less than eight months to be exact. She owed it to her son's father to conduct herself in a way that was appropriate to his memory.

Coveting another man was not appropriate. For a recent widow to harbor such carnal thoughts would be shocking by anyone's standards. It shocked her. Lord Almighty, it shocked her clear down to her toes.

It was a very good thing that she was moving out of his house. Not that anything would happen if she stayed. His actions tonight made it perfectly clear that he was anxious to be rid of her. Not that she could blame him. Poor man. Just look at how she and Noel had taken over his cabin!

The man didn't owe her a thing. Not a thing! She had absolutely no right to expect him to give up his socializing to sit home with her.

Even if it was their last night together.

Chapter 18

LOGAN did not go to the Golden Hind, or to any of the other six saloons in town. He did the very thing his leg forbid him to do, he walked. He walked through the cold dark woods to the hills above Deadman's Gulch. He gritted his teeth against the throbbing pain that began in his right knee and shot down his calf to his ankle. He walked until he limped so much, he could walk no longer.

He lowered himself onto a fallen log and rubbed the affected area. Some time passed before he found to his astonishment he was rubbing his chest, not his leg. It was only after he realized the futility of trying to make the pain in his heart go away that he pulled his hand away and concentrated on the physical pain in his leg, wishing he'd brought along his salve.

The sounds of the night closed in around him. An animal stirred in the nearby bushes. Logan sniffed and recognized the scent as that of a fox, checking him out, no doubt, in return. At another time, in another place, the fox might have had good reason to fear him. But not tonight.

From the distance came the unmistakable mating cry of a lone wolf; its long harrowing howl echoed through the hills. Logan wondered if he would ever again hear that familiar sound of winter without thinking of his own loss.

"Oh, Libby," he moaned aloud, sending the fox scurrying away in a wake of rustling leaves. All he'd wanted was to spend their last night together. That's all. Just one more night.

If she'd shown the slightest inclination of wanting to spend the night with him, nothing would have dragged him away.

It was late when Logan crept into the cabin. Libby, who had been listening for his footsteps for hours, lay perfectly still when he walked past her bed. She hoped that he wouldn't hear the unnatural pounding of her heart. For a moment she thought he had, for he stilled by her side. He was so near she couldn't breathe, and it wasn't until he moved away that she gasped for much needed air.

Hungrily, she watched him undress, his large frame but a dark silhouette in the dim light of the slow-burning fire. He rubbed his leg and she longed to go to him. But something, pride perhaps, but most likely fear of rejection, kept her frozen in place. He'd already rejected her once that night. She couldn't bear the thought of his rejecting her again.

And so for the very last time she watched him crawl into his bedroll. For the very last time, she monitored his breathing and wondered why it took him so long to fall asleep. For the very last time, she felt herself drift off, snug in the warmth of his protective presence. And because it *was* the very last time, she refused to give in to feelings of guilt.

Logan left the cabin shortly before dawn. Libby was changing Noel when he rose and quickly dressed. He murmured something about wanting to check out the snow level by his claim. His limp was more pronounced than she had ever seen it.

She made no effort to hide her concern. "Do you think that's a good idea?"

"Why isn't it?"

"Your leg . . ."

"Damn it! There's nothing wrong with my leg!"

He grabbed his blanket coat and left without as much as a cup of coffee, slamming the door after him.

"Fool man!" she muttered as she finished changing Noel. Plenty was wrong with that leg and the sooner he faced up to it, the better. But as much as his leg worried her, there was nothing much she could do about it. He flew off the handle at the least mention of it. Besides, she had her own problems to think about at the moment.

She glanced around the cabin and her heart ached at the thought of moving. For the last month and a half, this had been home. The truth was it was the only real home she'd known since leaving Boston.

Afraid that if she dwelled much more on her thoughts, she would be too depressed to work, she began gathering up her belongings with quick urgency.

By the time Sharkey, Thornton, and Appleby showed up promptly at eight as planned, she'd managed to convince herself that once she'd moved into her own house, she could put her feelings for Logan into perspective.

She offered them coffee and fresh-baked biscuits, and they gratefully accepted.

"You sure do make the best coffee and biscuits I ever tasted," Sharkey said. "What do you call it agin? The ingredient that makes the biscuits light as a feather?"

"Baking soda," Libby replied. "Hap sent an order for more with someone who was traveling to Sacramento City."

"Well, ain't that thoughtful of him?" Sharkey reached for another biscuit while she refilled his cup.

Thornton picked up Noel and looked startled when Noel spit up. "Oh, dear."

Libby reached for a cloth that she kept for such emergencies and rubbed the lapel of Thornton's fine wool coat. "I do believe it's as good as new." Thornton agreed, but he looked so uneasy, she took Noel from him. "Sharkey, will you grab Noel's cradle? And, Luke, you can carry Noel's clothes."

It took no more than an hour to clear her own few belongings and Noel's things out of Logan's cabin and arrange them in her new home. Big Sam and Beaker had been waiting at the house and had immediately pitched in.

The men had made a wood bed frame for her and Appleby donated an extra feather mattress he'd hauled in all the way from Sacramento City last fall. A crude couch had been made from a piece of lumber balanced between two wooden kegs and draped with heavy canvas.

Beaker had crafted a fine table with two chairs. But being a perfectionist, he was not satisfied with how one chair was seated, and set to work at once resanding one of the legs.

Everyone had contributed household goods. No two dishes matched, but it was all perfectly functional and Libby was already planning little touches that would give the cabin a more homey look.

"It's lovely!" she exclaimed when they had done all that could be done. She threw her arms around each of the men in turn. "Thank you. Thank you, thank you."

Big Sam rolled his eyes. Sharkey hiccuped. Luke looked pleased, Thornton smiled, and Beaker blushed all the way to the end of his considerable nose.

Meanwhile up in the hills high above Deadman's Gulch, Logan struggled to break through the ice and snow with a pickax. Despite the freezing cold air, sweat broke out on his forehead. The cold pierced his leg like a dull twisting knife.

Finally, he tossed the pickax aside and rubbed his hand up and down the side of his leg.

It was no use. The ground was too hard and his leg hurt like hell. He leaned against a tree, adjusting his weight, and popped a piece of willow bark into his mouth.

He wondered if Libby had moved out of his cabin yet. Sure would be nice to have his place back to himself. To sleep undisturbed. Eat when he wanted, what he wanted.

Yes, indeed, it sure would be nice.

He trudged back to where his gelding stood, his moccasins crunching against the hardened snow. After tying his equipment onto the saddle, he mounted and headed back to Deadman's Gulch.

Nearer to town, the snow was only inches deep and was fast turning into mush. Music and laughter drifted from the saloons as he dismounted and tied his horse to the railing of his porch. The good-natured laughter gave him pause. The saloons were packed solid and not one angry word, fistfight, or gunshot marred the congenial atmosphere.

He never thought he'd see the day.

He glanced across the dirt-packed road to Libby's newly built cabin. Smoke curled lazily from the stone chimney that stood tall above the shingled roof. He debated what to do. Should he stop in and see if she was all right?

Almost as soon as he thought it, he decided against it. Knowing Libby, she was perfectly fine. Besides, he was exhausted and his leg hurt to high heaven. All he wanted to do was to lie down on his very own pallet and get some shut-eye.

Inside his cabin it was dark and empty—so empty in fact that at first he thought she'd taken his precious few belongings with her. But all his things were there, his makeshift furniture, his extra knives and cookware. Not only was everything accounted for, but she had taken the time to put all his possessions back as she had originally found them. It astounded him to realize suddenly that he liked the room better Libby's way.

The baby's things were gone, just as Libby's were. The rain-ruined valise she'd insisted on keeping was no longer in its usual corner. Gone also was the annoying clothesline that had crisscrossed the room, and which had required him to constantly duck or face the possibility of being the first man to be hanged in Deadman's Gulch.

His pallet was neatly made up, the feather pillow plumped out, the extra pelts and blankets folded and stacked neatly at the foot.

Peace and quiet at last. He decided to catch some shut-eye before going to the Golden Hind. Sighing, he stretched himself out on the bed. It had been weeks since he had the luxury of sleeping on such softness. He couldn't even remember the last decent night's sleep he'd had.

Heaven. Sweet, sweet heaven. He could sleep when he wanted to sleep.

He turned over. That's when he caught a whiff of summer flowers drifting up from the depths of the pillow. Inhaling the lovely sweet fragrance, he caught a vision of Libby, soft and lovely in her blue calico. He blinked and the calico faded, only to be replaced with memories of Libby looking more earthy, but every bit as feminine in the buckskin dress he'd made for her.

He sat up, turned his pillow over, and lay down again. Sleep. All he wanted to do was sleep.

If only it wasn't so quiet.

Not that he missed Libby or the bab̄y, of course. It was the town. That's what it was. He was used to the miners a-shooting and a-hollering as Sharkey called it, and making all kinds of ruckus.

What was the matter with them? It was hours before curfew.

He rolled over and decided the reason he couldn't sleep was because it was cold. He pulled another blanket from the neat pile at the foot of the bed and spread it over himself. There now. Perfect. He lay down and closed his eyes.

Another blanket. That's what he needed.

An hour later he had piled every blanket on top of himself and he still couldn't sleep. Finally, he gave up and decided to make himself some coffee. Waiting for the water to heat, he limped about the room. His leg was numb and he thought it would help to exercise it. He threw another log in the fire and resumed his awkward gait.

He stopped in front of a chair and frowned. Picking the chair up, he lugged it to the other side of the fireplace and placed it exactly where Libby had arranged it. Soon, he was rearranging the furniture until everything was back to the way Libby preferred it.

And still the cabin seemed empty.

And all wrong.

He stopped in front of the door. Finally, he opened it and peered through the narrow crack at the little cabin across from his. Other than the funnel of gray smoke that rose from the chimney, there were no signs of life. He wondered what Libby was doing. Probably feeding the baby, he decided. Or changing his breeches. Or perhaps giving him a bath. He smiled to himself as he recalled his own experiences bathing the boy. Slippery as a fish he was.

He closed the door. The coffee was ready and he poured himself a cup. The coffee had the consistency and taste of wet ashes, but he drank it anyway.

It might as well have been thin air for all the good it did him. What he needed was something stronger and a bracing game of poker. At last, he was free to spend his evenings with the boys without feeling guilty or otherwise put upon.

He slipped on his coat and stepped out to his front porch and stretched. It was dark now and the air had grown colder.

His attention was caught by a moving shadow. Squinting, he watched the shadow walk up to Libby's cabin and knock on her door. Although it was too dark to make out the man's features, the unmistakable shape of a top hat told him it could be no other than Thornton Wellerton.

Not wanting to be caught spying, Logan ducked low

and crept closer to the railing of the porch to have a better look.

What in the name of sam hill was the matter with the man? Calling at Libby's house at this late hour. It had to be at least six o'clock, if not later.

Well, Libby would tell him where to go. The door opened. He could see Libby's lovely feminine form silhouetted against the light. She certainly gave the appearance of being glad to see the man. Squinting, Logan stretched forward to see more clearly.

He could understand her not wanting to hurt Wellerton's feelings, but to go as far as to let him in her house, now that was certainly above and beyond anything good manners required.

Besides, it was obvious the man was up to no good. The light revealed that he was dressed like he was going to one of those high-falutin social functions, like the ones they had in Boston. What in the world could Libby be thinking of to let the scoundrel inside at this time of night.

As soon as Thornton stepped inside the house and the door closed, Logan shot to his feet, forgetting to keep the weight off his leg. Cursing aloud as he was sharply reminded, he kept his eyes riveted to the closed door across the way.

She probably closed to door so as not to let in the cold air, he reasoned. That had to be it. Confident that Libby would explain that she had a baby to feed and would send the man promptly on his way, he waited.

And waited.

What in the name of sam hill was taking Libby so long to get rid of the nuisance of a man?

Cursing beneath his breath, he rubbed his hands together to keep warm. A man could freeze to death standing outside, waiting for a woman to say something that would take the average man thirty seconds or less to say.

What's the matter with that fool, Thornton, anyway?

Doesn't he know that a woman who's only recently given birth needs her rest?

Thirty minutes passed, an hour. Finally, Logan decided enough was enough. If Libby didn't have enough gumption to show the man out, then he would have to do it for her. He walked across the street with a determined stride—or at least as determined as his numbed leg would allow. From inside the cabin, he could hear laughter. Thornton's and Libby's.

He cleared his throat and pounded on the door.

The door opened and Libby appeared surprised to see him. "Logan. I didn't expect to see you." She gazed into his eyes for a moment before allowing her lids to drop down. "Are you all right?"

"Of course I'm all right. Why wouldn't I be?"

"I don't know." She looked up again and he caught a glimpse of concern in her eyes. "Your face is all red and your lips look blue. Are you sure you're all right?"

"I'm perfectly fine." His tongue seemed to do funny things in his mouth. Maybe he had suffered exposure. If he hadn't, he was about to. You think she'd extend the same courtesy to him as she had extended to that fool Wellerton and invite him inside.

"Won't you come in?"

It's about time, he thought irritably. But he maintained a civil voice. "I'm mighty obliged." He stepped inside.

Thornton, who was sitting in front of the fireplace, lifted his hand in a greeting. But the look he gave Logan was downright unfriendly.

Logan shifted his gaze to Libby, who was looking all flushed and pretty, her eyes shining bright, her hair held back with a blue ribbon that matched her dress. It was obvious she was waiting for some sort of explanation from him as to why he appeared uninvited on her doorstep.

"I . . . noticed your light on. I thought maybe there was something wrong. You know with Noel."

She looked confused. "My light? But it's only a little after seven o'clock."

"So it is. I guess I was thinking it was later."

A softness touched her face. "How very considerate of you to be concerned. But as you can see, I've got company."

Logan raked Thornton over with narrowed eyes. He made no effort to hide his contempt of the man. "So I can see. Well, it's getting *late*. I guess I'd better get myself home. Let you get your rest."

"It was very kind of you to stop by."

He glanced around the cozy room. Candles flickered on a table set for two. Noel was obviously asleep in the other room. Considering all the times that Noel had kept him up, why in the name of sam hill did the child have to sleep at this particular time? Didn't Noel feel an obligation in protecting his own mother from the likes of Thornton Wellerton? "Your home is quite cozy."

She flashed him a smile. "I think so too. As soon as I make some curtains . . ."

He held her gaze for a moment too long. "Curtains would be nice." Embarrassed to find himself staring, he cleared his throat. "I guess I'd better be going."

"Good night, Logan."

"Good night, Libby."

Ten o'clock!

That damned fool Thornton didn't leave her cabin until ten o'clock! Logan wouldn't have noticed, of course, had he not been peering through the crack of his open door where he had been watching Libby's house for the entire four hours it took Thornton to leave.

Trying to keep from freezing to death, Logan had wrapped himself mummylike in his bedroll in an effort to keep warm. Nevertheless, he was frozen to the bone. This only added to his ill humor.

It was indecent, that's what it was, to keep a new

mother up all hours of the night. Obviously Libby was too kindhearted to put the man in his place.

Obviously, this was a job for a man.

He slammed his door shut and turned, forgetting his body was completely encased in the confines of his bedroll. One step and he toppled to the ground with as much grace and rigidity as a falling tree.

Chapter 19

EARLY the following morning, Logan made it his business to *bump* into Wellerton, who was supervising his company of miners at Saddle Bar Creek. It irked Logan that the man was dressed in business attire in the middle of the gold mines.

Thornton supervised his mine as if it were a bank. All that was missing was a rolltop desk. He sat tall in the saddle of his fine black stallion and issued orders in the same tone of voice one would expect to hear in business circles. Just who did the scoundrel think he was?

Swallowing his irritation, Logan rode his horse next to Thornton's.

Thornton folded his map and greeted Logan with a guarded expression. "Good morning, St. John. What brings you to this neck of the woods?"

Logan managed a thin facade of civility. "Just happened to be passing by."

Thornton tucked his map in the pocket of his fine wool coat. "It seems to be a habit of yours."

"And yours seems to be keeping unseemly hours."

"Since when did you become interested in the hours I keep?"

"I'm not. But I am concerned about Libby. I thought she looked rather tired last night."

"Really? I thought she looked exceptionally lovely."

Logan looked him straight in the eye. "I guess I know her better than you do."

"If what you say is true," Thornton said, "then you

must know that Libby is quite capable of taking care of herself. If she was tired, she would have told me so. In fact, as I was preparing to leave, she pleaded with me to stay longer."

Pleaded. Logan couldn't imagine Libby pleading.

"Now, if you will excuse me," Thornton said, "I have work to do." Thornton tugged on the reins of his horse and headed up the hill toward the open mine shaft.

Logan stared after the man, mimicking his uppity manners. "I have work to do." He frowned in disgust. "I just bet you do."

In the days to follow, Logan became obsessed with the little cabin across from his. He monitored each visitor—and there were too damned many, as far as he was concerned. Big Sam, Sharkey, Beaker, Shakespeare, Appleby! At sight of the latter, Logan practically fell off his porch trying to get a better look. What was Appleby doing visiting a widow, and if his eyes served him right, going as far as to bring her gifts? Him a married man with two children!

Drawing himself upright, Logan decided it wouldn't hurt to give the man's memory a jolt or two.

In the days to follow, he made it his business to do just that on every possible occasion. "How're the little ones, Appleby? The missus?"

At first Appleby was only too happy to give Logan a full report. But he soon grew weary of the constant probing.

"What is it with you?" Appleby demanded that Friday afternoon when Logan had followed him from Libby's house to the general store and finally to the Golden Hind. "I told you three times already today how my family is. There're the same as they were yesterday and the day before that. I have not received a letter in nearly a month's time. So I have no choice but to assume that nothing has changed."

"You don't have to be so damned ornery about it,"

Logan grumbled. "A man has the right to show a little friendly interest."

"Friendly interest? Is that what you call it? Well, I call it jealousy."

Logan sputtered in denial. "Jealousy? If I wanted a family, I could have had one."

"This is not about family," Appleby charged, jabbing his finger against Logan's chest. "This is about Libby."

Logan pushed Appleby's hand away. "You're damned right, it's about Libby. A married man has no right to be taking gifts to another woman."

Appleby gaped at Logan in astonishment. "Gifts?" he managed at last. "I gave her a tin of baking soda."

"If you ask me, baking soda is a mighty personal gift for a married man to be giving a single lady."

"I'm not asking you," Appleby retorted. "And as much I would like to continue this discussion, I believe there's a law against any altercations within the boundaries of the town. Since you insist upon raising your voice, this no longer falls within the bounds of a friendly discussion."

"By all means, we don't want to break any laws." Logan spun on his heels and headed back to his cabin to take up his self-proclaimed duty as Libby's watchman.

It was almost time for Thornton to make his regular appearance on Libby's doorstep. Of all her visitors, Thornton concerned him the most. Partly because he came later and stayed longer than any other visitor. Mostly it was because Libby seemed so gosh damned glad to see the man.

Then there was Thornton's strange habit of singing to Libby some god-awful song from some god-awful opera.

It riled Logan that he couldn't have himself a friendly disagreement with someone without breaking the law, but it was perfectly acceptable for Thornton to shriek like a screech owl with a bad case of laryngitis whenever the mood struck him.

Long after Thornton had left for the night, Logan couldn't seem to keep his mind off the little cabin across the way. He lay on his pallet, his body rigid as he strained to hear the least sound coming from Libby's cabin. Through the cracks in the wall, he could see the light from her canvas-covered window.

He knew precisely how many times she got up at night to feed the baby, and made it his business to "bump" into her every time she walked into town for supplies.

On these occasions she was always polite to him and inquired as to how he was doing. He in turn tried to maintain the proper formality, but something always happened to tilt him off-balance. She looked at him in a certain way or gave him a smile that reached inside him. Sometimes their hands would accidentally touch. The latter occurred whenever he bent over to get a better look at Noel and to pry the blanket away from the baby's face.

At such times, he quickly brought their conversation to a halt and distanced himself. On one such occasion, he was so anxious to make his escape, he ran smack into Sharkey.

"Whoa," Sharkey said, "where are you going in such a fired-up hurry?"

Not sure where he was going, Logan nodded toward the Golden Hind. "Thought I'd get me something to drink. Want to join me? I'll buy."

Sharkey rubbed his whiskered chin. "I can't believe muh ears. It wasn't so long ago that you fellows wouldn't let me have a drink. Now you're offerin' to buy."

"You know what they say about looking a gift horse in the mouth?"

The two men walked side by side to the saloon. "Haven't seen you around much lately," Sharkey said.

"Been busy."

"I never thought I'd see the day that you were too busy to play poker."

They reached the bar. "Give us two beers," Logan said to Moe the bartender.

"Two beers coming up."

"You ain't holdin' out on us, are you?" Sharkey said.

Logan frowned. "Holding out on you. How?"

"Well, some of the boys and me were talkin'. We thought maybe you'd struck it big up there and think yerself too good for the likes of us."

The bartender pushed two foaming beers in front of them. Logan wrapped his fingers around the handle of the glass and took a long bracing swallow. He wiped his mouth with the back of his hand and swung around on his stool to face Sharkey. "There's snow up there. I'm not likely to find much at this time of year."

Sharkey shrugged. "Anything's possible."

Logan thought of Libby and Thornton together and slumped forward. "That's what I'm afraid of."

On the first day of February, Libby bundled Noel up in a warm blanket and headed for Hap's general store.

Hap, who was sitting with his feet propped up, stood and greeted her with a wide grin. "Good day, Mrs. Summerfield." He leaned over the counter toward Noel. "Whoosie, whoosie, goo, goo."

Noel rewarded Hap with a fixed stare. "I do believe he understands every word you said to him," Libby teased. "Don't you, Noel?"

Hap looked pleased. "He's probably the only person who ever understood me. What will it be today?"

Libby handed him her list and waited for him to gather up her order while she studied the bolts of calico that were half-hidden beneath a pile of harnesses. "I'll take ten yards of each," she said.

Hap nodded. "Ain't had much call for calico till you came to town. If you like, I'll cut it and bring it by later on today, along with the rest of your purchases. That way you won't have to carry them yourself."

"That's most considerate of you," Libby said. She heard it tell that Hap was lazy, but she personally found him to be most accommodating. She paid for her purchases and bid him good day.

Carrying Noel over her shoulder, she tramped through the muddied street toward her house. Upon reaching her front porch, she hesitated and glanced from one end of the town to the other. It was only after she was certain the street was deserted that she dared to stare openly at Logan's cabin.

Some times while she was busy taking care of Noel or doing one of her chores, she would get the strangest feeling. It was hard to explain. Perhaps it was only a coincidence that every time she had this feeling, she had only to lower an edge of canvas and peer outside to discover Logan on his porch. It was hard to determine if he was actually watching her house. But what else could he be doing?

And if he was watching her house, that made the other occasions—the times he walked right past her as if she didn't exist—that much more puzzling. Not that it mattered, of course, whether he ignored her or not.

Oh, but it did matter. No matter how much she tried to tell herself otherwise, the way he ignored her lately hurt her deeply. After what they had shared, how could he act like she didn't exist? If she had one sensible bone in her body, she would follow his example. That would be the wise thing to do, the proper thing. Not think of him.

Still, it was hard to forget how he'd taken care of her during her confinement. Harder still to forget the feel of his arms around her ... his hands ...

This last thought jolted her back to reality. With a quick glance around to make certain nobody saw her staring at Logan's place, she walked up the steps of her porch and into her house. Noel was still asleep and never opened his eyes the entire time it took her to carry him into his room and lay him on his stomach in his cradle.

She tiptoed back into the front room and picked up her sewing basket, intent upon finishing the little flannel nightgown she was making for Noel.

She tried to concentrate on her work, but Logan was very much on her mind. When she couldn't shake the troubling thoughts that assailed her, she abandoned her sewing and opened the little dream holder where she kept her gold locket.

She held the locket close to the window so that the light would pick up the feathery strands of Jeffrey's hair.

During the few months following Jeffrey's death, she had only to pick up the locket to see his face and feel his presence.

Today, by contrast, the locket elicited no strong emotions. She rubbed the locket with her fingers and tried to bring the memory of Jeffrey to mind. Much to her shock, she couldn't recall his face. Indeed, she had a difficult time remembering what he looked like at all. How was it possible to forget so completely? she wondered in dismay. What kind of woman could so easily forget the man who had been her husband?

With a deep sense of remorse, she snapped the locket shut and tried to remember Jeffrey's voice, his touch, anything. But the smiles and gestures that so readily came to mind were not Jeffrey's. They were Logan's.

Tears burned her eyes as she placed the locket back into the box. "Oh, Jeffrey," she whispered. "I'm so very sorry."

Noel cried out, and grateful for the respite from her tortured thoughts, she ran to his room. Lifting him in her arms, she held him close. "You're getting so big," she cooed. "Wouldn't your father be proud of you? Have I told you about your father? Well, let's see now. He was a banker. Yes, indeed and . . ." On and on she droned, in a desperate attempt to hold on to Jeffrey's memory. In the end, however, she was forced to concede that she was no longer the grief-stricken widow she'd been months earlier.

She toyed with a glimmer of hope. Perhaps this wasn't such a bad thing after all. Maybe it was natural and had nothing whatsoever to do with Logan. It could mean she had dealt with the past and was ready to tackle the future.

Of course, none of this explained why Logan commanded so many of her thoughts, or why his recent cold demeanor toward her affected her on so many levels. She couldn't imagine what she'd said or done to make him act with such indifference.

Unless . . . she sat forward in her chair. It suddenly occurred to her that Logan might have good reason to seem so remote. He'd provided her food and shelter, saved her life for goodness' sake. And what had she done to show her gratitude?

Not one single thing!

She had been in her house for two weeks and had not once thought to repay his kindness. Whatever was the matter with her? There simply was no excuse for her lack of good manners.

She decided it was an oversight that required immediate attention. She would invite him to dinner. It was the proper thing to do, and the fact that her heart beat faster at the thought only proved how anxious she was to live up to her social obligations.

Having made up her mind, she watched out of her window off and on for the remainder of the day until Logan returned home. Allowing enough time to pass so that he wouldn't think she'd been waiting for him, she then wrapped Noel in a warm blanket and carefully made her way across the muddied street.

Logan answered the door soon after she knocked. Upon seeing her, his eyes widened in surprise. "Libby. Is something wrong?" He glanced at Noel and ran his knuckle across one of Noel's chubby red cheeks.

"Nothing is wrong." Her heart was beating so fast,

she could feel even her smile quiver on her lips. "And you accuse me of always thinking the worst."

He smiled too, and she watched the little network of lines crinkle around his eyes. She caught her breath and found it necessary to remind herself what she was doing there. "I came to invite you to dinner."

His hand froze next to Noel's face. "Dinner?" He drew his hand away and looked at her as if she had taken leave of her senses.

She was beginning to have second thoughts. Maybe this wasn't such a good idea after all. "I made a pot of stew and . . ."

"I would like that."

Her heart skipped a beat. "You would?"

"Very much."

"Well, then." Suddenly she felt self-conscious, although there was no reason she should. This man had seen her under the worst possible circumstances. He had seen her naked, attended to her most intimate needs. It made no sense whatsoever that she should feel as shy as a bride in his presence now, on his porch, in broad daylight, while fully dressed, and discussing something as mundane as dinner. "Shall we say seven o'clock?"

"Seven would be fine."

"It won't interfere with your poker game, will it?" She knew how important his game was to him. "I could have dinner ready earlier . . ." She held her breath waiting for his answer.

"That won't be necessary."

She inhaled deeply. She couldn't believe it. He would rather be with her than play poker. Oh, Lord, now what? She backed down the steps. "I'll see you at seven."

Chapter 20

LOGAN waited until she had walked back to her own house before he closed his door.

Dinner, she had invited him to dinner!

Well, now, the least he could do was to make himself look presentable. A haircut, he needed a haircut. And a shave. It might not be a bad idea to take a bath. No sense exposing Noel to unnecessary germs.

He found Sharkey passed out at one of the tables at the Golden Hind. Cursing beneath his breath, Logan managed to rouse the man enough to drag him back to his house, where he plied him with coffee strong enough to raise the dead. Between cups, he splashed Sharkey's face with ice-cold water freshly drawn from the stream.

It took two full pots and the better part of the afternoon before Sharkey started to come around. "Dammit, Logan, what is that pois'n you're pourin' down me throat? Can't a man get drunk in peace anymore?"

"I need a haircut and a shave."

Sharkey rubbed his bloodshot eyes. "What's so damned impo'tant that you have to look all gussied up t'day?"

"Does a man have to have a reason for wanting to look his best?"

Sharkey struggled to focus his eyes. "It's Miss Libby, ain't it?"

"What?"

"She's the only woman in town. It's got to be her.

Every time I turn 'round anymore, someone's wantin' a haircut and shave to impress Miss Libby."

Logan felt his dander rise. "Who's been wanting a haircut and shave?"

"You know, Big Sam, Shakespeare, Beaker, Thornton."

At the mention of Thornton's name, Logan slammed the empty coffeepot back onto the stove.

Sharkey grabbed his head with both hands and moaned. "Take it easy, will ya? My head feels like it's 'bout to split open." He took another swallow from his cup. "As I was a-sayin', since Miss Libby came to town, I've made more money a-cuttin' and a-shavin' than I made in the last six months a-minin'."

"Maybe you ought to open up a barbershop. We could use one."

"Maybe so, maybe so." Sharkey stared into the fire. "There's an art to cuttin' hair. Minin' fer gold, that's no art. It's pure luck. An artist like me needs to express hisself better." He rubbed his forehead. "Well, let's get this job over with." He staggered out of his chair, his upper portion two strides ahead of his lower.

Logan watched Sharkey stumble around the room. "Before you start expressing yourself on me, you'd better have another pot of coffee."

At exactly seven o'clock that night, Logan arrived on Libby's doorstep. He ran his palms down the sides of his head to smooth his neatly trimmed shoulder-length hair.

His buckskins had been carefully brushed and aired outside. His skin smelled fresh with the scent of soap and water, and the slightest drop of beaver castoreum. The French valued the sweet musky fragrance and perfume makers depended on beaver men for their supplies. Trappers used castoreum as a tobacco sweetener, and he was convinced his old friends would laugh if they knew he was using it to impress a woman. He might not look like a city slicker, but he sure in hell smelled like one.

Had he been living in the wilderness, every hostile Indian and wild animal in the territory would smell him out and, as Sharkey would say, come a-calling. He'd be in mortal danger. Just thinking about it made him check the dark shadows on either side of Libby's porch before he knocked.

The door flew open instantly, and he was convinced it was because Libby was anxious to see him. She was dressed in her pretty blue dress and her rich golden hair was done up on top of her head. Tiny tendrils framed her face.

She looked mighty pretty, he thought, and the house provided a perfect setting with its warm and cozy glow. He was almost willing to concede there might possibly be an advantage or two to living in a man-made dwelling rather than the outdoors.

A table for two was set in front of the blazing fire. Candles flickered from the center of the calico-covered table, capturing them both in an intimate circle of light.

Feeling disarmed, he stepped back. "It smells good," he said, sniffing the succulent odors that drifted from the fireplace.

"We're having venison," she explained in a breathless voice that made him look at her speculatively. "Big Sam went hunting this morning. Bagged himself a fine stag. Insisted on giving me some fresh meat."

"That's mighty generous of the man." He picked a silver fork off the table and held it up.

"Thornton had one of his men bring me a set from Sacramento City."

"That was right nice of the man," Logan said politely.

Noel let out a cry and Libby made a quick check of the large black caldron hanging over the fire before she excused herself. A moment later she reappeared with Noel in her arms.

"He's growing quicker than a weed," Logan said,

chucking the boy beneath his soft rounded chin. He lifted his gaze to meet her eyes. They were more blue than green tonight, and sparkled as brightly as stars on a wintry night. "Pretty soon, he's going to be running around like a wild pony."

"I do believe you're right. Would you like to hold him while I check on dinner?"

"I'd like that."

Libby handed Noel to him and Logan held the little fellow over his shoulder. He patted the boy's back as he'd done many times before. Noel rewarded him with an impressive hiccuping burp. "That's what you get for being such a guzzler," he said, wiping off his buckskin shoulder with the cloth Libby handed him.

Almost without thought he checked Noel's breeches. For a change, the baby was dry. Looking up, he caught Libby watching him. Warm lights danced on her face and blazed in her eyes. "Well, now . . ."

By the time Libby carried a steaming bowl of venison stew to the table, Noel had fallen sound asleep; his little head rested in the crook of Logan's arm.

Logan felt that same sense of belonging he'd felt when Libby and Noel had lived with him, and he knew this was a dangerous thing.

"I'll put him back in his cradle," Libby whispered. "Would you mind opening the wine? The bottle opener is on the table."

He slid Noel into his mother's waiting arms. While she carried Noel into the bedroom, Logan examined the bottle opener but decided to use his knife to ease the cork from the narrow opening of the bottle.

He filled both their glasses, and when she returned, he held her chair for her, then took his own seat.

Dinner was delicious. Never had he tasted venison so tender. *Never had she looked so lovely.* Knowing he wasn't himself, he drank more wine than prudence allowed and kept his eyes purposefully focused on his plate. He could actually cut the meat with the damned fork he felt obliged to use, although he would have much preferred to use his knife.

"Is dinner always such a grand occasion in Boston?" he ventured. He felt an obligation to fill the silence that stretched between them.

It took so long for her to answer his question, he lifted his eyes. As soon as he saw the look of longing on her face, he regretted having brought up the subject of Boston.

"It was the one time of day that the family gathered together," she said at last. She studied him a moment. "Tell me what it's like to be a mountain man."

The question surprised him. "I've told you the important stuff."

"Which wasn't very much."

"I'm afraid you'd find the rest boring."

"Weren't you ever lonely?"

Funny she should ask that question. He'd been thinking about that word a lot lately, loneliness. "Not that I remember."

"Didn't you ever long for company?"

"I had plenty of company. Once a year us mountain men meet for rendezvous. We'd gather together to swap news and experiences, do some gambling, compete in various contests of skill and strength. As a boy I learned to read and write at the rendezvous. The other mountain men would take turns teaching us." He thought for a moment before adding, "I remember one man in particular. He taught us numbers. If we acted up, we had to sit and count the stars at night. Can't tell you how many nights I sat in the dark counting."

The story seemed to delight her. She clasped her hands beneath her chin and leaned toward him. "Did you ever finish counting the stars?"

He gazed at the stars in her eyes and decided there was only two stars worth thinking about. "Can't remember," he said vaguely.

"Oh, Logan, you must tell me more about these rendezvous."

"There's not a whole lot to tell. A rendezvous usually lasts several weeks. Believe me, that's enough company to see a man through an entire year."

After dinner, they sat on the bearskin robe in front of the fireplace. They lingered over their wine and talked about their childhoods.

Listening to her describe Boston, Logan grew relaxed and became mesmerized into a strange dreamlike state. It was the wine, he decided. Or perhaps it was the warmth of the room. His own cabin was always cold and drafty no matter what size fire he built.

Yes, he felt warm, strangely disoriented, so unlike himself. Suddenly he found himself talking about Catherine. Libby listened quietly as he spoke. He could only surmise by the sympathy in her eyes that she failed to understand the full circumstances of what he told her.

"It was wrong of me to marry her," he said.

"It was a very kind thing for you to do."

He looked at her incredulously. "Had I not married her, she might still be alive."

"You don't know that for sure. I think that what the Indians did to her had more to do with her death than anything you might have done."

Libby was wrong about that, he was sure. Had he been able to provide the kind of life Catherine had been used to, she would never have died. He was convinced of it. But what Libby said was comforting and he was willing to hold on to the thought, even if it was a lie.

So grateful was he to her for lifting the burden of guilt from his shoulders, if only for a while, he didn't even resent her talking about going home to Boston. He did, however, feel a sense of inner urgency to do something, say something. Several glasses of wine later, he did just that. "Marry me, Libby." His voice was low, pressing, so different than his usual voice.

Libby's mouth fell open and for several moments they sat staring at each other. "Why, Logan, I . . ."

She appeared stunned by his proposal, but no more than he was. The words had popped out of his mouth before he knew what he was saying. He sat up straight and stared at the fire. "I was only thinking of Noel," he stammered. "It's not right for the little fellow to do without a father."

"That's very kind of you," she said. "There aren't many men who would put a child's welfare before his own."

"There aren't many men who have the opportunity to be present when a child enters the world."

She lowered her eyes and blushed. "That's rightly so, Logan."

"I hope you don't I think I took advantage of your ... ah ... predicament."

"I never thought that."

"Naturally, I'd move to Boston with you."

"What?"

"If we got married. I'd move to Boston."

Libby smiled a sad smile. "You would hate Boston. Just as I hate ..."

"You were going to say just as you hate the West, weren't you?" She had never kept her feelings about the West secret. That's why it was so surprising that her honesty hit him like a blow.

"It just seems to take people and tear them apart. It's not just the land, it's everything. This gold fever. Look at the men in this town. Appleby, Keefer. Decent men with families back home. They came here with big dreams of striking it rich and returning home to their families. I wonder how many will ever see their families again."

"It must have been difficult when your husband died."

The look on her face told him he had sliced open a newly healed wound. "I kept thinking if only the banks hadn't failed. If only Jeffrey hadn't been bitten by the gold bug. If only I'd been a better wife ..."

"Don't!" He placed his hand over hers.

She met his eyes. "There had to be a reason that he thought the answer to his dreams could be found in the gold mines of this raw, untamed land."

"I doubt that there was anything you could have done. I think men are born with the need to hunt, whether it be gold, beavers, or female companionship."

She pulled her hand away. "Why do you suppose that is?"

"I don't know. Maybe it's nature's way of keeping us from getting too settled, too set in our ways."

"Maybe you're right." She bit her lower lip. "Logan . . . about your kind offer. I'm afraid under the circumstances, I have to decline."

"And what circumstances might that be?"

"My first marriage was for love. I couldn't possibly consider marrying for any other reason."

"Are you saying you don't love me?"

"Jeffrey's only been dead for a short while and . . ."

"I'm sorry. I had no right . . ." His eyes were riveted on her soft pink lips. "It was just a crazy idea." His mouth felt dry. He quickly took another swallow of wine before adding. "Besides, I'm not the marrying kind."

"I thought as much."

"And what do I know about children?"

"I would say you know quite a bit."

He stared at her in surprise. "Really?"

"It's no easy task getting a baby to fall asleep, and you did so quite easily just a short time ago."

He laughed. "I guess I rightly did."

"Nor is it an easy matter to help during childbirth."

"Well, now." He beamed.

"But as for Boston."

The smile left his face. "You're right. If it's anything like St. Louis." He grimaced. "All those people . . ."

"There are many more people in Boston."

"And all those buildings crowded together like a herd of cattle on a too small ranch."

"It's rather convenient that way. You only have to

walk a short distance should you wish to call on a neighbor."

"And I'd have to wear those city clothes."

Libby's gaze dropped to his buckskin shirt. "I can see where that would present a problem for you."

"And since Deadman's Gulch is no place to raise a child."

Eyes centered on the cleft of his chin, she agreed. "No place at all."

"Well, then, we agree. The whole idea of marriage was a crazy idea."

"But well meaning," she hastened to add.

"Oh, yes," he agreed, "definitely well meaning."

Chapter 21

LATER that night, Logan stood alone in his cabin, which despite the roaring fire still seemed dark and dreary. What a fool he'd made of himself. The last thing he needed in his life was the responsibility of a wife and child.

Take care of your mother, his father had cautioned him all those years ago. At five years old, it had been an easy promise to make, and so difficult to keep. He'd never forgotten the horror, nor the feeling of helplessness he'd felt upon watching his Indian mother die at the hand of a white man.

He hadn't been able to take care of his mother, nor, for that matter, had he managed to care for his father and later his bride. He was hardly a protector in any sense of the word.

Now that his own future was in question, he needed to devote his full attention to the problem of surviving in the wilderness with a bad leg. His lack of speed and agility made him an easy target for bandits or Indians. Without his usual stamina, something as simple as stalking a deer would be extremely difficult, if not altogether impossible.

But this was the least of his concerns. The cold dampness settled in his leg and the pain that resulted was enough to drive a man crazy. At times, the pain numbed his senses and slowed down his thought processes, putting him at even greater risk.

Panning for gold was becoming increasingly more difficult. If he couldn't even pan for gold along a river bank, how in the name of sam hill would he ever manage to walk waist deep in water to set his beaver traps?

Take away the means by which he supported himself, he had nothing. Was nothing. He was a man with nothing to give a woman, let alone a child.

Why, then, did spending one evening with Libby make him think he could do something he had no business doing? Be somebody he was never meant to be?

Well, it wouldn't happen again. Not ever. He was a trapper, a man of the mountains, and come spring he'd be heading north where he belonged, following the streams and rivers, answering the call of the wild. To hell with his leg!

Meanwhile, across the way, Libby sat on the bear robe staring at the slowly dying fire. *Marry me,* he'd said and the words echoed over and over in her heart. It was the wine talking. She knew it was the wine. She also knew that had it not been for Noel she would not have turned down his proposal.

No matter what her feelings for Logan, she had no choice but to put Noel's welfare first.

Promise me you'll take our child home.

She closed her eyes and pressed her knuckles against her lips. *I shall, Jeffrey, I promise.*

Hers eyes flew open and she vowed anew to do what was right by Noel and Jeffrey. But her resolve was nearly shattered by the echo of Logan's voice coming from seemingly nowhere. *Marry me . . .*

It was still dark the following morning when Logan was stirred awake. He sat up and rubbed his eyes. It took a moment for him to put a name to the infernal hammering that burst through the cracks of his cabin like a hundred charges of exploding gunpowder. Cursing, he fought his way from beneath the covers, quickly pulled his pants over his long johns, and charged outside. Even with Noel gone, it was getting so a man couldn't sleep anymore.

He looked to the end of the street where a large bonfire had been built to illuminate the area. There was so much activity that at first Logan thought gold had been discovered right at the edge of town.

But a closer observation made it clear that the lumber wasn't being used to build a sluice or even a flume. Before his startled eyes, the frame of a building was hauled upright, reaching higher than any other building in town and pretty much level with the surrounding treetops.

It didn't seem possible. The very same men who had, in the past, resisted any labor that didn't promise the wealth of gold, and who had been all too happy to rely on canvas nailed to the crudest frames possible for shelter, were suddenly as industrious as a colony of beavers. First building Libby's house. Now this.

He hobbled down the street on his still stiff leg, waving his hands and yelling to be heard over the infernal racket of hammers and saws. "Would someone mind telling me what's going on?"

Appleby heaved a plank over his shoulder, calling out in a voice that struck Logan as more indecent than cheerful given the ungodly hour. "Good morning, Logan."

Logan growled back in a voice he deemed more suited to the occasion. "It's more like the middle of the night. The sun's not up yet."

"We wanted to get an early start."

"I would say you accomplished that, all right. Now would you mind telling me what this monstrosity is doing in the middle of the street?"

"This is our new church."

Logan couldn't have been more astonished if they had said they were building a king's palace. "A church. You're building a church? Here? What do you want to go and do that for?"

Sharkey looked surprised by the question. "Got to build a church so the little one can have hisself a proper ba'tism."

Logan gritted his teeth. He should have known that

this latest madness would have something to do with Libby. "Did anyone tell you that it takes more than a church before you can have a proper baptism? It takes a preacher and . . ."

"Now don't you go a-worryin' your head about nothin'," Sharkey interjected. "Why ol' Genesis over there was a preacher befur he was a miner."

Logan glanced up at the bearded man who was clinging precariously to a high beam of the church. "Is that so?"

The man named Genesis waved a hammer. "Sharkey speaks the truth. I've seen an infant or two baptized in my day."

"What do you mean seen?"

Sharkey explained. "What Genesis means is that he went to preachers' school but he had to drop out befur he got pass the first chapter of the Bible. That's why we call him Genesis."

"But I know the first book of the Bible better than I know my own hand," Genesis explained.

Logan frowned. "Is baptism covered in the first book?"

"No, that's where Pastor Genesis will have to draw on his vast experience."

"Watching one or two baptisms is not what I call vast experience," Logan argued.

"Maybe not," Genesis agreed. "But believe me, when you've seen one baptism, you've seen them all."

"Either grab yourself a hammer or step aside," Big Sam barked. He threw down a plank of lumber, barely missing Logan's bare foot by an inch.

Logan looked from miner to miner, shook his head, and left. The whole damned town was plumb crazy. No doubt about it.

It snowed off and on during the second week of February, keeping the diggings buried and the men in town. For the most part, the hammering and sawing continued during each break in the weather. In between times, large sheets of canvas were spread over the lumber to protect it from the elements.

The finished church was enormous, clearly the largest building in town, with a fine pointed steeple, weatherproof doors, and redwood logs that had been sawed in half for pews.

The sun broke through the clouds minutes after Big Sam announced the church was officially complete. Applause greeted this welcome news, and the miners slapped each other on the back. Appleby pulled out his mouth organ and played "Nearer My God to Thee."

Big Sam and Sharkey waltzed together in the street. Sharkey batted his eyelashes, imitating a woman.

Laughing at their childish escapades, Libby stood in front of the church, holding Noel in her arms.

Logan walked up to her and she greeted him with a shy smile that told him that his absurd marriage proposal had not been forgotten by her, although thanks to the wine, his own memory remained blissfully vague. He only hope he hadn't made a bigger fool of himself than he thought.

"Did you ever see anything more beautiful in your life?" she asked.

His gaze remained fixed on her profile. "Never."

"You ain't seen nothing yet, Miz Libby," Big Sam said, gyrating past them. "As soon as the paint comes from Sacramento City, we'll finish it up, right and proper."

Sharkey twirled in front of them. "Hap sent a mule pack into Nevada City to pick up supplies. He should be back t'day or t'morrow, dependin' on how bad the trails are." He batted his eyelashes before spinning away.

Logan watched him, unable to believe his eyes. It was almost noon and Sharkey was still standing upright.

Appleby pocketed his mouth organ. "I think this calls for a celebration."

His suggestion was met with thunderous approval and the men headed toward the Golden Hind.

Logan remained behind. He ran a knuckle down Noel's chubby red cheek. Noel turned his head and started making little sucking noises. "I guess this little fellow is going to have himself a baptism."

Libby smiled. "He is at that."

"That's great."

They both started talking at once.

"Libby ..."

"I ..."

"You go first," Logan said.

"I wanted to ask you a favor."

"Ask me anything you want."

"You're going to think this is rather foolish."

"Nothing you say ... I mean I won't think it's foolish. I'd never think that."

She blushed. "Well, if you insist. I wondered if you plan to come to Noel's baptism."

Logan didn't know what to say. He hated to admit that he didn't know precisely what a baptism was, except that it had something to do with water. "I don't think so."

Her eyes filled with disappointment as she looked at him, but she didn't say a word. He ran his fingers through his hair. The last thing he wanted to do was disappoint her. Somehow, he must make her understand. "I'm not much for church ... I mean, I've never been ..."

She laid her hand on his arm. "I was hoping you would come. Please, Logan. Actually, I was hoping you would consider being Noel's godfather."

He stared at her incredulously. He wasn't sure what a godfather was, but it sounded mighty important. "A godfather? Me?"

Libby's eyes implored him. "It seems only fitting. You were the one who helped Noel into the world. You were the first one to hold him."

"Well, now, come to think of it ..." The warmth of

her hand was beginning to affect him and he wasn't thinking straight. "It does seem fitting that I be ... Noel's—what did you call it?—godfather."

Her face lit up and he was dazzled by the captivating smile she gave him. "Does that mean you'll be his godfather?"

"I suppose." He glanced down at his feet. "I mean if a proper Boston woman like yourself says it's fitting, who am I to argue?"

Chapter 22

PREACHER Genesis lived in a canvas tent just outside of town. He was a short, compact man with a bald spot the size of a half dollar, who peered at Logan through metal-framed spectacles. Seemingly delighted to have a visitor, the preacher pumped Logan's hand as if to force the last drop of water from a dried-up well, and invited him inside.

"You're the first visitor I've had since coming to California," Genesis explained. "Back home, people dropped in all the time. If someone got engaged or had a baby, I was the first one they told." His mind seemed to wander for a moment, but he soon caught himself and, apologizing profusely for his lack of manners, promptly cleared a pile of clothes off a wooden candle crate so that Logan could sit down.

Satisfied that he'd met his guest's immediate needs, the preacher drew up another crate and sat down beside him. "What brings you here?"

Logan placed his fur hat on one knee. "I came to ask you some questions." He hesitated. This was all so new to him. "They're of a religious nature."

"In that case you've come to the right place."

Logan was relieved to hear this. "Libby asked me to be Noel's godfather."

"That's quite an honor."

Logan knitted his brow and leaned forward. "It's not too much of an honor, is it?"

The preacher scratched his bald spot. "What do you mean, too much?"

"It's just that the name godfather . . . it sounds rather high falutin."

"Hmmm. Never thought of it that way before."

"Do I have to go around acting like . . ." Logan lifted his eyes skyward.

"No, no, no, nothing like that."

"I can still live my normal life and be a godfather?"

The preacher gave this a moment of thoughtful consideration before he replied. "It's hard to say. There's living a life and then there's living a life. You know what I mean?"

"Not entirely. But what I want to know is in living a life, is there room for a broad interpretation?"

"Depends how broad an interpretation we're talking about."

"Let's take for an example, can a godfather play poker?"

"Are you talking an honest game?"

Logan spread his hands open. "Honest as they come."

"Then I see nothing wrong with that."

"What about alcohol?"

"How broad an interpretation are we talking?"

"Enough to quench a man's thirst."

"See nothing wrong with that."

Logan began to relax. "What about women?"

"You're going to have to give me more to work with."

"You know a man has certain physical needs . . ."

"Ah, now, that's an area where you might be tempted to stretch the limitations beyond what's acceptable."

"What do you consider acceptable?"

The preacher looked flustered. Clearly, this was not covered in the book of Genesis. "I expect it means anything that's acceptable to you and the woman in question."

Logan breathed a sigh of relief. "That sounds reasonable. What else does a godfather have to do? Besides stay within acceptable limits?"

"Nothing more. Unless, of course, something happens to the mother."

"Libby?" At the thought of something happening to Libby, Logan's mouth went as dry as an old tobacco box. "You mean should something . . . I would be responsible for Noel's upbringing."

"Yes, with appropriate emphasis, of course, to his spiritual growth."

This last piece of news brought a frown to Logan's face. "I don't know anything about growing spirits."

"It's not as hard as you think. You teach him the Golden Rule, the Ten Commandments, and you take him to church on the Sabbath and you'll see all the spiritual growth anyone would ever need."

"The Sabbath part could be a problem in my line of work. Sometimes weeks or months pass and I never as much as see anything remotely civilized."

"This presents a challenge." Genesis thought for a moment. "I suppose under those circumstances it would be understandable to miss Sunday worship. As long as you make an effort to attend whenever possible." He stood and slapped Logan on the shoulder. "Now don't go getting yourself all worked up about this. I would say that Noel's mother is a healthy specimen if I ever saw one. Let's just think of you as insurance."

Logan wasn't sure he liked the sound of this. "Insurance, you say?"

"Think of it this way. You know how some of those eastern folks never go out without a pair of galoshes, even in the middle of summer when there's not a cloud in the sky. It never rains in the summertime in California, but they are always prepared. Trust me, your duties as a godfather will keep you as busy as a pair of galoshes in summertime." He laughed at his own joke. "You'll make a splendid godfather."

Logan left the preacher's tent determined to be the

best godfather a boy could hope for. He would protect
Noel with his life, that's what he would do. Why Noel
won't want for a thing, not a thing. Not if he had anything to do with it.

The night before Noel's baptism, Libby sat in front
of the fire, Noel's baptism gown spread across her lap,
and sewed the last stitch in place. She cut the thread
and stuck her needle into a pincushion she had fashioned out of sawdust and scraps of fabric. Holding up
the white cotton gown, she gave it a critical once-over.

The yoke was embroidered with tiny little flowers
and trimmed with a narrow white braid. The lace that
she'd taken such care to sew along the puffed sleeves
and round neckline was a bit too wide, but it was all
that Hap carried in his store and there was no time to
order more.

Satisfied with the finished garment, she carefully
pressed the dress with a hot brick and hung it over the
back of a chair. All that was left to do was to sew the
ribbons onto the matching bonnet.

She tiptoed into Noel's room to check on him. He'd
been fussy earlier, and she thought he might be coming
down with a cold. His soft even breathing assured her
that he was sleeping peacefully, and with a loving
smile, she tiptoed out of his room.

While gathering her sewing supplies from her chair,
she dropped a pin on the large bearskin she used as a
rug. She lifted the hem of her skirt and dropped to her
knees. The fur felt coarse to her fingers as she searched
the deep nap. It hadn't seemed anywhere near as coarse
the night she and Logan had sat together on that very
same rug. In fact, she distinctly remembered that on
that particular night, the rug felt soft to the touch.

Had it really only been eight days since he'd come
to dinner? It seemed like forever since she'd seen him.
She had, of course, bumped into him twice since. Both
times he'd been polite, but guarded, acting like he
didn't know where to look or what to say. She'd tried

her best to put his mind at ease. But it was hard with her heart beating so wildly in her chest and her tongue suddenly refusing to form the words she longed to say. She wanted him to know that she really did appreciate his kind marriage proposal, even though they both agreed it was not a particularly practical one.

Still, she couldn't seem to keep from asking herself "what if?" What if she had accepted his proposal? What if he were her husband? But the question that made her heart race was, *what would it be like to share his bed*?

Even now, posed as she was on hands and knees, the thought unbalanced her. She lowered herself to a sitting position and waited until her pulse had grown steady again. As soon as she gained control of her senses, she gave herself a stern mental shake and proceeded to search for the missing pin.

She jumped to her feet at the sound of a knock at the door. She knew it was Logan by his knock, but even the moment she took to brace herself before opening the door did not prepare her enough, and she greeted him with a wavering voice. "I . . . didn't expect to see you."

"I know . . ." He seemed to be having a difficult time looking her straight in the eye. "I have something for Noel." He handed her a rectangular package, tied with a piece of rawhide.

"How very thoughtful of you." She stared down at the package in her hands, wishing they could recapture the easy rapport they once shared. But that was before he'd asked her to marry him, before she knew how much she wanted to. "Do you want me to open it now or should I wait until after his baptism tomorrow?"

"Since I want him to wear this tomorrow, you'd better open it now."

Remembering her manners, she stepped aside. "Do come on in." Lord Almighty, they spoke to each other like strangers meeting for the first time.

She closed the door after him, crossed the room, and

placed the package on the table. She smiled nervously before she slipped the rawhide off and carefully pulled back the paper.

Inside was a little buckskin suit, identical to the one Logan was wearing, complete with a fringed capelet and rawhide lacing. With an appreciative gasp, she held the little outfit in front of her. "It's absolutely lovely! I've never seen anything so adorable." Her delight increased upon spotting the tiny moccasins to match. "Oh, Logan!"

Logan rewarded her with a broad smile. "Made it myself."

That explained why she'd seen him so seldom during the last week. She thought of all the times she'd peered through the canvas opening at her window to his cabin, not wanting to be caught gaping, yet driven by some inexplicable need to know what he was doing. It never once occurred to her that he was working on an outfit for Noel. "It's so tiny."

His smile faded. "It's not too tiny, is it?"

"Oh, no! It's perfect." For no good reason, she felt her face grow warm. "But then, you always were good at guessing sizes."

"I never guess a size," he assured her, his eyes dropping down the length of her as if to visually confirm her measurements.

Feeling naked and desirable beneath his gaze, she held Noel's suit in front of her as much to block Logan's view as to study the detailed handiwork. At first she thought the intricate design on the yoke had been embroidered, but closer observation revealed the little animal shapes had been created from tiny colored beads.

"Learned beadwork from a Dakota Indian," he explained. His eyes flared as he hungrily watched her fingers caress his handiwork.

"I've never seen such lovely work," she said. "And look at all this lovely fringe."

"Whangs," he said. "Trappers call them whangs."

"Whangs," she repeated.

"That's so the rain will run off."

"You just never know when that might come in handy," she said.

"If you like I can grease it up to make it really waterproof. Bear grease is the best."

"I don't expect that Noel will be out in the rain that much."

"No, I suspect not. You remember how to clean buckskins, don't you?"

The corner of her mouth lifted slightly. "Place them on an anthill."

He grinned. "I just might make a mountain woman out of you after all."

She caught her breath. "You . . . you said something earlier. About Noel wearing this tomorrow."

"For the baptism. It doesn't seem right to have a baptism and not be dressed properly."

He looked so earnest that she didn't have the heart to tell him that it was customary for a baby to be baptized in a proper white christening dress. "I quite agree."

"It seems the least a godfather can do is to see that his little godson has himself a proper outfit on such a special occasion."

"Noel doesn't know how lucky he is."

"I . . ." His gaze washed over her. "I'd better be going. Tomorrow is an important day and you need your sleep." He turned toward the door.

Reluctant for him to go, she reached for his arm in an attempt to delay his departure. He turned his head and looked back over his shoulder. Feeling foolish, she dropped her hand and stammered a good night. "I'll see you tomorrow."

His gaze flickered down to her lips. "Tomorrow."

"And, Logan . . . I'm much obliged to you."

After he left, she held up the little buckskin suit. She could only imagine what her staunch Boston parents would say if they knew that their grandson was going to be baptized in such an outfit.

The thought made her laugh.

The entire town of Deadman's Gulch turned out for Noel's baptism. All except for Cast-Iron, who took to the hills first thing in the morning, a-mumbling and a-grumbling, as Sharkey told the others, about the town a-going crazy.

The sky was a deep blue in color, with not a cloud in sight. The sun was warm, and the last of the snow around the newly built church had melted into pockets of mud. Planks of wood were positioned so that Libby could walk without slipping or otherwise muddying up her boots.

The church was already packed by the time Libby and Logan took their place in front of the pulpit.

While they waited for Pastor Genesis, Noel was passed like an offering plate from miner to miner. Everyone agreed that he looked right spiffy in his little buckskin outfit. Noel obviously loved all the attention. He cooed and gurgled and the miners cooed and gurgled back.

When it was Big Sam's turn, he held Noel with both hands, carefully cradling Noel's head in the crook of his muscular arm. "Gee, gee, gaw, goo, goo," the large man mimicked and Noel responded in kind.

"What's the boy sayin'?" Sharkey asked.

Big Sam rocked Noel gently. "Don't tell me you don't understand baby talk."

"Had no call to learn," Sharkey admitted.

"He said, when I grow up I want to be just like Big Sam."

Appleby laughed and slapped Big Sam on the back. "I'd say that since the little fellow has no hair and no teeth, he's got a purty good start."

This brought more laughter, and Noel was handed to Thornton, who made holding a baby look as unnatural as a bear giving birth to a lion.

"Will you look at this?" Big Sam scorned. "I've seen sacks of flour flung over the rumps of mules fare better."

Libby watched the men demonstrate the proper procedure for holding a baby and held back the urge to laugh.

"Got to keep the baby's center of gravity in line with the sun," Big Sam explained with such conviction, no one questioned his competence.

Thinking the minister had arrived, Libby glanced at the doorway upon seeing someone enter the church. Instead, it was her Chinese friend, Macao. Libby threaded her way down the center aisle to greet him. "Macao, I'm so happy you came."

The Chinese man bowed graciously. "It's very nice of you to invite me."

Libby pointed to an empty spot just as Preacher Genesis arrived, his Bible tucked beneath his arm. Dressed in a black flannel shirt and black trousers, with a piece of white linen tucked neatly into his collar, Genesis managed to appear appropriately dressed for the occasion.

The preacher took his place at the front of the church and adjusted his spectacles as he waited for everyone's attention.

When it took too long in coming, Big Sam stood up and yelled, "Dammit, everyone! Hush up!"

Appleby looked scandalized and quickly snatched Noel away from the big man's arms. "Didn't anyone ever tell you how to talk in church?"

Lowering his head in humiliation, Big Sam addressed the crowd in the most God-fearing, reverent voice he could muster. "Dammit. Can't you see Pastor Genesis is waiting?"

Appleby rolled his eyes upward and handed Noel to Sharkey, who handed him to Shakespeare, who handed him to Beaker. At last Noel reached the front of the church and Logan's waiting arms. Logan took his place beside Libby and they both faced the minister.

It took only a few minutes for Genesis to dribble water over Noel's head and announce him duly baptized. The infant looked startled, then let out an indignant cry.

"It's all right, little fellow," Logan said. He jostled the baby up and down, and in short order Noel stopped crying.

Libby smiled at Logan. "I told you that you had a way with babies."

Logan smiled back. *Family. That's how it felt. Like he belonged to a family.* "Well, now."

After the ceremony, the men crowded around to congratulate Libby and take another look at the wondrous child who had fallen asleep in Logan's arms.

Big Sam chucked Noel under his chin. "Now that we've got ourselves a properly baptized baby, I think this calls for a celebration."

"Wait a minute." Appleby waved a hand over his head. "I think we need to talk about something first." He waited for everyone to quiet down before he spoke his piece. "Now that we have a respectable church, I think it's high time that the rest of the town took on more respectability."

"We are r'spectable!" Sharkey shouted out.

Beaker concurred. "What could be more respectable than a mother and child, and now a church?"

The miners nodded in agreement and everyone began to talk at once.

"Hear me out," Appleby pleaded. He climbed onto one of the log pews so that he could be seen and heard by those in the back of the church. "I say that we need to tear down the eyesores of this town and put up proper buildings that would do our baby proud."

"It'll take too long," one miner pointed out. "We got gold to mine."

Hap Montana piped up, his bald head gleaming in the open doorway of the church. "It won't take long if we work together." It was a startling statement, especially since it came from a man whose chief occupation was to avoid work. A moment's silence followed as everyone turned to see if the speaker was, indeed, the owner of the sorry state of affairs known as the general store.

"There ain't much else we can do," Big Sam said. "I tried to mine my claim yesterday and the ground is still as hard as rock up there."

"That's my point," Appleby said. "While we're waiting for the ground to thaw, we could be putting our time to good use."

A lively debate followed as to how best to go about improving the town. Finally, Appleby took the floor again. "It's agreed then. We'll begin first thing tomorrow. We'll tear down the canvas buildings and construct permanent ones. Everyone agree?"

The miners let out a loud roar that made Noel's eyes fly open momentarily before fluttering shut again. Appleby's finger flew to his lips as he signaled the men to keep their voices low.

Choo-Choo stepped on the pew next to Appleby. "Fancy churches and buildings are all well and good. But that doesn't change the fact that you're asking a young mother"—he waved at Libby and then turned back to the men—"to raise her son in a town named Deadman's Gulch."

Moe the bartender called through cupped hands. "What are you saying, Choo-Choo? You think we should change the name?"

Shakespeare stepped on the pew next to Choo-Choo. "A rose by any other name will still be a rose."

"What the hell is that supposed to mean?" Big Sam demanded.

Appleby glared at the strapping black man. "Dammit! Can't you talk properly in church?"

One of the miners in the back pew shouted out. "It means that you can call Deadman's Gulch anything you want and it will still stink."

This brought jeering protests from the others.

"Hold it!" Appleby raised his voice to be heard. He

waited for quiet before he continued. "I think Choo-Choo has a good point. We can change the town all we want but unless we change the name, Libby isn't going to want to raise her son here. Isn't that right, Libby?"

Libby didn't quite know what to say. She didn't want to hurt the men's feelings. But nothing they did to the town was going to prevent her from leaving. Fortunately someone else spoke up, saving her the embarrassment of having to point this out.

"So what are we going to call the town? Roseville?"

"How about Lavender Gulch?"

Appleby waved for silence. "We're going to do this right. If you have suggestions, you write them down. At the end of the week, we'll post them in front of Hap's place. When everyone's had time to give each name due consideration, we'll take a vote."

Much discussion followed, but in the end it was decided that Noel would have himself a proper town with a proper name.

Chapter 23

IN the days to follow, Libby stood on her front porch and watched the canvased structures up and down Main Street disappear. In no time at all, wood frames began to rise in their stead. From early morning until late dusk, the air vibrated with the sound of hammers and saws.

By consensus, it was agreed that the men work on the general store first, to allow Libby a proper place to buy her supplies. It took only three days for the men to complete the simple, but functional square wooden building.

No sooner had the men finished and moved on to the next project than Hap and Libby went to work to ready the store for its grand opening.

Hap stood outside and supervised the placing of the sign on the false front, giving out as many orders as a general preparing for battle.

"To the right. More. More. To the left. Up. More. Down. Don't you know what I mean when I say down?"

Big Sam, who was having a heck of a time balancing himself on the roof, yelled out, "For someone who thought nothing of keeping crackers in the same barrel as the horse liniment, you sure are getting p'tickler."

At last the sign was nailed in place and the residents of the town gaped up at it like lifers about to be pardoned.

Grinning like a schoolboy playing hooky, Hap held

Noel in such a way that the little fellow could see the sign.

"See that, boy? Says 'Hap Montana's General Store.'" Noel gurgled and Hap nodded approvingly. "You're right, boy. It's the finest store this side of the Miss'ssippi." Hap thought a moment. "I like that. The finest store this side of the Miss'ssippi. Anyone want to make me another sign to put in my window?"

Choo-Choo volunteered. "Not sure I know how to spell Miss'ssippi though."

"What one do you want on your sign?" Sharkey asked. "The state or the r'ver?"

Hap thought a moment. "The river."

"I believe they're both spelled the same," Libby said tactfully.

"Is that so?" Sharkey asked, surprised.

Hap handed Noel back to Libby. "Let's get started."

Libby followed Hap inside the newly built store. The hardwood floors gleamed beneath several coats of bear grease and resin. Wide-open shelves lined the walls and a finely crafted counter ran the length of the store.

Earlier that day, she had helped Hap carry boxes of goods into the store. They'd stacked the boxes up against the back wall until over half the floor space was filled. Next came the job of unpacking the merchandise and arranging it on the shelves.

Libby placed Noel on a blanket in front of the woodstove and donned an apron. Hap pointed to a row of shelves on the wall opposite the counter. "You can start stacking the tin goods over there."

For the rest of that day and the following, Libby and Hap worked together to organize the store. It had been extremely difficult to convince Hap of the importance of keeping the household goods separated from the edibles. But once he finally saw the logic of it, they were able to finish the job with no further disagreements.

After the shelves had been neatly stacked, and the mining equipment hung on the back wall, Libby printed signs to hang around the store to help the customers locate the various goods at a glance.

At last everything was ready. Hap set the cash box behind the counter, changing its location several times before he found one that suited him. The scale for weighing gold was set next to the cash box. He then puffed out his chest, strutted between the carefully arranged displays, and inspected every last item with a look of unbearable importance.

"Yep, as I said before. No finer store this side of the Miss'ssippi." With a snap of his fingers, he signaled for Libby to turn the sign in the window announcing the official opening of the store.

Irritated by his pretentious air, she was tempted to tell him to turn his own sign, but decided against it. The man was entitled to feel important. At least for a day!

Hap unlocked the door and with a great flourish swung it open. The miners, who had been waiting impatiently outside, greeted him with hoots and hollers as they pushed their way inside.

Fearing that Noel would be trampled on, Libby quickly scooped him up in her arms.

The miners stocked up on tobacco and coffee and exclaimed at how easy it was to find what they wanted now that everything was arranged in proper order and carefully labeled.

The men were a bit startled to find Hap follow them around, watching their every move. Pity the poor man who made the mistake of picking something up to look at it and who didn't put it back precisely how he found it. Hap was on him like a cat on a field mouse. His face stern, he pointed a finger at the object in question until the hapless miner had carried it back to its proper place.

Normally a soft-spoken man, Hap took to shouting out orders like a general under attack. "Label out, you idiot. And you, Shakespeare, go back over there and straighten that harness."

Sharkey, particularly, took offense. "You think the man would be grateful for our bus'ness."

Libby had her hands full trying to soothe the ruffled feathers of the men. "He's naturally proud of his new shop. Give him time, he'll settle down."

But Hap did not settle down. If anything, he grew more overbearing during each passing day. He even went as far as to insist that his customers wipe their feet before entering.

He no longer whiled away his days reading old newspapers in glum silence. Instead, he priced his goods, checked his shelves, and made his customers obey the ever-growing list of rules and regulations for shopping in his store.

Since Hap no longer required her services, Libby busied herself making curtains for the newly built Golden Hind Saloon. The saloon was twice as big as the original. The baize-covered gaming tables took up only half of the floor space.

The dirt floor had been replaced by wooden planks and there was even a small portion set aside for dancing, although Libby couldn't imagine what use the town had for a dance floor.

The saloon was empty that afternoon while she worked. Nearby, Noel was taking his afternoon nap.

She stood on a chair in front of one of the saloon's windows and worked a red and white calico curtain along a thin wooden rod. She was so absorbed in her work, it wasn't until she heard a familiar voice that she realized she was no longer alone.

"Libby! Are you trying to break your neck?"

She nearly fell off the chair in an effort to glance over her shoulder at Logan. He grabbed hold of her waist and held her until she'd regained her balance.

"Lord Almighty, Logan," she scolded, tapping his hands away from her waist. "Don't go sneaking up behind people like that."

He stepped back. "I'm sorry, Libby. But you shouldn't be standing on chairs." He stared at the window. "I never heard of curtains in a saloon. Do you think it's, eh, proper for a saloon to look so feminine?"

"Curtains don't necessarily make a place look feminine." She straightened the hem of one panel. "They make a place look homey."

Logan looked unconvinced. "This is a drinking and gambling hall, not a place to raise a family."

She gave him an exasperated look and climbed down from the chair. Dragging the chair across the wooden floor to the next window, she pointed near his feet. "Would you be kind enough to hand me that pole?"

He picked up the wooden pole that had been whittled out of a tree branch and handed it to her.

"Do they have curtains in gambling halls in Boston?" he persisted.

"I wouldn't know," she said. "Until recently, I never as much as stepped foot in a gambling hall. Hand me those curtains, will you?"

He gathered up the curtains that lay across the bar and draped them carefully over his arm so as not to wrinkle them. She worked one panel, then another onto the pole, then climbed back onto the chair to slip the pole into the slots of the wooden brackets.

Logan held on to the chair as she worked. "Well, I've been in every gambling saloon on this side of the States and I can tell you that I've never seen a single one with curtains."

"Is that so?" she asked, unperturbed.

"I don't even know why we need all these windows," he continued. "Do you know how hard it is to make a window? And who knows when we'll ever get enough glass?"

"It is rather an inconvenience, I know. But look at the lovely view." She moved a curtain aside and gazed through the paneless window. "The snow looks mighty lovely on those mountains."

"You can see that exact view by standing outside on the porch."

Not knowing how to argue with such odd logic, she reached upward to adjust the gathers. The chair wobbled beneath her feet, but held by Logan's steady hand, it offered no real danger. Nevertheless, Logan refused to let her step down unassisted. Instead, he lifted her by the waist, holding her momentarily suspended in the air before easing her gently to the floor.

"Well, now," he said.

She glanced up at him and their gazes locked. "I think I'm all right." Her voice trembled slightly, her heart did flip-flops.

"I hope so." His voice sounded almost as tremulous as hers.

It wasn't until she pushed gently against his hands that he finally released her and jumped back as if caught stealing red-handed.

An awkward silence stretched between them.

He rubbed his thigh as was his habit when his leg bothered him, and she turned her attention back to the curtains, as if not to notice. She knew how defensive he became whenever she mentioned or otherwise noticed him favoring his leg.

"There," Libby ventured at last. "What do you think?" She glanced at him and when she discovered his eyes still on her, she stepped back to have a better overall view of both windows.

"They do give the place a bit of respectability," Logan admitted as he stepped back beside her. As if by mutual agreement, they began an in-depth discussion of the curtains.

"You don't think they're too red?" she asked. What she really wanted to know was where he'd been these last few days. But it would never do to admit that she noticed him gone. "We don't want to give the impression that this is a house of ill repute."

"The curtains *are* half white," he remarked, biting back the urge to tell her how beautiful she looked to him and how soft she'd felt in his arms moments earlier.

"That's true."

They stood side by side a moment longer staring at the curtains before she thought of something else safe to say. "You don't think that they're too full?" She turned to him and upon finding him staring at her lips added, "The curtains?"

He lifted his gaze, seeming to absorb her body and soul into the dark smoldering depths of his eyes. "I don't believe so."

Feeling a warm flush rush to her cheeks, she reached out to touch the hem. "What about the length? Do you think I should shorten them?"

"The length is perfect."

As they stood side by side, afraid to do more than share a quick glance, it became obvious to them both that they had very good reason to be afraid.

She never before suspected that so much could be said on the subject of curtains.

They discussed the weight of the fabric, the size of the checks, the particular shade of red, and might have continued in this mundane vein indefinitely had Noel not announced with a lusty cry that it was supper time.

In a frenzied rush that was meant to hide her rampaging thoughts, Libby collected her sewing supplies in one arm and Noel in another. In the process, she dropped her little gold scissors and a spool of thread.

Logan immediately retrieved her supplies and handed them to her. "Do you need help?"

"No, thank you," she said in a breathless voice. "I can manage." She walked a few steps backward. "It was nice seeing you." It was necessary to raise her voice to be heard over Noel's lusty cries. *Over the sound of her fast-beating heart.*

"Same here," Logan called back. "Oh, and Libby . . . you're right. The curtains do add a homey touch."

Chapter 24

IN the days to follow, the loud hammering and constant grating sound of sawing continued to echo from one end of the little valley to the other. The men started work at the first crack of dawn and worked until it was too dark to see.

The snow had melted on the upper peaks and the water rose above the banks of the river, filling the channels and running down the mountainside.

A few of the miners had already gone to check out the diggings, but most stayed in town to finish the task at hand.

Main Street became more clearly defined as one by one wooden buildings replaced the canvas tents and rag houses that had previously been scattered at random like so many dice.

Sharkey had his very own barbershop and set to work painting a tree log with white and red stripes to represent a proper barber pole. Now that he could better express himself artistically as he put it, he no longer wore out his elbow looking down the stiff neck of a whiskey bottle.

On the day Sharkey officially opened his barbershop, Libby dropped by to inspect his new premises.

"What do you think?" He took Noel from her arms and held the boy up. "Ain't this the finest barbershop this side of the Miss'ssip'?"

Libby readily agreed, despite the makeshift furniture, which included upturned whiskey barrels and a broken butter churn. "It's most impressive."

"I sent away fer one of those barber chairs." Sharkey straightened the row of barrels with a toe of his boot. "You know, the ones that go up and down."

"That's wonderful, Sharkey."

"And Hap ordered a full case of Ring's Verb'na Cream, like those fancy folks use. Makes the whiskers slide off eas'er than butter off a knife."

He brushed his fingers against the downy hair on Noel's head. "Noel will be needin' hisself a trimmin' soon. You know he has a whole year of free haircuts comin' to him."

"I think we have a while yet before Noel will be needing a haircut."

Choo-Choo entered the barbershop, wheezing like a steam engine. "There you are, Miss Libby. The boys be needing you to settle a little dispute."

"Oh, dear, I hope it's not serious."

"It has to do with naming the town."

Libby frowned in puzzlement. "But I thought the vote wasn't until next Saturday."

"It's not the voting that is causing all the fuss. It's deciding who gets to vote and what names they get to vote on."

Libby sighed and reached for Noel. "I'll see what I can do."

"You can leave him here with me if you want," Sharkey offered.

Libby smiled. "That's very generous of you, but I think the men might be more willing to listen to reason with a young one on hand."

Cradling Noel in her arms, she walked with Choo-Choo toward the group of men that stood in the middle of Main Street. As usual whenever Libby arrived on the scene, the miners whipped off their hats and began acting all self-conscious and polite.

"Now here's a sight for sore eyes," Beaker said.

"Pur-ty as a *pitchur*," another agreed.

Big Sam gained Noel's attention and then proceeded to make goo-goo sounds.

Despite the sea of friendly faces that greeted her, Libby sensed an edge of tension in the air. Seeing Macao and his Chinese friends standing back from the crowd, their faces dark and somber, she could guess the source of the tension.

She turned to Appleby. "Choo-Choo tells me there's a problem."

Appleby looked uncomfortable. "It's nothing to worry your pretty little head over."

"If you don't mind, I would like to make my own decisions as to what to worry over."

Big Sam rested a large dark hand on Appleby's shoulder. "What Luke here is trying to say is that we are conducting a dem'cratic process."

"Yeah!" Keefer shouted. "That means we get to choose what names to vote on."

Libby had never paid much attention to politics, but she knew the meaning of democratic process. "I thought anyone who had a mind to could submit a name."

"Yeah, well that didn't include no damned chinks!" Big Sam grumbled.

Libby directed a pointed look at the strapping ex-slave. "How many names have been submitted?"

Appleby glanced down at his notes. "Altogether? Ten."

"Well, now," Libby said. "It seems to me that ten is a mighty nice number to vote on."

Big Sam dropped his head and fingered his hat. Choo-Choo let out a hissing sound. Hap, who was standing on the steps of his store, scratched his hairless head. Feet shuffled, looks were exchanged, but nobody was willing to disagree with the town's only woman.

Appleby waited, and when no one spoke up, he prompted the crowd. "Well, men? What do you say?"

Sharkey, who had left his shop to follow Libby and Choo-Choo, spoke up. "I say if we hafta vote on ten names to keep our Miss Libby, here, happy, well then, it's a small price to pay."

Appleby scanned the sea of faces. When no further objections were forthcoming, he nodded his head, indicating that the matter was settled. "Very well. If no one has anything else to add, I'll read the names that we'll be voting on. Thornton and his men will be in charge of the ballot box. You get one vote and one vote only. Are there any questions?"

"Does that mean everyone in town has a vote?" Libby asked.

Appleby ran a finger along the collar of his shirt. "If you're asking if the chinks . . . eh . . . Chinese residents have a vote, I would say . . . eh . . ."

Libby smiled sweetly. "Oh, I know our Chinese residents have a vote. They are, after all, citizens of this town. What I was asking is if *I* get to vote?"

Appleby's mouth started flapping around like the tail of an old mule. Nevertheless, he failed to produce even one intelligent sound.

While the miners waited for their leader to respond, Thornton, who had been watching the proceedings with interest, obviously saw an opportunity to endear himself to Libby. He stepped forward, pulled off his fine straw hat, and gave a gentlemanly bow. "Naturally, you shall have a vote." He was so intent upon ingratiating himself with her, he didn't appear to notice Logan ride into town.

"That's most democratic of you all," Libby replied.

"It only makes good sense," Thornton said grandly. "A woman as intelligent as yourself should certainly have a say in important issues."

Logan sat in his saddle and listened to this exchange with growing irritation. He doubted that a single man would deny Libby a vote. But the way Thornton was carrying on, it sounded like he, alone, was making the decision.

He hoped that Libby could see through Thornton's ruse, but if she suspected Thornton's motivations, she sure in hell wasn't letting on. He nudged his horse forward until Thornton was forced to step away from Libby.

Thornton gave Logan a dark glowering look, before turning to the waiting crowd. "How many agree that Libby should have a vote?"

Shouts of approval exploded from the crowd. No one wanted to look bad in Libby's eyes. Even Big Sam gave his thunderous consent.

Appleby appeared relieved that the matter had been taken out of his hands. When the roar had died down, he cleared his voice and took on a self-important demeanor. "If there is no more discussion, I'll read the names that were nominated." He paused for a moment, then began, "The first name is Choo-Choo."

As his choice for a town name was announced, Choo-Choo grinned. Next to him, Sharkey made a contemptuous noise. "Of all the conceited, self-servin' . . ."

"The next name," Appleby called out, "is Barber-town."

Choo-Choo shot a mocking look at Sharkey. "You don't think that's self-serving?"

"Little Boston."

Libby sought out Logan, knowing that Little Boston had been his idea even before he gave her an acknowledging wink. Libby was so touched, she was forced to blink to keep her tears at bay.

"Libbyville."

Thornton squeezed her arm and whispered, "That was my choice. Do you like it?"

She nodded, although in reality she wasn't at all certain she liked the idea of having a town named after her.

One by one, Appleby read the nominations. Before announcing the last name on his list, he hesitated.

"Come on, Appleby!" yelled an impatient miner from the back of the crowd. "What are you waiting for?"

Appleby looked embarrassed. "I'm not sure how to

pronounce the last name on the list. It's the one that was nominated by, eh . . ."

Macao stepped forward. "Allow me." He said something in Chinese and bowed.

"What is this?" Big Sam growled. "We can't even pronounce the name, let alone spell it."

"If you don't like it, then don't vote for it," Appleby said. "Ballot boxes will be placed at strategic places around the town. You have a whole week to make your decision. You must cast your vote by noon next Saturday. If there are no more questions, this meeting is adjourned."

The crowed dispersed quickly. Since it was almost time for Noel's lunch, Libby headed straight for home. By the time she reached her front porch, Logan was already in front of his cabin, dragging his saddle off his horse.

She hesitated.

He looked up.

She started across the road. "I like the name Little Boston," she called.

He dropped the saddle on the porch and walked toward her, meeting her halfway between their two houses. "Really? I was afraid you'd think . . ."

"Think what?" she coaxed.

"That the name was too good for this town."

"Oh, I'd never think that!" she exclaimed.

He looked pleased. "Well, then . . ."

Noel started fussing. She eased him to her shoulder and began rocking him. "He's hungry."

"I'd better not keep you, then."

She hesitated. "I . . . I hope Little Boston wins."

Something flickered within the depths of his eyes. "So do I."

Chapter 25

DURING the next few days, the town was in an uproar. Signs were posted on every tree trunk, on every building, and on every fence post urging the citizens of the town to vote for this name or for that.

Give the Town Class, read one sign. *Vote for Libbyville. Barbertown,* read another, *the name that's a shave above the rest.* Sharkey was so proud of the slogan he made up, he was pretty near unbearable to live with.

"Do you get it?" he kept asking everyone he met.

"I get it already!" Big Sam growled, after being approached by Sharkey for the third time in as many hours. "And I still ain't voting for it!"

Noisy debates as to which name was in Libby's and Noel's best interests waged up and down Main Street.

One night, Logan lay on his pallet, his blankets over his head in an effort to drown out the noisy argument that was taking place outside.

"Anyone in his right mind would vote for Libbyville."

"You think so? Let me tell you somethin'. If yer mind was that gosh dern razor-sharp, you'd note for Barbertown."

Having just about all he could take, Logan stormed out of bed and plodded out to his porch. "Would you two quit your yelling!" he bellowed. "There's a baby asleep over there and it's past curfew."

At long last, voting day dawned. No sooner had the

sun risen than the miners began lining up in front of the various ballot boxes.

Thornton rode through town on his black stallion. With his coattails flapping behind him and his hat as tall as a stovepipe, he looked like an English lord. He stopped to talk with one of the men who stood guard next to a ballot box. Assured that all was under control, he touched his hand to the brim of his hat and rode on to the next voting booth.

It was after eleven-thirty by the time Libby arrived to cast her vote. Noel was dressed in his little buckskin outfit.

Sharkey and Appleby took turns holding him while Libby stepped into one of the little wooden voting booths that had been built for the occasion.

While she was inside, Logan appeared, and seeing his godson dressed in his little buckskin suit, he lifted the boy out of Appleby's arms.

Libby stepped out of the booth and gave Logan a dazzling smile. "Have you voted?"

"First thing this morning," Logan replied.

Noel started fussing and Logan jiggled him up and down.

"He's ready for his nap," Libby explained.

Logan smiled down at the boy. "Well, you go right ahead and take your nap, little fellow." He rocked Noel in his arms and soon Noel's eyes flickered shut.

The polls closed and Thornton swept by on his horse to pick up the ballots. Ignoring Logan, he tipped his hat toward Libby as he rode by.

"You do have a way with babies," Libby said, wondering about the scowl on Logan's face. She pulled the top of Noel's buckskin suit down over his middle, her hand brushing against Logan's. Their gazes collided for an instant before she lowered her lashes and pulled her hand away.

"He seems to like his buckskins," she said.

"Nothing more comfortable."

"I know." She lifted her eyes and bit her lip. "I miss

mine. The dress you made for me is rather big for me."
She gave an embarrassed laugh. "I can't believe how
enormous I was before I had him."

"I can alter it."

"Oh, I couldn't ask you to do that."

"Why not? It'll take me no time at all."

"If you're sure."

"Couldn't be surer. I'll stop by later and pick it up.
Meanwhile, I think we ought to walk over to the general store. It's almost time for them to announce elec-
tion results."

Already a crowd was gathered in front of Hap's
place and bets were being placed as to which of the ten
names would emerge the winner. It took almost an
hour for the men to finish counting and the crowd began to grow restless.

At long last, Thornton came galloping into town,
and a rousing cheer greeted him as he dismounted and
tied his horse to the hitching post in front of the store.

Appleby took his place on Hap's porch and faced the
waiting mob. Thornton handed him a folded piece of
paper and a hushed silence came over the town as all
eyes followed Appleby's every move.

Appleby carefully unfolded the paper and cleared
his throat. Logan reached over and squeezed Libby's
hand. She felt a surge of excitement and anticipation
that had nothing to do with the vote and everything to
do with his touch.

"Eh . . . the winner is . . ."

"Quit your stalling, Luke!" someone called out.

"I'm not stalling," Appleby protested. "I don't know
how to read the name."

"Let me," Thornton said. He said the Chinese name
so flawlessly, one would have thought it was his native
tongue.

The crowd was so stunned by this unexpected turn
of events, that for the longest while no one spoke.

Big Sam was the first to find his voice. "How could

this happen?" He pointed an accusing finger at Thornton. "You said one ballot per man."

Thornton did not take kindly to the implication. "Are you suggesting that my men failed to do their job?"

Logan stepped onto the porch. Noel was still sound asleep in his arms. "Before we start making false accusations, I suggest we calm down. We have a baby here trying to take a nap."

The men immediately complied with his wishes, and the argument continued in hushed whispers, but with no less intensity.

Sharkey pushed his way through the crowd and stood next to Logan. "I say if there's a pr'blem with ballot stuffin' we need to know it." His soft-spoken words were repeated by others for the benefit of those standing too far away to hear.

"Now see here!" Thornton protested, and was immediately hushed by the others. Looking taken aback, he glanced at Noel, and when it was apparent that the baby's sleep had not been disturbed, he began again, this time in a lowered voice. "As I was saying, my men and I made certain that everyone got one vote and one vote only!"

"Then would you mind explaining how this gobble-dygook of a name won?" whispered Beaker, waving his hand so everyone knew he spoke. His question was repeated until it reached Hap's porch.

Logan took it upon himself to point out what should have been obvious to everyone from the start. "The Chinese community is rather large. If every Chinese in the area cast a vote, I daresay they could very well outnumber us. Thornton and his men had nothing to do with it!"

While his response was being volleyed back and forth among the crowd, and was met with startled gasps, he shifted Noel from one shoulder to the other and wondered what in the name of sam hill he was doing defending the likes of Thornton Wellerton. He glanced over at Libby, who was watching him intently, her face soft with approval. Blast it all! Did she have to look so gosh darn pleased because he was defending the man?

Much to his relief, Appleby took command again. "If you recall, we decided that everyone living in and around Deadman's Gulch had a vote. Therefore I'm afraid . . ." He glanced down at the Chinese name written on the paper in his hand and shrugged. "Whatever this name is, is the name of our town."

While this statement swept through the crowd in a series of shocked whispers, Noel opened his eyes and yawned, and the meeting resumed in somewhat louder voices.

"Wonderful!" Big Sam wheezed. "No one including Noel will be able to pronounce it. Isn't that right, Noel?"

Macao quietly pushed his way through the crowd, bowed his head, and requested permission to speak.

Appleby motioned him onto the porch. The Chinese man stood between Appleby and Logan and faced the crowd. In a slow, singsong voice, he began, "I agree. The name might impose difficulties on this young man. For that reason, I suggest we use the English derivative."

"What's a div-a . . . whatever that word is?" Sharkey called out.

"Translation," Thornton explained.

Appleby glanced over the crowd, and when no objection was raised, he turned to Macao. "What is the English version?"

"It means 'She Who Wears Calico.' "

Choo-Choo spit in disgust. "That's just dandy." He spoke in a high, strained voice. "I live in a town named She Who Wears Calico."

A noisy dissent followed and it was only Noel's cry that got the crowd under control.

"Now see what you've done," Appleby chastised. "You've gone and scared Noel." He reached over and chucked Noel under his chin. "There, there, l'ttle fellow. It's all right."

Appleby directed his attention back to the matter at hand. "Does anyone have a suggestion? Libby?"

All eyes turned to Libby as she stepped forward and stood next to Logan. "I suggest we shorten the name to Calico."

"How about Calico Corners?" Sharkey yelled out, not willing to conceded fully that his own idea had been rejected.

"Calico Corners." Big Sam tilted his head from one side to another and repeated it again.

"Calico Corners," murmured the miners to themselves.

"By thunder," shouted Keefer from the back. "I think Noel likes that name!"

All eyes turned to Noel, who was lying in Logan's arms, his face dimpled in the biggest smile possible.

Libby was so overwhelmed by her son's first smile, it was all she could do to keep maternal pride from turning into sentimental tears. Her little boy was growing up right before her very eyes!

Noel's smile decided the issue. The miners agreed that from that day forward the little town of Deadman's Gulch would be known as Calico Corners.

Chapter 26

THERE was no question in anyone's mind that Calico Corners was the most respectable and refined town in the entire West. As the days grew warmer, the flowers that Libby had dug up from the surrounding hills and planted in the wooden window boxes began to bloom.

Every Sunday, the church bell, which was actually Choo-Choo pounding on a piece of metal with a rock, rang out as miners crowded inside. Everyone competed to sit as close to Libby and Noel as possible.

After church and if the weather permitted, the miners accompanied Libby on a leisurely stroll. The men took turns holding Noel. It was during one of these strolls that Libby mentioned how she wished Calico Corners had a post office.

As it was, the residents normally received mail every two or three months.

Appleby immediately jumped on the idea and called a town meeting. After everyone gathered in front of Hap's place, he announced that a post office was going to be built right next to Sharkey's barbershop.

"Who's going to be the postmaster?" Choo-Choo asked.

"That's a good question," Big Sam agreed.

Appleby scanned the crowd and suddenly his face lit up. "I think it only right that the position of postmaster go to a man who is not only refined, but who has a proper education."

Thornton smiled and stepped forward. "That's a

mighty generous offer, Luke, but I'm afraid running the mine is a full-time job."

Appleby regarded Thornton with cool detachment. "I was suggesting that we make Shakespeare our postmaster."

Shakespeare gaped at Luke in astonishment. "I'm not sure that I'm the right person," he stammered.

Logan, who stood next to Libby, holding Noel in his arms, disagreed. "Of course you are!" When Shakespeare continued to look unconvinced, Logan turned to the others. "How many think that Shakespeare is the right person for the job?"

A hundred or more hands shot in the air. Logan smiled at Libby. "See? What did I tell you?"

Shakespeare shook his head. "But you don't understand . . ."

"There's nothing to understand!" Appleby argued. "This is a democracy. Didn't you just see us take a vote? That means that you are the new postmaster whether or not you want to be."

Logan whispered in Libby's ear. "With logic like that, Appleby should run for president."

Big Sam waved his old felt hat. "All right, boys, now that we have ourselves an official postmaster, what do you say we get busy and build the best little post office in the West."

In less than three days, the building was finished and young Jimmy Hooper was hired to ride to Sacramento City to pick up mail. He was given a list of names and would be paid a dollar a letter.

The day he rode into town with a leather bag filled with mail, the miners ran from the saloons and shops along Main Street, throwing their hats in the air and shouting.

Curious as to what the commotion was about, Libby ran out to her porch. Upon catching sight of Jimmy, she pressed her hands to her chest and said a silent prayer that among the letters would be one for her.

It had been so long since she'd heard from her family, not since she'd left the boardinghouse. Perhaps that's why she was having such a hard time lately, recalling memories of home. Boston seemed so far away, like a half-forgotten dream.

Her thoughts were suddenly interrupted by the realization that Logan stood watching her from his own porch. Not even the distance between them lessened the heat of his gaze. Having had no time to brace herself, she was jolted by the river of hot blood that coursed through her body. Shaken by the effect and wanting so much to deny how the mere sight of him affected her, she forced an overly bright smile and waved.

Despite the distance between them, Logan had not missed the look of longing on her face before she was aware of his presence. It wasn't hard to guess that she was feeling homesick. Nor had he missed the annoying way his heart started hammering against his ribs as soon as he stepped outside and saw her. Did she know? Could she guess how he felt? Could she hear his heart pounding from where she stood? Did he only imagine the jolting impact when she glanced his way?

Whether he imagined any of this or not, it didn't much matter. It was going to be hard to lose her.

He'd become so accustomed to having her around, he'd almost forgotten that she would soon be gone. If Jimmy could make such good time traveling to Sacramento City and back, the roads, or at least the main ones, must be open. That could only mean that the stagecoach would soon roll through town, taking Libby with it.

He dreaded the thought of losing her, dreaded it so much, it was all he could do to keep from rushing across the street and begging her to stay. But it would be wrong. He knew it would be wrong. No matter how much they fixed up the town, it could never offer Libby the kind of life she had in Boston.

When he didn't return her wave, she waved again. This time she hung over the rail to make certain he saw her. Feeling sick at heart, cursing the day he met her and the circumstances that kept him from her, he lifted his hand in response.

Libby rose early the next morning. She quickly bathed and dressed before waking Noel. She was so anxious to collect her mail, she couldn't wait for him to wake on his own. In no time at all, she'd fed and bathed him, then dressed him in his little buckskin suit.

She was tempted to wear her buckskin dress. Logan had altered it as promised and the soft buckskin hugged the curves of her body so precisely, she blushed in memory of the night he had rubbed lifesaving warmth into her naked body. How was it possible for him to remember the exact width of her hips, her shoulders? To know how much room to allow for the fullness of her breasts? Surprised to find herself trembling suddenly, she put the buckskin dress away and settled for the safety of her calico.

The sky was partly cloudy as she stepped outside, and the air turned brisk whenever the sun took cover. Despite the early hour, a line of men, anxious for news from home, snaked from the post office all the way down Main Street.

In fine gentlemanly style, the miners insisted that Miss Libby, as most of them called her, go to the head of the line. Libby thanked each man in turn as she made her way toward the post office entrance where the line began.

Inside, a noisy dissent was in progress. Curious as to the nature of the argument, Libby peered through the open door into the small lobby of the post office.

She was shocked to see that Appleby had Shakespeare by the collar. Shakespeare's eyes bulged and his face was turning the most alarming shade of red.

"Luke Appleby!" she protested. "What is the meaning of this?"

At the sound of her voice, Appleby released Shakespeare and his face reddened. "I'm sorry, Libby, but we can't let an employee get away with not doing his job."

Libby looked past Appleby to Shakespeare, who appeared close to fainting. "I don't understand. What did Shakespeare fail to do?"

"I'll show you what he failed to do." Luke ripped open the little gate leading behind the counter and motioned her to follow him. He pointed to an enormous heap of mail that was scattered about the floor. "That is what he didn't do!"

Libby stared at the unsorted mail in dismay. "Why not, Shakespeare?" she asked. "Why didn't you sort the mail?"

Choo-Choo craned his neck to peer over the counter. "That's what I want to know!"

Shakespeare kept his eyes lowered as he stared at the floor. "Well ... I ... The truth of the matter is I can't read."

The miners who were close enough to hear this confession gasped in disbelief.

"What do you mean, you can't read?" Sharkey demanded.

Shakespeare's already red face turned scarlet. "I never had any occasion to learn," he explained. He glanced anxiously at Libby. "It's not that I was stupid or anything," he assured her.

He looked so forlorn, she gave him an encouraging pat on the arm. "I never thought you were."

Sharkey looked stunned. "What I want to know is how yuh can go 'round quotin' all that highfalutin lit'rary stuff if yuh can't read."

Big Sam folded his arms across his chest. "Yeah, how did you do that?"

"I grew up in a house directly behind a theater," Shakespeare explained. "I could hear the actors on stage from my bedroom window. After listening to the same plays night after night, I eventually came to memorize them."

"Well, I'll be!" Big Sam said, clearly awed.

Sharkey wrung his hands together. "This is a fine pur-dicament! A fine pur-dicament!"

The miners had now abandoned the orderly line outside and were trying to squeeze through the door to see what was going on. Those who were close enough to hear Shakespeare's startling confession demanded his resignation.

Shakespeare stood looking dejected and embarrassed.

Libby, feeling sorry for him, flew to his defense. Soon a noisy debate ensued. The miners put in their two bits' worth whether or not they had two bits' worth to say. Libby asserted her womanly rights and tossed in considerably more.

Meanwhile, Logan rode into town, a freshly bagged rabbit hung from his saddle. His way down Main Street was blocked by the commotion in front of the post office.

He cast a worried glance over the heads of the milling crowd to the open door of the post office. His anxiety increased upon hearing Libby's voice loud and clear. He'd heard that particular tone of voice a couple of times previously. Once, just before she threw a knife at him.

Grimacing against the pain in his leg, he dismounted, tied his horse to a hitching post in front of one of the saloons, and pushed his way through the crowd.

Inside he found Libby and Appleby practically nose to nose. They were surrounded by spectators who stared in openmouthed fascination at the most astounding display of feminine indignation the majority of them had ever witnessed. "You stubborn, mule-headed, knuckle-brained . . ."

Logan pushed his way to her side. She didn't miss a

syllable as he took Noel from her, freeing her to put her fists on her hips and continue her spiel unimpeded.

Logan leaned toward Sharkey. "Would you mind telling me what's going on?"

"Appleby asked for Shakespeare's r'signation."

"Why's that?"

"Can't read worth a pail of spit."

Logan straightened and moved Noel to his other arm. Any moment now, she was bound to run out of steam.

"All right," Appleby conceded at last. "What do you suggest we do? Continue to pay Shakespeare for doing nothing?"

"I never suggested such a thing," Libby said. "Shakespeare will learn to read."

Shakespeare looked startled. "I will? I mean I will!"

Sharkey looked dubious. "What are we s'pposed to do meantime?"

"Just leave it to me," Libby said. She turned to the men who stood waiting patiently to see how the matter was going to be resolved. "If you will be kind enough to leave, and I promise you that by tomorrow morning, we will have your mail ready for pickup."

There was a lot of a-mumbling and a-grumbling, as Sharkey described it, but in the end it was decided that another day without their mail wasn't going to make a whole lot of difference.

After the crowd had disbanded, Libby told Shakespeare to lock the door and put up the "closed" sign.

Logan circled the mountain of mail that was stacked on the floor, shaking his head. "You aren't going to sort this all by yourself, are you, Libby?"

"Of course not." She looked at him through the fringe of her lashes. "I was thinking that you might be kind enough to help."

He met her eyes. "Well, now . . ."

For the rest of that day, the three of them worked. Logan left for a short time to purchase cheese and dried meat from Hap, along with hot coffee.

Whenever it was Noel's feeding, Libby sat in a chair facing the wall and nursed him discreetly while the two men sorted and stacked behind her.

Shakespeare was taught how to read a few letters at a time. His first job was to go through the mail looking for names beginning with the letter "S."

"S for Shakespeare," he announced proudly each time he found one.

After he had sorted out all the S's, Libby asked him what letter he wanted to learn next. He thought a moment. "What's the letter for Libby?"

"L," she replied.

His mind made up, he gave her a determined look. "That's the letter I want to learn. L for Libby."

She drew some samples of the letter L on a piece of paper and laid it in front of him. "This is a printed L and this is how it looks in handwriting. See the way it loops on the top?"

Shakespeare traced the letters she wrote with the tip of a finger. "L for Libby."

While she worked in the back room with Shakespeare, Logan stayed in front and sorted mail into the tiny cubicles that were designed for the purpose.

It was dark by the time Libby joined him, bringing him a stack that had been presorted by Shakespeare. "Here's some more S's," she said.

His fingers brushed against hers as he took the stack from her.

She pulled her hand away quickly and pressed it against the cool fabric of her skirt. Suddenly she was having a hard time breathing. "Shakespeare's catching on quickly."

Logan glanced through the door leading to the back room. Shakespeare was sitting on the floor bent over a stack of mail. Next to him, Noel slept in a box lined with newspapers and fur skins for warmth.

Logan turned to face her fully and she heard him inhale. Her heart nearly stopped as she recognized the smoldering flames in his eyes as desire. His heated gaze dropped from her eyes to her lips and she trembled with anticipation.

The saner more rational part of her told her to back away, to leave at once while she still could. Tenacity made her stand firmly in place, helped in part by her own aching need to be near him.

"Is . . . is everything all right?" she ventured.

He lifted his eyes away from her lips. "Why wouldn't it be?"

Disconcerted by the thoughts that assailed her, she blurted out the first thing that came to mind. "I thought maybe your leg was bothering you . . ." She regretted her thoughtless words even before she felt his withdrawal. Too late, she tried to amend her error, only to make matters worse. "You've been standing on it for hours."

He turned away brusquely. "Nothing's wrong with my leg!" He began shoving envelopes into evenly spaced slots.

Stung by his abrupt manner, she quietly left the room, fighting back hot tears.

Less than an hour later he motioned to her from the adjoining doorway. Anxious to end the tension between them, she followed him into the other room, prepared to apologize.

He never gave her a chance. Instead, he handed her a letter. "I believe this is for you."

She took the envelope from him and immediately recognized the neat dainty handwriting as her mother's. "Oh, Logan!" She flung her arms around his neck. "Oh, thank you, thank you!"

It felt so good to be in his arms, her body pressed next to his. When she looked up at him, her heart sang out with elation and joy. For in his eyes was more than desire this time, more than passion. What she saw was love.

What he saw filled him with awe and wonder. It was love. In her eyes. Love for him. He could see it. Feel it. Taste it. God help him, he could even touch it. Why had he not known that such a miraculous, wonderful thing existed?

Feeling like he was floating on a cloud, he lowered his head and angled his mouth against hers. He traced the soft fullness of her lips with his own, before plunging his tongue into the secret recesses of her mouth.

Pleasantly surprised by her response, he raised his head and looked deeply into her eyes as if to confirm what her lips told him to be true. He then slipped his hands from her waist to her buttocks and jerked her toward him until she was pressed hard against his torrid body.

"What's Noel's letter?"

No sooner had Shakespeare's questioning voice penetrated her runaway senses than she pushed Logan away with quick urgency. He looked startled at first, then glared at Shakespeare in annoyance.

Libby reached out to touch his arm beseechingly. It wasn't Shakespeare's fault. Logan gave her a long hard look before turning back to his work.

Her cheeks flaming red, she turned toward Shakespeare, ready to stammer her way through some sort of explanation. Fortunately, Shakespeare's head was lowered, his full attention focused onto the envelope in his hand. It was obvious he'd noticed nothing out of the ordinary.

She struggled to find her voice. "Noel's name begins with the letter N. I'll show you." She glanced back at Logan. His back was straight, his shoulders squared.

It occurred to her that Logan's kiss had only confused matters between them. Neither one of them had wanted for this to happen. Now that it had, how could they not acknowledge the feelings that went with it?

Heaving a heavy sigh, she followed Shakespeare into the other room, her mother's unopened letter still clutched in her hand.

A short time later she sat on a wooden crate close to where Noel was sleeping and tore open the envelope.

Her fingers shook as she unfolded the parchment letter. Aware, suddenly, that her mouth still burned with the memory of Logan's kiss, she wet her lips with her tongue in an effort to cool them down. She'd been shaking ever since she'd left Logan's arms.

Before commencing to read, she glanced through the open doorway and, just as she supposed, found Logan watching her. He looked as confused and shaken by what had happened as she felt.

She quickly averted her eyes to the letter she held in her trembling hands. It took a great deal of effort to concentrate on the ornate handwriting that filled the page.

Her mother wrote about Christmas and the blizzard that struck Boston two days before. The Christmas menu was described down to the last detail. Each guest was mentioned by name, along with her mother's usual astute observations.

It bothered Libby that the letter failed to bring the usual warm memories of home flooding back. It was as if the family members mentioned in the letter were little more than strangers. Feeling guilty, she reread the letter. *Your Aunt Alice is expecting again, although, naturally, she didn't breathe a word about it to a soul. But I could see it in her eyes.*

After rereading the letter, Libby slipped it back into the envelope and tucked it into her pocket for safe-keeping. Her mother was always talking about what she could see in a person's eyes. Libby shuddered to think what conclusions her mother would draw if she were in the room with her now.

Conscious of her still flaming cheeks, she kept her head lowered and her eyes carefully averted as she went back to work.

She and Logan spoke not a word to each other in the hours that followed. Fortunately, Shakespeare's incessant chatter filled the uneasy silence that stretched between them. He was delighted with his ever-increasing knowledge of the alphabet and his confidence grew with every stack he sorted.

Libby praised his successes and gently pointed out any errors. But it was hard to keep her mind on her work after what had happened earlier with Logan.

Despite her resolutions, she couldn't seem to keep from staring at Logan's back as he worked. She found a certain satisfaction in rediscovering the little details that she'd taken for granted in the past.

She loved the way his fringe—whangs, as he called them—hung from his arm as he raised it to insert a letter in an overhead slot. It still intrigued her to watch his broad shoulders test the limits of his buckskin shirt. Allowing her gaze to follow the outline of his hard, lean hips to his strong, sturdy thighs, she was reminded of the many nights she'd lain in the semidarkness of his cabin and secretly watched him undress.

How she hated to admit even to herself that every night since moving into her own cabin, she wished she were back with him.

She might have stood there in the foyer of the post office watching him indefinitely had he not glanced over his shoulders and caught her in the act. With a guilty start, she bent over to sort the last stack of mail.

When at last the mail had been sorted, the three of them stood gazing proudly at the mail-filled slots. Shakespeare was ecstatic. "I can't believe it," he exclaimed. "I can read. I can actually read."

He was so pleased with himself, Libby didn't have the heart to tell him there was more to reading than simply recognizing the letters of the alphabet. There would be time enough later to break this news to him.

Exhausted from the long day, Libby decided to take Noel home. Logan offered to escort her, but she insisted that he stay awhile longer to help Shakespeare finish up.

Logan followed her outside. "Libby, about what happened . . ." He searched her face.

Chapter 27

IT was two weeks before the novelty of Calico Corners having its very own post office wore off, and the line of miners in front diminished in length. With each passing day, Shakespeare grew more proficient in his job. He became so good at what he was doing, he was soon able to sort the mail within a day of receiving it from Sacramento City.

Although the nights were still cool, the days grew gradually warmer. More and more miners exchanged hammers and saws for pickaxes and gold pans and returned to their claims. The men left early in the morning, and as a rule didn't return until after nightfall, at which time they were either disgruntled or elated, depending on the day's haul.

Although the miners never resorted to their earlier bouts of wild behavior and followed the laws agreed upon to the full extent, Libby sensed a tension settle upon the town. It was nothing she could put her finger on. But it was as apparent to her as the covering of fine dust she was forced to wipe off her furniture each day.

Although she questioned several men, no one wanted to admit there was a problem. Even Logan shrugged off her concerns. "The men are homesick, is all."

She accepted this explanation until that particular Wednesday afternoon when she stopped to talk to Macao, and inadvertently learned the truth. Earlier in the week, she had sent some of her baking soda biscuits to the area in the hills known as Chinatown.

Macao stopped her in the middle of Main Street to tell her how much he and his friends had enjoyed them.

Afterward, Appleby followed her into the general store and cornered her in front of the candlewax display. "I don't think it's a good idea for you to be seen in public talking to Macao." He spoke softly so as not to be heard by the other customers. "There's still those in town who resent the fact that the Chinese are the ones who named the town."

"Macao's my friend," Libby replied.

"I don't want you to get hurt."

"Hurt? How?"

"Some of the boys are afraid that the Chinese will be running the town before long."

"That's ridiculous," Libby protested. "They're not interested in running the town. They only want to have a say. What's so wrong with that?"

"You know it's against the law for the Chinese to stake a claim. Up until now, we've kind of looked the other way. It didn't matter much. We thought there was enough gold for everyone."

"Isn't there?"

"I don't know if there is or not. But now that the boys know how many Chinese are in the area, they decided it's time to enforce the law."

"So the Chinese can't mine for gold?"

"That's right, Libby. The problem is Macao and his men have decided to retaliate by picking up gold in the cover of night. Now that the waters are beginning to recede, nuggets can be found along the banks of the river."

Libby gave a satisfied nod. "Well, it serves the miners right." She studied Appleby's face, sensing there was more. "Is there something you're not telling me?"

He rubbed his chin and said nothing.

"Luke Appleby, I insist!" One or two of the other miners in the shop turned to look at them, and she lowered her voice. "I insist that you tell me everything."

"Very well." Appleby waited until the other customers had turned back to what they were doing. "Benjamin Jacobs took it upon himself to post shotgun guards along the riverbanks at night. The guards have orders to fire at anyone seen picking up nuggets."

Libby felt sick. During the last few weeks, she'd come to care for these miners and it had been easy to discount the town's earlier reputation for lawlessness. The weather had kept the men from mining their claims. The lust for gold had lain as dormant as the snow-covered ground. She knew this, of course, knew that once the men could return to the diggings, greed would once again become the ruling force. She supposed it was only inevitable that hate and prejudice would also rear their ugly heads.

Appleby looked so concerned as he studied Libby's face, she couldn't help but feel sorry for him. He had only her best interests at heart. "I'm much obliged to you, Luke, for being honest with me."

"I think it's only right that you should know the danger you and Noel could be in should you continue to befriend Macao."

"Macao is my friend," she said simply. "Nothing is going to change that."

During the two weeks following the kiss in the post office, Libby's sleep had been filled with disturbing dreams. But now that she knew about the shotgun guards, sleep was altogether impossible.

One night after hearing what sounded like gunfire in the distance, Libby crept out of bed and lifted a window, hoping to prove she was mistaken. Shivering against the cold night air, she stuck her head outside. A line of bobbing Chinese lanterns traveled along the crest of a distant hill. This time, there was no mistaking the sound of gunfire.

Early the next morning, she cornered Logan just as he was saddling his horse. Since the night spent at the post office, they'd spoken only on rare occasions. But this was no time to let personal feelings interfere.

"Logan, I couldn't sleep last night for the shooting in the hills."

With a grim nod of his head, Logan reached beneath the saddle flap to tighten the girth. Judging by the shadows beneath his eyes, he, too, had lost his share of sleep in recent nights.

"Can't you do something about the situation?" she pleaded. "Someone is going to be killed."

Logan's jaw tightened. "There's nothing I can do. They're only following the law."

"What kind of law allows for a man to be shot down for doing nothing more than pocket a few nuggets?"

"I can't change how things are, Libby. If I could I would, don't you know that?"

Suddenly they weren't talking about unfair laws; they were talking about the two of them. Unable to think of a suitable reply, Libby watched in silence as he mounted his horse and rode away.

The next night Libby was awakened by a loud knocking. She threw a shawl over her linen nightgown and hurried to the door. "Who is it?" she called out.

"It's Macao."

She fumbled with the bolt and threw open the door. "I've been shot," he said hoarsely. "My shoulder . . ."

"Oh, no!" she gasped, horrified. "Quick, inside!" She slammed the door shut and led him through the dark room to the couch. She lit a lantern and set it on a nearby table.

She was shocked by how he looked. His face was pale, almost waxen in appearance, and one of his sleeves was soaked in blood. She quickly reached in her sewing basket for her gold scissors. After cutting the red-stained tunic away from his shoulder, she examined his wound. "The bullet's going to have to come out."

Macao nodded his head ever so slightly, but said nothing.

With clarity of thought that surprised her given the circumstances, she calmly sized up the situation. She guessed the bullet was deep, which meant it would require an experienced hand. Logan was the only man she knew who was qualified to perform such a task.

"Stay here," she whispered. "I'm going for help."

"No!" He reached for her arm, but he was too weak to hold on for long. "Don't know . . . who to trust."

She squeezed his alarmingly cold hand and felt it tremble in the curve of her fingers. "I can trust Logan." She spoke with total conviction. "And so can you."

His head rolled back, and his eyes crossed as he struggled to stay conscious. He was growing weaker by the moment, and he obviously knew his choices were limited. "Do what you must, Missee Libby." With a dull thud his head fell back against the couch.

She pressed a clean flour sack against his wound. "I'll be back in a minute." She opened the door and held her breath as she monitored the sounds of the night. Except for the musical strains of a fiddle filtering from one of the saloons, the night was quiet.

She ran down the steps and across the road to Logan's cabin. She banged on the door with both fists. "Hurry," she whispered to herself. She only hoped he was home and not playing cards. To her relief, the door swung open. She was so glad to see him, she could barely talk. "I need your help!"

Logan looked startled. "Is something wrong with Noel?"

"No," she whispered urgently, "it's Macao. He's been shot."

"I'll be right there."

Not wanting to leave Macao alone a moment longer than necessary, Libby raced back to her cabin, leaving the door ajar. The Chinese man failed to stir when she pressed the cloth against his wound to stop the alarming flow of blood.

Logan arrived moments later and with practiced fingers felt Macao's pulse. Libby found his commanding presence comforting. Right now, she needed someone strong. He straightened and drew his knife from its sheath. "Run the blade through the fire."

Grateful for something tangible to do, she took the knife from him and dropped to her knees in front of the fireplace. She ran the blade through the flames as she had watched Logan do in the past. Behind her, Logan lifted the slightly built man onto the table.

Logan held the lantern high as he leaned over Macao's motionless body. "The bullet is deep. It may have damaged a nerve. We need alcohol."

Libby handed him the knife and reached in a cupboard for a bottle of whiskey.

"We need clean cloths and you'd better bring a blanket. He's going into shock." As an afterthought, he added, "We also need pincers."

Libby raced around the room gathering up the things he asked for. In her haste, she accidentally knocked over the little dream keeper that Macao had given Noel, and it fell to the floor with a clunk next to Logan's necessary bag. Fearful that this was a bad omen, she quickly scooped up the box and placed it on the mantel.

Logan set the lantern down and stretched out his leg.

Libby bit back the urge to ask him about it or to let on that she noticed his discomfort. Instead, she set the supplies on the table and took her place opposite him.

Taking the knife in his hand, he looked across at her. "Ready?"

Her heart fluttered nervously. She'd never witnessed surgery, but knowing that Macao's life hung in the balance, she swallowed her fears, lifted her chin, and nodded. "Ready."

Logan leaned over Macao's still body and carefully

worked the tip of his knife into the wound at his shoulder.

Libby averted her eyes and willed herself to remain strong. Except when he requested more cloths or alcohol, Logan worked in silence. She watched his face, looking for something that would tell her if Macao was going to make it. The last time Logan had looked so intense was the night she gave birth to Noel. Only then, he looked wild, almost panicked. Tonight, he was in full control; his jaw was clenched in concentration, his brow lined with deep furrows.

At last he dropped his knife into a basin of water and called for the pincers. Their fingers touched lightly as she handed them to him. His eyes met hers and for a moment they shared their unspoken concern for the man who lay between them.

Logan carefully worked the pincers into the wound. Time passed. She jumped when Logan cursed, and chanced a worried look at Macao's face. The man lay so still, it was hard to know if he was still alive.

Finally, Logan straightened and held the pincers up, a bloodied bullet caught in the metal grip.

Libby breathed a sigh of relief and grabbed a handful of clean linen, which she carefully pressed against the wound while Logan washed his hands in the basin of water she'd set out for him.

"I'm going to have to sew that up," he said. "I'll need a needle and thread."

She waited for him to take over for her, then rummaged through her sewing supplies until she located several needles. "Which one will work best?" She laid them out on the edge of the table for him to see.

He chose the fine-pointed bone needle he'd crafted himself. She handed him flaxen thread, but he decided to use buffalo sinew.

"It's easier to work with and it's stronger," he explained. "I have some back at the cabin. Here, hold on to this." He indicated the cloth pressed against the wound. She moved to his side and placed her hands according to his instructions.

He checked Macao's pulse. The face of the unconscious man was pale and clammy to the touch. "He's breathing steadily." Logan surprised her by laying his hand against her cool pale cheek.

"Are you all right?" he whispered, his eyes filled with concern.

She bit her lip and nodded, and apparently satisfied, he headed toward the door. "I'll be back in a minute." As an afterthought, he added, "Don't let anyone else in."

Logan returned moments later, bringing with him a leather pouch filled with various supplies. Locating the card wrapped with buffalo sinew, he threaded the bone needle and with nimble fingers quickly sewed up Macao's wound.

"Where did you learn to do surgery?" she asked.

"In the wilderness." He refused the scissors she offered him, preferring to use his knife to cut the thread. "A trapper better know how to take care of himself, otherwise he isn't going to last long. I know one trapper who was forced to cut off his own leg."

Libby's eyes rounded in disbelief. "How awful. Is he all right?"

"Last I heard, he was fit as a fiddle."

She replenished the water in the basin with fresh hot water and handed him a bar of lye soap. He carefully scrubbed his hands and his supplies while she wiped away the blood from Macao's shoulder.

"That's about all we can do for now. Do you want me to take him back to my cabin?"

She glanced back at Macao's face. He was still a ghastly white color. "I don't think we ought to move him."

Logan checked the patch of matted beaver hair that stopped bleeding, in his opinion, far better than any other styptic. "Why don't you get some sleep? I'll watch him."

"Logan ... thank you. I don't know what I would have done without you."

"It could be dangerous, you know, his being here." She lifted her chin. "No matter. He must stay."

Macao woke before dawn. He was weak but lucid and, at Libby's gentle but firm prodding, drank a cup of hot tea. Logan had added the crushed leaves of the yerba buena plant to the tea. The plant, which was used to ward off fever, grew almost exclusively above the hills of what was now known as San Francisco. The city had originally been called Yerba Buena after the noble plant, and Logan could not understand why San Francisco was thought to be an improvement on the former name.

Logan carefully removed the matted beaver fur from Macao's wound. "No redness," he said, "and so far no sign of fever."

While Logan applied wild mountain mushrooms to the wound, another infection-fighting method he swore by, Libby poured Macao more tea. "Would you like something to eat?" she asked. "I can heat up some of the biscuits you like so much."

Macao shook his head. "Nothing to eat." He glanced anxiously at the door. "I must leave while it's still dark, Missee Libby. If anyone knows I'm here, it could mean trouble for you and your little one."

"You're not going anywhere," Libby insisted. "Now lie back and get some rest." He needed no further encouragement. He laid his head against the pillow and in only a few moments his even breathing told her he had fallen fast asleep.

Logan drew the blanket over Macao and once again checked his forehead.

Logan looked exhausted and his limp was more pronounced than usual. She watched him slump down in a chair and pop a square of willow bark into his mouth. She walked over to him and ran her hands along his back and neck. He tensed beneath her touch, but soon the rigid tautness left his body. A contented sigh escaped him, and as her fingers moved down the length of his back, his sigh was followed by a moan of pleasure.

Her hands absorbed the essence and the feel of him until at last she was forced to pull away or risk flinging herself into his arms. He surprised her by spinning around and grabbing her by the wrist. With a soft, anguished sigh, he pressed her hand against the warmth of his neck.

Heart pounding, she stroked his head with her other hand. The feel of his dark silky hair against her palm filled her with pleasure. "I don't know how I can ever thank you for saving Macao's life."

He kissed the knuckles of her hand and released her. "I'd better go," he said, knowing that if he didn't leave, he might do something he would later come to regret.

"Yes, you'd better," she agreed. *Because if you don't leave at this very moment, I won't be able to let you go at all.*

"Don't let anyone in."

"I won't."

With a nod toward Macao, Logan held Libby's gaze a moment longer than either could bear, before opening the door a crack to make certain the way was clear.

No sooner had the door closed behind him than Macao spoke in a low, weak voice. "That's a good man, Missee Libby."

She rushed to his side to see if there was anything he needed.

"Is it possible that you and he . . . ?"

The ache in Libby's heart deepened. "My place is in Boston and Logan belongs up north in beaver country."

Macao looked surprised. "I thought it was only us Chinese who were bound to the rules of our birthright."

She cleared her voice and changed the subject. "You should eat something. You lost a lot of blood."

"I must leave."

"You're in no condition to go anywhere."

"I cannot stay here. My presence puts you and your little one in grave danger."

"The miners would never hurt me or Noel."

"They would not mean to. But there is much hatred for my countrymen. Hatred does strange things to a man's mind."

"Please, let's not talk about hatred." From the next room came the sound of Noel's cry. Libby was torn between trying to persuade Macao to stay and attending to her young son's needs. "Please, Macao," she begged, "please stay. After I feed Noel, I'll fix you some breakfast."

"You are a good friend," Macao said, his voice almost inaudible. "I shall never be able to repay your kindness."

"The only thing I want is for you to make a complete recovery."

Noel's first tentative cries had now turned into high-pitched wails.

"Go to your son." When she hesitated, he added, "We will discuss my situation later."

Taking this to be his promise to stay, she left the wounded man's side and hurried to Noel's room. "Good morning, young man."

At the sound of her voice, Noel stopped crying. She picked him up, holding him close, and was almost overcome with the love she felt for him. "You aren't going to grow up hating anyone, are you, my dear sweet son? Promise Mama."

Noel cooed as she changed him, and then nursed hungrily at her breasts.

After attending to his physical needs, she carried him out to join Macao, but the room was empty and there was no sign of him anywhere outside.

She hated having to wake Logan, but felt she had no choice. After wrapping Noel in a blanket, she donned her shawl and slipped out the door.

The sun was just beginning to spread its warmth across the valley. A bird warbled from a treetop, filling the clear morning air with its lovely sweet song. Compelled to act as normal as possible, she resisted the urge to quicken her steps.

Logan's door opened before she knocked and she wondered if he had been watching for her. Or had he simply sensed her presence as she had so often sensed his. "He's gone." Her voice was hushed, but even so, Logan stepped outside to glance up and down the street before hustling her inside and firmly bolting the door shut.

"He was afraid his presence here would cause problems for Noel and me."

"I'm afraid he's right."

"This is terrible! All this hatred."

"I don't suppose you have to worry about hatred in Boston."

Libby laid Noel on the table and moved the blanket away from his face. "I wish that were true." She felt a guilty start at the realization that she'd never given the matter much thought in the past. She'd heard the talk in the elegant parlors and at the fancy dress balls, heard the hatred directed at the Italians who had recently flooded the city. Still, she'd not considered the implications or thought to take a stand. "I'm afraid Boston has its own prejudices."

Logan folded his arms across his chest. "Why, Libby, I can't believe my ears. You can't mean it. Calico Corners has something in common with Boston?"

"Don't make light of this, Logan. This is too serious. Would you watch Noel while I go to Chinatown? I've got to know if Macao's all right."

He grabbed her arm. "I can't let you do that. It could be dangerous and you have Noel to think about."

"Are you saying I would be a better mother to Noel if I stay here and do nothing to help someone in need?"

He released her and turned to stare at the fire, his hand on the mantel. "I'll go."

"I can't ask you to do that."

He turned his head to meet her gaze. "You didn't."

Chapter 28

DURING the week to follow, Logan made nightly trips to the wooden shanties that clung to the hills above Calico Corners in the area known as Chinatown.

Macao lived in a flimsy wooden shack with two other men. During each visit, Logan changed Macao's bandages and dispensed whatever healing plants he'd brought with him.

After each visit, he stopped at Libby's house, knowing how anxiously she awaited his latest report on Macao's condition. What he told her varied little from one night to the next. The wound was healing, with no sign of infection. For the most part, Macao seemed to have regained his strength.

At first Libby received his reports with relief and thanksgiving, but gradually she grew uneasy and suspected that Logan was holding something back. Logan denied it, and she decided it was only her imagination. But when he appeared on her doorstep late that Friday night, he looked troubled.

Logan sat warming himself by the fire while she poured him a cup of hot tea. She then sat down on the hearth next to his feet and braced herself for the bad news she was certain he'd come to tell her. "Logan?"

He regarded her solemnly. Not even the light from the fire could chase away the shadow of worry at his brow.

"He has no feeling in his right arm."

For a moment she stared at him in relieved silence. Compared to the fate she'd imagined, this was encouraging news. Macao was still alive and that's what counted, but she kept her thoughts to herself. Logan would never understand.

In the short time she'd known Logan, she'd come to realize that a trapper prized physical strength and endurance above all else. She understood this, at least in part. An injured leg—or in Macao's case, an injured arm—could make the difference between life and death in the wilds.

She also knew that, unlike Logan, Macao was a man of the soul. While Logan communed with nature, Macao tapped into the spiritual world. While Logan heeded the wind, Macao took counsel from his long-departed ancestors. His physical being held little or no significance to him.

Still, Logan looked so depressed, she probed for more. "Is . . . is there anything else?"

Her question brought a dark look to Logan's face.

"Isn't that enough?" he asked bitterly, and she knew he was thinking of his own leg. Regretting her careless words, she laid her hand on his arm. "I didn't mean that like it sounded. But knowing Macao . . ."

As if regretting his brusqueness, he covered her hand with his own and nodded. "He lacks spirit. He does nothing but sit and stare into space. He keeps saying that he's going home horizontally."

Libby gasped. "He thinks he's going to die?"

"I'm afraid so. And you know for a Chinese man, to die on foreign soil is the worse possible fate."

Libby closed her eyes momentarily, feeling a strange kinship with Macao. She knew all too well how it felt to be deprived of home and loved ones, to be so consumed by homesickness that it was almost impossible to perform the normal duties of everyday life. "Do *you* think he's going to die?"

"I think a man dies when he wants to die."

She inhaled deeply. She pulled her hand away and stared into the fire, her forehead wrinkled in thought. She had precious little money left from her savings and was reluctant to dip into the funds she'd put aside to pay for her travel expenses back home. She would if she had to, of course. She'd do anything for a friend, even if it meant taking in more wash to replenish her funds—a chore she dreaded above all else.

It wasn't until after Logan had left for the night that another idea occurred to her.

The Golden Hind Gambling Hall and Saloon was packed to capacity that Saturday night. The men were growing restless and bored. The weather had turned cold again, and temperatures had dipped below freezing. The ground had frozen up at the diggings and the mines had produced slim pickings.

Logan sat at the table watching the cards being dealt. Although he frowned in concentration, his mind was not on the game; he was thinking of Macao. The man grew more listless with each passing day. Logan had purposely avoided stopping at Libby's house earlier that evening. He hadn't wanted to tell her that her friend had stopped eating altogether, and that his already slender frame had been reduced to mere bones.

"Your bid, Logan," Sharkey prodded.

Logan picked up a stack of gold coins from his cache and placed them in the pot. With a grin, he fanned his cards on the table.

A collective groan rose as the other men threw down their cards.

Beaker glared down his pointed nose at Logan. "Your deal."

Logan picked up the cards and shuffled them. They were the thin Spanish cards that he preferred. The Golden Hind was the only place in town that used these particular cards. He looked up as Benjamin Jacobs walked up to the table.

"Mind dealing me in?"

Swallowing back his dislike of the man, Logan dealt the cards. "Aren't you on guard duty tonight?"

Benjamin lifted a corner of his mouth as if he relished the thought. "From midnight till dawn."

"How many chinks you gonna git tonight?" a man called from one of the other tables and laughed.

Benjamin yanked out a chair and sat down. "Many as I kin," he replied.

Logan picked up his own cards, aware of a buzz of excitement behind him.

Sharkey's voice cut through the murmur. "Why, look who's come to visit us."

Big Sam turned from the rowdy group at the bar and shouted, "Why, if it's not Miz Libby. The most beautiful lady in the West."

Logan swung around in his chair to see for himself. "What the hell . . . ?"

Seemingly oblivious to the attention she was drawing, Libby whispered something in Appleby's ear. Thornton stood by her side holding Noel straight out in front of him like the boy was the dasher of a butter churn or something.

Big Sam cursed and stormed across the room, waving his arms about his body like a broken windmill. "What did I tell yer 'bout holding a baby? Where's the center of gravity?" He reached for Noel and demonstrated, cupping the baby's head in his powerful black hand as he pointed to the baby's middle. He glared at Thornton. "The center, you jackass!"

Meanwhile, Appleby walked to the middle of the empty dance floor. "Gentlemen," he said grandly, hooking his thumbs into his bright red suspenders. "The lady requests your undivided attention."

"The lady always has me undivided attention," one of the miners yelled out. This was followed by loud hoots and hollers.

Libby walked to the center of the dance floor. "Thank you." She waited for the crowd to settle down before she continued in a clear voice. "The reason I'm here is because I'm taking up a collection for a very

worthy cause. One of my friends, a gentlemen by the
name of Macao, wants to go back to his homeland."

Logan groaned inward as Libby made it clear what
she had on her mind. Fool woman! Didn't she know
the danger she was putting herself in? The miners
pretty near worshiped Libby and her son. But whether
the men's affection for Libby outweighed their hatred
for foreigners was anybody's guess.

Not wanting to chance it, Logan rested his hand on
his gun, ready for action at the first sign of trouble.

"I would be most grateful for any donations to this
very worthy cause." She paused a moment and let her
gaze travel from one man to the other, beseeching as
many as was possible by way of a sweeping glance. "I
know from experience how very generous all of you
are. I come to you tonight as a friend."

Logan's jaw tightened as he watched her. She
couldn't have looked more cheerfully unconcerned if
she were asking for bids at a box-lunch social!

Logan glared at Thornton. Why hadn't the damned
man stopped her? He had to know the danger she was
putting herself in.

Following her appeal, a tense silence filled the
room. The kind of silence that precedes trouble.

Across from Logan, Benjamin Jacobs, the man responsible for Macao's injuries, flicked the extended
handle of his mustache with a finger.

Logan decided to act before things got out of hand.
He swung his stiff leg around and stood. Although he
spoke to the crowd, his eyes were on Libby. "I think
the lady has a splendid idea. I say that ten percent of
any winnings should go to the cause."

Jacobs looked meaner than a rattler as he turned to
object. But before he could speak his mind, Appleby
piped up. "I feel lucky tonight. What could ten percent
hurt?"

Big Sam, satisfied that Noel's center of gravity was
being properly considered, gave an enthusiastic nod.
"Winning always put me in a charitable mood."

Sharkey let out a loud guffaw. "I guess that explains why Big Sam ain't too char'table. He pretty near nev'r wins!"

This brought a round of laughter from the others. Logan relaxed as the tension left the air. He sat down and gave Benjamin a mocking look. "What about you, Jacobs? How's your luck running tonight?"

While the cards were being dealt, Libby walked from table to table to personally thank each of the miners.

Shakespeare beamed as she planted a kiss on his forehead and wished him luck. Since learning to read, he seemed less inclined to quote the playwright. His confidence growing daily, he even ventured to try out a few quotes of his own. "Lady Luck's smile couldn't be any prettier than the smile that graces your face."

Libby's cheeks deepened to a lovely rose color. "Why that's beautiful, Shakespeare."

She thanked Logan, who met her gaze with eyes filled with hidden messages. Not brave enough to decipher them until she'd reached the safety of her own home, she tucked them away in her heart and quickly averted her gaze to Benjamin.

Her smile faded for a moment. It was no secret that he had been the one to put that bullet in Macao. She was sorely tempted to give the man a piece of her mind, but sensing Logan tense by her side, she thought better of it.

Instead, she offered him her hand and, speaking loud enough for all to hear, said, "I appreciate your help, Mr. Jacobs."

Benjamin was so disconcerted by the sudden attention, he pretty near swallowed his tobacco. But since everyone was clearly on Libby's side, he had no choice but to take her offered hand.

By the time she and Thornton left the saloon, practically every miner in the place was ready to donate the very shirt off his back toward the cause.

The men resumed their positions around the game tables. Each one of the miners was convinced that Libby had brought him luck, and the bids began to escalate as the competition grew.

Logan watched Benjamin sort his hand, surprised that the man responsible for shooting Macao continued to remain at the table.

"You understand, don't you, that ten percent of your winnings will go to send the man you shot back home?"

Benjamin gave Logan a penetrating look. "Too bad I'm feeling unlucky tonight."

"I'm mighty sorry to hear that," Logan said, placing his bet.

"Count me out," Sharkey said.

"Me too." Appleby tossed his hand down and called to the bartender to bring him another beer.

Benjamin picked up a stack of gold coins. "I'll raise you." He fanned out his hand with a great flourish, so sure was he that he'd lost. "I have a no-pair hand," he announced triumphantly.

It was Big Sam who called out Logan's hand. "Why, look what we have here. Another no-pair hand."

Sharkey leaned over Logan's shoulder. "Yep! Looks like no-pair to me. That means the hand with the highest card wins."

"That's your hand, Benjamin," Big Sam said. "The king beats Logan's jack."

Benjamin's mouth dropped open. "How did you do that?"

Logan managed a facade of innocence. "Do what?"

"You know what! Make it so that I won!"

Logan feigned a wounded look. "You're not suggesting I cheated, now, are you, Benjamin?"

"I'm not *suggesting* anything," Benjamin said thickly. "I'm out and out *saying* you cheated."

Big Sam spread his hand over his chin. "I never heard of a man who's winning accuse the other of cheating."

Benjamin glowered. "What do you have to say, St. John?"

Logan shrugged his shoulders. "I believe ten percent of your winnings comes to around twenty dollars in gold."

Chapter 29

IT was nearly midnight by the time Logan left the Golden Hind. A canvas bag heavy with gold dust, gold coins, and nuggets dangled from his hand. The generous cache clinked together with each step he took.

Overhead, stars shone brightly from a velvet black sky. In the distance, a coyote let out a yipping howl and then fell silent. Had Logan been living in the wilds, such a sound would have brought him sitting upright in his bedroll, keeping him awake until every sound and shadow and odor had been carefully measured, and the possible reason for the coyote's warning cry had been determined. But tonight, Logan focused only on the light shining in the distance that told him that Libby was still awake and was quite possibly waiting for him.

He quickened his pace, pausing only momentarily in front of her house before he climbed the steps leading to her porch. He knocked gently so as not to awaken Noel.

Libby called through the door. "Who is it?"

"It's me, Logan."

The door opened and Libby stood looking at him with eyes that seemed to caress him with their softness. He was so positive she had been waiting for him, it was all he could do to keep from jumping with joy. If only his leg didn't hurt from sitting so long.

"I'm sorry to bother you this late."

"It's not all that late."

"I wanted to give you this." He held up the leather pouch. "This is ten percent of tonight's winnings." What he didn't say was that he had seen to it that pretty near half had come from the man responsible for Macao's injuries.

Libby took the pouch in her hands and almost dropped it. "So much," she gasped. "I had no idea."

"May I come in for a moment? I know it's late but . . ."

"Please, do come in." She stepped aside to let him in, and it was then that he noticed Thornton sitting by the fire, holding Noel over his shoulder. The domestic scene had the same effect as a blow to his stomach.

Thornton nodded curtly. "Logan."

Swallowing his dislike of the man, Logan nodded in kind. "I'm surprised to see you here so late."

"I could say the same about you," Thornton said.

"Would you like some coffee, Logan?" Libby asked.

"No, thank you," Logan said thickly. He plunked himself on the chair across from Thornton and stretched his hurting leg toward the warmth of the fire.

Libby set the bag of gold on the table. "I can't tell you how obliged I am to you and the others. Would you give everyone my thanks?"

"I'd be more than happy to." Logan tried to ignore the visual daggers from Thornton.

"It will mean so much to Macao."

Thornton's look darkened. "I told you, Libby, that asking for help was totally unnecessary. I would have gladly paid for Macao's fare home myself."

"I'm most grateful for your generosity, Thornton. But I'm afraid it might have put you in a difficult position. The only way I could think to avoid future repercussions was to get everyone involved in paying Macao's fare. That way, no one person need take the blame."

Thornton shifted Noel from one shoulder to another. "I hope you'll at least permit me to arrange for Macao's journey to Sacramento City. In fact, several of my men will be heading in that direction day after to-morrow. It would be a small matter to arrange for Macao to leave with them."

"That's a wonderful idea!" Libby exclaimed. "What do you think, Logan?"

Logan forced a wooden smile. "A wonderful idea."

"Then it's settled." Libby clapped her hands together and glanced from one silent man to the other. After a while she took her sleeping son from Thornton and cradled him in her arms. "I'll be right back."

She left the room, leaving the two men to sit glaring at each other. Upon her return, Logan and Thornton made an unsuccessful bid to hide their contempt for each other beneath a demeanor of polite tolerance.

"Are you sure I can't get you some coffee?" she asked Logan.

"It's getting late," Logan said, staring pointedly at Thornton.

Thornton gave him a frosty smile. "Don't let us keep you."

"I wouldn't think of it," Logan replied, making no move to leave.

Libby sighed. In all honesty, she was exhausted. Noel had kept her awake the night before, and Macao had weighed heavily on her mind for quite some time now.

But since neither man showed the least inclination to leave, she did her best to make conversation. As the hour grew later, she decided that if she didn't take matters into her own hands, no one was going to get any sleep.

She stood abruptly. "I think I'll bid you both good night."

Thornton looked embarrassed and promptly rose to his feet. He reached for his hat and gloves.

Logan stood lazily as he watched Thornton don his ridiculous beaver hat. Sakes alive, had he known how absurd the hats looked, he might have taken up another profession. "I'll walk you out," he said graciously.

Thornton glared at him. "How very thoughtful of you." He took Libby's hand in his own and gazed into her eyes. "Thank you for a most enjoyable evening." He drew her hand to his mouth and kissed it.

Libby blushed. "Why, Thornton, you are such a gentleman."

"And you are such a lady." He smiled smoothly and released her hand. He opened the door and waited for Logan.

Libby turned to Logan. "Thank you again, Logan, for everything you've done for Macao." She gave him her hand. Logan took it in his, and with a smooth motion that surprised even himself, he pulled her into his arms and kissed her firmly on the mouth. Releasing her, he walked past Thornton and took great satisfaction at the man's shocked expression.

With Libby's lovely sweet essence still on his lips, Logan limped the short distance to his own cabin. Once inside, he didn't bother to turn on his light or stoke the fire. He didn't need fire. His body was burning as it was. He lay down on his pallet and stared at the ceiling. He could still envision Libby's stunned look after he kissed her. He'd be lucky if she ever talked to him again!

What in the name of sam hill had possessed him? Not only had he succeeded in making a spectacle of himself, he'd embarrassed Libby in the process. And for what?

Unable to sleep, he climbed out of bed and peered through the open door. A soft light flickered from her cabin windows. She had not yet retired. What was she doing? he wondered. Hating him? What?

After the two men had left, Libby stood in front of the fire, gazing unseeingly at the dying flames. Her lips still burned with the memory of Logan's kiss.

She should be angry, furious, at such out-and-out impudence. She *was* angry and furious, she told herself. How dare the man make a public spectacle of her. Just because she allowed him to kiss her that night in the post office gave him no right to think he could kiss her whenever he darned well pleased!

Still, the most unexpected thing about the kiss was not the familiarity that such behavior inferred, and which Logan, no doubt, intended. It was the shivery, hot, and desirous feelings left in its wake.

Such ardent feelings horrified her and filled her with a deep and sorrowful remorse. As much as she loved Jeffrey, he never once set her heart afire the way that Logan was able to do. Nor had Jeffrey ever filled her body with such deep longing.

Oh, Lord, now she was comparing Jeffrey with Logan. Not only was this unfair to Jeffrey, it filled her with unspeakable guilt that weighed upon her shoulders like a heavy boulder.

She reached for the little carved dream box that had been Macao's gift to Noel and opened the lid. It surprised her to find the box empty. She was so certain she had placed the locket containing Jeffrey's hair inside the box for safekeeping. Finding the locket missing, she fought back panic.

It had to be in the room somewhere. It had to be! She dumped her sewing supplies on the floor and frantically pawed through the spools of thread and scraps of fabric. She scrambled across the room to check under the furniture and to run her flattened palms over the deep nap of the bearskin that was stretched in front of the fireplace. She rummaged through boxes and her apron pockets. Every nook and cranny, including the bookshelves in the bedroom, were given a thorough search. The locket was nowhere to be found.

Feeling defeated, she sank to her knees, her eyes blurred with tears. Without the locket and Jeffrey's hair, it was harder than ever to capture her late husband's face in her mind's eye. Nor could she remember her husband's kisses. Not with any sort of clarity. Not with any feeling.

How could she with Logan's kiss burning like hot cinders upon her lips?

What was it about this strange, raw land that made everything so much more intense, including desire?

As shameful as it was to have to admit to such things, she couldn't deny the indisputable fact that had Thornton not been present that evening, she would have welcomed Logan's kiss with wide-open arms.

Chapter 30

MACAO left town that Monday. He was wrapped in blankets and placed in the back of a wagon heading for Sacramento City. Thornton assured her that his men would make the arrangements for Macao to board a ship heading for Canton.

Libby wished her friend well and watched as the wagon pulled out of town. A group of Chinese men stood huddled together as their leader was driven away. A few planned to stay in Calico Corners, but most of them had decided to head for San Francisco where they could band together with others to fight the unfair laws that prevented them from owning property or earning an honest living.

A cold wind blew down from the snow-covered mountains, but the sun was warm, and Libby decided to plant the wildflowers she had dug up from the hills in the front of her house.

Actually she was waiting for Logan. She had not spoken to him privately since he'd taken undue advantage of her two nights earlier, but she decided it was time to tell him exactly what she thought of his scandalous conduct.

Just thinking about that night disarmed her and she ended up digging a hole that was far too big for its purpose. Realizing what she'd done, she stared down into the hole in dismay. She was so lost in her thoughts that she failed to notice she had a visitor.

"Good morning, Mrs. Summerfield."

Startled, she looked up, and upon seeing Genesis,

she smiled. "Preacher Tucker." She stuck her spade in the ground. She was wearing a blue sunbonnet to protect her complexion from the sun and the blue ribbons fluttered in the wind. "Why aren't you at the diggings?"

"I decided to seek my treasures elsewhere."

"Don't tell me you've found yourself a mother lode that no one else knows about."

"More or less. Except, I intend to share it with everyone. I'm going back to being a full-time preacher."

Libby was delighted to hear this. "That's wonderful."

"I got to thinking that the Lord works in mysterious ways. He brought you and Noel into town and as a result, we have the prettiest little church that one could want. It seems such a waste not to put it to good use."

"I wholeheartedly agree." She was so touched that Preacher Tucker thought she and Noel were sent by the Lord, she threw her arms around him.

Genesis blushed and looked almost relieved when she pulled away. He cleared his throat, straightened the white ribbon around his collar, and adjusted his wire-framed spectacles that Libby had inadvertently pushed askew. "As I was saying, it seems only fitting that I do my part. From here on out, I'm making it my business to assume full-time pastoral duties. I've already written to the church to tell them of my intentions to continue my pastoral studies through the mail. In addition to my studies and Sunday services, I shall visit the sick and conduct proper Christian funerals." He leaned closer. "Of course I would much rather perform weddings and baptisms, but there isn't much call for such happy occasions out here."

"I can't tell you how happy I am to hear this. I think a full-time pastor is exactly what this town needs."

"It does my heart good knowing that I have your full approval. I guess I'd better let you finish your . . ." He glanced down at the hole she'd dug as if seeing it for the first time. "Bless the Lord, did someone die?"

"Oh, no. Nothing like that." She gave him a sheepish smile. "I'm planting flowers."

"Flowers, you say? I see. Well, if you have no need for my services, I'll let you get back to work. See you on Sunday."

He peered dubiously into the hole once again, before heading in the direction of the church. Libby watched him, thinking how much livelier he stepped now that he had made the decision to follow his true calling.

Before turning back to her work, she noticed Logan watching her from across the street. Thinking about the liberties he'd taken with her, she fought the erratic beat of her heart. She was angry at him and she best not forget it!

"Logan St. John! I want to talk to you." She stormed across the street and planted herself squarely in front of him, hands on her waist, her eyes flashing with blue-green fury. "You had no right, no right at all to . . ." her voice faltered, but she boldly pressed on, "kiss me."

"I apologize," he said curtly. "It won't happen again."

"You told me that last time. At the post office."

"This time I mean it."

She withered beneath his dark angry scowl. Or was it the hurt in the depth of his eyes that made her feel vulnerable and confused? Hurt that only someone who knew him on intimate terms would have seen. Hurt that made her desperate to explain that it wasn't really his kiss she objected to. It was the way his kiss made her forget Jeffrey and her promise to him. Forget her responsibility as Noel's mother. Forget everything.

She swallowed hard. "You know that I'm leaving soon. Going back to Boston. It's not a good idea for us to become close."

He let out a deep sigh, and the anger and hurt faded until honest regret was ingrained upon his every feature. It was at that moment that she knew pretense was no longer possible. Their feelings for one another must be fought against, but they could no longer be denied.

By early March, all the roads from Sacramento City were open. Mule packs and wagons filled with supplies and dry goods began to arrive in town. Windowpanes and buckets of whitewash were among the first things to arrive, along with Sharkey's up and down barber chair.

The latter caused a great commotion in the town as the miners lined up to take their turns riding on the chair. Sharkey was so proud of his chair, he showed rare patience in allowing the men to take advantage of his generosity. But he soon grew weary of the endless lines outside his door.

Finally, he resorted to his usual business tactics. "If you wanna try out the chair, you have to pay for a haircut first. It's only fair."

The men complained, but they paid Sharkey to cut their hair whether or not a haircut was needed. No price was too high as long as they could try out the remarkable chair.

As the supplies continued to arrive, the miners set to work finishing up the town. The canvas was pulled off Libby's windows and replaced with glass. The uneven panes were riddled with blemishes and other imperfections that distorted the view. But enough sun filtered through the mottled glass to fill her front room with light and warmth.

Libby was so delighted with her new windows, she laid Noel on a blanket beneath them so he could enjoy the natural light. For hours, he was contented to gaze at the beam of sunlight and watch the tiny dust particles that danced above his head.

Meanwhile, the miners whitewashed the church until it gleamed like a large white jewel. They then began to work on the wooden buildings along Main Street until one by one, each business had a fresh new coat of paint.

Libby found Hap Montana standing in front of his sparkling white general store. He fingered his suspenders and looked unbearably smug. "Wouldn't you say the whitewash makes a difference?"

"Indeed I would," she agreed, stepping out of the way so that members of the Sign Brigade, as they now called themselves, could pass, hauling the sign for the assay office over their heads.

While two or three members of the Sign Brigade stood on the roof adjusting the sign and nailing it in place, a crowd of miners stood below shouting instructions.

The loud voices were still ringing in Libby's ear as she followed Hap into the general store. Hap offered to hold Noel while she made her purchases and she was all too happy to let him. Noel was growing so rapidly, her arms ached at the end of each day from carrying him.

"Look what I have for you," Hap said. He indicated a wooden crate. "Baking soda."

Libby already had more baking soda than she could ever hope to use in a lifetime, but not wanting to hurt his feelings, she thanked him. If nothing else, she could make a table out of the sturdy wood box.

Hap agreed to deliver her purchases after closing hours. Thanking him, Libby walked the short distance back home.

In front of Logan's cabin, Jim Bridger snorted softly and scraped the ground with a hoof before lowering his head to nuzzle at the scattering of hay at his feet. As far as Libby knew, Logan hadn't ridden his horse in days. Indeed, he hadn't left his cabin except to feed the horse and fill the nearby trough with fresh water.

Was he ill? she wondered. She decided to make it her business to find out.

Still cradling Noel in her arm, she made her way to his front door and knocked.

His voice sounded muffled and distant. "Go away!"

"It's me, Libby," she called, pressing an ear against the door.

A short silence followed before he spoke again, this time his voice less gruff. "I'm busy. Come back another time."

She stared at the closed door. Busy doing what? she wondered. Propriety demanded that she take him at his word, but she'd long since learned to play by less rigid rules than the ones dictated by Boston society. So, it was in grand western style that she reached for the door handle and walked inside.

Logan was sitting on the floor, his bared leg extended over a steaming black kettle. His face was twisted in agony as he stared up at her, but whether from pain or hurtful pride, she couldn't tell.

"I hope you're satisfied," he said curtly.

She closed the door behind her and laid Noel on the bear robe far enough from the fire for safety's sake. "I haven't seen you in days. I was worried."

"As you can see, there's nothing to worry about. Now if you would kindly leave me in peace . . ."

"Your leg . . ."

"Is fine!"

The leg looked anything but fine. Closer observation revealed that the leg was uncommonly red and the knee was swollen to twice its normal size. It angered her that he stubbornly refused to acknowledge how bad his leg really was.

Feeling her own stubbornness come to the fore, she snapped her head around and confronted him. "It doesn't look fine," she retorted. "It looks dreadful."

His face darkened with fury. "You know nothing about it," he shouted.

"Is that so?" she shouted back. "Well, if your leg is so gosh darn fine, what are you doing huddled over this ridiculous kettle!"

"All right, dammit, the leg's not fine. Does that make you happy to hear me say it?"

Knowing how hard it must have been for him to finally admit the truth, she was tempted to take him in her arms. But this was no time to show sympathy or compassion. She'd tried such approaches in the past and neither one had worked.

She glared at him. "If your leg is giving you trouble, then why don't you do something about it?"

"What do you think I'm doing, dammit!"

She sniffed contemptuously. "You think a little steam is going to help that leg? Ha! And you think you know so much!"

"Since obviously you're such an expert in these matters, suppose you tell me what I should do!"

"What you need is a full soaking in hot water."

He curled his lip back. "How do you suggest I do that?"

She straightened. "I'll show you how!" With that she dashed out of Logan's cabin and raced across the street to her own front porch. She lifted the wooden wash barrel that she used for her own bath and hauled it across the street. With no small amount of difficulty, she lugged the tub through Logan's narrow door.

Logan seemed to take some satisfaction in watching her struggle. He folded his arms across his chest and gave a disparaging frown. "If you think I'm going to sit in that, you'd better think again."

She intentionally ignored him as she emptied a bucket of cold water into the tub and then reached for the steaming kettle. It took three more kettles of hot water before there was sufficient water in the tub to adequately cover him. He said nothing as she worked. Indeed, ignored her. It took an additional kettle of cold water before the bath was ready.

"Take your clothes off," she commanded.

"I will not!"

"Why are you so stubborn?"

"I am not stubborn!" he said stubbornly. And then, "Do you have any idea how much it's going to hurt to get into that thing?"

She almost relented and softened her stance. But she

knew that would be a mistake. She picked up the skillet and held it over his knee. "Do you know how much it's going to hurt when I drop this thing on your leg?"

He looked up at her aghast. "You wouldn't!"

"Don't tempt me," she said.

For several long moments they stared at each other like two foes waiting for the other to make the first move. Suddenly the hard lines on his face softened and he surprised her by bursting into laughter. "Well, now, Libby," he sputtered between guffaws. "You always were good at getting me into hot water."

She lowered the skillet and tried to suppress a giggle. But the warm sound of his laughter was infectious, and she soon found herself laughing along with him.

She almost choked on her mirth, however, when he pulled his buckskin shirt over his head and tossed it aside. The sight of his bared chest brought a blush to her face, and she quickly averted her eyes. "I'll be back later," she said hoarsely.

"Stay!"

Confused, she looked up. He was watching her with bright blazing eyes and she couldn't help but wonder if he was enjoying her discomfort. "I might need help."

"Very well." She spoke primly, casting a starched, even look at him. But there was nothing prudish or even proper at the way her heart was beating against her ribs. She backed away from him. "I'll wait over here." She knelt down on the bearskin next to Noel, who was still sound asleep, and kept her back toward Logan.

"You can look," Logan said from behind her.

Her heart galloped faster than a runaway horse. "I wouldn't think of invading your privacy."

"It never bothered you before."

She was so shocked by this accusation, she glanced over her shoulder and gasped slightly at the sight of his naked limbs. She quickly averted her head. Her face flaming red, it was with great difficulty that she managed to find her voice. "What are you saying?"

The water splashed behind her as he lowered himself into the tub. "I was simply making reference to all those times you used to lie in bed at night and watch me undress."

Ashamed of her little secret, she quickly denied it. "I did not!"

"You most certainly did," he insisted smoothly. "I could tell by your breathing."

"My breathing was perfectly normal!" she exclaimed, then realizing she'd given herself away, she covered her mouth with her hand.

He laughed aloud, and she picked up a stray moccasin and threw it at him. He was sitting waist high in the water and already she could see the tense lines at his brow were beginning to fade.

He leaned his back against the rim of the tub and sighed. "You're right, Libby. The hot water helps."

Her earlier embarrassment forgotten, she filled the kettle with fresh water and hung it over the fire to heat. "I think you should have a doctor look at that leg."

"I did have a doctor look at it."

Surprised, she turned to face him. "Oh? What did he say?"

"He told me to stay out of the saddle, stay away from cold weather, and quit wading through icy cold streams."

"And why haven't you done what he said?"

"Because those are things I have to do."

Later, after he had finished soaking and was lying prone in front of the fireplace with his leg propped up in front of him, she ventured to ask him his plans for the future.

He looked confused by the question. "I'm going to do what I've always done."

"And if your leg doesn't heal?"

"I'm a trapper, Libby. I don't know anything else."

Chapter 31

EVERY day for the next week, Libby arrived at Logan's house promptly at noon to fill the tub with hot water. He fought her every step of the way until she was ready to throttle him. She called him stubborn and pigheaded; he called her overbearing and pushy.

The arguments were necessary and on some level, both accepted this. If they weren't yelling at each other, and calling each other names, they would be saying all the wrong things, the things they couldn't afford to say because she was going home to Boston, and he was going up north to set his traps.

And so they waged a loud and verbal war that was, in reality, a war fought privately in their hearts, every moment they were together.

Every moment they were apart.

The hot baths helped his leg, but after a week of fighting his rampaging feelings for Libby, he grew restless and irritable.

The swelling of his knee had gone down, and that had to be a positive sign. The only problem was the ache in his loins made up for any progress made in alleviating the pain in his lower limb.

Late that Friday afternoon in mid-March, he decided to pay a visit to his favorite saloon and was surprised when he found the once spirited gaming tables all but deserted.

Moe the bartender bitterly explained. "It's been like this all week. Between the time the men spend in the gold fields and in sprucing up the town, they're too tired to show up here."

Disgusted, Logan limped back to his cabin and was surprised to find that during his short absence, several men had gathered in front of his place. The very same men he had hoped to find at the gaming tables.

Sharkey was the first to spot him. "Hey there, Logan. We were lookin' for yer. We have somethin' i'portant to talk to you 'bout. Don't we, boys?"

Logan gritted his teeth. He wanted to play cards, and they wanted to talk. "Well say what you have to say, dammit!"

Big Sam stepped forward and flashed his wide grin. "The boys and me are just about finished with the town."

"Yep," Sharkey concurred, "we've all spruced up our places."

"It's about time," Logan growled. "Now maybe a man can get himself some uninterrupted sleep."

Sharkey glanced at the others before he continued. "We have only one eyesore left."

Logan looked up one side of the street and down the other. Every last building and every last fence and every last hitching post glistened beneath a coat of fresh paint. Somebody had even gone overboard and painted a rock that rested by the side of the street. "I don't see any eyesore."

"We were referrin' to your diggin's here," Sharkey said.

Logan stepped back. He was so astonished, he forgot to favor his leg and he immediately suffered the consequences. Swearing beneath his breath, he rested his hand against a tree and shifted his weight. "My diggings? What's wrong with my diggings?"

Big Sam pointed to the dreary shack in question. "It gives the town a bad name. Isn't that right, boys?"

"I'm not allowing my house to become all sissified, and that's final."

Appleby, ever the diplomat, took charge. "Now before you go getting yourself all in a stew, I think you ought to consider something very seriously. You're a godfather, ain't that right?"

Logan frowned. "I don't see what one has anything to do with the other."

"Now hear me out," Appleby said. "Look what's right across the street from you. Your little godson. And when he looks out his bright new shining windows, what does he see? Does he see a town he can be proud of? Or does he see an eyesore?"

"He sees an eyesore!" the men yelled out in unison.

Logan considered this. Preacher Genesis hadn't said anything about a godfather having to fix up his house. He started toward his porch. "I don't have time for this foolishness . . ."

Appleby stayed him. "You won't have to worry about a thing. Will he, boys?"

"Not a thing," Big Sam agreed.

Appleby slapped Logan on the back. "You just give us the word and we'll take it from here."

Logan was torn between doing what's right by the boy and protecting his privacy. Finally, he relented, but mostly because he was outnumbered. "Not too sissified," he warned.

"Wouldn't think of it. Would we, boys?"

"And none of those calico curtains."

Appleby looked less confident about promising this. "You'll have to take that up with Libby."

Forcing aside his reservations, Logan limped back into the house and slammed the door shut behind him. He told himself it would only be a temporary inconvenience. Besides, winter was about over. Just as soon as the ache in his leg subsided, he'd head up north to beaver country. He had traps to set.

According to Hap who'd heard it from one of his suppliers, first-class pelts, or plus as they were called by mountain men, were bringing top prices. Probably because there were even fewer free trappers than usual this year. Most had headed for the gold fields of California.

Word was that the north had never known such cold weather and bitter storms. This was good news as far as Logan was concerned. It might be May before beavers began to shed their winter coats. With any sort of luck, he might still be able to get enough pelts to see him through the summer. Maybe not prime pelts, but good enough to sell.

But that meant he'd have to leave sooner than expected, regardless of his still ailing leg. The truth was that if he hoped to trap any beavers worth something, he'd have to leave no later than early April. That was only two weeks away.

Meanwhile, the least a godfather could do was to see that his godchild had himself a decent view.

During the next three days Logan's shack was practically rebuilt from the ground up. The miners cut out two square holes for windows, one on either side of his front door, before anyone thought to ask Hap about the availability of window glass. When it turned out that Hap's supplies were depleted, Logan pretty near froze to death until canvas sheets were stretched across the frames and nailed in place.

Big Sam built flower boxes and matching shutters for the windows. Sharkey and Beaker tore down the porch and replaced it with one that didn't sag. Last came a new roof and a paint job.

Logan stood in front of his house and demanded to know why they painted it yellow. "Of all the sissified colors. It looks like a giant gold bar."

"We ran outta whitewash," Sharkey explained.

Logan was still staring at the house several minutes later when Libby walked out of her front door carrying Noel. "It's lovely," she called to him. She hurried across the street to join him. "What do you think, Noel? Did you ever see a prettier house in all your born days?" She held Noel up so he could see.

Logan gazed at her pink cheeks and soft lips. "Do you really like it?"

"Absolutely. Now all you need are some calico curtains . . ."

"Calico curtains would be nice."

"And flowers in your flower boxes."

"I don't know anything about planting flowers."

"If you like, I would be happy to plant them for you."

"That would be mighty kind of you."

She glanced at his leg. "Would it be too much for you to hold Noel while I fetch my gardening gloves and spade."

"No trouble at all."

"He's getting heavy."

He took Noel in his arms and bounced him up and down. "Indeed he is."

"I won't be but a minute," she said.

"Take your time. My leg is much better." It still hurt, but he had no intention of letting on how much.

"The hot baths must have helped." She blushed prettily and dashed back to the house, her skirts all aflutter, her hair flying in every direction. He couldn't take his eyes off her until she had disappeared into the house. He lowered his head and buried his nose next to Noel's sweet-smelling skin.

Noel delighted him with a dimpled smile that lit up his chubby round face. "Well, now . . ." Logan broke into a wide smile.

Libby came out of the house and hurried toward them, her face set with a sense of purpose. "I brought some cuttings from my garden," she said. "Poppies and lupines. I never thought I would become an expert on wildflowers."

"Don't they have wildflowers in Boston?"

"Not really. Unless you drive out into the country." She gave him a quick smile and set to work planting the flowers. She chattered freely as she filled the window boxes with soil.

It was her way to talk incessantly when she was anxious or fearful. That's how he knew his presence was affecting her, by her nonstop chatter. Just as her presence was affecting him.

He wondered how he let the two of them grow on him so. Mother and son. He had no business feeling the things he felt for them. No business at all. He was nothing but a lowly trapper, with nothing of value to his name. All he had to offer was a bad leg and no future.

"There," Libby announced at last. She brushed her hands off. "It won't be long before you'll have flowers."

He should have told her right then and there that he'd never see those particular flowers come to bloom. He was leaving in less than two weeks. But the words wouldn't come, and so he kept his misery to himself.

She gave him an uncertain smile and for a moment, but only a moment, he imagined things were different. That he wasn't who or what he was. That his body was sound and his future bright. "Here," he said brusquely. He handed Noel to her.

Looking confused, she stared as Logan backed away.

"I have things to do," he explained. He grabbed his gold rocker and heaved it onto his horse. He cursed the leg that kept him from running—more than that, kept him from loving.

Later that afternoon, Logan returned from his claim, feeling worse than before. He'd mined maybe fifteen, twenty dollars' worth of gold that day, and he was feeling it. The cold from the water had pretty near reached clear down to the bone in his leg. He decided that if he was going to leave in two weeks' time, he'd better stay away from the cold and the dampness. If that meant soaking his leg twenty-four hours a day in hot water, then that's what he intended to do.

He glanced across at Libby's house before climbing the steps leading to his porch. Smoke curled slowly from her chimney. Noel's clothes flapped from a rope that was strung between two trees. But otherwise, all was quiet.

Inside, he made himself a cup of coffee and settled down on his pallet to read the paper he'd picked up from the general store. The paper was several days old.

He turned the page to find a continuation of the story he was reading when a sudden commotion outside caught his attention. He should have known the town wouldn't remain quiet and peaceful for long.

His leg had stopped aching, but it wasn't until he tried to stand that he realized it had grown numb. The damned leg was getting worse. He was sure of it. How was he ever going to manage to sleep outdoors again, with only the ground as his bed and the sky as his cover? How would he ever manage to wade through the icy cold rivers to set his traps?

Still not accustomed to windows, he peered through his open door to the group of men who were gathered in front of Libby's house. "Now what?" he muttered.

His curiosity getting the best of him, he hobbled out to the porch and down the steps.

Libby's voice drifted toward him. "It's truly the most remarkable thing I've ever seen."

Logan stretched to his full height, trying to see over the crowd. Beaker stood by Libby's side, blushing like a summer peach. "I was lucky to be able to find maple trees in the area," he said. "And Hap just happened to have a parasol in the shop. Said he never thought he'd sell it."

"It's absolutely perfect!"

Logan pushed his way through the ranks of men. Finally, he could see the small wooden wagon set on four wheels that was the object of attention.

"Let's see how the little fellow likes it!" Big Sam suggested.

Libby laid Noel in the bed of the wagon, which was lined with a woolen blanket. She then straightened and placed her hands on the wooden bar that served as a handle.

"Move outta the way, boys," Sharkey ordered, waving his hands in front. "Make room, make room."

The men moved aside, leaving a path clear for the push cart. Libby pushed and the crude wooden wheels began to turn. The cart bounced up and down and poor Noel looked positively startled.

Sharkey shook his head. "The way he's a-rattling and a-shaking away, his teeth are likely to fall out."

"He's got no teeth," Big Sam pointed out.

"And he ain't gonna git any at that rate."

One of the wheels sank into a gopher hole. Gripping the wooden handle, Libby pulled the cart from the hole, but the back wheel caught on a rock.

Applebee frowned. "What it needs is rubber tires."

"What we need is a proper boardwalk," Big Sam exclaimed. "Why every decent town from Sacramento City to San Francisco has itself a proper boardwalk."

"He's right," Sharkey agreed.

Beaker looked profoundly relieved when it was decided that the lack of a boardwalk was responsible for Libby's difficulty in pushing, and it was no fault of his cart.

After much discussion, the men decided to remedy the situation the first thing in the morning. Big Sam carried Noel's cart onto Libby's porch before joining the others, who had already rushed off to gather lumber and tools.

Suddenly there was just the two of them, Libby and Logan. Three if you counted Noel. A-standing and a-staring at each other, as Sharkey would say, a-gazing at each other.

Libby was the first to speak, her voice as soft as velvet to his ears. "It's time for Noel's feeding."

Now was as good a time as any to tell her that in less than two weeks time he would be gone. "Libby, I . . ."

She took a step forward, her lovely forehead shadowed with concern. "What's wrong, Logan?"

She was so close to him, he could smell her delicate fragrance. She smelled like wildflowers and warm sunshine. Trying not to inhale, he tore his eyes away from her dewy soft lips. "Nothing's wrong." *Everything's wrong.*

He met her gaze and almost drowned in the lovely blue-green depths of her eyes. It was obvious by her shadowed brow that she didn't believe him.

He glanced toward Noel, who was starting to fuss. "You'd better go."

"Are you sure you're all right?"

He forced a grin and backed away from her. "Couldn't be better." He turned and limped back to his own front door. He hated the cowardly lie he told. He could feel her eyes on his back and this only added to his guilt. But the lie couldn't be helped. He wasn't ready to tell her he was leaving—not yet.

Chapter 32

IT was barely light the following morning when Logan awakened to the sound of hammering and sawing. He lay on his pallet, his leg propped upon a stack of furs, and wondered if there would ever be an end to what the residents of the town would think up next.

The hammering continued all that day and the next. For the most part, Logan ignored it. He was too busy soaking his leg in hot water and rubbing every possible kind of ointment into his knee. He had less than two weeks to get his leg back in shape. Less than two weeks to tell Libby good-bye.

In little more than a day, Calico Corners had itself a proper boardwalk.

Upon completion, the miners stood along Main Street while Libby tried it out. With Noel in the cart, she strolled past the line of men as if she didn't have a care in the world.

When she reached the end of the newly laid planks, Beaker and Appleby lifted the cart to the other side of the street, allowing her to continue her stroll.

Sharkey was so touched, his eyes watered. Sniffling like a small child, he dabbed his face with a corner of his red bandanna. "I haven't seen anything like it since I left Hoboken."

Everyone agreed. Libby pushing Noel in his cart was a sight to behold.

* * *

That night, the men were in good spirits and their good-natured laughter greeted Logan as he entered the gambling saloon. Well, now, he thought, the town was finally back to normal. And it wasn't any too soon.

He sensed a lucky streak coming on. Yes, indeed, a lucky streak. His intention was to turn the twenty dollars' worth of gold he'd dug up a few days earlier into a few hundred dollars. Enough money to buy provisions for his trip up north. He carefully set his bag of gold dust on the table and waited for the others to do the same.

Appleby laid a single gold coin on the table.

"Why did you stop?" Logan asked.

Appleby looked puzzled. "Stop?"

"Where's the rest of your money?"

"That's all I'm betting tonight."

Logan frowned. What was this? He turned to the others. "What about you, Sharkey?"

"That's it for me too."

Logan sat back in his chair and surveyed the saloon, taking careful note of the gaming tables. There wasn't enough money in that room to satisfy a miser. "Suppose you men tell me what in hell is going on!"

Appleby exchanged glances with the others before he began, "Libby . . ."

Logan tensed immediately at the mention of her name. It seemed that he couldn't bear to hear her name anymore without feeling overwhelmed by a stampede of emotions. "What about Libby?"

"She said that it was sheer folly to gamble away all our gold." Sharkey waved his hands, trying to get the others to back him up. "Didn't she, boys?"

"Those were her exact words," Shakespeare said. "Sheer folly."

Appleby leaned across the table, his face earnest. "She said we'd never manage to bring our families to California or to save enough to go back home if we didn't start saving."

"That's what she said all right," Sharkey said. "She

said it was plain loco to blow our money on a-gambling and a-drinking."

"First time I ever had money in my mattress," Big Sam said proudly. "It's like sleeping on rocks. Now I know why rich folks look so serious. They don't get no sleep."

Logan couldn't believe his ears. Libby had been in town for only three months, and nothing was the same.

He'd put up with all the building and painting. He allowed himself to become Noel's godfather. Why, he'd been right generous, come to think of it, in how much he'd tolerated. Just thinking about it made his head spin. He'd hardly complained when Libby insisted upon hanging curtains—*curtains* of all things—in the saloon and gambling hall. And he'd said nothing when she took over his house. Then there were the times she'd tried to cook him alive in those hot baths.

But she had gone too far this time. Now he intended to complain. He intended to complain loud and clear. And maybe, just maybe, while he was telling her what he thought about her latest interfering ways, he would get up enough nerve to tell her good-bye.

Early the next morning he parked himself in front of his new window and watched Libby carrying a basket of clothes in one arm and Noel in the other.

He waited for her to walk around to the side of her house where she normally did her wash. While he watched, he carefully rehearsed his speech.

Certain words needed to be emphasized. Words like meddling and brazen. *Words like good-bye* . . .

Squaring his jaw, he ripped open his door and barreled across the street in a loping gait.

Noel was in his cart beneath the shade of an oak tree. His little hands waved as he cooed to himself. Nearby, his mother was bent over a washtub scrubbing clothes.

The fetching sight of Libby's behind dulled the sharp edge of his fury. He cleared his throat, trying to maintain the full extent of his anger. It was the only way he could maintain the necessary distance from her.

Libby straightened and turned. "Why, Logan, what brings you here so early?"

"I have something important to say to you."

She wiped her hands on her apron. "It sounds serious."

"It is." He stopped, trying to remember the speech he'd prepared. But he couldn't concentrate. Not with those big blue-green eyes planted squarely on his face. Not with the distracting soap bubble that was centered on her slightly upturned nose.

"You have something on your nose."

She looked startled. "What?"

"Right here." He touched his finger to the bubble and wiped it away.

"Thank you."

The smile she gave him made his heart do flip-flops. "The boys said you talked them into curtailing their gambling."

She looked pleased with herself. "I most certainly did. It makes no sense for them to throw their hard-earned gold away on the gaming tables."

"It's their only recreation."

"When they bring their families out here, there will be other ways to occupy their time."

He opened his mouth to argue, but when he couldn't think of anything to say, it occurred to him that he could argue with her all he wanted and it wasn't going to make his task of saying good-bye any easier. And that's what he really came to do, say good-bye.

"Libby . . . I . . ." Damn it! Did she have to look so soft and appealing. "Forget it!" He turned.

"Logan . . ."

He stopped midstep.

"Why don't you say what you really came to say?"

He turned to face her. "What makes you think I came to say anything that I haven't already said."

"It's just a feeling I have. Now would you please

stop beating around the bush? If you have something to say, then just say it!"

He was startled by her sudden outburst. "I have no right to say what I want to say. Me being a rough, uneducated mountain man and you being a . . . fine lady."

"That's hogwash!"

"But you are a fine lady."

"I meant your being a rough and uneducated mountain man. Why I've never met a man as educated as you . . . Look how you nursed me back to health the night I came into town. And you helped with Noel's birth just like you were a doctor."

"I never went to school."

"That doesn't mean you're not educated."

"I don't know anything about opera."

"I don't know anything about wild animals." She glanced away. "Sometimes I wonder . . ."

He looked at her hard. "What? What were you going to say?"

She bit her lower lip. "I wonder how I can teach Noel about nature and wildlife. He won't learn that in Boston."

"Boston is still in Noel's best interests."

"I know that. And I must think about his future."

"I couldn't agree more."

"He'll need other children his age. Besides, I promised his father I would take his son back home."

At mention of Noel's father, Logan frowned. "Do you still think of him much?"

"Jeffrey?" She looked so stricken by the question, he immediately regretted having asked it. "Yes, I think of him a lot," she admitted. "He was the perfect match for the woman I used to be." Her voice grew stronger as she spoke, as if she was anxious to try out a new idea. "I'm a different woman than I was when I was married to Jeffrey. I'm stronger, more independent. If Jeffrey and I were to meet now, I'm not sure . . ." Oh, but she was sure. Jeffrey would have hated this town, and most certainly would have disapproved of the rough-mannered miners she had come to love in recent months. She shuddered to think what Jeffrey would say if he knew that one of his son's favorite playmates was a runaway slave.

As much as it hurt her to think it, she could no longer deny the truth; Jeffrey belonged to a woman who no longer existed.

Logan stood watching her, a look of regret and sadness on his face. "You were always strong, Libby. I'd bet on it. Maybe that's why you came out west. Not just because of Jeffrey, but because of your own free spirit. Did that thought ever occur to you? Did you ever stop to think that maybe you wanted to escape Boston?"

She loved him for thinking her strong and free-spirited. But he gave her more credit than she deserved. "If that's true, then I was deluding myself. Boston is my home. It will always be my home."

"I know." He glanced away. "When . . . when do you plan to return to Boston?"

"Thornton says I should plan to leave soon. Otherwise, I'll meet with bad weather on the East Coast."

A muscle tightened at his jaw. "Thornton's right." A moment of awkward silence stretched between them before he added, "As Noel's godfather, it seems only fitting that I help with expenses."

His offer touched her, and she felt a pang inside. "That won't be necessary. I still have money left from my savings and some of the miners have been paying me to do their laundry."

"Let me pay your fare."

"That's very kind of you, Logan, but it's really not necessary . . ."

"It's the least I can do for my godson. Please, Libby. Let me do this one thing for him."

She sensed it was important to him, and for that reason she accepted his offer. "That's most generous of you."

He braced himself. "I'm leaving in two weeks' time. Heading north where I belong."

"So ... so soon?"

His eyes met hers. "It's time, Libby."

They both knew it was time.

Her eyes filled with tears and he wanted to die.

He wrapped his fingers around her arm. "Don't cry, Libby. Don't do this to me." She bit her lower lip and reached up to touch his cheek with her hand.

Her touch ignited something within him. The look on her face melted through his last defenses. Moaning her name, he crushed her to him.

"Oh, Libby!" He ran his lips across her forehead and down her cheeks, turning the stream of tears into liquid fire, before covering her mouth hungrily with his own.

Wanting to absorb his every essence, she raised herself to feel the full impact of his lips on hers. The hot flame of his tongue slipped inside her mouth, and quivers of delight ran through her.

Shamelessly, she arched against him and buried her fingers in his hair. Her breasts tingled against his chest, and she felt an aching longing radiate from the deepest part of her.

When at last he pulled away, it was as if someone had ripped her apart.

His eyes smoldered as he looked at her, seething with fires of passion and desire, but more than anything, love. It was the love that touched her the deepest. It was love she heard when he spoke.

"I'd better go, Libby, before we do something we both regret."

"Please stay, Logan," she pleaded.

"Libby. Listen to me. If you really care for me ... I beg you not to make this any more difficult for me than it already is."

"But ..."

He touched his finger to her lips. She clung to him for one last time before he pulled away.

Chapter 33

LOGAN walked into the Golden Hind later that night. He'd spent the last few hours in his cabin battling the raging need that burned inside him. He wanted so much to go back to Libby and finish what they both had started. But that would be a mistake. He knew it would be a mistake. A big mistake.

Still, he wanted her so much he couldn't think straight. Her sweet hot lips had burned a hole in his resistance, and before he knew it, he'd been halfway back to her house before he noticed she had company.

Thornton! Damn the man! Choosing that exact moment to make his appearance, a large bouquet of wildflowers in hand, his face plastered with an oily smile.

Grimacing against the memory, Logan scanned the crowded room until he spotted Cast-Iron Peters.

He walked up to the man and slapped him on the shoulder. "What do you say, Cast-Iron? Feeling lucky tonight?"

Cast-Iron only had one facial expression: contemptuous. "I always feel lucky."

Logan pulled out a chair in front of an empty gaming table. "Have yourself a seat."

Cast-Iron hesitated. "I don't want to waste my time with no two-bit bids."

Logan grinned. "I wouldn't think of insulting you."

Cast-Iron nodded once and sat down.

Big Sam sauntered over from the bar and sat next to him. "Count me in."

Logan shuffled the cards. "Don't you have to consult with your financial adviser?"

Big Sam looked surprised. "You mean Libby. She won't care." He leaned over the table. "I got money to burn."

Logan gave Big Sam a narrow-eyed glance. "Is that right?"

"Lookie here." Big Sam pulled a leather pouch from inside his shirt and set it in the middle of the table. Inside was a gold nugget the size of a fig.

"Holy smokes!" Sharkey exclaimed as he leaned across the table to have a closer look.

Soon everyone in the saloon was scrambling to get an eyeful of Big Sam's treasure.

"Calm yourselves down." Big Sam grinned good-naturedly. He stood and held it up for all to see.

The miners exclaimed and marveled over it.

Big Sam couldn't resist an audience, and he took great pleasure in recounting his tale. "I was walking along Devil's Bar minding my own business. There it was right on the ground in front of me. I couldn't believe my eyes."

"Let me see that." Appleby picked up the nugget and examined it. "Where's the rest of it?"

"What do you mean rest? There is no rest!"

"There sure 'nough is," Sharkey insisted. "Look." He pointed to the one ragged end of the rock.

Logan followed Sharkey's finger. "I'll be damned if he's right. Looks like a big chunk is broken off."

"Where'd you say you found that," one of the miners called from the back. "Devil's Bar?"

"It's mine," Big Sam said, grabbing his nugget back.

"The one in your hand might be yours," Sharkey argued. "But it seems to me a man's not got a right to anythin' not in his own hand."

Appleby nodded. "Sharkey's right."

"I say every man for hisself," Benjamin said, heading for the door.

"Now wait just a minute!" Sharkey grabbed his hat

and chased after him. This started a mass exodus as everybody pushed and shoved their way outside.

Logan sat debating with himself. A nugget the size of Big Sam's could keep a man going for quite some time. It would certainly mean that he could forgo the trapping season and wait until fall. Hell! He could wait a whole year if necessary. He could wait for however long it took his leg to heal.

He'd be rich. *Rich!* He would never have to trap again.

He knew, of course, that his chances of finding the missing half of that gold nugget were almost nonexistent. The others had an advantage over him. They could walk faster, cover more terrain, take shortcuts through streams and rivers, climb over rocks and fallen trees. Only Logan would be forced to take the long way around.

Common sense told him that any attempt to search through such rough terrain would only do more injury to his leg, negating any progress he'd made in recent weeks.

Still, it was tempting. Damned tempting. He'd be rich enough to move to Boston and not have to worry about making a living.

He'd be rich enough to give Libby the kind of life she deserved. His chances weren't good. Practically nonexistent. No sane man would pursue such odds. But it was all that he had at the moment, a chance, the slimmest possible chance.

With this last thought burning inside, he grabbed his hat and followed the last man out the door.

In no time at all, news of Big Sam's remarkable find had traveled from one saloon to the next, sending miners scrambling back to their cabins for their knapsacks. The night thundered with the sound of horses as one by one the men sped out of town.

The race was on!

Libby rose just after dawn the following morning. It

had been a long sleepless night filled with burning memories of being in Logan's arms. The kisses they shared. The glow of love in his eyes.

On many levels she was shocked by the torrid thoughts that kept her twisting and turning through the night.

She'd gone through the process of motherhood, had seen her body go through the most amazing changes in the process, but never had she imagined she was capable of feeling such longing, such passion, such an all-encompassing need.

Anxious to get an early start on her chores before Noel woke, she dressed, brushed her hair, and slipped outside, closing the door quietly behind her. Unconsciously, she found herself staring at Logan's cabin, her pulse quickening in anticipation. She longed to go to him. To tell him the things in her heart that she couldn't say yesterday.

But sensing his absence, she felt her spirits drop. It was then that she noticed his horse gone.

She drew her shawl around her shoulders as she walked to the creek to fill her bucket with water. Something was not right.

Normally at this time of day, the chimneys were smoking and the smell of bacon, salt pork, and coffee generally filled the air. Today, there was not a soul in sight. The town was deserted.

She spent the remainder of the morning doing her chores and taking care of Noel, but she was troubled by the miners' absence. Every few minutes or so, she stopped what she was doing to glance out her window at Logan's cabin. His smokeless chimney told her that Logan had probably been away for several hours or more.

Would the men have gone up to the diggings so early? she wondered. And if so, why had Logan gone with them? He told her he was leaving Calico Corners in two weeks. So why would he chance doing more damage to his leg? It made no sense.

It was a lovely clear day, the air was cool and sparkling, and the sky cloudless. But it would be far colder up at the diggings.

Distracted by her troubling thoughts, she left her chores unfinished and decided to go to the general store. Hap would know where everyone had gone.

She put Noel in his cart and pushed him along the boardwalk. It puzzled her that every business in town was closed, even the general store. Where was everyone?

The sound of horses broke the almost eerie silence, and feeling a sense of relief, she spun around to greet them.

But it was not the miners riding into town; it was strangers.

The leader was a grim-looking man with an eye patch. The man reined his piebald horse in front of her and signaled the others to stop. Folding his arms across his lap, he impaled her with one stone-cold eye.

"Howdy, ma'am," he said politely. "My name is Thomas Flint. Me and the boys here are looking for someone. I wonder if you could help us? His name's St. John."

There was something about the man she didn't trust. He was smiling at her, but the smile failed to soften the hard glint of his eyes or the rigid line of his mouth.

Her heart fluttered nervously. "St. John, did you say?"

"Logan St. John."

She pretended to give the matter some thought. "I can't say that I've heard of the man." Telling that lie was no easy matter. Not when the mere mention of Logan's name started her heart pounding and brought a flush to her body.

"Are you sure, ma'am?" Flint was looking at her hard. "Think carefully." He glanced at Noel, and Libby felt a knot in her stomach.

"I'm certain," she said too quickly, too . . . everything. "There's no one in this town by the name of St. John."

One of the other men took off his hat and wiped his forehead with his arm. "Come on, Flint. What is this? You said this was the perfect town for us to hang out in once you took care of your business with St. John."

"Perfect!" sneered a scar-faced man. "Did you ever see such a sissy town in your life?"

"Will yer look at that?" yelled a man on a flea-bitten roan. "A saloon with ruffled curtains, for chrissakes!"

All the men except for Flint began to laugh.

"Stop it!" Flint roared.

Flinching, Libby tightened her grip on Noel's cart.

One man rode his horse next to Flint's. "No. You stop it, Flint. You said Deadman's Gulch was perfect for us. You said nothin' about women and children. Dammit, it eve' has a church. And enuf flowers to poll'nate the in-tere state."

The other men echoed out in agreement. "I ain't stayin' here," one cried out.

"The same goes for me!"

The men rode down Main Street, leaving a cloud of dust in their wake.

"Wait!" Flint called. "Come back, you scoundrels!" Flint hit his horse with his whip. "I'll make St. John pay for making an ass out of me. If it's the last thing I do!"

Horrified at the venom in his voice, Libby stood frozen in place as the men rode out of town. Despite the warm sun, she shivered against the gooseflesh that rose along her arms.

Fearing the men would return, she waited until the sound of horses' hooves had faded in the distance, then quickly wheeled Noel home. She didn't breathe easy until she had carried him inside and firmly bolted the door.

In the hours to follow, she maintained an anxious vigil in front of the window. Where in heaven's name was everyone?

Logan. Oh, dear God, where could you possibly be?

Her mind conjured every conceivable possibility that would explain his absence. Perhaps he'd left Calico Corners for good, to head up north. But he wouldn't do that, would he? Without saying good-bye?

She was almost ready to believe that he had when she remembered that the rest of the miners were also missing. Logan had to be with Big Sam and the rest.

But what if he wasn't? What if by chance he should happen to meet that awful man, Flint, unexpectedly? Since there was only one main road leading into town, it was a distinct possibility.

It was late afternoon before Logan rode up to his cabin and dismounted. With a cry of relief, she raced across the street and flung herself into his arms.

Startled, Logan wrapped his arms around her waist. "Well, now, this is what I call a welcome home."

She pulled away from him. "Where have you been? Do you know what I've been through?"

He searched her face, his forehead creased in a worried frown. "What is it, Libby? What's wrong? Is Noel . . .?"

"Noel's fine." She glanced around to make certain that that awful man Flint wasn't spying on them. "Come to the house." She turned and hastened back across the street. Logan followed at her heels, hammering her with questions.

"Libby, talk to me. What's going on? Libby!" She waited until they were safe inside and the door firmly bolted before she explained.

Logan listened to every word as if they were flecks of gold that must be weighed. "You say the man's name was Flint? Was he wearing an eye patch?"

"He most certainly was!" The dark look on Logan's face confirmed her suspicions that the man was dangerous. "Obviously you know this man."

"I'm afraid so. The man was here last December. Tried to push his weight around. So you told him you never heard of me, uh? I'm surprised he took your word for it."

"I don't think he did." She shuddered as she recalled the look on Flint's face as he glanced at Noel. "It was the other men . . ." Just thinking about how the men had made fun of the town made her bristle with indignation.

"They had the nerve to call this a sissified town. You should have heard how they attacked everything in sight. Lord Almighty, they even made disparaging comments about the curtains I hung up in the saloons."

"No!"

"Indeed they did! And another thing. They criticized the church."

"Unbelievable!"

"They said we had enough flowers to pollinate the state."

"They said that?"

"They most certainly did!" Libby's eyes blazed. She looked so indignant that Logan couldn't contain himself a moment longer. He threw back his head and laughed.

Libby stared at him as if he'd taken leave of his senses. "I fail to see what's so funny," she said. "This is a very serious matter. Why I could have been . . . Noel could have been . . ."

Logan winced inwardly. He knew all too well what Flint was capable of. "I know, Libby. That's what's so astounding. You single-handedly scared Flint and his men out of town." He was so thankful that she and Noel were not harmed that he grabbed her by the waist and whirled her around the floor, absorbing the feel of her lovely slim body pressed against his.

The effort cost him in the way of pain. He released her and grabbed his leg.

"Logan?"

He sank to the floor and rubbed his knee. "It's all right. The cold got to it. I should never have gone up there."

She dropped to his side. "Gone where?"

"To Devil's Bar."

"Why did you?"

He told her about the missing half nugget. "I thought ... I wanted ..." He wanted it for Libby. For Noel. For the three of them. "One of Thornton's men found it. The rich keep getting richer." He made no effort to keep the bitterness from his voice.

"I never thought you cared about getting rich."

"It's not the money, Libby."

Her gaze dropped down to where he was rubbing his leg. "Let me," she said. She pressed her fingers against his knee. He stiffened at her touch, but only for the instant it took her to prove her competence in such matters.

Surprised by the wonderful warm sensations that seemed to flow through her fingers, he allowed himself to relax before realizing what a mistake that was. "That feels so good," he whispered. The sweet, lovely fragrance of her filled his head.

Her eyes never leaving his face, she increased the pressure of her fingers. She worked the knee before moving her palms upward to his thigh to bring a moan of pleasure to his lips.

"Do ... do you want me to fix you a hot bath?" she stammered.

"You'd better not. Unless you're prepared to join me."

For several moments they stared at each other. Finally, he lifted a brow as if to repeat his warning.

Heart pounding, her hand tightened around his thigh.

His breath escaped him in a hissing sound. "You'd better stop, Libby."

"Stop what, Logan?"

"You know what."

She applied more pressure with her fingers.

"I mean it, Libby. If you don't stop right now, I'm not going to be responsible for what happens." He grabbed her hand and pulled it away from his leg. A moment of tortured longing crossed his face, followed by a shadow of agony as he released her.

She laid her hand on his arm. "Don't push me away," she whispered.

"Dammit, Libby. Can't you see this is not right? You deserve better than me. Noel deserves better. You're going to Boston and I'm going up north. And that's the way it's going to be. We're never going to see each other again after next week."

"Neither one of us is going anywhere tonight." This time her voice was strong and firm with conviction.

He looked at her in astonishment. "Libby! Surely you can't mean . . . you're not suggesting . . . I care for you too much to take advantage of you. I could never . . . It's unthinkable."

She sat so still, no one could possibly guess how fast her heart was beating. "I'm not asking you to take advantage. I'm asking you to hold me."

He grabbed her by both arms. "Dammit, Libby, why are you doing this to me? You know that physically . . ."

She pulled away from him. "Physically? You mean your leg? The very same leg that you've insisted all this time was just fine? You think that's going to prevent you from . . . ?"

"I mean that you deserve better than me. You deserve a man who is whole and can give you a better life. I'm a trapper. That's all I'm ever going to be. And when I can't trap anymore, then I'll be nothing."

Keeping her eyes on his face, she let her hand drop to his sturdy thigh. She'd been afraid, so afraid for his safety earlier. She had been convinced that she would never see him again. And all the time she feared for his safety, she regretted the many times she failed to tell him how she felt about him. She wasn't going to make that mistake again.

"I love you, Logan St. John."

He opened his mouth, but if he meant to protest, she effectively stopped him by letting her fingers inch closer to his crotch. She saw the struggle in his face, heard the pain in his voice as he spoke. "Libby, our feelings for each other can't change a thing."

"Maybe not." She traced circles with her fingers and flattened her palms against his upper thigh. She'd never in her life been so forward with a man. But then she'd never wanted a man more than she did at that moment. Nor had she met a man quite as stubborn. "But it does give me a mighty good reason for doing what I'm about to do." Her fingers brushed against him and she felt a surge of joy upon finding him fully aroused.

"In the name of sam hill . . ." He gasped, grabbing her by the shoulder. His eyes burned like molten lava. "My God, Libby. What did you stop for?" He slipped his arms around her waist and crushed her to him.

"One night," he moaned between kisses. "We can only have this one night." Saying this helped him put aside his guilt for taking her when he had so little—next to nothing—to give in return.

Lifting his head, he nuzzled against the warmth at her ear as he coaxed her backward in his arms.

"Oh, Libby, I've dreamed of this so many times. All those nights you lay in my bed."

"You too?" she whispered.

He smiled and cupped her face in his hands. The loving look she gave him filled him with a happiness he never knew possible. "You mean, you wanted me, even then? You weren't just watching me undress out of curiosity."

"I wanted you," she admitted.

Her confession brought a wide smile to his face. "Well, now . . ."

He fumbled impatiently with the hooks and eyes at her bodice. With an awkwardness that was remarkable in its efficiency, he slipped the yards of calico from her body until her dress lay in a puddle at their feet. He could hardly breathe as he undressed her.

He shivered in anticipation as he began to remove

her dainty white linen chemise. He'd seen her nakedness before, knew the loveliness that awaited him. But
this was different. Those other times, she wasn't his to
take.

But she was his to take tonight.

And he intended to make it a night to remember.

For it was all that they had left to them.

He touched the silky strap that divided her shoulder,
savoring the touch of her velvet-soft flesh as he slipped
the narrow band slowly down her arm until one lovely
full breast was revealed to his hungry eyes. Her breast
spilled into his palm and he likened its soft skin to water lilies.

Gasping with pleasure, he teased the lovely dark
nipple between his teeth, tasting the sweet nectar that
filled his mouth like an earth-warming spring. He
never felt more like a man than he did at that moment
suckling at her breast.

Her skin warmed him like sunshine. Her kisses like
the rain were sometimes gentle, sometimes urgent, but
always nurturing and satisfying, washing over him
with a purity that took his breath away.

Her hands tugged at his shirt. Smiling at her impatience, he nonetheless tried to hold her back. They only
had one night and he intended to make the most of it.
Slowly he peeled away her chemise until every inch of
her exquisite body was revealed to him anew.

With a sense of wonder, he found all of nature rep-
resented in her lovely feminine form.

"Oh, God, Libby. You're so beautiful."

Pulling off his own shirt, he tossed it aside. He
wrapped his arms around her. Hands spread on the
lovely curves of her hips, he drew her closer until his
throbbing male hardness pressed against her lovely
feminine warmth.

The log in the fire rolled and heaved, sending a sudden hot flame upward and casting a warm orange glow
over them.

He moaned with pleasure as she ran her palms

across his muscular chest and down his back. His breath caught when she reached down to unfasten the hooks on his trousers. His heart almost stopped when she released his pulsing hard phallus from its rawhide confines and took it lovingly in her hand.

He stilled for a moment, as he so often stilled to savor a sunset or the first glimpse of new-fallen snow. And as he paused to take in the full wonder of it all, a fire blazed through him until his entire body had been torched. He lowered his head between her breasts. "You're driving me crazy," he moaned against her.

Laughing softly, she squeezed him once again, and this time his body could lie still no longer.

Pushing her back as gently as urgency would allow, he settled on top of her, the tip of his manhood perched upon the soft nest of curls that beckoned to him.

He resisted the urge to straighten his injured leg. His leg reminded him of his inadequacies and tonight he wanted to be perfect in her eyes.

"Oh, Libby," he gasped. "You've driven me crazy from the moment you first appeared on my doorstep." He pulled back and gazed at her lovingly. Torn by the need to bury himself within her and the need to prolong the sweet agony of dancing on the brink of heaven, he sprinkled hot kisses up and down her body. Intense pleasure filled him as he explored every lovely little peak and valley of soft warm flesh and felt her quiver beneath his touch.

Only when she pleaded with him to stop did he enter her. A cry of ecstasy mingled with hers as he surrendered himself to the fiery heat of her feminine sheath.

Later, as they lay in each other's arm gazing into the dying fire, Logan felt a sense of stunned disbelief by what had happened between them. Never had he been with a woman who gave so completely of herself and demanded so much in return.

It had never occurred to him that it could be like this; that physical love could touch the soul as well as the body. All those years in the mountains, battling the wild and savage land, had taught him nothing about love and life. All those women he'd had, his marriage—none of it had taught him what it meant to be with a woman. Not until that moment had he known how truly magnificent it could be—was surely meant to be.

He hugged her closer, feeling the stirrings of his loins once again. Pressing next to her, he smiled in apology. "I can't get enough of you."

She nuzzled up close, telling him in so many different ways that the same was true for her.

They made love, talked love, and in every way possible expressed their love for each other for the remainder of the night. They stopped only long enough for her to attend to Noel's needs. As she nursed Noel, Logan held her wrapped in his protective arms, covering her nakedness with his own. He loved to stroke her breasts as she nursed. The flow of her milk was like music to his sensitive fingers. There was nothing else in nature that compared.

After each feeding, he carried Noel back to his room to lay him gently in his cradle. His heart filled with tenderness as he stared down at the sleeping child.

Leaving the warmth of Libby's arms, the cold night air pierced his knee with knifelike swiftness. After the initial stab of pain, he felt a burning sensation similar to being pricked with a thousand blunt needles. Nonetheless, he resisted the urge to rub his leg or otherwise try to relieve the pain. Instead, he hastened back to her side to escape back into her arms where they made love again. Sweet, passionate love that allowed no room for physical afflictions. In her arms, he forgot about his leg. Forgot about his uncertain future. Forgot that the two of them would soon be going their very separate ways.

In her arms, he felt whole again. She made him feel whole.

Chapter 34

IT was late afternoon when Logan walked into the Golden Hind. The saloon was empty. Most of the miners were up at the diggings. Logan limped up to the bar and ordered a double whiskey.

Moe the bartender lifted a questioning brow, but said nothing. Logan made quick work of the whiskey and ordered another.

All right, so she's going back to Boston. What's the big deal? He always knew that. Boston is where she belongs. Where Noel belongs. And just because they spent one night together . . .

He picked up his glass and gulped down his drink. One beautiful glorious night, he amended.

A few more drinks and the memories of the night spent with Libby began to grow fuzzy.

"It wasn't really that great," he slurred, head hanging over the bar. "Nothing could be that great, right?" He focused on the bartender.

Moe had suddenly sprouted two heads. Both heads wagged from side to side as he refilled Logan's glass. "Whatever you say."

It was dark by the time Logan staggered into his cabin. Not bothering to light his lantern, he stumbled around the room until he located his bedroll. Tucking it under his arm, he left the cabin, mounted his horse, and headed up to the hills. He couldn't bear the thought of lying in his own bed, knowing that Libby was so close. After last night, every minute away from her had been torture.

The sting of the cold night air cleared his head. He rode his horse to a protected place in the hills amid a cluster of cottonwoods. Reaching his destination, he remained on his horse, senses alert. It was a dark moonless night and the tall trees blocked out what little starlight there was.

Logan sniffed the air, mentally sorting out the odors until every last one had been identified. He could smell squirrel fur, rabbit, owl, could pick out the tangy smell of the wild blackberry bushes that grew nearby. The slight stirring of the wind carried the scent of coyotes. Another sniff and he determined that they were probably a few miles away. The same wind told him that there was no sign of man or bear in the area, and that was the important thing.

Satisfied, he dismounted his horse and pulled his bedroll from the saddle. The ground was level and relatively free from rocks. He chose his position carefully, picking out a spot that allowed him to view the trail below. With Flint on the prowl, he couldn't afford to get careless.

He stretched out beneath the stars and arranged his weapons by his side, ready to grab in an emergency.

It had been months since he'd last slept outdoors. He remembered how difficult it had been to get used to sleeping inside a man-made building.

Strangely enough, he found it equally difficult to adjust to sleeping outside again. The slight rustle of leaves overhead distracted him, as did the rushing sound of the river in the distance.

He lay on his side in that hazy state just before sleep and wondered why Noel hadn't yet awakened for his two o'clock feeding. Thinking something wrong, he opened his eyes. It was then that he remembered it was not possible to hear Noel from this distance. Nor could he see the light from Libby's cabin as she rose to tend to Noel's needs.

He turned over. He was surprised at the many ways he remained connected to Libby and Noel, even after they had moved out of his cabin and into their own. It had been unconscious on his part; he hadn't even known until now how connected he'd been to them. It wasn't his nature to be so dependent on another human being. Not his nature at all. He was a man of the mountains, he told himself. The great outdoors had nurtured him from childhood, been home and family to him, friend and foe. He knew the outdoors like he knew himself—maybe even better.

Tonight, nature was a stranger.

Libby paced a trail from one window to the other as she watched Logan's house. Noel was asleep and time hung as heavy as a chain around her neck.

Three days. It had been three days since she and Logan had spent the night together. She'd not seen him since.

She felt hurt . . . confused. She'd never been with a man other than Jeff and they had waited until they were married before sharing much more than a chaste kiss.

There was nothing chaste about Logan's kisses and certainly nothing chaste about how she'd returned them . . . Just thinking about it brought a blush to her face, followed by a liquid warmth that radiated outward and spread throughout her entire body.

"Oh, Logan, where are you?" She was convinced that his leg was acting up again and he was trying to keep it from her.

When at last Noel awoke from his morning nap, she bathed and dressed him and laid him in his cart. She then pushed him up the boardwalk toward the center of town. Someone had to know where Logan had been spending his time.

The town was deserted except for Cast-Iron Peters, who leaned against a post in front of the general store, whittling away on a piece of wood. No one else was in sight, although a few horses were tied to the hitching post in front of the Golden Hind, indicating that some of the miners had already returned from the diggings.

Although Cast-Iron never spoke to her or otherwise acknowledged her, she always greeted him politely. Today was no different. "Good morning, Mr. Peters."

As usual, she received no response.

She walked past him and froze at the sound of a loud cracking sound that ripped through the stillness. Before she could identify the sound, a sign fell from a false-faced building and crashed to the boardwalk, startling the horses.

One bay reared on its hind legs and pulled free from the hitching post. With a wild whinny, the horse galloped toward her.

She opened her mouth to scream, but nothing came out. Swallowing panic, she spun around just as the horse raced past. She watched in horror as Noel's cart went flying off the boardwalk and onto its side.

She didn't recognize the scream as her own. Not until Cast-Iron's steadying hand clamped down on her shoulder.

"It's all right, ma'am."

Libby turned toward the voice and could hardly believe her eyes. There was Noel all safe and sound in Cast-Iron Peters's burly arms.

Relief flooded through her. She grabbed her son and held him close. A cry of thanksgiving trembled on her lips.

The commotion had brought others on the run. Sharkey ran bowlegged out of his shop, waving a pair of scissors. "You're mighty lucky, Miss Libby. I thought for sure you and the baby were a goner."

"They would have been too," Hap concurred from the door of his general store. "If it hadn't been for old Cast-Iron here. I believe we have ourselves a hero."

"I believe you're right," Libby said, smiling up at the man, who looked embarrassed by all the attention.

"I didn't do nothing," Cast-Iron mumbled.

"I don't know about you, but I call a-savin' a

mother and her child a-doing somethin'," Sharkey insisted. "I think this calls for a cel'bration."

Appleby stuck his head out of the barbershop, his chin half-covered in soap suds. "Before you go drinking yourself silly, Sharkey, how about finishing the job you started here?"

"Ah, shucks, Luke. You know what the matter with you is? You take life too ser'ously." Sharkey shuffled back to his shop. "As soon as I finish up Luke, here, the first round of drinks is on me."

Logan rode into town after dark and stopped at the Golden Hind. The high spirits of the men surprised him. As far as he knew, not much had happened in the diggings, not since one of Thornton's men had found the other half of Big Sam's nugget.

Sharkey was the first to greet him. "Look who's here. Where you been a-hidin'?"

"Hiding? Not me. What's going on?"

"You mean you ain't heard?"

"Don't tell me you finally struck it rich?"

"Naw, not me." Sharkey turned to the others. "Logan here ain't heard the news. Why we have ourselves a hero. Cast-Iron, take a bow."

Cast-Iron grinned and looked embarrassed.

Logan couldn't remember Cast-Iron ever cracking a smile before, let alone displaying anything that even slightly resembled civil manners. "So what did Cast-Iron do?"

"Why he saved Miss Libby and Noel from sure death."

A gut-wrenching pain shot through Logan as he stared at Sharkey. "He what?"

"Yessiree. Snatched them out of the way of a gallopin' horse. Just like that."

No sooner were the words out of Sharkey's mouth than Logan had spun on his heels and dashed back outside. He headed toward Libby's cabin on foot and pounded on her door.

She looked pleased to see him. "Logan! Where in the world have you . . ."

He took her hands in his and pushed his way inside. "I had to see for myself that you're all right."

She pulled away from him and the initial delight on her face dissolved into an angry scowl. "What do you care?"

"What are you saying? Of course I care."

"And how am I supposed to know that? You walked out of here the other morning and disappeared without a word."

He rubbed his whiskered chin. "Libby, I do care. If anything happened to you, I don't know . . ." The words caught in his throat.

He had such a deep need to protect her, protect Noel, protect the two people in all the world he cared about. But there was only one way he could do that.

"Libby, you must leave for Boston. It's not safe here for you. You might have been killed." Just thinking about her recent close calls made him want to carry her to Boston himself. "First Flint and now this . . . You've got to leave before Flint comes back."

Her eyes widened. "You think he'll come back?"

"You can bet on it. You said it yourself, Libby. This is no place to raise a child."

"I know but . . . it's strange. There's so much I hate about California. The harshness, the violence. The fact that a man with a gun can declare himself judge and jury. But I'm really going to miss the miners and . . . you." She looked up at him and the raw honest emotion on her face tore him apart. "I'll miss you."

"Oh, Libby." He gathered her in his arms and held her so close their hearts seemed to beat as one. He was filled with remorse that he had so little to offer her. He couldn't even offer her something as basic and simple as a proper home.

He lovingly cupped her face in his hands, knowing that every detail he memorized would only haunt him for the rest of his life, and still he couldn't help himself.

She gazed back at him with tenderness, and as the full impact of her love for him took effect, he felt a squeezing pain. It nearly killed him to know that love was the enemy at the moment and had to be fought at all costs. For it could force them to make the wrong decisions—decisions they might both come to regret.

"You must go back to Boston," he said.

"Please, Logan," she pleaded. "Come with me."

"I can't, Libby. You know that I can't."

"Then I'll come with you!"

He was so startled by her declaration, he stared at her dumbfounded. "You can't possibly know what you're saying. A trapper's life is no life for a woman. For a child."

At the mention of Noel, she bit her lower lip. Not even her love for Logan would let her do anything that was not in Noel's best interests.

Chapter 35

TWO days later Libby stood outside by the clothes-line, staring with unseeing eyes at the basket of wash that was waiting to be hung up to dry. It was so difficult lately to concentrate on chores. How could she? With Logan commanding her every thought?

How was she going to find the strength to say good-bye to him? How would she ever get through the days, the months, the years, without him?

So depressed was she by her bleak thoughts that she didn't hear Thornton ride up. Indeed, she was so startled by the deep masculine voice that cut through her thoughts, she jumped.

"I didn't mean to startle you," he said in apology.

He sat upon his fine black stallion watching her in such a way that she was convinced that her red flaming cheeks had given her thoughts away.

Embarrassed to be caught daydreaming, she forced a smile and tried to look pleased to see him. "What brings you here this time of day?" He would normally be at the mines during the day.

He dismounted and tied his horse to a bush. "I had some good news I thought might cheer you."

"Oh?"

"Word is that the stage will resume its regular run next week."

Libby pressed her fingers into her palms. "Really?"

"They finally cleared away all the debris on the road leading to Nevada City. I know you're anxious to leave." He studied her face. "I thought you'd be happy about this."

"I am," she assured him, and since his face was dark with skepticism, she tried to sound more enthusiastic. "Of course I am. It's just hard to believe. I've been trying to get home to Boston for so long." Much to her surprise, she burst into tears. "Oh, dear. I don't know what's the matter with me."

Thornton handed her a clean linen handkerchief and wrapped his arm around her. "Don't apologize. I'm sure you're just overwhelmed with the prospect of going home."

Grateful for his understanding, she took the handkerchief from him and wiped away her tears. It occurred to her that he was probably the only man in California who had a clean handkerchief.

"I feel better now. Thank you." She lifted her chin and handed his handkerchief back. Something in his face made her step away from him. She considered Thornton a good friend, but the look he gave her went beyond friendship.

Not knowing what to say suddenly, she pulled one of Noel's wet nightgowns from her basket and shook it out.

"I didn't tell you all the good news," Thornton said, watching her closely. "At least, I hope you think it's good news. I'm thinking about returning to Boston with you."

"Really?" She flung the nightgown over the line. "What about your mine?"

"As you know, I've been fairly successful. But most of the easy stuff has already been mined. As I told you before, to mine any more would require us to blast away solid granite. That would require far different equipment than is presently available. I need to return to Boston to make arrangements for such equipment to be transported out here, along with men trained to handle it."

"I see."

"Then you won't mind having me as a traveling companion?"

Traveling alone with an infant was something that Libby had dreaded. "I wouldn't mind at all."

He shot a finger across his mustache. "It's my hope that you would also allow me to pay my respects to you and your family in Boston."

Libby blushed. "Why, Thornton, I would be most honored."

Thornton looked pleased. "Perhaps you could do me the honor of attending a play with me. I know how you love the theater."

"I would like that," she said, trying with all her might to sound enthusiastic. But her voice was flat and she knew she fooled no one.

Thornton smiled, but she could see the hurt in his eyes and she felt guilty. He pulled a wet blanket out of her basket and hung it neatly next to Noel's nightgown. "Then it's agreed? We leave next Friday?"

"Friday?" She mustn't think, she told herself. She mustn't think of Logan. Mustn't think of leaving him. Of never seeing him again. Mustn't think. "That's . . . that's only a week away."

"Do you need more time? We could go the following week. But keep in mind that the longer we postpone our trip, the greater our chances of bad weather when we reach the East Coast."

"Of course, you're right. Next Friday will be fine."

He looked pleased. "I shall make the necessary arrangements."

Moments later Noel awoke from his nap. She walked over to his cart and picked him up. She held him close, pressing his warm little body next to her chest and dropping a kiss on his velvet-soft brow. His hair felt soft and silky to her touch. "We're going home, little one." *Yes, yes, I must concentrate on thoughts of home.* "And won't your grandparents be happy to see what a big boy you are?" *Concentrate.*

"Oh, Noel, we're going home. Just like I promised your poor dear papa."

For the next two days, Libby tried to find the right moment to break the news to Logan that she would be leaving town within the week. Perhaps knowing that she was leaving would make it easier for him. At least he wouldn't have to worry about her safety should Flint return. Maybe if he knew she was leaving, he'd leave too. Then they'd both be safe from Flint.

Her chance came late that Monday afternoon when she glanced out her window just as Logan returned home. She picked up Noel from the floor, wrapped him in a blanket, and carried him to Logan's cabin.

The door flew open and Logan looked pleased to see her. "Come in and have some of my terrible coffee." He took Noel and placed him at a safe distance from the fire.

She sat at the table and watched him pour two cups of coffee. She tried not to think of the time spent with him in the past. The nights she lay in bed watching him, monitoring his breathing, feeling the warmth of his presence. She tried not to think of a lot of things. "The reason I came today is I wanted to tell you before you heard it from someone else."

He raised his eyes and his face grew still. It was obvious that he'd guessed what she'd come to tell him.

Still, she had to follow through. It was the only way she knew to maintain control. "I'm going home. We're leaving Friday. Thornton is going with me."

He lowered his eyes and stared into his coffee cup. A silence stretched between them. It was as if he, too, were holding on for dear life. When at last he spoke, his voice was strained. "It's best, Libby. You know that."

She swallowed hard. "I wish things could be different. That you would come with me."

He regarded her with dark troubled eyes. "If I thought for one moment it would work. That you and

I could make a life together in Boston, I wouldn't hesitate a moment."

"After what happened between us the other night, I know it could, Logan." She clutched at his arm, the need for control forgotten. "I know it could. If you really loved me."

His eyes flared with anger. "Don't ever question my feelings for you."

"Then let me go with you."

"No! I lost one wife to the wilds. I'm not about to make that mistake again." Seeing her stricken face, his voice softened. "We always knew this day would come, Libby. Let's not make it worse than it already is."

"Nothing could be worse than this!"

He stood and pulled her to her feet, taking her into his arms. "It's what your husband wanted for his son. It's what's right."

She laid her head against his chest and he felt her tremble. "Libby . . . I . . ."

She pulled away and studied his face as if searching for something she was unable to find there. Wordlessly, she spun away from him and hurried toward Noel.

"Libby!"

She froze in place, and he sensed her fight for control. When at last she turned to face him, her face was composed. "It's best," he said again. He loved her too much to say what he wanted to say, was desperate to say. Didn't dare. For he knew how fragile her composure—his own composure—really was.

Miserably, he watched her bundle Noel in her arms. It pained him to think he would never again lay eyes on the boy. The hurt increased to a point of torture as he watched her walk away. She never looked back as she crossed the street and disappeared inside her house.

But even after both doors between them had been shut, he feared she would hear the silent cry of his less than noble heart, *Don't go, Libby. Don't leave me.*

Chapter 36

THE decision to leave Calico Corners without saying a final good-bye to Libby was the most painful, most difficult thing he ever had to do. It was also the most necessary.

His only hope was that she would understand the reasons why it must be this way.

It was still dark when he fought his way out of his tangled bedclothes. Not bothering to light the fire that had died during the night, he dressed in the dark. He grabbed his saddle and stepped outside.

Jim Bridger nudged him with a velvet-soft nose. He threw the saddle over the horse, then loped back to the house for his bedroll and other supplies.

The last thing he grabbed was his rifle. But before mounting the horse, he walked out to the middle of the street and stood for one last time in front of Libby's house. How long he stood in the dark shadows of the night, he couldn't say. But he stood long enough for the mist to seep through his clothes, long enough for the faint glow of dawn to touch the horizon.

He might have stood there forever had Noel not cried out, snapping him out of his reverie.

He knew every one of the child's distinctive cries by heart. This particular one was the full-fledged lusty cry that preceded each mealtime. The cry stopped abruptly, telling him that Libby had eased a milk-swollen nipple into Noel's mouth.

Logan squeezed his lids tight to hold back the moisture that had suddenly blurred his vision. Cursing himself, he mounted his horse and rode out of town.

Every inch of him was filled with an excruciating pain that ate away at his core. No sooner had he skirted past the last building than he rode his horse hard in a desperate attempt to put as many miles behind him as possible. In a way it worked, for eventually the pain began to diminish and a bleak, empty void took its place.

Only then did he dare to stop his frantic pace and let his horse rest.

He traveled all that day and into the night. He ignored his tired muscles and painful leg until he was convinced that he was so exhausted that nothing, not even memories of Libby, would interfere with his sleep. It was almost midnight when he finally dismounted and set up camp.

He slept little, if any, and when at last the first sliver of dawn touched the peaks of the mountains that loomed over him, he felt a sense of relief that the long night was over.

Overhead the sky was still dark and studded with stars. Shivering, he buried himself deeper into his bedroll. The pain in his leg had gone from a dull throb to a piercing ache. It was a painful reminder that his days as a trapper could be few in number if not altogether at an end.

He rubbed the circulation back before standing, then walked slowly until the stiffness was less pronounced. But it wasn't his leg that gave him pause. It was a sense of foreboding that came out of nowhere.

Alerted, he tensed to test the air around him. After identifying even the softest of sounds and the faintest of odors to his satisfaction, he scanned the rocky cliffs that rose ahead, his eyes quick and sharp. He found nothing to suggest there was danger lurking nearby.

Still, he kept a watchful eye as he tied his bedroll to the saddle. He reached into his necessary bag for some of the beef jerky he'd packed. After biting off a mouthful, he dug deeper into one of the pockets of his leather bag for the willow bark to relieve the pain in his leg. He drew out a rectangular piece and as he did so, something fell to the ground. He stooped over to pick it up.

It was a gold locket. Libby's gold locket. He released the catch with his thumb and studied the cluster of golden hair. He thought of Libby cutting a piece of her dead husband's hair so she would have something to give to Jeffrey's son. He knew how much the locket meant to her.

He snapped the lid shut with a curse. Of all the damned luck. How did the thing get in his necessary bag? He considered mailing the locket back to her at some later date. But by the time he reached a town big enough to have a post office, she would have already left Calico Corners, and he had no idea what her Boston address was.

As he considered his options, he lopped off a piece of rough bark with his knife and popped the square piece into his mouth.

He couldn't go back.

But the locket means the world to her.

He couldn't trust himself to go back.

But Libby was saving the locket for Noel.

If he went back he would do something he had no right to do. Dammit! He dare not go back. Not even for his godson's sake. Not ever!

How could he not?

Libby stood in the center aisle of the general store and stared at Hap in disbelief. "What do you mean, Logan's gone?"

Hap glanced at Sharkey and Big Sam, but when neither stepped forward to answer Libby's question, he gave a sigh of resignation. "He came in here for supplies day before yesterday. Said he was going up north."

"But that's not possible!" Libby protested. "He wouldn't leave without saying good-bye."

She didn't want to believe it was true, not even after

she left the general store and headed straight for Logan's house to see for herself.

Much to her alarm, she discovered that although the crude furnishings remained, including a pile of valuable pelts, his personal belongings were gone.

Still not wanting to believe he could take off without as much as a good-bye, she laid Noel in front of the darkened fireplace and tried to control her emotions. But she was hurting too much to keep the tears at bay. "Oh, Logan, how could you?"

She stayed in his house all that day, absorbing the essence of him that still lingered in the room to taunt her.

It was nearly dark when Big Sam and Sharkey arrived and found her sitting on the pallet, her face buried in one of the buckskin shirts Logan had left behind. Between the two of them, they tried to persuade her to go home.

Big Sam regarded her with eyes filled with worry. "If you don't get your sleep, Miz Libby, you ain't gonna be fit for travelin' tomorrow."

"Big Sam's right," Sharkey agreed. "That stagecoach is due might' early."

"I'll be ready," she whispered. There was no reason to stay any longer, now that Logan was gone. "I'm going to miss you both." She hugged Big Sam and wrapped her arms around Sharkey. "If you ever come to Boston . . ."

They hugged and cried and hugged some more. Finally, Big Sam scooped Noel into his strong dark arms and he and Sharkey escorted Libby home. After they left, she took off her calico dress and put on the buckskin dress Logan had made her. She wanted to surround herself with reminders of him and nothing reminded her of him more than the warm soft dress he'd made with his own two hands. She was still dressed in buckskin when she fell exhausted and depleted onto the bed.

* * *

He was crazy to go back. But once he made the decision, it was as if he was caught in some strong magnetic force that had taken control of his every thought and deed.

He had traveled all day, stopping only long enough to let his horse drink from the cool rushing springs he found along the way. His fear was that if he lingered one moment longer than necessary, he would not make it back in time. And she would have left with Thornton, never to be seen again.

And there was so much he had to tell her. So much that must be said. Maybe, they could be together. There had to be a way. Despite his leg. Despite the fact that he was a trapper and possibly even an ex-trapper, there had to be a way.

During the warmest part of the day, when the hot rays of the sun penetrated his leg and the willow bark had taken effect, he managed to convince himself that his leg was on the mend. On some deeper level, he knew, of course, that he was deluding himself. But it was a pleasant delusion and one that made the long hours in the saddle more bearable.

It was nightfall by the time he reached the mountain trail. It was dangerous to try to navigate the sharp twists and turns in the dark. But he had no choice, not if he wanted to reach her in time.

He reached the summit without mishap. He reined in his horse and stopped to absorb the sounds and odors around him. It was a habit acquired in his youth after he and his papa were attacked by a small band of Indians. It was only by sheer skill that they'd escaped, but the lessons learned never left him.

His body tensed. He reached for his revolver. But it was not the memory of that long-ago brush with death that had alerted him. His inner alarm had been triggered by some primal instinct. He cocked his gun and waited.

Sensing his uneasiness, his horse nickered softly. A short distance away, an owl let out a low hooting sound. The nocturnal cry would normally have set his mind at rest. But not tonight.

The slight breeze carried the distinctive odor of a wolf's den, but there was no smell of humans or bear. Nothing that would be cause for alarm. Still, he remained fully alert. He sniffed the air and listened, his sharp keen eyes measuring every shadow, every movement.

His gun held in readiness, he urged his horse forward. It puzzled him that Jim Bridger revealed none of the usual signs that signaled danger. How could his horse's instincts be so out of accord with his own?

Without the slightest hesitation, the horse followed a sharp turn, but even this failed to put Logan's mind at ease.

The sound of water rushing along the wooden flume obliterated the normal sounds of nature. There were no worrisome scents in the air, nothing at all that should cause alarm. Still, he scanned the darkness around him, convinced that something was amiss. Never before had he occasion to doubt his own instincts. He wasn't about to doubt them now.

He reached the trail leading downward, but decided to take a short detour to a spot that overlooked the valley below and Calico Corners. After dark, the most that could be seen normally from such a vantage point was a pinpoint of light.

Tonight, however, a reddish glow ten times brighter than any gas lantern or campfire greeted his startled eyes and struck terror in his heart. Calico Corners was on fire!

With a thrust of his hand, he replaced his gun and urged his horse back toward the trail. With no thought for his own safety, he rode helter-skelter down the mountainside with only the faint light of the silver half-moon to lead the way.

The pounding sound of his horse's hooves beat out the silent cry of his heart. His leg hammered unmercifully against the rigid moist flank of his racing horse, but none of this mattered to him. The only thing that did matter was that Libby and Noel were in danger.

And he was so far away.

Chapter 37

HOME. At last she was home in Boston. But rather than feeling joyous, Libby was overwhelmed with feelings of confusion and fear. She ran along the same crowded streets she had roamed as a child.

She tensed her body and listened to the city sounds as Logan had taught her to listen. They were all there—the familiar sounds of home. The clink of milk bottles being delivered in the early morning hours. The clip-clop of iron horse shoes upon the cobbled streets. The loud clang of the anvil from the blacksmith shop a block away from her house.

It struck her as strange that the familiar sounds of the city would suddenly seem so harsh and forbidding.

The smell of the freshly baked bread from the bakery, combined with the salty smell of crab and lobster from the nearby fish market, seemed far less forbidding, though nowhere near as welcoming as she had supposed.

It surprised her that she felt like a stranger. If only she could find the house she grew up in. Maybe, then, she'd feel at home.

She could see it now, in the hazy distance. She jumped off the pier and began to swim through the icy cold water toward the house. Her mother waved to her from the veranda. Her father called to her from a second-story window, telling her to go back.

Her limbs grew heavy, leaden, dragging her beneath the surface of the water. She could no longer breathe.

Gasping, she sat up in bed, clutching her throat. Her

brain in tumult, she fought through a maze of confused senses. But it was a muffled choking sound coming from Noel's cradle that jolted her to full wakefulness.

Before she could name the source of the danger, she jumped out of bed and made a mad dash across the room. Gathering Noel in her arms, she glanced in alarm at the bright orange glow outside the bedroom window. She fought against the terror that froze even her lungs. It was no time to panic.

Forcing herself to think rationally, she held Noel close and dashed through the door leading to the other room. The room was filled with smoke and her throat tightened in protest.

The metal handle of the front door felt hot. Using a portion of Noel's blanket, she yanked the door open. Smoke and flames clawed at the doorway. With a startled cry, she slammed the door shut and spun around to face the side window. That's when it hit her full force. The house was surrounded by fire.

And there was no way to escape.

By the time Logan thundered into town, the flames had spread from one end of Main Street to the other. Urging Jim Bridger onward, Logan flew past the church just as the steeple collapsed, sending sparks flying across his path. His horse reared in panic.

Cursing beneath his breath, he reined until he had the horse under control, then quickly dismounted. He landed on his bad leg. He let out a muttered oath. Momentarily dazed by the pain, he fought his way through blinding smoke and scorching heat.

He hobbled on one foot and dragged his other leg behind him. Chunks of blazing wood fell around him.

The entire frame of Libby's house was in flames, including her wooden porch where a group of men worked frantically. Buckets filled with water were hauled with speedy precision from one man to the next all the way from the creek.

Thornton's usual soft-cultured voice was harsh and relentless as he issued orders to his men.

The entire porch and front entrance were completely engulfed in flames. Logan ran to the side of the house where Thornton had just broken through the wall with a hatchet.

Logan called to the others. "Bring the water over here!"

No sooner had he spoken than gallons of water hit the side of the house. The water sizzled and evaporated as it doused the hot flames and sputtered steam.

Logan tried lifting his leg through the hole. His leg felt numb and heavy and refused to budge. He had no control over it. He slumped to the ground. Thornton gaped at him in surprise and valuable seconds were wasted. "Go to her, dammit!" Logan shouted.

Thornton, moving quicker than Logan had ever seen him move, squeezed himself through the jagged opening and disappeared. Snapping orders to the men, Logan watched the gaping hole like a hawk. What was taking so long, dammit! What was Thornton doing in there?

Much to his horror, the front wall collapsed inward and flames shot upward. Shouting Libby's name, Logan scrambled toward the opening.

A heavy weight landed on his shoulder and he felt himself being dragged away from the house. His senses spun in protest. He fought the dark hands that held him, but the viselike grip remained. "Dammit, Big Sam, let go of me."

"You can't do anything," Big Sam cried. "It's too late!"

"No! I won't have it. Let me go!" He pulled free from Big Sam, only to find himself being held by the others. A wild, desperate struggle followed.

Big Sam's voice roared above the rest. "Let the fool man go."

Logan scrambled on his one foot and hopped forward, his eyes blinded by flames and smoke. "Libby!"

His cry was filled with such anguish. If only he'd not left her, she would still be alive. "Oh, Libby, Libby, will you ever forgive me?"

A shadow appeared in front of him and he recognized the ash-covered face as Thornton's. "Libby . . . ?"

"She's fine!" Thornton shouted back. "Take the baby!" No sooner had he spoken than Noel was thrust into Logan's arms.

Logan handed Noel to Big Sam just as Thornton and Libby stepped away from the burning house.

"My God, Libby!" He couldn't believe his eyes. Not even after he took her in his arms and, hobbling on one foot, carried her to safety. He set her down on the grass and cupped her face in his hands. "I thought I lost you," he whispered.

She took his hand in her own. "Hold me," she cried. "Oh, Logan, please hold me."

The hill overlooking Calico Corners looked as grim as the aftermath of a battleground that morning as the full extent of the horror was illuminated by the morning sun. Exhausted miners were sprawled everywhere. A few fire-weary men had suffered burns and were soaking hands and arms in buckets of water. Several more stood in the fast-moving stream, letting the icy cold water swirl around their ankles as they splashed cold water onto blistered skin.

Some men sat staring into space, their soot-covered faces as still as wooden masks. Others gathered in groups of two or three to share their harried experiences in hushed voices.

Libby sat huddled beneath a blanket. Noel slept in her arms peacefully. She stared down lovingly at her fair-haired son and said a prayer of thanksgiving for his safety.

Logan and Thornton had worked on the fire line for most of the night. So far as anyone knew, no one had been seriously hurt, but a few of the miners had been trapped and it had taken heroic measures to free them.

Logan had crept back to her side at the first light of dawn, his face black with soot.

"How is Noel?" His voice, thick and hoarse from the exposure to smoke and heat, worked its way through her dazed senses.

"He's coughing a bit, but otherwise he appears to be as healthy as ever." She watched Logan chew down on a piece of willow, a sure sign that his leg was causing him pain. Her heart went out to him. "Are you all right?"

Logan wrapped his arm around her shoulder. "I was so sure I lost you." His voice was but a hoarse whisper, but it was emotion not smoke that thickened his voice, this time. "Lost Noel."

In the dying embers of the fire, Logan's eyes glowed brightly, but it was a brightness that could only come from an inner source.

She lifted her hand to his face. "Oh, Logan," she whispered back. "Do you know how I felt when I discovered you gone? I thought I'd never see you again."

He pressed his cheek into her palm. "I thought it would be best, Libby, if I just left."

"How could you think such a thing?"

"I don't know. I can't seem to think at all lately. I had some crazy notion . . ."

"What crazy notion . . . ?"

He stared at her in silence. He'd come back to tell her that he thought they could find a way to be together. But that was before the fire, before he knew how his leg would fail him in ways that had nothing to do with trapping, and everything to do with protecting the woman he loved.

"What crazy notion, Logan? Tell me . . ."

"Forget it, Libby, it was nothing." He pulled his hand away. "The reason I came back was to give you this." He reached into his pouch and pulled out the locket.

Her face brightened as she grabbed it away from him and held it in her hands. She had lost all her worldly possessions in that fire, but not the one object she cherished the most. She couldn't believe her eyes. "Where did you find it?"

"In my necessary bag. I have no idea how it got there, unless you dropped it the night I performed surgery on Macao."

Her fingers flew to her mouth. "I remember now. It must have fallen out when I knocked over the dream keeper. Oh, Logan, I can't tell you how much this means to me."

"I know, Libby. I know."

Sharkey hurried toward him, waving his hands. "I just saw Flint."

Logan stiffened. "Did you say Flint?"

"Sure 'nuff. Over there. He was a-watchin' the flames with the damnedest smile you ever did see. And some of the boys and me found an oil can over there by the river . . ."

Logan didn't wait for Sharkey to finish. He rose to his feet and stared in the direction Sharkey pointed.

"Don't go," Libby pleaded. She reached for his hand. "Please."

He gave her a tortured look. "What he did . . . It almost cost you your life. Don't ask me to forget that." He pulled away and nearly bumped into Thornton, whose bedraggled and weary appearance gave him a masculine dignity that Logan had previously thought lacking.

Next to Thornton, Logan felt inadequate. It was painful to admit, but Thornton had proven to be the better man, his stamina relentless through the long and difficult night. It was Thornton who had saved Libby, who had saved Noel, who had saved the two people in all the world that meant the most to Logan.

Logan would never forget that. Nor would he forget how he had personally failed Libby. "Take care of her," he said.

The two men exchanged a brief look as if to confirm the meaning behind those four simple words. Logan wanted Thornton's promise that he would care for Libby forever.

To his credit, Thornton accepted this unspoken mandate without the slightest travesty. He laid his hand briefly on Logan's shoulder. Thus the pact between them was rendered binding.

It happened so quickly that even Libby seemed oblivious to the brief, but no less solemn exchange.

Logan squeezed her hand and turned without further word. Anger and bitterness waged inside him as he headed down the hill. He was determined to make Flint pay for what he'd done.

But only some of the anger and even less of the bitterness were directed toward Flint. He blamed fate or whatever else it was called that had brought Libby to him. He had been content in his life before he met her; content to be who and what he was. Would have been content to spend the rest of his days in blissful ignorance, not knowing how much he missed, knowing even less how very miserable and empty his life really was.

Logan and Flint caught sight of each other at the same moment. But it was Flint who had the advantage. Before Logan could get his leg moving, Flint was already hightailing it back to his horse.

Realizing the futility of a foot chase, Logan spotted Big Sam's bay. It took some effort to force his leg over the wood and hide saddle, but once he was mounted, the odds were even, and he was in the game.

With grim determination, he tightened his grip on the reins, dug his heels into the sides of the horse, and took off after Flint.

Counting on Flint to follow the road, Logan veered through the woods and took a deer trail he knew crossed the road on the way to the river. The wind blew through his hair as he raced the horse through the heavy growth of trees. On occasion, he was forced to duck to avoid a low-growing branch. Upon reaching

the road again, he slid off the horse awkwardly, waited
a moment for the pain to subside, then tied his bay out
of sight.

Hearing Flint's horse race toward him, Logan drew
out his gun and waited.

The miners crowded around when Logan returned
some time later with Flint in tow. Their town in ashes
about their feet, the men wanted blood and they made
no effort to hide it. "String him up" came the unified
cry. Let the fool man hang for what he did to their
town.

Flint, dazed from Logan's grazing bullet, was
dragged off his horse and carried to one of the few
oaks in the immediate vicinity to escape the fire.
Standing in his saddle, Benjamin tied a rope to a
branch. The other end was forced over Flint's head and
drawn tight around his neck.

Libby, who had been watching from a distance,
could watch no longer. Leaving Noel in Shakespeare's
care, she ran down the hill. "Wait!" She grabbed
Logan by the arm. "Are you going to let them hang
this man without a trial?"

"The lady wants a trial," Benjamin yelled.

"I'll be the judge," said another. "I find this man
guilty as charged."

"Hang him!" The words grew into a chant that was
taken up by the miners until it was a deafening roar.

Libby never took her eyes off Logan's face.

"Stay out of this," he warned.

"Logan, don't let them do this."

"Don't you understand? Flint burned down their
town. He robbed the men of their homes."

"It was my home too!" she cried. In the silver light
of early morn her face was veiled with devastation and
despair. Tears filled her eyes as she gazed past the men
to the smoldering remains of the town.

Her words were a stunning blow to Logan. All this

time, he'd thought she hated the town. But she called it home . . . Home.

Why this affected him so, he couldn't say. It wasn't his home. Could never be his home. His home was the wilds, the mountains, the woods and streams.

Nonetheless, he was affected by her outburst.

But it was the honest raw emotion in her face that he found so devastating. His need for revenge left him. He felt drained and spent. "Cut him down."

Benjamin turned on him, his face twisted with anger. "Are you crazy?"

Logan grabbed Benjamin by the collar. "I said cut him down!"

Benjamin searched the crowd for support, but the miners' eyes were riveted upon Libby's face, and the silver streams of tears that trailed down her cheeks. The tension left the air.

Sharkey blew his nose and sniffled. Choo-Choo wheezed. Big Sam's eyes glistened as he began to speak for the very first time of being dragged away in his youth from his native African home.

"I never thought to have a home after that," he said. "The tobacco plantation where I toiled beneath the hot blazing sun was not home. Deadman's Gulch was not home." He wiped away his tears with the palms of his hands. "But Calico Corners. Now that was home."

Hap sat on the grass, rocking back and forth, staring into space. He clutched a can of baking powder, the only thing he had managed to salvage from his beloved store. Appleby sniffled by his side, too overcome to play a tune on his mouth organ.

Even Benjamin's eyes took on a suspicious sheen.

Libby's tears provided the glue that bonded the residents of Calico Corners together. Honest and open grief replaced any need for revenge.

Chapter 38

BY the time the sun had cast its golden glow upon the charred remains of the town, the miners had already rounded up every possible horse and mule in preparation for their trip to Grass Valley where they planned to purchase canvas tents and other supplies. Appleby had talked the men into taking Flint into town and turning him over to the alcalde.

Logan rounded up a mule for Libby and Noel. "Is this Crazy Man?" she asked suspiciously.

"No, it's Man Killer."

"What?" she cried out before seeing the teasing tug at the corner of his mouth. She stared openly at the face she had come to love so dearly during the last few months. She reached up to wipe away a black smudge from his forehead.

"Are you coming?" she asked, her voice trembling with tears she was determined not to shed.

He closed his hand over hers. "I can't."

She bit her lip and glanced away. "But your leg . . ."

"Is fine!" He regretted his harsh retort even before the hurt spilled from her eyes and spread across her face. He wanted to apologize, to tell her that the pain in his leg was nothing compared to the pain in his heart at losing her.

Losing Noel.

Losing the part of himself that only existed when he was with her. He tightened his fingers around her hand and pressed his lips into her knuckles.

"Take care, Libby."

"I guess this is good-bye," she whispered.

He always knew it would be hell to say good-bye. But this was far more difficult than anything he could imagine.

The leader of the group gave a low whistle. The caravan began to move forward.

His eyes never leaving her face, he cradled Noel in his arm and held the mule steady with his free hand while Libby mounted it. Before placing Noel in her arms, he dropped a kiss onto his velvet-smooth forehead. "You take care, little fellow, you hear?" He squeezed his eyes tight before lifting his head to meet Libby's gaze.

He laid Noel in Libby's outstretched arms. "Libby . . ." He spoke her name as if it were ripped from some part of him that had never before been touched.

She made no effort to hide the deep longing on her face. "I didn't want to say good-bye like this," she cried softly.

He didn't want to say good-bye at all. "Oh, Libby, I can't . . ." He stopped as Thornton rode up to take his place by Libby's side.

Thornton's face was hard and grim, and Logan was reminded that he'd made the man promise to take care of Libby. It had been the right thing to do. He knew it was right. Thornton was the better man. He'd proven that during the fire. He would take care of Libby. Give her everything she deserved. Protect her.

Libby's hand gripped his. "What were you going to say, Logan? What can't you do?"

"I can't wait to get started," he said quietly. "I have a long journey ahead."

She looked stricken, but said nothing as her mule began to move forward in line. Her hand was pulled from his grasp, taking with it a vital part of him, taking away everything he'd ever cared about.

Logan kept Libby's gaze in his own as the procession wound its way up the mountain toward the jagged peaks.

He watched until he could no longer see her face.

He watched until the last of the horses and mules had disappeared from sight. He watched until the watery blur of his eyes obliterated even the mountain from view.

Only then did he turn and limp pass the dying ashes, which was all that was left of the town.

He was drawn to the spot where Libby's house once stood. The sun glinted off some metal object, catching his eye. He bent over to investigate and found a tin can filled with baking soda. The can was scorched and still warm to the touch, but otherwise intact. He gazed at the can for several long minutes before dropping it into the leather pouch at his side. It was the only thing of Libby's that was left. Except for memories. And the scent of her that seemed to linger despite the acrid smell of fire.

Everything of Libby's that he held dear would fade with time. He would see to that.

He was a free trapper and it was time to answer the call of the wild.

Still, it was with a heavy heart that he searched for his horse. It was nearly nightfall when he found Jim Bridger in the woods nearby. The gelding gave a nervous wicker as Logan approached.

The horse had been burned slightly in the fire. Logan dug in his necessary bag for a fish bladder filled with salve and applied it to the raw spot on the horse's left flank. The horse whinnied and stomped his foot in protest. "There, there, fellow," Logan said soothingly.

He led the horse to the stream to drink from the cool waters. After the horse had his fill, Logan mounted and with one last lingering look at the remains of Libby's cabin, he began the long journey north.

The caravan of mules and horses snaked along the narrow trail toward Grass Valley, carrying the grim-

faced travelers over the mountain pass. Libby was
oblivious to her surroundings. She kept her head lowered. Once they began the ascent up the mountain,
she'd not looked back. Still, the vision of Logan's face
was so fixed in her mind, she could think of nothing
else.

At first, Thornton tried to make conversation, but
when he received no response, he soon gave up and
fell in line behind her.

It was late afternoon by the time the weary travelers
reached Grass Valley. It was a bustling town, twice as
big as Calico Corners. What surprised Libby most was
the number of women who strolled along the boardwalk or could be seen riding in the springboard wagons that filled the streets. Even more startling were the
number of children. Libby couldn't believe her eyes.

When had all these people arrived? All these families? Children?

No sooner had they reached the heart of town than
the majority of men—including Sharkey, Shakespeare,
Big Sam, and Appleby—headed for the saloons to
quench their thirsts. Libby was grateful to Thornton for
offering to stay with her.

She was exhausted and her body ached from the
hours spent on the mule. Noel was heavy and it was
such a relief when Thornton took him from her arms
and escorted her to the hotel, where he booked separate
rooms.

Libby's room was at the top of the stairs and had a
balcony that overlooked Mill Street. The proprietor
had offered to give her one of the back rooms, away
from the street, but Libby wanted the luxury of looking
out her window and watching the many families that
strolled up and down the boardwalk below.

Thornton laid Noel on the bed with his usual awkwardness. Despite Big Sam's instructions and the best
of intentions, he never could manage the knack of
holding Noel. "I think it would be wise if you stayed

here and got some rest. I'll arrange for some refreshments to be brought up."

Libby sat on the bed next to Noel. His breeches were wet, but his little buckskin suit was dry and had kept him warm. "I'm really not hungry. What I need are some clean clothes for Noel." Everything but the precious few things she'd grabbed before making her escape had been lost in the fire.

Thornton nodded. "I'll see what I can find." He hesitated at the door as if he was afraid to leave her alone. "I won't be long."

He closed the door after him and his footsteps faded away.

Libby poured the tepid water from the pitcher into the porcelain basin and washed the road dust off her hands and face. She than bathed Noel. His darling smile failed for once to lift her spirits, and she felt a sense of guilt for being so despondent in his presence. Wrapping him in a large Turkish towel, she settled in a chair next to the window to nurse him. She eased a nipple into his little pink mouth. The lack of tingling made her suspect her milk supply had dropped. His frantic sucking efforts confirmed it.

Luckily, Noel was more tired than hungry, and he soon fell asleep at her breast. She gently inched a finger into his mouth and released her nipple. She then laid him in the center of the bed. The feathered pillows provided ample protection from drafts.

She wandered onto the balcony. From where she stood, she could see the mountains that separated her from Logan. *You were always strong,* Logan had once told her. *I'll bet on it.* She closed her eyes. *Oh, Logan,* she thought, *it was you who made me strong. But now that you're gone* . . . She drew herself together. Somehow she had to find a way to get through the rest of the day. And every day after that.

Pulling her gaze from the mountains, she studied the steady stream of bullock carts and wagons that passed by.

A tap at the door announced Thornton's return, and she hurried to let him in, holding the door open while he maneuvered a silver tea tray into the room.

"The proprietor was kind enough to arrange for some bread and cheese, along with tea," he explained. He tossed her a package. "I picked up a few things for Noel at the general store."

Libby tore open the package. Inside were cloth diapers and a warm woolen bunting.

"I'm afraid that's all they had for infants," Thornton said. "We'll have to wait until we reach Sacramento City to purchase more."

"It'll do for now," Libby said.

"Anything is better than that ugly outfit he was wearing," he said, referring to the buckskin suit.

"It's not ugly!" The words were out before she could temper the sudden anger that ignited within her.

He looked startled and then apologetic. "I didn't mean to say anything to upset you."

He looked so contrite, she immediately regretted her hasty words. "I'm sorry, it's been a very long day and I'm tired."

"There's no need to apologize, my love." He poured her a cup of tea. "Here you are. This will make you feel better."

Surprised by the familiarity of his address, she took the china cup and saucer in her hand. A moment of awkward silence passed between them before she asked, "Did you make our travel arrangements?"

Thornton carried his own cup across the room and sat down in the chair opposite hers. "I did. However, I had a slight problem."

Libby's cup froze halfway to her mouth. "Which was?"

"There's a shortage of space on all departing liners."

"Really? I find that hard to believe. I thought it was coming to California that was the problem, not leaving it."

"From what I was told, I gather a lot of men are giving up and going back home. They've had enough."

"Maybe gold fever is about to end."

"As long as there's gold to be had, I'm afraid there will always be gold fever."

"So were you not able to book our passage?"

Thornton hesitated a moment. "I was able to attain a private cabin, at great cost, as you can imagine."

"I'm so sorry." Regarding him over the brim of her cup, she took a quick sip. "You could only book *one* cabin?"

Thornton cleared his throat and tugged on his collar. "If you'd rather that I not travel with you . . .?"

"Well . . . I . . ."

He stared at her accusingly. "If I recall, you had no qualms about living with St. John all those weeks."

She was so shocked by the sudden hardness in his voice, she almost dropped her teacup. "I had no choice."

Thornton looked stricken as if he suddenly realized he'd overstepped his boundaries. "Libby, I didn't mean to suggest . . . Perhaps you'd rather that I stay behind and wait for the next available space."

Libby set the teacup on the tray. They were both tired, she decided, which explained the strain between them. Anxious to smooth things over, she searched for an alternative. "I know you're anxious to return to Boston for your business. Perhaps you should travel ahead."

She sensed his hesitation. A shadow played across his brow, suggesting an inner conflict. "I couldn't bear to think of you and Noel alone in the city. Nor for that matter traveling aboard ship without benefit of a male protector."

"I've been without a male protector for over a year." She didn't want to sound ungrateful to him for his concern, but the truth of the matter was she still smarted from his earlier references to Logan.

"But not in the close quarters of a ship. I daresay

that many of those men haven't seen a woman in a year or two."

"What do you propose we do, Thornton? Wait until such time that we can book two cabins?"

"I'm afraid that would take longer than either of us care to wait." He cleared his throat. "I do have another possible solution."

"I would be most anxious to hear it."

"I hope you don't think me too forward, but under the circumstances . . ."

"Please feel free to speak your mind."

"Very well, if you insist. If you would agree to becoming my wife, we can then feel free to travel in one cabin."

The proposal wasn't completely unexpected, although she thought he'd wait until they'd arrived in Boston before speaking so boldly. What was unexpected was how trapped she suddenly felt. "Your wife?" she stammered, stalling for time.

She tried not to show how little the idea appealed to her, indeed, repulsed her, but apparently she failed. For his face flared red with humiliation and dismay.

"I know it's only been a year since your husband died. I planned to wait until we reached Boston before making my intentions known. But under the circumstances, it seems it only makes sense to find a preacher to marry us at once."

"I . . . I don't know what to say."

"There's only one thing you can say, Libby. Please say that you will marry me. It would simplify our travel arrangements."

She glanced at Noel, painfully aware that what was said in that room over the next few minutes would have a profound impact on his future. "That hardly seems like the proper reason to get married."

Thornton followed her gaze. "Please don't misunderstand, Libby. My intentions have always been to ask for your hand in marriage. Under normal circumstances, I would have waited for a more appropriate time." When she made no reply, he added, "I can assure you that I would be a proper father to Noel."

She met his eyes.

"He would be groomed for the family business just as if he were my own flesh and blood."

What he was offering was no small thing. Noel's future was of major concern to her. Without the benefit of marriage, her prospects were slim, indeed, if not altogether nonexistent.

"Please say you'll marry me."

She closed her eyes. She was convinced he would be a good father to Noel, and no less of a husband to her. In many ways, he reminded her of Jeffrey, and if it wasn't for her feelings for Logan, she might have welcomed his generous offer. But without the all-consuming passion she knew with Logan, the most she could hope for from any future marriage was mutual respect. She inwardly cringed at the thought of such a passionless future, even as she concentrated on Noel and what was best for him.

"I'm very honored, Thornton," she began. "Please don't think that I don't appreciate everything you're trying to do . . ."

"Don't say anything more." He stood up. "We shouldn't be talking about this tonight. You're tired. I'm tired. We've both been through a terrible ordeal. I'll let you get some sleep and we'll discuss this in the morning."

"Tomorrow won't change how I feel," she said. "I'm sorry, Thornton, but I don't want to give you false hope."

Thornton's face darkened. "It's Logan, isn't it?"

"Please, Thornton—"

"Isn't it?" His loud sharp voice bounced from wall to wall, waking Noel. "Answer me!"

Stunned by the change in him, she nodded, unable to find her voice. Suddenly she felt very much afraid.

He looked at her incredulously. "But why? What can he possibly offer? Dammit, Libby, what can you see in him?" His voice rose above Noel's piercing cry. "The man has nothing. Is nothing."

She scooped Noel off the bed and held him tightly in her arms. A sudden silence filled the room, playing against her already taut nerves. "I love him." It was the most direct explanation she could give.

"He's no good for you, Libby! I can offer you so much more. A house ... Libby ... bigger than any on Bunker Hill. And diamonds. You'll be the envy of every woman in Boston. I can take you to the theater. We'll travel abroad. Think of it. Libby, I can give you everything your heart desires."

She listened to him and felt a sense of sadness to think that she might have been tempted in the past by what he had to offer. But not now, not after what she'd been through these last several months, not after experiencing widowhood and motherhood, and under Logan's loving guidance the full blossom of womanhood.

"I'm sorry, Thornton. I really am sorry."

He straightened. "Is there any way I can persuade you to change your mind?"

"I'm afraid not."

To his credit, he accepted her decision with gentlemanly grace. He bid her good night and left. Although she was relieved that he chose not to pursue the matter further, it saddened her that he thought love was something to barter for. She wondered if he was capable of feeling true love. Perhaps she should envy more than pity him. For surely he would never have to feel the torture she now felt.

And indeed, it was torture, and it grew worse as she thought of Logan on the trail alone, heading north. She worried about his leg, and prayed it wouldn't be too cold. She worried about him meeting with hostile Indians or wild animals. She closed her eyes and said a prayer for his safety.

Later, she lay in bed and stared at the ceiling of the hotel room, and considered all that had happened to her. Was it selfish of her to deny Noel the kind of life that Thornton offered? She loved Noel more than life itself. She would do anything for him. Yes, even marry a man she did not love if she thought it was best for Noel.

The fact that she had no other prospects hit her with cold reality. She'd thought so much about going home, it never occurred to her to consider her options once she got there. She resisted the idea of being supported by her parents. With no real marketable skills, her prospects looked grim, indeed, but no more grim than the thought of being married to a man she didn't love.

She turned on her side and pounded her feather pillow with a fist.

It was Logan she loved and the thought of never seeing him again was too painful to bear. A dark agonizing despair rose up inside that was almost overwhelming in its bleak reality.

Chapter 39

THE morning dawned warm and sunny with not a cloud in the sky.

Her heart heavy with despair, it took all her effort to get through her morning ablutions. She dressed Noel in his buckskin outfit that she had brushed and aired before retiring. It looked almost as good as new. She knew how Thornton hated it, but it was such a practical, not to mention darling, outfit that the bunting he purchased paled in comparison.

The general store was two doors from the hotel. Libby reached the store just as Sharkey and Big Sam were coming out.

Big Sam grinned and made goo-goo sounds for Noel's benefit. He took Noel and lifted him in his arms.

Libby watched her son's face melt into a delighted smile as he looked up at the beaming black face. "He's going to miss you two."

"No more than we're a-gonna miss him," Sharkey said.

"What's your plans, Miz Libby?"

"I'm going to book passage on the stage to Sacramento. Are either of you going in that direction?"

Big Sam and Sharkey exchanged glances.

Sharkey tugged on an earlobe. "We've been a-talking, Big Sam and me, and we decided to go back to Calico Corners."

Libby looked from one to the other. "But there's nothing left."

"That don't mean we can't rebuild," Big Sam said. "I still have my gold nugget. It should be enough to purchase lumber and tools to build us a mighty nice town. Mighty nice indeed. Maybe you and Noel will come back and visit us one day."

She wiped a tear away with the tip of her finger. "Who else is going back with you?"

"Most everyone who's got a sens'ble bone in his body," Sharkey said. "Appleby, Shakespeare, Genesis, Cast-Iron . . ."

She laughed. "I don't believe it. Cast-Iron?"

Big Sam grinned. "Even Benjamin, if he behaves himself."

"Hap, too, if he ever gets himself away from the general store," Sharkey added.

Libby shook her head in wonder. "I wish I could be there with all of you."

"You'll be there in spirit, Miz Libby. 'Cuz you're the one that taught us what a hometown is all about."

"Now, now," Sharkey said, throwing his arms around her slender shoulders, "don't you go a-cryin'."

"I can't help it," she sobbed, her tears rubbing onto his flannel shirt.

Big Sam slipped an arm around her waist, and the three of them, four counting Noel, stood huddled on the boardwalk, oblivious to the curious stares of passersby.

After the three of them had said their good-byes, Libby slipped inside the general store, her eyes still blurred with tears. She was greeted by a pleasant woman by the name of Sarah Tuckford, whose mass of copper curls was matched only by the number of freckles on her face. Sarah was the wife of the store's proprietor. "Why, you poor thing. You must be Libby. What a terrible ordeal you must have been through. These mining towns are nothing but fire traps, if you ask me." She cooed as she looked at Noel. "What a precious darling baby!" She took Noel from Libby's arms.

In the back of the store, Hap's scolding voice could be heard. "I've never seen such disorganized merchandise in my life!"

Embarrassed, Libby gave Sarah an apologetic smile. "You should have seen the terrible condition of his first shop."

Sarah discounted Hap's complaints with a wave of her hand. "Harry will handle him. He's used to difficult customers. Now, tell me about that dreadful fire."

"Indeed, it was quite dreadful," Libby agreed. "I'm afraid we lost everything."

Sarah studied Libby's buckskin dress and Libby suddenly felt self-conscious. "I was wearing this when the fire broke out. What I'm looking for is . . . something to travel in. I don't think my family would appreciate me showing up in Boston dressed in buckskin."

"We'll find something for you to wear. Come upstairs with me." Holding Noel over her shoulder, she led the way through a narrow door and up a flight of stairs to the private apartment on the second floor, where she and her husband resided.

After Noel had been placed on a clean sheet on the floor, Sarah opened up a chest and pulled out a dress. She held it up for Libby to see. "You look to be my size."

"It's beautiful," Libby exclaimed. The lightweight wool dress was a lovely beige color and trimmed in brown. A full gathered skirt was attached to a fitted high-necked bodice. Full balloon sleeves were edged in white pelerine cuffs that matched the collar.

"I was wearing that dress when Frank proposed marriage."

"Then you must keep it . . ."

"I want you to have it," Sarah insisted. She shrugged her shoulders. "Where in the world would I ever wear such a dress in this town?"

"But it has a special meaning for you."

"Yes, it does. And it will bring you good luck, just as it brought me. Here, try it on."

While Libby tried the dress on, Sarah rummaged through an old trunk until she found a pair of side-buttoned boots.

While Libby finished dressing, Sarah fussed over Noel. "What a darling little outfit!"

Libby finished buttoning up one boot and started on the other. "His godfather made that for him."

"His godfather must be very special. I've never seen such a practical outfit. I can't believe the clothes that people bring out west. I see them getting off wagon trains dressed in silk and velvet dresses like they were going to a fancy dress ball. Sakes alive! Some of them bring more ruffles and lace with them than any woman in her right mind should ever have to wash and iron! Now this . . ." The woman fingered Libby's discarded dress. "This is what I call practical."

Libby smiled at her. She'd felt an instant rapport with the woman almost from the moment she'd first walked into the store. Now she knew why.

Libby straightened. The dress was a little loose around the waist, but otherwise fit perfectly.

"It looks lovely on you!" Sarah exclaimed. "Come and look." She pushed a chair aside to clear the way to the beveled mirror.

Libby stared at her reflection. It had been so long since she'd had the luxury of a looking glass, she hardly recognized herself. She moved closer to have a better look. As would be expected, her breasts were fuller, but her hips were still slender. The sun had turned her skin two shades darker during the trip to Nevada City, and this made her hair appear lighter in color.

But these were subtle differences and did not explain why the woman she saw reflected in the mirror seemed like a stranger to her.

"You look absolutely beautiful," Sarah was saying. "Just like a grand lady from Boston." She leaned closer. "The kind of lady that would turn the head of that nice handsome man Mr. Wellerton."

Libby turned her head. "You know Thornton?"

"He was in here yesterday, buying baby clothes. What a nice man. And so handsome." She gave a coy smile. "This dress has already inspired one marriage proposal."

Libby turned to face the mirror once more. "You're right, Thornton would love this dress." And so would Jeffrey. And so would her parents, her parents' friends, and everyone else back in Boston. She felt closed in, suffocated. The dress seemed too confining. Desperate to free herself, she reached for the china buttons.

"What are you doing?" Sarah asked.

"I do appreciate the offer, Sarah. It was most generous of you, but I simply can't wear this dress. It's simply not me."

Sarah looked confused. "I don't understand."

Libby took the dress off and felt a sense of relief wash over her. Taking a deep breath, she reached for her buckskin dress. "This is more my style."

"It's very attractive on you," Sarah said. "But what do you suppose they'll say in Boston?"

After getting dressed, Libby picked up Noel and dashed down the stairs to the general store calling Hap's name.

The store owner looked up from his ledger and nodded toward the door. "He's gone and I can't say I'm sorry."

"He's not as bad as he seems," Libby said as she rushed by him. She called back over her shoulder, "Thank you, Sarah."

She raced out the door and glanced up and down Mill Street hoping to catch sight of the men before they left town. But apparently she was too late. She did, however, catch sight of Thornton strolling along the boardwalk with a young dark-haired woman.

Libby raised her hand and waved. "Thornton."

Thornton turned.

"Wait for me." She waited for a stagecoach to pass before crossing the dirt-packed street to the other side.

Thornton's face was cool and impassive as she approached. The slender beauty slipped a possessive hand through the crook of his arm.

"Have you seen Big Sam or Sharkey?"

"The whole group of them left," Thornton said icily. "About ten minutes ago."

Libby felt crushed. "They . . . they left?"

"Went back where they belong," he said with a sneer. "To that hellhole called Calico Corners. Come along, Cynthia."

Thornton and the woman sauntered away. Libby stood watching them, not knowing what to do or where to turn. She decided to hire a horse. Surely, she could catch up with Big Sam and the rest as they headed back to Calico Corners.

She rushed back across the street toward the livery stables and almost bumped into a portly woman who was surrounded by three young children. She apologized profusely, but the woman was too busy fawning over Noel to notice.

"What a darling outfit!" the woman exclaimed. "Look, children, look at the darling baby."

Libby smiled as the two little girls and a tall skinny boy gathered around to peer at Noel.

"I want a suit just like that," the boy said.

"Me too," said the oldest of the two girls.

Much to Libby's surprise, she soon found herself surrounded by a crowd. Everyone oohed and aahed at Noel and his little buckskin suit.

It took a while, but she finally managed to free herself from the admiring crowd and find the livery stables. She walked up to the fleshy man who was shoeing a horse and introduced herself.

"I need a horse to take me to Calico Corners."

The man shook his head. "You and everyone else. That must have been some gold strike to send everyone scurrying over that mountain."

"Gold has nothing to do with it," she said.

"Don't worry. I ain't gonna tell anyone. Do you think I want everyone to desert this town? It could put me out of business."

"Yes, I see what you mean. Now about that horse . . ."

"I'm 'fraid you're out of luck. Those men cleared me plumb out of all the extras." He indicated the row of empty stalls in back. "I can sell you a mule real cheap."

Libby's heart sank. "A mule."

"He's over there."

She followed the man's finger. "That's Man Killer. I can't ride that mule. I have a baby to think about. We could both be killed."

He shrugged. "That's all that's available."

Libby left the livery stable feeling depressed and discouraged. She returned to her hotel room to nurse Noel, and while he slept, she stood on the balcony watching the street below.

Thinking she recognized someone, she stepped closer to the railing to have a better look. There was no mistake; the driver who had abandoned her outside of Deadman's Gulch that past December was loading crates onto the bed of his parked wagon across the street from the hotel.

Anger welled up inside. She rushed from the room and stormed down the staircase.

Just wait till she got her hands on that awful dreadful man!

"Mr. Thornborough, isn't it?" she called as she dodged around a bullock cart and started across the street.

The man turned. "That's Roseborough. Harvey Roseborough at yer serv'ce."

"Mr. *Rose*borough, I have a thing or two to say about your service." Everything about that long-ago night came back in painful detail. The fear, the icy waters, blindly racing through town, the stray bullet. *The warm caress of Logan's hands.*

In an effort to erase the last and most vivid memory, she allowed her voice to rise another octave. "I could have been killed because of you ... you ..." She called him every name she could think of.

A crowd began to gather, but Libby was too incensed to notice.

Finally, a man dressed in a brown suit and vest stepped between her and the unfortunate driver. "My name is Mr. Whittaker. I own this wagon. Mr. Roseborough is my employee. Any complaints you may have must be directed to me."

Libby gave the man her full attention. "I would be most happy to direct my complaints to you," she said, and then proceeded to tell him how she had been abandoned outside of Deadman's Gulch. The townsfolk gasped in shock as she described how she had been shot.

Since it was obvious where the crowd's sympathies lay, Mr. Whittaker had no choice but to make amends. He voiced his apologies and gave his employee a stern look. To Libby, he said, "How might we make amends for the inconvenience that was caused?"

Libby placed her hands on her hips. "It was hardly an inconvenience, Mr. Whittaker. Because of Mr. Thornborough ..."

"That's Roseborough," the driver interjected.

Libby glared at him. "I was nearly killed!"

Mr. Whittaker appeared flustered. "I assure you that nothing like that will happen again. And as a token of goodwill, I shall have my driver take you wherever you like. Sacramento. San Francisco. You name the place."

"I wish to go to Calico Corners."

"I never heard of it," Mr. Whittaker said.

"It used to be called Deadman's Gulch," she said, glaring at the driver. "As Mr. Thornborough well knows!"

The driver looked about to protest, but Mr. Whittaker stopped him. "My driver will personally see that you arrive in Calico Corners safe and sound. Won't you, Mr. Thorn ... uh, Roseborough?"

Chapter 40

THE pounding sound echoed along the granite walls of the mountain and bored like a relentless drill into the hazy fogginess of Logan's mind.

He stirred from the bed of pine needles where he'd been forced to lie for weeks now.

He'd traveled no farther than the hills above Calico Corners when his horse reared back on its haunches and threw him. He'd landed on his bad leg and the pain had rendered him unconscious. How many hours or days he'd lain on the ground, he had no way of knowing. All he remembered was when he finally gained consciousness, a mangy coyote was gnawing away at the whangs on his buckskin.

He'd managed to reach his knife and plunge it into the coyote, but with no strength to protect himself further, he feared the animal's blood would only attract more predators.

Somehow he managed to brace his leg to his rifle and scoot along on his posterior until he found an empty cave. The cave offered some protection from the elements, although it lacked the depth necessary to keep the temperature from dropping too low. During several long nights, he nearly froze.

His leg was red and swollen. For days, he'd floated in and out of consciousness. It was always a sound that pulled him from his dazed stupor. A baby crying. A woman's voice. In the hazy fuzziness that followed, he called their names. But his lips and throat were too parched for more than a whisper to escape.

The sheer act of speaking did, however, bring a clarity of thought that lasted only a moment before his instincts took over. He breathed in the air, hoping to detect a possible rescuer. But for days on end, it was coyotes he smelled and coyotes he heard. And whenever he took the trouble to look, it was coyotes he saw, standing guard outside his cave, their thick red tongues hanging out of their drooling mouths.

But the constant banging was not coyotes. His mind still foggy, he decided it was tom-toms.

He reached for his rifle. He'd used the last of his bullets soon after his accident. On the slightest possibility that a trapper was within hearing distance, he'd fired out the universal distress signal that had been worked out by a group of trappers years earlier at a rendezvous. One shot, silence. Two shots, silence. Three shots. But no one came.

Blackberries grew in abundance, and at moments of lucidity, he inched his way a few feet outside the cave to pick them. For added nourishment, he chewed on the buckskin whangs or rather what was left after the coyote had finished with them. After many days, he started on the rawhide laces of his moccasins.

If he were to guess how long he'd been in that cave, he'd say twenty days. The swelling on his knee had gone down. He'd lost a lot of weight and his clothes hung loose around his body.

He shook his head to clear it. He had to concentrate on the message sent by the tom-toms. The pacing of the drumbeats puzzled him. Indians rarely rapped out a message so slowly.

He had no idea how weak he was until he tried sitting up. Dizziness assailed him. As if to sense his vulnerability, the coyotes that guarded the cave began to yip and howl. It was this threatening sound that kept him from blacking out. He would belong to the coyotes soon enough, but he had no intention of serving himself to them on a silver platter. They can bloody well wait.

The coyotes' cries faded in the background and his eyes drifted shut. Noel was crying. He needed his breeches changed. Libby laughed, a sweet musical sound that filled the very air around her with a lovely gurgling sound that he associated with spring. She had a summer laugh too. And a winter laugh that reminded him of snowflakes falling to the ground in a crystal whirl.

Her laughter faded away and she called his name. Her voice was urgent and persistent. His eyes flew open and his finely tuned senses grew alert. Something was different. And then he realized the tom-toms had stopped.

He sniffed, but all he could smell was the lingering dank order of the wolf family that had once dwelled in the cave, and the eternal coyotes outside.

Gritting his teeth against the pain, he inched his way toward the opening of the cave. The coyotes had moved away from the cave. So there *was* something . . .

Keeping his leg rigid, he inched himself along the ground by his arms until he could look over the valley below. The banging sound had started up again. Perhaps because the sound had grown closer, he realized his earlier mistake. It was not Indian drums he heard. Someone was chopping wood.

Raising himself on his elbows, he was able to see men in the distance. There were six in all. Knowing they would never see him, he nonetheless waved his hand and pushed a few loose rocks down the mountainside. Failing at his feeble attempts to create an avalanche, he untied the rifle bracing his leg before he remembered he was out of ammunition. He crawled back into the cave and tore though his leather pouch in search of bullets. Damn! Had he really wasted that much ammunition in the first few days following his accident?

He dumped out the contents of his possibles bag and pored over the last of his survival tools. The charred can of baking soda rolled away as he pawed through the clay Indian beads, the vials of bear grease, and fish bladders filled with resin and camphor in search of a stray bullet. It was a well-stocked bag and included everything from a cork and length of string to be used for fishing, to a bone needle and flaxen thread. But there was not a single bullet to be found.

Damn! he muttered. With a violent thrust of his arm, he scattered his belongings. It was then that his eye fell on the tin can that had rolled next to the jagged wall of the cave. Libby's baking soda.

The can reminded him of something from his youth. During one of the several rendezvous he'd attended with his father, his hero, Jim Bridger, had entertained the young ones by disappearing in a cloud of smoke. Logan recalled how he'd begged Jim Bridger to show him how to make such smoke at will.

Jim revealed the source of his magic, but only after swearing young Logan to secrecy. Recalling that magic formula now, Logan reached for the can. Baking soda had been a key ingredient. Also needed was alum, which he knew could be found in the Indian beads, and sulfur. This last he kept to clear the nasal passages.

Everything he needed he found in some form or other among his supplies. For the next hour or so, he pounded and scraped until he had a pile of shavings in front of him. To this he added baking soda, scraping the caked powder with the tip of his knife. At last, he reached for his buckskin fire bag and drew out his flint, steel striker, and charcloth.

Sharkey was the first to see the smoke. "Will you look at that!" He pointed and next to him Big Sam straightened and narrowed his eyes. The smoke was yellow in color, floating upward in little clouds.

"Looks like a signal of some sort," Big Sam said.

Appleby dropped the ax and wiped the sweat from his forehead. "You mean like an Indian signal?" He glanced around anxiously. "You don't suppose we're about to be attacked by Indians, do you?"

"Last I heard tell, there ain't nothin' but friendly Injuns 'round here!" Sharkey said, but he was tugging down on his hat as if to protect his topknot just the same.

Big Sam jostled him with an elbow. "What's the matter, Sharkey?" he teased " 'Fraid Indians might put you out of the haircutting business?"

"I ain't afraid of nothin'," Sharkey grumbled.

"I'm mighty glad to hear that," Appleby said. "You and Big Sam can go up there and see what's causing that smoke."

Big Sam laughed and slapped Sharkey on the back. "Don't look so worried, Sharkey. I ain't planning on letting anyone give me a haircut but you."

The two men mounted their horses and headed toward the trail leading up the mountain. The smoke cleared and they were tempted to turn around.

It was Big Sam who decided to keep going. "We're almost there," he said. "It won't take but another few minutes. We've come this far, we may as well have a look."

It took a half hour altogether to reach the opening of the cave. At first they didn't recognize the wasted man who lay unconscious on the ground, the metal striker still in his hand.

Sharkey dismounted his horse and crept slowly into the cave opening, ducking his head beneath the rocky overhang. "I'll be damned!" he exclaimed. "It's Logan!"

Chapter 41

LOGAN fought his way through a dark tunnel. A male voice echoed from a far distance. "We thought you were a goner for sure."

Shadows floated around him. Forms darkened and moved closer. Instinctively, he reached for his rifle only to knock over a lantern.

"Whoa, there, boy. Where do you think you're going?"

Logan stared into the dark familiar face that began to take shape in front of him. "Big Sam?"

"In the flesh," Big Sam replied. "And right here is Sharkey."

Logan turned his head. Sharkey wiggled his fingers and gave him a silly grin.

"Where am I?" Logan asked.

"In Calico Corners," Big Sam replied.

"Calico ..." Logan closed his eyes as he recalled the ordeal of the last few weeks. "How did you find me?"

"You made enough smoke to be declared a human volcano," Big Sam said. "How'd you do that?"

Recalling how Libby's baking soda had saved his life, Logan managed a weak smile. "Jim Bridger's secret."

Sharkey looked puzzled. "Your horse made the smoke? Well, I'll be."

Sharkey slipped pillows behind Logan's back until he sat upright. He then handed Logan a cup of hot steaming coffee. "You'd better get some food down you."

A wedge of white goat cheese and soft piping-hot biscuits seemed to materialize out of nowhere.

Logan fingered a biscuit, but took only a single bite. Food would have to be digested slowly for the next day or so. He'd eaten sparsely in the last few weeks and it would take time for his body to adjust.

He began to feel better, though, and his head was clear enough to take in his canvas surroundings. He was in a tent. Outside was the sound of hammering and sawing. Strange as it seemed, the sound that once drove him to distraction sounded like music to his ears. "See you're at it again."

Sharkey grinned. "Yep. In no time at all, I'm gonna have myself the biggest and the bestest barbershop in the gosh dern terr'tory."

"Maybe you can help us with a little disagreement," Big Sam said. "I think we should build us a saloon first. But Sharkey here's gone soft in the head. He thinks we should build a church."

Not a church, Logan thought. That would only remind him of Libby. "I say build a saloon and a gambling hall. A man's got to have himself a proper place to spend his free time."

Big Sam grinned. "Well, now, I see your mishap did no harm to your thinking."

"Got any more of those biscuits?" Logan asked.

"As many as you want," Sharkey said. He set a basket full of biscuits next to Logan. "Help yourself."

Logan reached for one but his hand froze halfway to his mouth. He looked up at Big Sam. "No one makes biscuits like this except . . . "

Big Sam exchanged glances with Sharkey. "We didn't tell Miz Libby you were here. We didn't think you were going to make it and . . ."

Logan's heart raced. "What do you mean, tell her? She's here? In Calico Corners?"

Big Sam nodded. "She's helping us to rebuild the town."

Logan dropped the biscuit and stared at Big Sam. "Has the woman gone crazy or what? This is no place to raise a child! She knows that!"

"We tried to tell her that," Big Sam said. "Didn't we, Sharkey?"

"We did. Honest. But she ain't hearin' none of it."

Logan looked from Sharkey to Big Sam. "What do you mean, she won't hear of it?"

"She said this is where she wants to raise Noel."

Logan couldn't believe his ears. "That's crazy." He rubbed his forehead with both hands. "What else did she say?"

Sharkey tugged on an ear. "Said she's stayin' right here until you get some sense into you and admit that your trappin' days are over."

Logan stared at Sharkey through his fingers. "Oh, she did, did she? Well, we'll see about that!" He overturned the basket of biscuits as he struggled out of bed.

"Now hold on there, Logan. You ain't going nowhere." Big Sam threw his body against Logan's. Logan was too weak to fight him. "If you want to see Miz Libby, Sharkey will go and fetch her."

It was by far the better plan, but Logan was determined to do it his way. "I have to go to her."

Big Sam released him. "You're not in any condition to go anywhere."

"I said I have to go to her," Logan repeated, this time louder. Big Sam looked puzzled and he couldn't blame him. How could he explain that in order to prove to Libby that they had no future together, she had to see him for what he was: a man without a profession. A man without a home. A man who couldn't even walk, let alone ride a horse.

He didn't have the strength to fight Big Sam and he considered this for several moments before motioning the man to come closer. "Tell me what it was like to be a slave."

Big Sam looked surprised. "Now what do you want to know that for?"

"They tied you up?"

"Sometimes."

"Chained you?"

Big Sam tugged on the collar of his shirt. "I don't want to talk about this."

"They had complete control over you."

"Dammit, I said . . ."

"They controlled your every hour."

"If you don't shut your mouth, I'll—"

"Your every thought."

"No!" Big Sam shouted. "Not my thoughts. They couldn't control my mind."

"They controlled minds," Logan said.

"But not mine," Big Sam insisted. "That's why I had the courage to escape. Others could have escaped, but they didn't. They let white men fill their heads with fear."

"But you didn't, Big Sam. You have spirit, and it was this burning spirit that set you free."

"I never looked at it that way before, but I guess you're right."

"I have to go to Libby. I have to let her see me as I really am. It's the only way I can set her free. I know that a man of your great wisdom and intelligence would understand. Help me to set her free."

Big Sam stared down at Logan for several moments before stepping aside. "If you got your mind made up, I'm not stopping you. But if anything happens, you have only yourself to blame."

Sharkey offered to give Logan a shave and haircut, but Logan resisted. Libby was going to see him at his worst. There wasn't going to be any more pretending, especially about his physical affliction.

Sharkey fashioned a set of crutches out of tree limbs, then he and Big Sam helped Logan out of bed. After Logan left the tent, Sharkey confronted Big Sam.

"Do you mind a-tellin' me what all that talk about spirits and sl'very was 'bout?"

Big Sam shrugged his shoulders. "Search me."

"You mean you let him go wi'out knowin' what the hell he was tryin' to do? Some wisdom and intell'gence you have."

Big Sam grinned and glanced in the direction of Libby's tent. "I have a funny feeling I have more wisdom and intelligence than even I know about."

Logan hobbled along Main Street on his crutches like a man possessed. He fought off dizziness and weakness. He had to make her understand. Her place was in Boston. She must know that. Boston. Not here. Not with him.

His resolve weakened as he made his way through the tent city. Her presence was everywhere. Each tent had a small vegetable garden in front, divided by a neatly graded walkway.

One tent was designated as a church, with a little white cross in front and a neatly printed sign. Another had a sign that read *Shakespeare's Theater*. A barber pole marked Sharkey's tent, and next to that Beaker's wood objects were displayed in front of his tent, including a baby cart just like the one he'd made for Noel. Hap was already set up for business, and his voice could be heard harping on a customer who had apparently displaced some merchandise. Next to Hap's general store was a tent marked *Luke Appleby, First Mayor, Calico Corners*.

Everyone, it seemed, had found a home in this place called Calico Corners. Everyone that is, but him. It struck him as strange that this should affect him. His home was in the wilds, he told himself. Up north, in what was left of beaver country! Not confined to a town where a lot of people were forced to live in close proximity.

As he continued passing the row of neatly placed

tents, reading the signs, he suddenly saw one that made his heart stop. The sign read *Libby's Bakery*.

He hobbled the remaining distance and tore open the flap of the tent. Tossing his crutches to the ground, he hopped inside on one foot.

Libby stood in front of a table rolling out dough. She lifted her lovely blue-green eyes and stared at him dumbfounded. At the sight of her, he stilled as he so often stilled when coming across something in nature of such indescribable beauty that the full splendor of it could only be absorbed over time.

Even his heart seemed to freeze midbeat until he'd had a chance to sort through her every essence, from her lovely fragrance to the faintest sound of her breathing. As his overwhelmed senses gradually adjusted to the overload, he felt himself grow stronger. His heart began to beat so fast he thought it would jump out of place. He couldn't seem to breathe fast enough to keep up.

"Logan!" Her voice was barely louder than a whisper and took a long time in coming. It was as if she, too, was obliged to absorb him fully before she could respond. She wiped her flour-covered hands on her apron, her gaze never leaving his face. "What happened to you?" Her eyes drifted down the length of him to take in his bandaged leg. Dark tortured eyes clung to him. "Your leg . . ."

"The leg feels terrible," he said gruffly. Let her know the truth, dammit! Maybe then he'd drive some sense into that head of hers. Maybe if he could see himself mirrored more accurately in her eyes, he could control the rampaging need to take her in his arms. Perhaps if he didn't look at her . . . Only he couldn't tear his eyes away. No matter how hard he tried. "The leg is no good to me at all!"

She looked so devastated by this, he was almost overcome by the need to hold her and comfort her, to repeat the lies of the past and tell her his leg was on the mend.

But knowing what a fatal mistake that would be, he hardened his heart and forced an even harsher tone. "What the hell are you doing here? Why aren't you on the way to Boston? What about your promise to your husband?"

"I promised Jeffrey to take our child home," she stammered, looking confused.

"And?"

"I realized that home for me is Calico Corners. It can never again be Boston."

Staggered by this news, he stared at her, willing his knee not to buckle under him. Finally, he managed to find his voice again. "What about Noel's education?" The outer edges of darkness began to claw at him again as the effects of the past few weeks began to bear down on him. He shook his head slightly and forced himself to continue. If ever he needed to be strong, it was at this moment. "There are no schools here, no families. Dammit, Libby! What kind of a mother are you?"

Despite his cruel attack, her blue-green eyes were soft with concern for him. "Oh, Logan, I was astounded when I arrived in Grass Valley. Some of the men had sent for their wives and children. There's even talk of building a schoolhouse. We can do the same thing here, in Calico Corners. By the time Noel is old enough for school, he'll have everything he needs right here."

Logan felt that his very foundation had been pulled from beneath him. With Noel's future no longer an issue, there was nothing left to do but to admit to the truth. Knowing that she was here in town, accessible to him in a way not possible if she were in Boston, would make it that much harder to stay away from her. It would be so tempting to put his own needs above hers. But he must never do that. He loved her too much.

"Dammit, Libby. Do you know how hard this is for me? Knowing that I can't give you the kind of life that you deserve?"

"This is where I want to be," she said. "I want to raise Noel with the people who love him. Big Sam, Sharkey, and Hap."

He glanced around. "Where's Noel?"

Libby nodded. "Cast-Iron took him for a walk."

"Cast-Iron?" He shook his head in disbelief. "What about Thornton?"

"Let's not talk about Thornton," she pleaded softly. I want to talk about us."

"There isn't any us!" he snapped and almost doubled over in pain.

Libby cried out and ran to his side. "Please, Logan, sit down." She pulled a barrel that served as a chair toward him. She looked so worried, he didn't have the heart to argue. He sat down and stretched his leg out in front of him.

"Can I get you something. Some tea? Anything?"

He shook his head, but his gaze fell on a can of baking soda inside a wooden crate used for a cupboard.

He picked up her hand and held it to his lips. This woman who had turned his life inside-out and upside-down had also saved it. There had to be a way to express his gratitude and love without sacrificing her future. But he was a simple mountain man and though he knew what must be said, the actual words eluded him.

He knew her one weakness was her son. There was nothing she wouldn't do for Noel and he counted on this. "What Noel needs is a real honest-to-goodness father."

"I don't think he would ever find a better one than you."

Unable to keep his hands off her, he touched his fingertips to her lovely soft cheeks. "What kind of father would I make? I can't even provide for myself, let alone a family. All I know how to do is to set traps and sell pelts. And now I can't even do that."

"There's a lot you can do," she insisted.

"No!" He dropped his hands and closed his eyes. He

wanted to prove how much he loved her. And the only way he knew to do that was to walk out of that tent and never return.

Libby's hands fell to his shoulders. "Look at me!" Her voice softened as she added, "Please."

He took a deep breath and did as she asked. "You deserve so much more than I can give you," he said.

She backed away from him and lifted her head in the way that she did whenever she met opposition. "Don't I have anything to say about this?" When he failed to reply, she drew a piece of paper from her apron pocket. "These are the people in Grass Valley who want a buckskin suit like you made for Noel."

Confused, he glanced at the paper then back at her. "What are you talking about?"

"I'm talking about starting a business."

He laughed at this. "Me? I'm a trapper, Libby. I know nothing about business."

"Trapping *is* a business," she said stubbornly. "And considering that beaver is out of fashion and has been for quite some time, I would say that anyone who was able to make a living from selling beaver skin as you have done has very astute business sense."

"I never thought of it that way." He took the list from her and scanned it. He shook his head in disbelief. "This many people want buckskins?"

"Oh, Logan, you should have heard the fuss they made over Noel's little suit. And that's only the beginning."

"Do . . . do you think it's possible?" He gazed deep into her eyes. "Oh, Libby. Do you think I could . . . a businessman. Me?"

"With a shop of your own," she added.

"And a sign . . ." He shook his head. "I don't know, Libby."

"You won't have to set traps, or ride a horse, or sleep out in the cold ever again," Libby pointed out.

"Where will I get the skins?"

"You can buy them from free trappers," she said.

"I'm sure you have a few friends who will be willing to do business with you."

The thought of himself sitting on the other side of the bargaining table made him laugh. "Come to think of it, I do."

His laughter seemed to encourage her and she ran her hand along one side of his gaunt whiskered face. "I thought I would never see you again," she said softly.

"Oh, Libby!" He pulled her onto his lap and kissed her. "Libby Summerfield," he whispered between kisses. "If you're crazy enough to think I can be a businessman, I wonder if you're crazy enough to—" He pulled away so he could study her face—and that's when sanity took hold. What in the name of sam hill was he thinking? He couldn't propose marriage with his future so undecided.

"What were you going to ask me?"

"Nothing."

She put her hands on her waist. "Logan St. John, don't tell me nothing."

"I was going to ask you to be my . . . personal baker."

She looked unconvinced. "You were going to ask me to be your wife."

"I most certainly was not." He breathed deeply and tried not think about her lovely sweet fragrance. "If I did happen to ask that question, which I wasn't, what would you have said?"

"I'd say it was about time that you decided to get down off your high horse and ask me to be your wife."

He looked at her in astonishment. "That's not what you said the last time I proposed."

"That's because it was the wine that proposed back then," she said.

"Does this mean you accept?"

She pulled back to look him square in the eye. "Does this mean you're asking?"

A slow grin spread across his face. "Just so there's

no question, I'll ask you again. Libby Summerfield, would you do me the honor of being my wife?"

"It's about time you got off your high horse and—" She never got to finish what she was going to say, because he had pulled her into his arms and proceeded to give her the most thorough kiss possible under the circumstances.

"I love you," he whispered. "I only hope that you never come to regret . . ."

She stayed his words with a finger to his lips. "I love you too."

All at once weakened and strengthened by her declaration of love, he pulled away and pointed to the opening of the tent. "Get my crutches."

"What?"

"My crutches, dammit!"

She retrieved his crutches and handed them to him, then stepped back to watch him struggle to his feet. "Are you coming with me?" he asked.

She looked startled. "Where are we going?"

"We need to get the men started on building a church," he explained. "The saloon can wait."

He was outside the tent and halfway up the street before she caught up with him. "Don't tell me you've gone and got yourself some religion."

"Religion has nothing to do with it," he said, grinning. At that moment in time, his crutches felt like wings. "A man needs a place to have himself a proper wedding, wouldn't you agree?"

She smiled her lovely sweet spring, summer, fall, and winter smile all rolled into one. She had to lift her voice to be heard above the loud cacophony of hammers and saws. But what she said was music to his soul. "Welcome home, Logan."

He dropped his crutches and took her in his arms, right there in the middle of tent city for all to see. "Welcome home, Libby."